Running Wild

by

J.L. Sheppard

Hell Ryders MC Book 1

Running Wild

Contact Information: info@thewildrosepress.com

Cover Art by *Diana Carlile*

The Wild Rose Press, Inc.
PO Box 708
Adams Basin, NY 14410-0708

Visit us at www.thewilderroses.com

Publishing History
First Scarlet Rose Edition, 2016
Print ISBN 978-1-5092-0698-8
Digital ISBN 978-1-5092-0699-5

Published in the United States of America

Whose rules would she play by...his or hers?

A woman moaned.

Allie hadn't meant to look, but unwillingly, she turned her head. The door wide open, so inevitably, she caught sight of them. She stood there seeing, yet unbelieving, frozen with her eyes glued to an image she'd never forget no matter how much she craved to.

Jace.

Shirtless sitting up on the edge of his bed, his head angled back, eyes closed, lips parted. A dark-haired woman draped over him, kissing his neck, her legs wrapped around him. Her black leather skirt hiked up to her waist, his hands cupping her bare ass.

Her heart clenched, squeezing in her chest so hard it hurt. Deep and searing her from the inside out.

Jesus.

How it hurt.

And she didn't know why.

He wasn't hers. He was a biker who couldn't stand her. Single, free to screw however many scantily dressed women he wanted.

Her brother warned her bikers did it often, and still somewhere deep inside, she held hope Jace was different. He wasn't just a biker, he was the man who took his niece to dinner weekly, the man who'd roughed up her ex-fiancé, then held her while she cried.

It was more than that, too. She wanted to believe the man who affected her in a way no other man ever had, the man whose arms she'd felt safe in couldn't be anything like her brother described.

Dedication

To my feisty, crazy, beautiful little sister, Jackie. This
one is just for you.

Author Acknowledgments

A big thank you to my family and friends for their continued support. To my editor, Sharon Pickrel, I'm forever thankful for all I've learned and your hard work. Last but not least, to my publisher, including everyone who works behind the scenes, thank you for giving me the opportunity to reach countless readers, and especially, for believing in my stories.

Chapter One

Sitting in coach on an American Airlines flight with her headphones blasting music into her ears to drown her rambling brain, the urge to cry her heart out overwhelmed Allie again. The urge gnawed her raw every five minutes when she remembered again how her life had turned to shit. She swallowed and held those damned, pesky tears at bay. She couldn't and wouldn't have a meltdown in public.

Allie wanted to cry since the moment she made the decision to leave the only life she'd ever known behind, but she couldn't. Having made the decision days ago, to accomplish it, she had to pretend all was well, so no one discovered her plan and stopped her.

Seven days ago, her life became, not just crappy or shitty, but fucked. She didn't like to curse and only did when warranted. Now, it was.

With her heart lodged in her throat and trembling hands, she packed a duffel bag and took off, knowing she'd never return. She wanted no part of it, not anymore, not ever. Still, it was the life she'd led for three years, the life she'd been primed to lead for twenty-two years before that, and it hurt to leave it behind. Hell, it was devastating to leave it behind, but she didn't have much of a choice.

The seatbelt sign lit. Relieved, she heaved a sigh. Finally, they were landing. She couldn't wait to get off the plane. She hated flying though she'd done it often even as a kid. Turning off her music player, she pulled up her seat and took another deep breath, forcing her tears to dry. One managed to slip out. Hoping it wasn't the opening of the flood gates, she wiped it away quickly, then focused her attention on holding them in.

Before she realized it, people around her unbuckled their seatbelts, stood, and retrieved their bags from the overhead compartments. She took her purse and duffel bag and deplaned. Walking through Santa Rosa's airport, the big step she'd made slammed into her, leaving her breathless. She should've thought this through. She should've left her father a note, so he wouldn't call the police and report her missing. She should've at least called Tyler before unceremoniously dropping in and invading his life. What if he didn't have room for her? What if she showed up at his house and he wasn't there? Too late to turn back now.

Allie walked outside, stepped into one of the many cabs lined outside the airport, and gave the driver Tyler's address. Twenty minutes later, she arrived at a one-story house in the small town of Wadden, outside Santa Rosa. It looked empty, and worse, from the outside, it looked like it was in the process of being remodeled. A large dumpster with pieces of cabinets and furniture stood beside the house.

She should call him, but her cell phone was one of the many things she left behind, and buying another one right then was not her top priority. She gave the cab driver another address, his work address, and prayed. She highly doubted he'd be at work at three p.m. on a Saturday, considering he mentioned a time or two he didn't work weekends, but she had no choice. She

2

hoped she'd at least get some information from someone who knew where she might find him. If not, she'd stay at a hotel and regroup.

Ten agonizing minutes later, she stood outside a mechanic shop with a sign that read, Ryders' Custom Rides. She paid the cab driver, slung her designer purse over one shoulder, duffel over the other, and walked toward the door with a small sign that read, Office. Pulling the door open, she automatically rested her sunglasses on the top of her head and froze.

Never had she seen that many tattooed, big, scary-looking men in one room together. Not that there were many, just three, but three more than she'd ever seen. That they were bikers didn't come as a surprise. Tyler told her about the motorcycle club he joined. Still, apart from Tyler, who she didn't consider a "biker," she'd never met bikers before, only heard stories, and they unnerved her.

The office was large for a garage and messy. A dark counter lined the entirety of it. Behind it, a desk and two computers. In front of that, three foldout chairs, and beside it, another door. The large office didn't feel big. In fact, it felt like a cramped bathroom. The three men in it took up all the space, and their intense gazes were deadlocked on her.

She took a deep breath and managed to find her voice. "Hi, I'm looking for Tyler."

It got her several curious looks and lifted brows. After several long moments, one of the men, in his early thirties, wearing a black tank, the length of both arms tatted so they looked like sleeves, spoke. His dark, hooded gaze ran up and down her body. "No one here by that name, honey." His voice was deep, rich, and thick.

Unnerving, no one had ever called her honey.

She ignored his gaze as it continued to trail down her body. "I figured since it's Saturday. Will he be back Monday?"

"No one here by that name," he repeated. "No one ever here by that name."

What he meant hit her. Tyler didn't work there. Tyler never worked there. The sudden urge to cry came. She blinked the tears away, telling herself she would not cry in front of tatted, ripped, scary men.

"Fuck." She had no idea where Tyler lived or worked. And now, she had no freaking clue how to find him or what the hell to do.

She had no clue why he'd lie. They were close, spoke at least once a week, sharing their lives, laughing, and joking. Her father disapproved of her speaking to Tyler. She'd hid it from him for a long time. When he'd found out, he nagged her until finally she told him she'd cut all ties.

The three scary men were now looking at her like she was from another planet. She flushed. "Sorry."

"Heard the word before, doll." This came from the man standing to her left. Dark hair framed his face, his eyes were a light hazel, and he wore a white, V-neck shirt that exposed some of his tattoos. Like the others, he wore a black, leather vest. On the right part of the vest, a patch read, Hell Ryders MC. Under it, another patch read, Road Captain. She had no idea what it meant and disregarded it.

"I suppose you have." She looked away from him, took a deep breath, and met his stare again. "May I use your phone?"

"Need a ride?"

Her attention darted toward the last man. He stood to her right, wearing no shirt, only a black, leather vest. Hard to ignore, primarily since he was sculpted with six-pack abs, the whole nine yards. Blond with bluish-green eyes, out of the three, he scared her the most because those eyes looked dead.

"Um…well, yeah, but I need a phone, too."

"You can ride on the back of my bike," he said without meeting her gaze. His attention glued to her chest.

Was he insane? She would *never* get on the back of a bike with a tatted, half-naked man with dead eyes.

She brought her large, designer bag to her chest.

His gaze snapped to her face. "'Cause you got a fancy bag, I can't check out the digs?"

What? God, really? She didn't even know how to respond.

The other two men chuckled, obviously finding this amusing. "Tyler wouldn't mind sharing," Tatted Sleeves said through a chuckle.

Gross. Her and Tyler? No way, but she wouldn't tell them they weren't a couple. If they had so little respect for her thinking she was taken, she couldn't imagine how much worse it'd be if they knew the truth.

Her cheeks flamed. She'd run from one nightmare to walk into another. "How do you know if Tyler will mind?" she snapped, her voice filled with fury. She should've kept her mouth shut. They were not the type of men you riled. She just couldn't help it. She was exhausted, scared, and needed a good cry.

Two of the three laughed. Dead Eyes didn't find it amusing. "Prefer my taps without attitude."

What? Did he just…Yep, definitely another nightmare. Screw borrowing a phone. She rather walk.

She turned on her heel and reached for the door just as a roar of bikes sounded outside. A hand grasped her elbow and pulled her back around to stare into those dead eyes. Fear clogging her throat, she forgot to breathe.

He leaned in until a hair's breath away.

She tried to yank her arm away. He tightened his hold until it hurt. "Let me go."

The roar of the bikes grew louder and louder and then died.

"You wanna ride, you come to me."

Not likely. "Don't hold your breath." She snatched her arm away.

He released her, but stayed close.

The door to the side of the office slammed open, and then she heard the voice she'd been dying to hear for seven long, agonizing days.

"Allie?"

She angled her head toward the sound of his voice, and her gaze met his. His dark hair still cut short, but not as short as when he'd been in the military. Tall, six-foot-two, broad-shouldered, and built.

Her heart swelled in relief.

His eyes softened in that tender way they always did when they met hers. Then they sliced to Dead Eyes, every muscle in his body clenching. When he spoke, his voice was a low growl. "Step the fuck away from her."

Chapter Two

"Allie?" Army said when he walked through the side door into the garage's office.

Jace "Trigger" Warren's steps quickened, pushing through his brothers until he stood beside his army buddy and club brother.

That's when he saw her.

Fucking beautiful, so beyond anything he'd ever laid eyes on, the impact of seeing her hit him square in the chest, a deep burn he swore touched his soul. She was that beautiful with long, dark hair and clear, hazel eyes. She was classy, too. He could tell by her face, her perfectly manicured nails, and the expensive purse she had angled across her chest.

Beautiful and right then, terrified out of her goddamned mind. Not hard to figure out why.

Ripper, a.k.a. Dickhead, was shirtless, smirking, and standing too close—so close if he bent over, he could reach her lips.

Trig hated it. His muscles tensed and throbbed in protest, the bitter taste of envy in his mouth. In that heated moment, all he wanted to do—tear Ripper to fucking shreds so he'd never have to see that terrified look on her face. He didn't have time to wonder why, too consumed by the anger burning, too focused on not taking that anger out on his brother—Ripper, a dick, but his brother nonetheless.

She was that beautiful and classy, and he'd stake his life she was sweet as hell too, the perfect combo.

Her eyes, deadlocked on Army, softened and welled, and that deep burn inside him became a throbbing ache radiating out of his heart.

"Step the fuck away from her," Army growled, and then scanned the room, meeting his eyes for a split second before he moved on and warned, "Off fuckin' limits."

His chest tightened. He held his breath, hoping the ache would subside. Fuck. Army's girl? How the hell was it possible? The man fucked everything in sight.

Ripper crossed his arms over his chest, but didn't step away from her. "Know the rules, Army. No one's off limits unless it's an old lady."

The sudden urge to claim her as his own rose, but Army beat him to it. "Family's off limits, fucker."

Family? His heart hurt then. It hurt more than it had when his dad left, when his mom told him he was worthless, and when he'd left his sister behind to make something of himself.

Ripper took a menacing step in Army's direction. "Immediate family."

The air thick with tension. Army pissed, in the midst of one of his tempers, and Ripper fishing for a fight. Fists would fly. It would happen eventually, so Trig was trying to figure out how to whisk her away before all hell broke loose.

His gaze gravitated to her.

Jesus. How could anyone be that beautiful?

Army closed the distance between him and Ripper. "Yeah, fucker, she's my sister. Now. Step. The. Fuck. Away."

Shit. His sister. She looked familiar. Army had a picture of them in his room. In the picture, though, she was turned to Army, laughing. You could only see her profile. She being Army's sister just amplified how fucked he was. If he didn't stand a chance before because she was too beautiful, too classy, and too fucking perfect, no way in hell he'd ever have a chance now. His brother's sister, she'd know what a piece of shit he was. No doubt Army would warn her, and she'd run in the other direction.

Prez pushed his way through the brothers. "Stand down."

Maybe this shit wouldn't come to blows.

The tension in his shoulders lessened. He forced himself to tear his gaze away from her and reassess the situation.

Yeah, he'd been wrong.

Army was fisting his palms, and he only did this when he was close to striking. Ripper still hadn't wiped the smirk off his face.

"What's goin' on?"

"Family's off limits," Army snarled.

Prez's gaze sliced to her. She cowered away. Prez then said what he'd hoped. "Family's off limits."

Ripper looked at her. His gaze traveled up and down her body, making his stomach knot, and then Ripper smiled. "Remember what I said."

What had the bastard told her? He'd kill him. He clenched his jaw, taking a deep breath, and attempting to control his anger. It didn't help. He took a step in Ripper's direction.

"Off fucking limits, fucker," Army barked.

Ripper smirked. "She wants to ride. She rides with

me."

That's when all hell broke loose.

****

He held her tightly, one arm around her waist, the other cupping her cheek, pressing her against his chest, holding her captive, his deep masculine scent filling her. He was warm and strong, and it made her feel safe. That felt great after the dreadful week she had.

She didn't know what he looked like. Her gaze had been glued to Tyler when the fight broke out. All she knew about this man—he was tall and big, smelled great, and he wore a white tank and leather vest.

"W-what?" she stammered. "Let me go!" She put her hands in between them and pushed with all her might.

He released her immediately. Her feet hit the ground moments before she put distance between them. She tilted her head back to stare into the eyes of the man who'd carried her out the door. It took a while because he was tall, as tall as her brother.

One look and a deep, startling feeling settled in her gut. That feeling knotting her stomach got worse each second. And she didn't know what it meant.

Whoever he was, he was hot, so hot he could've made a career out of it. He had dark eyes and dark brown hair the same shade as hers. Every feature on his face was chiseled as if carved from stone: a strong brow, a square jaw, and thick, sinful lips. The scar marring the side of his lip, the bulging muscles lining his shoulders, arms, and chest were well defined too, and she knew this with certainty. Not a minute before, her face had been plastered against his chest.

He crossed his arms and barked, "Stay here."

God, his voice was hot, even laced with anger. The low rumble touched her in places she refused to put much thought into.

She was tired of being treated like crap by these men, but she didn't want to fight Hot, Angry, Badass Biker. Not like she could fight any of them, anyway. At five-foot-six with a small frame, she weighed no more than a hundred and twenty pounds. Exhausted, moody, and now scared Dead Eyes hurt her brother, she didn't have the strength to fight anyone.

"But Ty—"

He clenched his perfectly squared jaw. "He's fine. It's over."

"W-what?"

He didn't respond, instead he grabbed the duffel bag off her shoulder and set it on the ground.

At least this one was sort of nice. He kept his gaze on her face, and he relieved her of the little she brought. She looked away and sighed heavily. Her eyes watered. She met his gaze, curious to see if he noticed. Her luck, he had.

His expression hardened, a muscle in his jaw twitched. "Army's fine. He can take care of himself."

Army? What the…

He must've seen her confusion. The next second, he said, "Your brother. He's fine."

The door to the office slammed open. She angled her body to peek from behind him and saw her brother. His lip torn and bleeding, he gave her his million-dollar smile. She ran toward him, slamming into him, and wrapped her arms around his waist. He chuckled, placing his arms around her shoulders, and squeezed her tight.

She sighed. For the first time that day, a relieved sigh. She found her brother. She wasn't alone in the world.

He cupped her cheeks and pulled away to look at her. "Missed your brother, eh?"

With tears brimming in her eyes, she nodded.

He kissed her forehead. "None of that. I've survived worse."

Yes. He'd served in the military: two tours in Iraq and one in Afghanistan, but she always worried about him and always would.

His gaze darted behind her. "Thanks for getting her outta there, bro. I owe you."

"Naw, you don't."

She turned hesitantly, and Hot, Angry, Badass Biker's gaze met hers for a brief moment. He picked up her duffel bag and handed it to her brother.

Feeling the heat of her brother's gaze, she directed her attention to him. "Allie, this is Jace. Served together on our last tour." Tyler then introduced her. "Jace, this is Allie, my baby sister."

She glared at her brother, playfully. "Haven't been a baby for twenty-four years, Ty."

He laughed. God, how she'd missed him. She especially missed seeing him laugh. For so long, even before he enlisted, he hadn't laughed. Even though they spoke on the phone and he often laughed, seeing and hearing were two different things.

Addressing Jace, he said, "How'd I know that was coming?" He chuckled, then faced her. "So you've come to visit me, finally."

God, she should've called, should've given him a heads-up. She just couldn't. "Um...well..." She hesitated, looking away from him. Those damned tears she held back clouded her vision.

Tyler's face hardened. An angry look completely erased his earlier amusement.

"It's…" She spared a glance at Jace. Her cheeks flushed, hating she couldn't control her emotions. Her gaze darted back to her brother then she blurted, "I left."

Her brother's eyes widened. "You left? For good?"

She nodded. "I know I should've called to let you know, and I know you have your own life. I don't mean to intrude. I know this is an inconvenience for you—"

His eyes narrowed. "Allie." His voice firm. "Have you fuckin' lost your mind?"

Fuck. Silent, but warranted. She never thought staying with her brother would be permanent, but she hoped to crash with him while she looked for a job and found a place of her own. She could've gone anywhere, but she wanted to be close to him, the only family she had left.

"Allie?"

Her gaze darted back to him. "It's okay." She reached for her bag. "I can go—"

He grabbed her wrist firmly, preventing her from getting her duffle. "Allie, you aren't going anywhere. Why you think this is inconvenient for me, I have no fuckin' clue. Remember, anytime, anyplace?"

She remembered. She'd never forget the words he ended each letter and call with.

"You're my fuckin' sister. When have I not been here for you?"

He didn't wait for her to answer. "Never. I've always been here for you despite Dad's fuckin' threats."

Dad's threats? She meant to ask, but he looked beyond pissed and continued to ramble, so she let him.

He stuck his finger in her face. "You're fuckin' staying with me, Allie."

Chapter Three

His fingers on her wrist tightening, Tyler hauled her through the garage doors and into a long, narrow hallway.

The garage was much bigger than she'd thought. It went for what seemed like a mile and led into a large living room with several haphazard couches, where several men were seated, drinking beers, and watching a game on a big screen TV. Tyler didn't stop and introduce her. He didn't even look their way. He continued dragging her into another long hallway lined with doors and up a flight of stairs. At the top, he made a right into another hallway. Opening the last door at the end, he allowed her in first.

It had to be Ty's room. Everything in its place. In the middle, the made, cherry wood, king-size bed with a navy-blue comforter. To its left, a dresser topped with several colognes and a picture frame. In the frame, a picture of Ty and her. He had his arm around her shoulder, staring into the camera with a big smile on his face. She was smiling too, but her face was turned to him. To the right of the bed, a closet, an armoire, and a door that probably led to a bathroom.

Ty unceremoniously dropped her duffel on the floor, the sound resonating around them. She faced him, then, and finally, let herself cry. The next instant, her head lay against his chest, and his arms wrapped around her.

He ran his hand up and down her back in a soothing motion. "Shh…It's okay, Allie. Your big bro is gonna fix this."

She pulled away to look at him and shook her head. "I don't want you to fix anything, Ty. I want to start over. I have money saved. I could've gone anywhere, but I wanted to be near you."

He sucked in a breath, trying to stay calm.

Tyler and their dad didn't get along. In fact, they hadn't spoken since her father disowned him eleven years ago. Even before, Tyler and their father hadn't gotten along. She had no idea why. Neither one of them ever told her. When he'd turned eighteen, he joined the Army. Her father disapproved. He wanted Tyler to follow in his footsteps and become CEO of his real estate company, Holden Holdings, LLC.

She'd been fourteen at the time and kept in the dark about much of it. What she did know, she'd learned from hearing her parents fight after they thought she'd gone to bed. Much of that fighting was her father forbidding her mother from contacting Ty. She didn't know if her mother followed through.

Ty never mentioned if he still spoke to their mother, but their mother gave her the letters Tyler sent her. She always wrote back and gave her mom letters to send off. She knew he received them because every letter he wrote he told her so. This went on for two years. She never learned why her mom continued to disobey her dad, but she didn't care. She had Ty.

Two years later, she saw Tyler again. On leave at the time, he surprised her by showing up at her school. With their mom covering for her, they'd spent the entire week together until he had to go. Before he left, he bought her a prepaid cell. After, they communicated when he wrote and when he called.

She graduated from high school a year and a half later. Their mom had just died, and their dad had been stuck in a meeting at work and unable to attend, but Ty had gone to her graduation. They continued to call and write throughout her college years and after, when her dad hired her right out of college. By then, Ty had been out of the military for a year.

Allie still had that prepaid cell and all his letters. They were the first two things she'd packed when she decided to leave.

"Tell me what happened."

She wiped her face and took a deep breath. "I hate my job," she blurted for some insane reason. True. Her dad had practically forced her into the accounting profession, but it wasn't the point. "You know Wyatt?"

He nodded. She'd told him about Wyatt and talked about him often though they'd never met.

"He's a lawyer, handsome, well-off, and from a prominent family. We've been dating for a long time, and well…he proposed, and I said yes because I loved him …" She paused, gathering the strength to admit what she had to. "What you don't know is that he's a cheater, too."

Tyler's eyes narrowed. "He cheated?"

She nodded.

The muscle in his jaw jumped. "On you?"

She nodded.

"Fuckin' bastard."

"About two months ago, I caught him cheating, confronted him, and broke off our engagement. I didn't tell you. I was…" She shrugged. "Devastated, and he kept sending me flowers and saying how sorry he was. I gave him another chance. I…" She looked away from him, and then met his stare again. "I know this sounds crazy, but I didn't trust him after what he did, so I hired a PI and caught him cheating again. I sent him the pictures and broke it off."

"That's not crazy, Allie. That's smart. Better now than when you're married with kids."

"Dad showed up that night and said I should give him another chance because he was a good catch. Like I care. I mean…" Tears brimmed and spilled. "I don't care if he's well-off and handsome. Don't I deserve someone who loves me enough not to cheat?" Her voice trembled.

"Yes, Allie, you do. You're beautiful, talented, and hard-working."

She smiled softly. "You have to say that. You're my brother," she whispered, wiping her tears with trembling fingers.

"I wouldn't say it if it wasn't true."

She swallowed. "Dad said all men cheat. That it's normal. He said—"

"All men do *not* cheat. If a man knows he's got a good thing, he doesn't cheat, Allie. Trust me on this."

"Would you cheat, Ty?"

"Allie," his voice laced in emotion. "I find a woman I love, I'll never fuckin' cheat. Ever. That's a promise to you, to her, whoever the hell she is. I don't have a woman 'cause I haven't found her."

"I asked Dad if he'd cheated on Mom," she whispered.

He clenched his jaw.

"He said because I was old enough now, I should know he's had a mistress for thirty years." Her voice broke. Something in his eyes told her he already knew. "You knew?"

He looked away from her and nodded.

"I thought the world of him, you know. Well, except for what he did to you." She hesitated before she said, "After he left, I sat in bed for a long time thinking, and I realized everything around me was a lie. I hate my job. Hate it, Ty. I knew I'd hate it. I didn't want to study business. I wanted to be a teacher. I did it for Dad, and I did it because Mom agreed with Dad. I hate my big, fancy apartment in the city. I wanted to live in the suburbs, but Dad said I needed to show people I lived well. I didn't want to meet Wyatt, but Dad said I had to. He'd given him his word, said he could meet me, and he doesn't break his word.

"I'm a pushover and I met him, and then he asked me out. I knew that was Dad's intention, so I agreed thinking I'd go on one date, and then blow him off. I couldn't. Dad kept pushing him at me, inviting him over for dinner, and I started falling for Wyatt's lies. Next thing I know, I'm planning a three-hundred-thousand-dollar wedding with a man who's cheated on me multiple times.

"I told Dad I wasn't going to marry him, and he said I had to because it would connect two very prominent families, and it would help the company!" By this point, she half-heartedly yelled her frustration. "The company? Really? What about his only daughter? Why am I not important enough to make my own decisions? Why doesn't he care about my happiness?"

The tears came in droves then, streaming down her

face. About damned time. Tired of hiding and suffering in silence, she wasn't ashamed either, not with Tyler.

"It's a lie, Ty, and I can't live a lie anymore," she whispered.

He grasped the back of her neck and pulled her into a hug. She cried and cried, and after a while, the tears dried.

"I'll fucking kill Dad," he said, angrily.

She believed him. It's why she'd waited a week before coming and hadn't called ahead of time. "Ty, you can't. You're all I have left, and I don't want to visit you in prison."

He chuckled humorlessly, the anger in his eyes abating. She smiled her best fake smile, then looked away.

"Did he hit you, Allie?"

Her gaze snapped back to him. He wasn't joking. She swallowed, hating herself for what she would do next. "No."

He lifted her chin, gaze scanning her face for endless moments, and then he released her. "I'll call Dad. Tell him you're with me, so he doesn't call the cops."

"No, I'll do it."

He shook his head. "No, you aren't. I don't want him fuckin' with your head. I'm not telling you never to speak to him again. That's your decision, but I'm telling you, you need time, and you're getting that time. I'm making sure of it."

A command, one she wouldn't take lightly considering he never commanded her to do anything. She didn't have the will to fight him anyway.

"Rest easy. I'll be back later." He then walked out

the door and shut it behind him.

****

"What's the deal, Army?"

Trigger wanted to know, but couldn't summon the courage to ask, so he was glad when someone else did.

"My dad's a fuckin' dick," Army replied snidely, still in a foul mood. Army didn't often get angry, but when he did, it was nasty, and it could last days.

"Yeah, well, thought you knew that, bro."

Rake. The damned brother couldn't say anything without sarcasm. Annoying as hell, especially when you were in a bad mood, and Trig usually was.

"Yeah, I knew, just didn't think he'd be a dick to my baby sister."

Army's sister. He couldn't believe his luck. Finally, a girl worth something walks into the garage, and she's related to his brother, meaning off limits.

She wasn't just pretty. She was beautiful. All it took—one look, and she had him. On the thin side, but she had curves, fantastic legs, dark, long hair, and hazel eyes that turned olive-green in the sun. Even wearing slim-fitted jeans and a loose, white blouse, she was something. Not like it mattered; she had class and money, the type who had gone to the best private schools and took etiquette lessons. Women like that wouldn't look twice at a biker like him. They steered clear of men with rough pasts who grew up in trailers.

Still, never in a million years would he have guessed a girl looking as sheltered as her was related to Army. He'd known Army for seven years now, and never had the brother mentioned he'd come from money. He had known he had a sister.

"Hate to break this to you, but there's nothin'

'baby' about your sister," Dash said with a smile.

Trig thought the same thing, but he'd never in a million years say that shit aloud. Stupid considering Army's nasty mood, not to mention, he'd just punched another brother in the face for claiming her.

Army's eyes hardened and flared, his shoulders tensing. "You want a broken nose, too?"

Dash shrugged. "Naw, thanks, gotta tap tonight."

Sure, he did. Bikers, especially with cuts of Hell Ryders MC, all had their share of "taps" meaning girls willing to roll in the sack with no strings attached.

Army pulled his phone out of his pocket, dialed a number, and brought it to his ear. "Asshole." His greeting. It got several chuckles from his brothers. "I'm calling to inform you, you're done fuckin' with my sister. She's with me. Don't even think about calling the cops. She came on her own 'cause her piece-of-shit cheating, lying bastard of a father wants to fuck with her life. You aren't fuckin' with it anymore. You're never fuckin' with her again. You try, you're dealing with me."

Army paused, looking like he would reach through the phone and strangle his father. "She quit the company. She doesn't want that fancy ass apartment, and you know what else? She isn't marrying that cheating bastard either."

With those final words, he ended the call, stormed out of the room, and into the kitchen. A moment later, a crashing sounded and echoed through the room.

Rake took a pull of his beer. "Bet you fifty bucks Army's gonna need a new phone."

Trig barely heard it, still thinking about the last words Army barked. He couldn't explain why, but the knowledge of it made his blood boil. Fisting his hands, he stood and headed toward Army. At the threshold into the kitchen, he paused. Army stood with his back to the door, both hands in fists at his sides. His phone lay in pieces at his feet.

"Brother."

Army turned.

"Looks like you need a new phone."

Army nodded. Still, the pissed-off look didn't abate. He headed past him. Trig placed a hand on his shoulder. Army paused. His rage-filled gaze met his.

"Let it go. She'll be fine." He didn't know why he'd said it because he wasn't sure he believed it himself. He didn't know the whole story. In fact, he knew only what he'd heard, but if being in the service taught him anything besides being one hell of a marksman, it taught him how to read people. He had the feeling staring into Allie's eyes she'd run. An instinct and perhaps it was nothing but nonetheless there. Following those instincts kept him alive a long time, so he'd stake his life there was much more to the story than Allie would ever admit, even to her brother.

He wouldn't tell Army, not yet, not until he was sure, and he didn't think it mattered. Army had instincts of his own, good ones, and he'd seen for himself how much he cared for his sister. With certainty, nothing bad would touch Allie. Her brother wouldn't allow it.

"You coming?" Army asked.

"Always down for a ride."

"Let me check on Allie." Army headed down the hall and up the stairs.

He followed, unwilling to admit he wanted to check on her himself. He stood behind while Army knocked on his bedroom door. It parted, and she came to view.

Even prettier than he remembered, she wore a blue robe, reaching mid-thigh with her hair wet from the shower. Her eyes were swollen and red-rimmed like she'd been crying—a lot.

Fuck. Why did that knowledge make him want to bash her cheating fiancé's head in? He looked away, his ears perking up to see how she sounded.

"Hey, you okay?"

"Yeah," she whispered. Even her voice was fucking beautiful, soft and so feminine.

"Talked to Dad already, so you don't have to worry about that shit anymore. If he calls you, don't answer."

"He can't. I left my phone."

Through his peripheral vision, he caught sight of Army's body tensing. He couldn't blame him. The thought didn't please him either.

"Allie, Christ, Allie." He sounded pissed again. "You traveled across the country alone without a cell phone?"

She shrugged, unfazed by Army's temper. Luckily, because the woman raised protective instincts in him, wanting to beat the shit out of her ex and her father, wanting to hold her when she was fighting tears. He didn't know how he'd react if Army's temper made her start fucking crying again, and he didn't want or need to find out.

"I know it was stupid. I just didn't want Dad or Wyatt to call."

Wyatt had to be the fiancé. What a stupid name. Lucky, stupid bastard.

He gritted his teeth.

Army sighed heavily, running his fingers through his hair. "You could've turned off your phone."

"Yeah, but then when I turned it on, I'd have messages."

"You ignore them then."

"Ty, it's over, and I made it okay. I'm fine."

"Yeah, you are...Gotta get a new phone. I'm buying you one."

"Let me give you some money—"

He shook his head. "Don't even think about it."

"I have money."

"Save your money. I take care of you now."

She laughed, softly. "I'm twenty-five, Ty. I have a lot saved, and I'll start looking for a job Monday. I'll be out of your hair in no time."

"You aren't gonna go anywhere, Allie. You're living with me."

"Yeah? Oh, what are you going to do with me when you bring a girl over?"

A teasing glint in her voice, he hid a smile.

"You let me worry about that, 'kay?"

She chuckled.

Trig couldn't help himself then. He looked in her direction. Her gaze met his for a brief moment, then went back to her brother.

"Take a nap. I'll be back; then we gotta talk."

She nodded. Army faced him, then turned back around to her. "Oh, and I'm bringing you your Camaro."

She smiled a smile that reached her eyes then closed the door behind her.

Beautiful, classy, and she drove a Camaro.

Fuck.

****

Trig sat astride his Harley, waiting for Army who'd been inside the store for close to an hour.

"Yo," Army shouted.

Looking up, he spotted him walking his way, a bag in hand. "Ready?"

Army lifted his chin.

He started his Harley, waited for Army to pack the bag, and start his bike. "You need more time to cool off?"

"Probably wouldn't hurt, but I gotta get back. Have to explain some things to her. Just gotta prepare her, you know…She's—"

He looked away from him and gazed across the parking lot. "Classy."

"Yeah. Never told you, and you'd never guess, but I came from money."

"I'm seein' that."

"I gave it up 'cause I wanted to make my own way, doing my own thing. Never regretted it. But I fuckin' regret not telling her what I knew about that life, what I saw, and why I left. Maybe she would've realized it sooner. Maybe she would've been a teacher like she wanted. Maybe then, she would've never met that prick who cheated. And maybe she wouldn't be in my room crying her eyes out."

"Brother, she's pretty, looks sweet and smart, too. A man lets go of a woman like that, he's a fuckin' idiot."

Shit. It slipped. He had to be more careful. His gaze shot to Army, hoping he wouldn't be the next one with a broken nose.

Army smiled, shocking him. "She is. All of it. I

was serving when she was in high school, but we'd talk and write as much as we could. She'd tell me about guys. She only got real serious with one her senior year. He played her. When I got back, I paid him a visit."

He chuckled. "Scared the shit outta him, but he never messed with her again. After that, she went to Columbia, got her bachelor's, and worked while she finished her master's. Sometimes, I wonder how the hell we're related. Dad's a dick. Mom was a pushover, and Allie's nothing but sugar."

Trig could see that, totally, and he could tell she wasn't afraid of much, not even her big brother's nasty temper.

"What I regret the most is not being there for her." Army's eyes had a faraway look to them, like reliving something in his mind.

"Army, from what you said, sounds like you were."

Army shook his head. "I was, but I wasn't."

That, he understood. Completely.

Chapter Four

A knock sounded on the door. She parted it and found Tyler. She moved away to allow him in. "Hey."

"Hey, you sleep?"

"Yeah, like an hour." She was still exhausted, but she figured if she wanted to get any sleep tonight she shouldn't sleep longer. Besides, her stomach started to rumble.

He handed her a phone. "My number's saved. Added the garage's and Jace's, too. In case you can't get a hold of me."

Silently praying she'd never have to use Jace's number, she mumbled, "Thanks."

He ran his hand through his hair. "Have a seat. I gotta explain a couple of things to you."

She sat on the edge of the bed and waited for him to do the same. He didn't.

"The club. Remember I told you about it?"

"You said they were like family."

He nodded. "Yeah, they are. The guys you met today are brothers. There's more of them. We work together, live together, and ride together, but Allie, they aren't the type of men you're used to—"

She smiled. "You mean rich cheaters?"

He chuckled. "Only a few have steady women or are married. They're called 'old ladies.' The rest play the field."

Her eyes widened. "They call their wives 'old ladies'?"

He fought a smile and nodded.

"And their wives don't mind?"

He grinned and shook his head.

She shrugged. "I guess it's a biker thing."

"Yeah, it is. We got thirty here in town. Like I said, most play the field. When I say that, I mean they rip and dip, and they can 'cause there're women who don't care as long as the guy's wearing a cut. They take what's offered and leave. No strings attached.

"Living with me, especially living here at the compound, you're gonna run into a lot of these guys. You'll run into the women who are okay with being just that, too. It's club life. We live by our own rules, we don't judge 'cause we're family. We eat, work, and play together."

He paused then added, "They aren't your type, Allie. They're rough around the edges, crude, and partake in questionable activities. You get me?"

She understood, completely. In fact, he didn't have to tell her any of this. She knew exactly the type of men they were, having been crudely initiated earlier. Then again, from her experience, the type of man didn't matter. Her ex-fiancé was the opposite of them and ended up cheating. "Ty, I appreciate everything, but I think I should get a hotel until—"

He sat beside her and held her hands in his. "What're you afraid of? What're you uncomfortable with?"

Reason why she loved her brother, whatever she wanted, whenever she needed it. It had always been that way with him. "You know I've never been one to judge, Ty, but think about it. I know what I look like. I know what I appear to be, what I've been my whole life. I don't fit in here with your life. I won't judge them, unless I catch them cheating on their old ladies," she half-heartedly joked. "But they'll judge me."

"What'd they tell you?"

It totally caught her off guard. She didn't want to admit exactly what happened. "What?"

"Before I got here. What happened?"

She avoided his eyes, knowing it'd be easier to keep the truth from him. "Well…"

"Don't lie, Allie."

She met his stare again. "It wasn't bad."

"Ripper."

"Is that his name? Ripper?"

His eyes narrowed. "He's not gonna mess with you, not after—"

"Ty, I'm not letting you get into fights with your family over me."

He flinched like she'd struck him.

She hadn't meant to hurt him, so she attempted to rephrase. "I know they mean a lot to you, and I don't want to come between you—"

He shook his head. "Allie, they're my brothers by choice. You're my sister by blood and choice. You get me?"

The magnitude of his words hit her square in the chest, spreading warmth all over. What he'd said meant the world to her. God, she loved her brother. Understanding completely, she nodded.

"I love you, Allie, you know that, right?"

"Yeah, Ty, and I love you, too."

He gripped the back of her neck and pulled her into

his embrace, kissing her head. "Remember, anytime, anyplace."

She smiled. "Anytime, anyplace."

****

Near seven p.m., Allie hadn't eaten in close to twelve hours. Her stomach growled so loud she didn't know how Ty hadn't heard it. She followed Tyler down the stairs past the living area and into the kitchen dining area. Larger than she expected, dark cabinets lined the right side where the stove, refrigerator, and double ovens were. Marble countertops circled half the room and separated the formal dining area from the kitchen.

The moment she walked in, voices died, heads shifted, and gazes hit her. She didn't recognize any of them, but figured she'd be polite. "Hi."

It got her several chin lifts, much better than being scanned from top to bottom like a piece of meat. She smiled and looked toward her brother.

He opened the fridge, cursed then shut it. "Looks like we're getting take-out tonight." He glanced around the room. "My bad, Allie, this is Blaze, Cuss, and Trick." He paused, shifting his attention to them and said, "This is Allie."

Blaze was blond, blue-eyed, and tall. She could tell, since sitting on a stool, he was taller than her. Cuss looked in his early twenties, his hair so dark it looked midnight blue, and his eyes were round and big, a captivating sapphire-blue in color. Trick appeared mid-twenties, probably around her age. He had long, dark hair pulled back in a ponytail, and he wore a black shirt with the sleeves cut off.

Blaze took a sip of beer and chuckled. "Pleasure to meet the reason Ripper's got a broken nose."

Trick's gaze hit her. "Class act like you, it'd be my pleasure to show you the ropes."

Cuss shook his head just as her brother jumped to her defense. "There'll be no showing her anything."

He laughed. "She ain't my type. 'Sides, I think you made your point earlier."

Her cheeks heated.

"He's messing with you," Blaze told her. "Don't pay mind to it."

She smiled softly and nodded.

Her brother rolled his eyes then faced her. "What're you in the mood for?"

"At this point, anything will do."

He lifted a brow. "Even Chinese?"

Chinese was not her favorite, and Ty knew this. At that point, she was so hungry she'd eat raw chicken. She laughed. "Yeah, Ty, even Chinese."

He shook his head. "I know this great Italian place. I'll take you there."

"You thinking of takin' her to Anthony's?"

She turned. Cuss's sapphire gaze met hers, that captivating color enthralling. Like a fly caught in a web, she had to fight to look away.

Ty nodded. "Yeah."

"Might wanna give Trig a call. Place is usually packed Saturday."

"Where is he?"

Cuss shrugged. "Fuck if I know."

"Right." Ty fished his phone out of his pocket and brought it to his ear. "Trig. Thinking of takin' Allie to Anthony's tonight." He paused for several seconds, listening to the other end. "Meet you here." He snapped his phone shut. "Gotta get my keys." He strode out, telling her to wait for him there.

He'd been gone a minute when two others entered. She recognized them immediately. How could she forget the warm welcome they'd given her?

Tatted Chest and Tatted Sleeves.

Seeing those two, she'd known the moment would eventually come, but she hoped she would have more time.

Tatted Sleeves closed the distance between them, stopping only a foot away. "Honey, could've told us you were related to Army."

Like it would've made a difference, considering she didn't know who Army was until later and considering they'd thought she was Tyler's woman and still hit on her.

Tatted Chest drew closer. "Know what you're thinkin', Doll, and yeah, it would've made a difference. Family's off limits."

"No hard feelings, yeah?"

She had the feeling this was some sort of apology. Releasing a breath, she nodded. "No hard feelings."

"Name's Bud," Tatted Chest said then nodded toward Tatted Sleeves. "This is Dash."

"Alyssa."

Bud lifted his brow and grinned. "I think I like 'Doll' better."

She smiled. "If you get to call me 'Doll,' then I get to call you 'Tatted Chest.' "

He threw his head back and laughed. Dash grinned and shook his head. "You're gonna fit in nice here. Damn shame you're off limits."

"Unless you wanna rile that brother of hers, suggest you call her something else," Cuss warned.

Bud turned to Cuss. "Any ideas?"

Blaze's brows furrowed. He looked her up and down then grinned. "Classy."

"I say we vote," Dash said.

"The only thing you're gonna do is clean your blood off the floor if you don't step away from her."

She jolted at the sound of his voice. Rough, deep, and thick. That deep, startling feeling reignited in her gut. She didn't have to look to know who the voice belonged to. In fact, not wanting to be reminded how hot he was, she tried her hardest not to look.

Bud and Dash turned to him, paving the way for her to get a glimpse, and that unsettling feeling intensified.

Shit. Hotter than she remembered, his dark hair, short on the sides and longer on top, was disheveled like he'd been running his fingers through it. Still, it was too appealing. He wore a blue-collared polo that fit snugly against his broad chest and a pair of faded jeans. His expression made her lose her voice. Looking angry again, his square jaw clenched, the muscle in his jaw jumping.

Dash shrugged. "Just talkin' to the girl."

"Don't gotta be that close to talk," Jace shot back.

"You see Doll upset?" Bud asked.

Jace's eyes narrowed, taking a menacing step in their direction.

The perfect moment to interrupt, so she did. "They weren't bothering me."

The muscle in his jaw jumped again. He angled his whole body toward her. His gaze met hers and held for a long moment.

The heat of everyone's gaze was on her, but she

couldn't look away from his eyes. A powerful emotion shined through their deep, dark depths.

She saw it.

She felt it.

She just didn't know what it was or why he showed it to her, but it knocked the wind out of her.

"Thought we'd agreed on Classy," Blaze spoke, breaking their moment.

Thank God for Blaze. She didn't know if she would've ever summoned the courage to look away.

She faced Blaze. "I thought we'd agreed on a vote though I get unlimited vetoes."

"Fuckin' shit. You tryin' to bargain with bikers?" Cuss asked.

Still a bit shaky, she tried to hide it with a smile.

Trick chuckled. "Yep, gonna fit in real nice here."

"J!" The squeal tore her gaze away from him toward the threshold into the kitchen just in time to see a girl slam into Jace's side and wrap her arms around his legs. Five, maybe six years old, she had dark hair like Jace, but hers was long and curled at the ends. She wore a frilly pink dress and white sandals, matching the barrette in her hair.

Resting his hands on her back, Jace looked down at her, smiling.

And holy shit, could Hot, Angry, Badass Biker smile, a great smile that softened the harsh lines on his face, making him that much more attractive.

"You said hi to Mia and Lynn?"

She nodded, and then she turned to them. Her gaze scanning the men then landed on her and held.

"Is that who I think it is?"

The girl's smile widened a second before she

turned to look behind her where Tyler stood. She nodded.

Tyler shook his head, grinning. "Naw, can't be. She's too big." He kneeled and opened his arms.

The little girl jumped on him, hugging tightly then pulled away. "J told me you're coming with us."

Ty nodded. "Yep, you in the mood for pizza or spaghetti?"

She shrugged. "Don't know yet."

Her brother chuckled, then met her stare. He lifted his chin, a silent signal it was time to go.

She turned to Blaze, Cuss, and Trick. "Nice to meet you guys." She then faced Bud and Dash. "See you around."

Allie strode toward her brother, feeling the heat of Jace's gaze. She avoided looking at him, avoided his eyes because she didn't think she could handle seeing anything else in them. He made room for her to walk past him.

"Della, this is my sister, Allie," her brother introduced. "Allie, this is Della, Trig's niece."

Her brows furrowed. "Trig?"

"That's my uncle. He takes me out to dinner every Saturday. I call him J. His real name is Jace, but everyone calls him Trigger or Trig because he was a sniper in the Army, and he was really good and—"

"Del, you gonna write her a book?" Jace teased.

Della looked to her uncle and giggled. "Maybe."

Her jaw dropped, her gaze gravitating to him, unable to believe what she heard. She couldn't wrap her mind around a hot, angry, badass biker who took his niece out to dinner every Saturday. Not to mention, it went against the speech her brother gave her.

Jace's gaze went to her. She quickly looked away from him to his niece. "Nice to meet you, Della."

"Nice to meet you too, Allie."

Chapter Five

Trig didn't know whether to thank his lucky stars or curse fate. No doubt he wanted to see her again. He'd wanted that since the last time he saw her and realized she'd been crying. That, in itself, bothered him. He shouldn't care. He didn't get attached. He couldn't afford to. If that wasn't enough, she was way out of his league and deserved more than someone like him.

Yes, she was beautiful, but he'd seen plenty of beautiful women. He'd had them, too. There was something else, something about her. He felt it in the pit of his stomach every time he looked at her. He didn't know what it was, only knew it was more than lust.

All it took—one look, and the woman had him doubting shit, thinking about shit he shouldn't be worried about, and craving shit he had no business wanting.

So when Army called him and told him about Anthony's, coincidentally where he took Della every Saturday, he'd jumped on it. But it didn't mean it was a good idea. It was a bad idea. The woman was beautiful and off limits. He needed to remember that and feared the more time he spent with her, the more likely he'd forget.

He swung open the door leading into Anthony's, allowing Della and Allie in first, Army trailing behind. He then headed to the hostess and gave her his name, requesting a table for four instead of two. A moment later, they were seated in a booth. Della and Allie sat first, then slid in. He sat beside Della, and Army next to Allie.

Allie, eyes on Della, with a smile on her face, asked, "So what's good here?"

"The spaghetti's my favorite, but I get pizza sometimes. The pizza's really good. I like cheese. That's my favorite."

"That's my favorite, too."

"J likes pepperoni, and so does Ty. They can eat an extra-large by themselves, really fast."

The waitress stopped at their table and asked if they wanted anything to drink.

"Della, Sprite?"

She nodded. Trig ordered a Sprite and a beer, for himself.

"Allie? Still drinking beer?" Army asked.

She nodded.

Shit. Beautiful, classy, drove a muscle car, and drank beer? He was so fucking screwed.

Army ordered two beers. The waitress left to retrieve their drinks.

"So, Allie, what're your plans for tomorrow?"

"Need to get some shopping done. I wasn't thinking clearly when I packed. I need a suit for interviews."

"Let me arrange to have your stuff shipped here."

She shook her head. "New beginning… Besides, that stuff is useless to me here. I kind of get the feeling this town's more low key than the city."

The waitress returned with their drinks and garlic bread, and then they ordered two extra-large pizzas half-cheese, half-pepperoni.

"I have to go to the restroom," Della announced.

He cringed inwardly. He loved taking his niece out to dinner, the movies, anywhere really. He loved spending time with her. She was beautiful, sweet, and reminded him of his sister, but he hated this part. She was too little to head into the women's bathroom alone, and he hated taking her into the men's.

"I have to go too. Mind if I come with you?"

Damn. Allie must've read his mind.

Della nodded. He stood and helped Della out then watched them go.

"Don't worry. Allie's good with kids."

His gaze shot to Army, sitting across from him. "Not worried, brother. In fact, I'm relieved."

Army quirked a brow.

"You have a daughter one day. You take her out alone, she's young like Della is, and she needs to go to the bathroom, you'll know what I mean."

Army smiled and shook his head. "Hadn't even thought of that."

"Allie looks better."

"Yeah. Don't know if I should trust it though. She hides shit, and I got this feeling in my gut there's something she's not telling me."

His brother noticed, and it hadn't even taken a day. "What'd you think it is?" When the question went unanswered, he asked, "That bad?"

He shook his head. "I don't want to say it 'cause I hope to God I'm wrong."

Fuck. She had run, and where he came from women only ran from men for one reason. The thought it happened to Allie turned his stomach.

The girls returned, and the waitress came by with their food. They ate, drank, and talked. Allie mostly talked to Della and Army. She only looked in his direction twice. Only then had he allowed himself to glance her way.

Torture of the worst kind, ignoring her and ignoring how he felt, but he had no other choice. No one could ever know. Didn't mean he didn't notice shit. He noticed how she took a sip of her beer, her lips on the rim of the bottle, how she managed to still look classy and so fucking sexy it made his cock twitch. He noticed how she listened to his niece like she was the only one at the table, how she laughed softly with guarded eyes, and how she looked at Army like he was her fucking savior.

All of it made him want her more. He wanted her in a way he'd never wanted another woman, for more than a night, for more than sex. He wanted her for keeps.

Fuck.

No other choice. He *had* to keep his distance. She was too fucking good for him, and off limits.

Chapter Six

Allie had managed to get through the past three days with little effort.

Sunday, her brother drove her to the mall. She bought a black skirt suit and black heels to match. She also purchased several leggings, a pair of sneakers, and workout shirts. He drove her to the grocery store where she purchased necessities: shampoo, conditioner, lotion, and so on.

Monday, since her Camaro was in the process of being shipped, she'd borrowed her brother's SUV to pick up a newspaper and search for job listings. She'd also borrowed his laptop, checked listings online, sent off her resume, and lined up three interviews Tuesday and another Friday.

Now with three interviews down, she felt good, like she was on her way to getting her life back on track. With a master's in Accounting and three years of experience at a large company, she was confident in her abilities and certain she'd get offers from at least two of the jobs she interviewed for. She wouldn't make near as much money, but she didn't need to make so much. Living costs in a small town were nowhere near what they were in New York City.

In no time, she'd have a job, and she'd find a place of her own. She hadn't mentioned this to Tyler yet. He had this crazy idea she should live with him. He was in the process of remodeling his house and claimed there was plenty of room for her.

On a high, she decided to go for a run. She hadn't run for more than a week, and her body craved the exercise. After changing into a pair of leggings, sports bra, shirt, and sneakers, she headed downstairs. Passing the living room, she spotted Cuss and Dash, sitting on the couch, the television on full blast. Her gaze gravitated to the picture on the screen. Hard not to considering it was a 70" flat screen TV.

Dash and Cuss shifted on the couch, turning to her. Their eyes wide, their mouths hung open. "Hey, Classy, ain't that you?" Cuss asked.

Yes, it was a picture of her smiling. Under it, the caption read, "Accountant from Holden Holdings, LLC. Missing."

Her stomach turned. The room around her spun, bile rising in the back of her throat. She really hoped she wouldn't barf in front of bikers. Completely freaking humiliating, worse than crying.

"Fuck, brother, she looks like she's gonna retch."

She swallowed, attempting to ignore the nausea and wiped the sweat beading on her forehead with the back of her hand.

Shit. Fuck. Totally warranted.

A man came on the screen, her cheating ex-fiancé, Wyatt.

"When did you notice your fiancée was missing?" a reporter, off camera, asked.

Such a good actor, his brows creased, expression of worry etched across his face, like he loved her, like he hadn't cheated multiple times, like he hadn't beat the love she had for him out of her. "She's been gone since

Saturday. She's my world, my rock, and I'm scared to death something has happened to her."

His world? His rock? She knew his plan. It didn't take a genius to guess. She'd have to fly to New York and sort out the mess he made, and then he and her father would try to get her to stay. If that didn't work, they'd make her.

She fisted her hands until the sting of her nails biting into her palms began to hurt. The sudden urge to scream ripped through her. She couldn't. It wasn't how she'd been taught to deal with her problems.

"Doll, you engaged?" Bud asked. He and several others had since walked into the room.

Her gaze sliced to his. "No, I'm not engaged," she snapped. "I broke things off because he cheated. I caught him with *three* different women."

She lost it, and it was the reason why everyone was now looking at her like she'd grown another head. She hated getting so emotional, hated more she showed it. Her father hated it, too. Every time her mother got emotional, he got angry and walked out, so she'd taught herself to hold all her "womanly emotions" in check, all the time.

A strand of hair came undone. She pulled it back into her ponytail. "Fucking asshole thinks he can control me. I'll show him," she mumbled under her breath. Turning on her heel, she ran into the kitchen, picked up the phone, and dialed information for the number to the New York City Police Department. They transferred her a moment later.

"Detective Mason."

"Detective, my name is Alyssa Holden, and I'm calling to inform you I am *not* missing. I know exactly where I am and so does my father." She heard chuckling behind her and ignored it.

"Are you telling me your father lied to police?"

"I'm telling you he knows I left and why I left, and I'm twenty-five, which means I can disappear if I want."

"Ms. Holden, your fiancé filed the report. Is there a reason why you left without telling him?"

"Detective Mason," her voice laced in fury. "He is not my fiancé. Before I left, I broke off the engagement. Not that it is any of your business, but my ex-fiancé cheated, reason why I broke off the engagement, and it's also the reason why I don't have to tell him I left or why I left."

"Right, Ms. Holden. I need you to come in, in person, so I can see you for myself."

She rolled her eyes even though she knew chances were she'd have no choice. "Right, I'll be there in a day or two, and please call off the media storm."

He chuckled.

She slammed the phone down on the receiver. "Fuck," she muttered under her breath. Warranted, she didn't want to go to New York. She didn't want to see Wyatt or her father, but now, she had no choice.

Turning, she spotted the maelstrom of bikers and froze. How much they'd heard of her conversation, she had no idea. In the middle, stood the man she hadn't been able to forget since she set eyes on him, rekindling that now familiar feeling in her gut.

His dark eyes deadlocked on hers, the muscle in his jaw jumping. Angry, but what else was new? Not too far-fetched to assume why. Men didn't like emotional women. Men didn't like dealing with drama. She'd created a scene and put them in the middle of it.

Why she cared what this biker thought and paid no mind to any of the others, who obviously found it amusing considering the wide smiles on their faces, was beyond her. Still too angry and wrapped up in what Wyatt had the nerve to do, she didn't put much thought into it.

Still, her cheeks flushed. She lifted her chin and strode toward them. She had no choice. It was the only way out.

They made way for her, everyone except Jace. She side-stepped to move past him, pausing in front of Bud. "Sorry I snapped at you." She then walked out, intent on doing what she'd planned—running.

It helped.

It always helped.

****

"Brother," he greeted Army, phone to his ear. Trig tried to keep his cool, but it was hard. They had a situation, and it wasn't good. "It's Allie."

"What happened?"

"Don't know the whole story. What I do know is someone reported her missing, and she's on the news."

Army let out a curse.

Exactly his thought. Compared to his brothers, he didn't find any of this funny. He'd bet his life her dickhead father in cahoots with her cheating ex-fiancé were trying to manipulate her, and it worked. From what he overheard, she planned on heading to the city, giving them the opportunity to spew shit about how sorry they were, how everything would change. Maybe then, she'd give it another go and stay where she obviously didn't want to be.

"Where is she?"

"From the looks of it, she went for a run."

"Shit. I'm on a guard, but I'll be there by the time she gets back. Don't let her leave."

"What're you gonna do?" He bit the side of his mouth, knowing he shouldn't have asked. He couldn't let on he cared.

"No other option. Gonna go to New York."

About to hang up, Army said, "Thanks for the heads-up, bro."

"No problem." Ending the call, Trig headed outside the garage and waited. He wouldn't chase her, figuring she needed to run like he needed to ride. He'd let her have it, but when she returned, he'd be there, and he wouldn't let her out of his sight.

****

Allie was exhausted, drenched in sweat, and it felt great. She'd needed a run for days, and after Wyatt's infuriating stunt, she needed it more.

As she headed into the garage, she pulled up the bottom of her shirt and wiped the sweat off her face. Taking a deep breath to slow her heartbeat, she looked up and found Jace only feet away, wearing a black wife beater under his cut, and jeans hanging low on his waist. Her stomach clenched at the sight; he looked so good. Her gaze drifted to his, his on her stomach, undisguised lust written on his face.

Her cheeks flamed.

His gaze shot to hers and hardened. Like it was her fault he caught a glimpse of her bare stomach. Like it was her fault he liked what he saw. Like he hated he liked what he saw.

He took a step, schooled his features, and then he

casually asked, "Good run?"

Damn, he was good. He so easily disguised what he felt, what she caught a glimpse of.

"Yeah."

He crossed his arms over his chest. "Your brother's on his way."

She didn't know why he told her. She said nothing.

"He wants to talk to you."

Talk to her? About what? Oh, God. Jace told her brother about her tantrum! Why else would Jace be waiting for her? Why else would her brother want to talk to her?

"You told him?" she asked, abashed, her face heating. "Why would you... I'm allowed to have feelings, you know." She believed it. She just didn't think she was entitled to show them, but instinctively, she defended herself. "I know I lost it, but I'm entitled to feel. Just because—"

"What're you talkin' about, Allie?"

The way he said her name with his deep voice made a shudder run though her. She fought to ignore it, and then she fought to remember why she should be angry.

"What're you talkin' about, Allie?" His voice grew harsher.

Why did that make her shiver? "I'm losing my mind," she mumbled under her breath.

He closed the feet between them until he was so close she had to tilt her head back to look at him. "I'm talkin' to you."

"I know, but I have a lot on my mind right now, and I was side-tracked for a second. And I'm not sure I want to talk to you after you called my brother to tell on me."

He leaned toward her. A breath away, she lost track of thought because his lips were so close she could almost taste them. Powerlessly, her gaze gravitated to them.

He clenched his jaw, swallowed then mumbled a barely coherent, "Fuck."

She snapped out of her trance. Her gaze went back to his.

"It had to be done."

Letting her anger get the better of her again, she stomped her foot. "I know I lost it. I would've told him."

His gaze went to her foot, then back to her eyes. The sides of his mouth twitched, fighting a smile. "It's not about you losin' it. It's about you going to New York where your dickhead of a dad and ex-fiancé can fuck with you."

Her heart stopped beating. For a moment, she relived the moment, watched it unfold again and again. Then her heart started pounding again, so loud she swore he could hear it. He didn't move away from her; he stayed close and kept his eyes on her.

She'd been a bitch for no reason. That didn't sit well with her. She released a breath. In doing so, her shoulders slumped. "I'm sorry. I think I misunderstood."

"You gonna let me in on what you misunderstood, Allie?"

He said her name again, and he said it so softly like he cared. She loved it, loved how he said it and how it made her feel.

She didn't want to admit it because she felt like an

idiot, but she did anyway. "I thought you told him about my temper tantrum."

"Your what?"

The words were harsh and loud causing her to jump away. "My temper tantrum."

He lifted a brow and nodded, what she understood to mean a silent command she continue.

"I was upset, and I let it show."

He shook his head once. "Not gettin' you."

"Women aren't supposed to show when they're emotional. They're—"

"Who the fuck said that?" he shouted so loud she jumped again.

She hesitated. The real question? Who hadn't said it? Everyone had: her father, her mother, Wyatt. The list went on.

His eyes widened and flared. He clenched his jaw so hard she thought he'd crack his teeth. "Right, your dickhead of a father and that shit of a fiancé you had." He ran his fingers through his hair. "You feel it. You show it. Get me?"

She nodded.

In the distance, a bike roared. He moved away from her but never lost hold of her eyes.

Chapter Seven

Her brother wouldn't take no for an answer, so Allie was on a flight to New York with him *and* Jace. It meant the flutter in her stomach had been on overdrive for the last several hours.

She hadn't wanted to interrupt Tyler's life more than she already had, but deep down, she was glad he'd insisted. She *needed* him. Had he believed her, she would've come up with a plan to avoid the unavoidable—seeing her father, seeing Wyatt, but she didn't have much hope any plan would work. Men like her father and Wyatt didn't take no for an answer. Lucky for her, neither did her brother. The difference? Tyler had her best interests at heart. He let her choose, and his instincts were dead-on. When he sensed she needed him, nothing stopped him from being there.

She fiddled with her music player attempting to soothe her nerves, but it didn't help. Tyler glanced at her every so often. His eyes would soften, and he'd smile. Jace noticed, too. His gaze snapped to her hands and hardened, and then he'd spare a glance at her face. Not even then would he hide the hardness in his expression. He let her get her fill until she looked away.

She had no idea why her brother wanted Jace with them considering her father wouldn't come near with Tyler around, considering one look from Tyler and Wyatt would run for the hills. Her brother was that scary when angry. Still, Tyler told her Jace would go with them.

After she explained what happened, he'd been so angry she hadn't wanted to upset him more, and she hadn't even asked why. Why Jace agreed to come when it became more and more apparent with each of his glances, every one more menacing than the last, he didn't like her and he didn't want to be there, she had no clue. Because of her nerves, she didn't put much thought into it either.

The plane landed with a small thud. Instinctually, she reached for the arm rests, gripping them for dear life.

"Still scared of flying?" Ty teased.

She laughed softly. "I'm not scared. I'm terrified. There's a difference."

He chuckled. "Think you're cutting off Jace's blood supply, Allie."

She shifted. Her gaze shot to her hand on Jace's forearm. She flushed, looked up to meet his gaze, and mumbled, "Sorry."

For some reason, he grinned, revealing a heart-stopping smile. She released him, then quickly looked away. Before she knew it, they deplaned and hailed a cab. Tyler opened the door for her, and she climbed in. Jace entered through the other side. Tyler slid in behind her, and she scooted farther, making room until she felt Jace's arm against her, the natural heat of his body mingling with hers, tempting her to seek more of that warmth and curl herself against him.

Tyler instructed the driver to drive to the police station. Twenty minutes later, they arrived. Jace opened his door, stood, and held out his hand to help her out.

The action was mystifying, so gentlemanly and unlike any man she'd ever dated.

His gaze locked on hers, she placed her hand in his, tough, calloused, and masculine. His fingers tightened around her hand, and heat shot up her arm. He pulled her up and out of the cab easily. She forgot where she was, what she meant to do as his gaze bored into her. No other man had this effect on her. He was the first. She sure as hell hoped he wouldn't be the last. Even now, after his kind gesture, he didn't seem fond of her. The corded muscles in his shoulders were tense, his mouth tight.

"Allie."

She jumped at the sound of her name, turned, and found Tyler staring at her. It hit her then, where she was and why. Striding past him, she went into the police station. Her brother hot on her heels while Jace retrieved their bags from the trunk of the cab. She went to the reception area and asked to speak to Detective Mason. A moment later, a lean man in his early thirties wearing a pair of khaki Dockers, shirt, and tie greeted her.

He held out his hand. "Ms. Holden, I'm Detective Mason."

She took it and shook it firmly. "I wish I could say it's a pleasure, but this is a bit of an inconvenience."

The door opened, then closed behind her.

Detective Mason's eyes drifted to it, his posture tensing. "Can I help you?"

She turned and spotted Jace, blocking most of the doorway and holding two duffel bags. "You help me by helping her." He sat a chair away from Tyler, dropping the bags at his feet.

"A friend?"

She faced Detective Mason. "My brother, Tyler, and his friend, Jace."

He nodded. "I'd like to talk to you in private, Ms. Holden, if you don't mind."

He led the way into a small room, and she took a seat. He sat across a wood table in front of her.

"As you can see, I'm not missing. I'm here, but I only plan on staying a night. My brother didn't kidnap me. His friend didn't kidnap me either. I left because I wanted to. Are we done?"

His gaze intensified, piercing her, but then he smirked. "In a rush?"

"Yes, I want to go home."

He straightened and leaned closer. "I can argue your home is New York. You've lived here your entire life."

"My home is wherever I want it to be, Detective. Right now, it's not here."

"Can you explain why a woman would leave her home, her job, her life from one night to the next without planning ahead?"

She could. She just didn't want to.

"You're running from something, Ms. Holden."

Allie lifted her chin defiantly. "I'm running from a life of lies, Detective Mason, and it's none of your business." She stood and turned on her heel.

"Where'd he hit you, Ms. Holden?"

She froze, her heart pounding so loudly she thought it'd beat out of her chest. She wanted to run, but knew it'd do no good. He was a cop, after all, and a good one. He'd read her from one look. Maybe even before that.

She swallowed, faced him, and sat.

His expression softened. "You can press charges."

No, she couldn't. It wouldn't make much of a difference anyway. Wyatt was one of the top defense attorneys in the state, loaded, and had friends in high places. It would be her word against his. She'd be vilified. "I just want to go home, Detective."

"You're a smart woman, graduated top of your class at Columbia, but I'll tell you this anyway. Being gone isn't going to erase what happened. It won't make it hurt less."

She nodded.

"You can go, Ms. Holden. I won't keep you longer."

She stood and headed toward the door. When she reached the threshold, she turned and found him staring her way. "I'm sorry I was rude." She smiled weakly. "Thank you, Detective."

He smiled, shaking his head. "I deal with crooks, rapists, and murderers. You were a breath of fresh air, Ms. Holden."

Her smile widened.

****

A knock sounded on her door. "About time," she mumbled under her breath.

After their trip to the station, they headed to her Manhattan apartment. Tyler insisted she box up her stuff and arrange for it to be shipped. She agreed, considering she needed more than a duffel bag of clothes and the few things she'd recently bought, so she spent the better part of the afternoon doing that while Tyler and Jace watched a football game on TV and drank beers. Half an hour ago, Tyler left to pick up dinner, and Jace jumped in the shower.

Glad for the packing break, Allie straightened and hurried to open the door.

The breath rushed out of her, her heart stopped dead, then started pounding again, loud and fast. "Wyatt," she whispered, cursing herself for not looking through the peephole.

Wyatt had ways to get by the front desk of her building. Namely, his good looks. Tall, just an inch under her brother's height, but thinner with brownish, sun-streaked hair, cut short, he wore a black suit and tie. Right then, his brows were creased, the same worried expression she'd seen on TV marred his face.

"What are you doing here?" she asked, hoping he couldn't hear the panic in her voice.

He didn't respond. Instead, he stepped through the door, shut it, and embraced her. She stood frozen. He wasn't much for blatant displays of affection, not in public, not in private. But it wasn't the reason why. The last time he'd touched her, it hurt. He meant it to.

"Alyssa, I've been out of my mind with worry," he whispered against her ear.

She fought not to move, but inside, she cringed.

"I've missed you so much." He drew away from her slightly then finally released her.

Unwillingly to make any sudden movements, she slowly took a step away. "You shouldn't be worried considering we're over." She whispered, purposefully. Making him angry would only make her more afraid.

He sighed heavily, his eyes softening before he shoved his hands in his pockets. "I know I've messed up, but I'm a different man now. I haven't been with anyone since—"

"You know why this is over, Wyatt. Don't make

me remind you."

"I'm sorry. I love you, Allie."

"Don't call me Allie," she snapped.

She shouldn't have snapped, but she couldn't help it. He never called her Allie. Until recently, no one had ever called her Allie but Tyler.

Instead of snapping back like she imagined he would, he held up his hands. "I'm sorry—"

Thanking her lucky stars for the reprieve, she softened her voice. "I don't want your apologies, Wyatt. It's a little too late for that. I forgave you once. I'm not forgiving you again, especially not after...You need to go."

That did it, what she wanted to prevent.

His eyes hardened. He grasped her wrist, his fingers pressing into her flesh in a painful grip.

She let out a small gasp. Fear and panic overwhelming, she fought, placing her other palm over his chest to shove him.

"I'm not leaving, and you're not leaving, Alyssa." His voice harsh and ominous. "Don't make me—"

His words died suddenly. The next instant, his back slammed against the door. His hand still held hers. She stumbled forward, then straightened. Her head shifted. She spotted Jace.

His hand wrapped around Wyatt's throat, the other arm resting against his chest. "Let her go, asshole."

Relief swarming her, she pressed her lips together, silently thanking him and her brother too.

Wyatt's gaze sliced from hers to Jace's then back again, but he didn't release her. "That was quick, Alyssa."

Jace's hand around his throat tightened. He yanked

Wyatt away from the door then banged his whole body against it again, the impact causing a loud, echoing thud. "Look who's fuckin' talking. I'm not gonna ask you again."

Finally, Wyatt released her.

Immediately, she took several steps away. "You need to go."

"You've fallen, Alyssa. Going from me to…" His gaze shot to Jace. "This…"

Her lips parted to deny there was anything between her and Jace, but Jace beat her to it.

"That's where you're wrong, 'cause I got her, and I'm not fool enough to cheat. I got her, and I'm smart enough to know there's no one like her. Classy, sweet, smart, and fuckin' beautiful. Her skin's like silk. Her pussy tastes and feels like fuckin' heaven. And I knew all that from one fuckin' look."

Her jaw dropped.

He lied through his teeth, but his voice had been laced with emotion, like he meant it with every breath in his body. For a moment, she let herself believe he wanted her that much, and it gave her hope. Maybe someday, someone would want her that much.

She shook her head, forcing the fantasy away. Neither one of them seemed to notice. Wyatt and Jace continued to stare each other down, sharing silent not-so-nice words.

"So this is how it's gonna go. I'm gonna release you, and when I do, you're gonna leave, and you're never gonna see or contact her again. You're gonna leave 'cause if you don't, I'll be tempted to beat the cheating bastard outta you.

"You're gonna leave 'cause her brother's gonna be

here any second, and if he's sees you here, he's gonna flip his lid. Trust me when I tell you, you don't wanna catch that man in a temper. So I'm gonna let you go this one time 'cause quite frankly I'm thanking God every second of every day you cheated. It means she's warming my bed now instead of yours, but don't take this for kindness. I'm not kind, and you hurt my woman, so you see or contact her again, that face of yours is never gonna look the same, and you're gonna have a hard time getting pussy. Get me?"

Wyatt's gaze met hers. Jace released his hold on his neck and punched him in the gut. Wyatt doubled over, wrapping his arms around his waist, and groaned loudly. She let out a small gasp, then immediately put her hands over her mouth. Jace grabbed the front of Wyatt's shirt and slammed him against the door again.

"That's for puttin' your hands on my woman. No one touches what's mine. Let that be a lesson. And 'cause you've proved you're a fuckin' idiot, I'll tell you this, a man, a real one, doesn't put his hands on a woman who doesn't wanna be touched. Now, don't mother fuckin' tempt me, asshole. Walk away, and don't say another word. Don't even look in her direction."

Jace let him go.

With those last words and without sparing a glance in her direction, Wyatt straightened his shirt, opened her front door, and walked out.

Allie watched him go. For a long moment after, she stared at the door, wondering where the hell she'd gone wrong. She'd never wanted a relationship with Wyatt. From first glimpse, something about him turned her off, but her father pushed and pushed until she gave in. She ignored her instincts and fell for Wyatt's lies. In the end, he showed her why she should've trusted herself. He showed her the real him—a monster.

"You okay?"

The muscle in his jaw jumping, and still, his voice had been tender.

"Yeah, I'm okay. Thank you."

Tears began to choke her. She walked away as fast as she could. Inside her room, she closed and locked the door behind her, and then she sprinted into her closet. Taking a seat in the farthest corner, she cradled her knees and dropped her head. Only then did she let the tears cascade down her face.

She wasn't sure how long she sat there crying, but it was long enough she started sobbing. She sobbed so hard there came a point she thought she'd never be able to stop. When the thought occurred, her bedroom door slammed hard against the wall, and she was forced to swallow her sobs. She wiped her tears and blanketed the emotion from her face just as he came to view. Tears choking her, the flutter in her stomach hit her with full force.

Handsome, even in a T-shirt and jeans he was handsome in a rugged biker kind of way, so different from anyone she'd ever dated and still too appealing. She bet her life he didn't take an hour to get ready. She bet when he found the woman for him, he'd treat her like gold. She knew this because of everything he'd said. A man who couldn't give himself completely to a woman couldn't speak like he had.

His jaw dropped and that angry expression always there disappeared. What was left? A rugged biker looking at her in the tender way she'd seen men look at women who'd lost hold of their emotions.

In the haze of her grief as she looked into his tender dark eyes, she realized why every time she looked at him that flutter in her stomach came and what it meant. It meant he was a man she could fall for without so much as trying.

"I'm fine."

Jace sighed heavily, closed the distance between them, and lifted her off the floor. Cradling her against his chest, he strode out of the closet. The feel of his body, the warmth permeating it, soothed her. She didn't want him to let her go.

She sucked in a breath, knowing with certainty had she fallen for a man like him no one would've ever hurt her. "I can walk. I'm fine."

He softly set her on the bed. "You're not fine, Allie."

"I will be."

He sat beside her then nodded. "Yeah, you will, but you need to get that pent-up shit out."

"I don't need you here to do that. I was doing that just fine alone... You...you're a biker, and bikers—"

"I'm a man, and no man likes to see a woman cry. A man with half a heart tries to console that woman, no matter who she is."

Had he just said that? Jesus. He really made it hard for her. Angry most of the time, but then he said things like that and did things like lift her off her closet floor and hold her close. It made her think there was much more to him than her brother said. "What?"

"I get you've been surrounded by pricks, dickheads, and cheaters, so I'll repeat it. A man with half a heart tries to console a woman who's crying. A man who's not a prick, dickhead, or cheater doesn't tell a woman she can't express how she feels."

He was still looking at her that tender way, and it made her want to believe everything he said. Worse, it made her think he cared. Right then, she couldn't look at him and not think these things, so she looked away.

Resting his elbows on his legs, he ran his fingers through his hair. Without meeting her eyes, he said, "You love him." He said it like it pained him to admit it.

Wanting to know if in fact it had, she looked at him. She knew she'd know staring into his eyes. His head cast down, not looking at her. She said nothing.

"Do you?" He turned to her. His brows furrowed, his expression pained, really like it hurt him to have her admit it.

The flood of tears came and slid down her face. She let them. "I loved him. I never…" She let the words trail off. "We were introduced by my father. There was something about him I didn't like, but my father insisted I give him a chance. I did. We dated. After a while, I fell for the lies."

She shook her head. "I don't want to be the woman who blames herself, but I do because a part of me knew. I let my father make the decision for me like I let him make every other decision in my life."

With one swift movement, he hauled her toward him. Cupping the back of her head with one hand, the other firm on her back, he pressed her against his chest.

"Cry, Allie, fuckin' let it out."

She did.

After several long moments, he said, "I meant what I said."

She pulled away from him. Still close, so close if she moved a fraction of an inch, his lips would touch hers.

"You—"

"I know. If I feel it, I show it, right?"

His jaw clenched. He didn't say or do anything for several moments, and then as if reluctantly, he nodded.

Chapter Eight

Allie crying in his arms, crying those silent tears, holding back the gut-wrenching sobs he'd heard before. Her small body, pressed against his, trembled.

He was helpless, powerless to undo what had been done. The only thing he could do—beat the shit out of the asshole who'd hurt her. He would have, too. He'd wanted to bash the bastard's head against the door repeatedly until he physically suffered the pain she felt inside, but the fear in her eyes held him back. She was class, beyond fist fights, blood, and revenge.

Pressing her tighter against him, feeling like the luckiest trailer trash on earth, he whispered, "I meant what I said." He admitted it because he wanted her to know all he said, he meant. More importantly, he wanted her to know her worth.

She pulled away from him slightly. Still, she was so close if he moved a fraction of an inch, he could press his lips to hers.

He hadn't finished his thought. Meaning to elaborate, he began, "You—"

"I know." She smiled the saddest smile he'd ever seen. "If I feel it, I show it, right?"

He meant that too, but that hadn't been what he wanted her to know. He wanted her to know he meant what he said to her ex-fiancé. She was classy, smart, sweet, and fucking beautiful beyond words. He wanted her to know, and yet he knew he made a mistake, acted irrationally, letting how he felt act for him instead of rationale. Knowing he should have never done what he attempted, he hesitated.

To keep the words at bay, he clenched his jaw, and so he wouldn't be tempted to say it again, he didn't speak for several moments. Then, finally and reluctantly, he nodded.

Coward. Scared. Tempted.

He was all of it.

He hated not having the guts to tell her, but knew he'd done the right thing. She was grieving for the man she'd loved and lost and didn't need another man proclaiming shit. She was off limits, and most importantly, her ex was right. She was out of his league and deserved better than him.

It had been clear to him from first glimpse, but one look at the apartment building where she lived with a doorman and reception area, and the knowledge slammed into him. One step into her apartment, and it seared his soul. Because her Manhattan apartment wasn't an apartment but a penthouse. Extravagant and lavish, the type of stuff he'd seen in movies: two bedrooms, two baths, full kitchen, dining room, living room, and a study. Lined with floor to ceiling glass windows that gave you an amazing view of the city no matter what room you were in. Everything in it expensive. Expensive in a way you didn't have to know anything about designers or décor to know its value.

"Allie," he managed. "You'll find someone one day who'll think the sun rises and sets on you, and you'll think the sun rises and sets on him."

She smiled. "Is that biker philosophy of some

kind?"

Fuck, no. That was him being a wuss, but he wouldn't admit it. He wiped her tears with his thumbs, then chuckled. "Naw, just me."

Staring into her eyes, he savored the feel—her against him, her eyes on him, giving him that sad, fake smile.

Woman like her, faking a smile for him made him feel like the luckiest trash on earth.

The moment broken with a single knock on the door. His protective instincts jumped to the forefront, he tore himself away. "Go in your closet. Take your phone. Stay there. Don't come out."

She didn't argue. She didn't ask questions. She nodded like she trusted him to take care of anything.

Luckiest trash on earth.

He dashed to the front door and looked through the peephole then swung it open.

"Brother, what took you so long?"

"Hiding Allie."

Army tensed. "What?"

He ignored it. He needed to get Allie first. Not wanting her to worry, he headed to her room, opened the door, and instructed her to come out.

"Trig, what the fuck?"

Trig caught sight of Allie coming out of her closet, wiping her face before he responded. "Ex showed up."

Army unceremoniously dropped the take out bags on the dining room table. "What?" His gaze snapped to Allie and hardened. "He touch you?"

Allie's gaze shot to his. He nodded, knowing she'd understand his silent command. He gave her free rein to tell him first, whatever she wanted, whatever she didn't.

Why he did that, he didn't know. Army was his brother and hers, and he should know the bastard put his hands on her.

"It wasn't a big deal."

Army's hands in fists, his jaw hardened. "Alyssa Marie Holden, a man puts his hands on you, it's a big fuckin' deal."

"Ty, he grabbed my wrist. It wasn't a big deal. Besides, Jace handled it."

Army's gaze shot to him.

He nodded.

"Jace slammed his head against the door several times, then punched him. Oh, and he thinks Jace's replaced him."

Trig tore his gaze from Allie to look at Army, wondering how he'd take this piece of information. The pent up anger had to go somewhere, and he didn't think Army would be opposed to beating his ass, considering he made it look like his classy baby sister was dating a biker.

"He looked scared. I mean, he didn't even try to fight back, Ty." Allie's voice alight with amusement.

The tension coiled around Army faded.

Allie closed the distance between her and Army. She smiled big, thrilled he'd roughed up her ex. "He won't be coming back."

Army crossed his arms over his chest. "May I ask why you were crying then?"

She crossed her arms, mimicking her brother. "May I ask why it took you more than an hour to bring dinner when you know I'm starved?"

Trig's lips twitched, hiding a smile. He knew her game. She wanted to keep the details from her brother because Army, in an instant, would find her ex and beat the living daylights out of him. That would probably get him arrested.

Her game, though, would only succeed in riling him. Army should never be riled, especially since he'd been practically foaming at the mouth moments before. Nonetheless, she did it and in the cutest possible way, proving he'd been right. She wasn't scared of her brother in the least.

His gaze shifted to Army.

Surprising, Army too, fought a smile. "Alyssa, don't rile me. Answer the question."

She lifted a brow. "Tyler, don't rile me, and let me eat."

Army threw his head back and laughed, then shook his head. He pulled out his chair and sat mumbling, "Damn woman, you're the only one who gets away with pulling this shit with me."

She smiled, cheekily. "I know."

Shocked as shit, Trig smiled, then followed her into the kitchen.

"Ty, you know you could help," she said over her shoulder.

"I got dinner."

Trig helped her grab plates, utensils, and headed back into the dining room. The square table, made from a deep, dark wood, seated four. Allie sat to her brother's right, he to his left. They dug into the food immediately. For several moments, no one spoke.

Allie broke the silence. "Both of you should take the beds. I'm smaller and can sleep on the couch."

Trig, in the process of swallowing, almost choked. He gave her his best angry, disbelieving gaze. "Fuck, no."

"What the fuck?" Army said, simultaneously.

"You have to admit it makes perfect sense. I'm smaller. A lot smaller. Both of you are—"

He shook his head.

Army shoved a fork full of meat in his mouth. "Allie, I'm not letting you sleep on a couch."

"No—" She began to protest.

Trig took a sip of beer. "I'm taking the couch."

Allie's gaze snapped to her brother. "Why don't you let me take care of you for a change?"

"I'm a man, Allie, and I'm your older brother. I take care of you. Always."

She shrugged. "Fine, be stubborn." Her gaze shot to him. "Both of you can sleep on the couch and wake up grumpy." She shrugged. "See if I care."

Trig took a bite, and then, because he couldn't help it, he chuckled.

Allie lifted her brows. "It's not funny."

He swallowed before he answered. "A man doesn't let a woman sleep on the couch."

Her eyes softened, and she turned her attention to her plate. After a moment, she met his gaze. "Thanks for beating up my ex."

"I didn't beat him up." He wished he would have, but he couldn't. Even knowing she wouldn't mind, he wouldn't have.

"He roughed him up, but..." Army's gaze shot to him. "...you should've."

"Deserved worse, but not something I wanna do in front of a woman."

She surprised him by saying, "He had it coming, so thanks."

He took a gulp of beer. "That means I have your permission to beat the shit outta him next time I see him?"

"I got dibs on kickin' his ass," Army said.

She laughed. "It's a moot point. Don't think either one of you will ever run into him again considering we're leaving tomorrow."

"You're forgetting I'd pay good money for a flight to come here and kick his ass, Allie."

Trig would do it right then if he could. "I second that."

She met his stare and smiled softly, a smile that was just for him.

Yeah, he was the luckiest trash on earth.

****

"Allie, why haven't you packed?" Army asked.

It was morning, and they were scheduled to leave early that afternoon.

Allie poked her head out of the closet, pointed at the boxes in the corner. "What do you call that?"

Army walked toward her. "What about the rest of this stuff?"

Trig agreed. From the look of the three boxes stacked in the corner, she'd barely packed anything. He'd been inside her closet the night before, and it was huge. He couldn't recall how much she'd packed in there. He'd been focused on the tears streaming down her face and the sadness emanating from her hazel eyes, but he bet she hadn't packed much of that either.

Allie sighed then headed into the closet. Army followed her. Trig right behind. Once inside, his gaze raked the entirety. As he'd predicted, she barely packed a thing. Her closet, bigger than the trailer he'd lived in growing up, was nearly filled. The right side was lined with shelves small enough for her shoes. At the far end, another series of shelves stacked with purses. To the left were her clothes: dresses, skirts, pants, blouses. In clothes alone, what she planned to leave behind was four times what he owned and probably worth more than his GI bill.

"I have what I need."

Army's arm shot out, pointing out the rest of the clothes, shoes, and bags. "What about the rest of this?"

That would've been his question.

"I'm donating it. My friend—"

"You should take most of this with you," Army insisted. "And donate what you don't want, but come on, you're gonna tell me you don't want any of those designer purses, that you don't want some of those shoes?"

Her shoes. Damn. They were all heels, high as hell and hot. She had them in every color and style, with straps, without, closed-toed, sandal-looking ones, sling-ons. Some even had red bottoms instead of the normal black.

She sighed. "I don't need them. Where am I going to wear half this stuff in a small town? It's too fancy."

He had to agree with her, and yet those fuck-me heels she should take. Any man would appreciate them. On her, they'd hand over their balls.

"It's a small town, but we got nice restaurants. Not far to the opera and—"

"I hate the opera."

"You should take the shoes," Trig said without thought.

Their attention turned to him. Her jaw dropped.

Army's eyes widened.

Shit. Maybe he shouldn't have blurted that. Too late to back down now. "When you start dating, you'll want them, and your man will appreciate them."

Army smirked. "You giving my sister dating advice?"

Shit. Why the fuck had he given her advice on how to turn on another man?

She smiled. "Fine, I'll take some of the shoes, but I don't want—"

"Allie, you should take some of the clothes and purses, too," Army insisted then looked to him.

"Women get tired of wearing the same shit. You should take the clothes and purses, too."

She chuckled. "And you know this because?"

"Gotta sister and a niece."

"Fine. You've both exasperated me, but I'm not taking the furniture." She paused, her eyes narrowed on Army. "Ty, I'm serious. Do *not* have it shipped."

"It's your stuff."

She turned away from both of them, grabbing purses from one of the shelves. "No, it's stuff Dad insisted I buy. I didn't even get to pick out my bedroom furniture." Facing them with purses in hand, she finished, "I don't want it."

He hoped he didn't run into her father, ever. He did, he'd have to teach the bastard a lesson, and he didn't think she'd like that.

Chapter Nine

Her phone rang. Allie dashed out of the bathroom with a towel tightly wrapped around herself and into her brother's room to pick it up from the bed where she'd dropped it. Looking at the caller ID, she smiled.

She picked it up and brought it to her ear. "Hello."

"Ms. Holden?"

"Yes, this is she."

"This is Regina Carter from Merriweather Group Corp. I've called to inform you we've decided to hire someone more suitable for the job."

"Oh." She couldn't help the disappointment in her voice. This was the third company who'd called to inform her they wouldn't hire her despite her degrees and three years' experience at a larger company.

"While your resume is impressive, we've decided to go another way."

She'd been to four interviews the week prior. The interviews had gone well, too well, and she left feeling confident she'd be hired. Friday, she received two calls from two different companies to say the same. She couldn't understand why, so she asked, "I mean no disrespect, but may I ask the real reason?"

A long moment of silence at the other end. Regina, the human resources manager who'd interviewed her, contemplated whether to tell her. "This stays between us."

Allie swallowed, a hollow feeling forming in the pit of her stomach. "Yes, of course."

"We didn't receive good recommendations from your previous employer. They cited tardiness, missed work days, and the inability to perform at a high standard."

In an instant, all the love she once felt for her father vanished. He'd done this. To her. Her father hired her out of college, but she started at the very bottom. She'd been hired as an accountant's assistant, although she was a certified public accountant, and she worked her butt off, days, nights, and weekends to make it to the top, to gain his approval, and to gain the approval of her co-workers.

"I understand you worked for your father's company, Ms. Holden. It came to my attention, via the news media, you left recently. It wouldn't be farfetched to presume there is some family issue between the two of you. Because I figured as much, I spoke to several employees. Because of the comments they made, my hands are tied. I cannot hire you regardless of your experience."

Her father was a bigger asshole than she'd thought. It was one thing to make false claims about her work ethic to suit his motives, another completely to force his employees to do it. She should've expected it. Her father would do anything and everything to get his way. More than anything, he wanted her to return to New York and marry a man who hurt her. All to give his company publicity and make more money.

"I understand. Thank you for your honesty." She hung up then slumped on the bed and ran her fingers through her wet hair, wondering what the hell she should do now. She had to find a job, the sooner the better. Unused to being inactive, she was antsy. Perhaps, though, it was a blessing in disguise. With her father bad mouthing her skills, she'd be forced to look for a job outside the accounting profession she never liked. Though she didn't know who'd hire her without experience.

She sighed heavily, then dressed, intent on heading downstairs to make dinner. Tyler told her she didn't have to cook for him, but she did. A little she could do to help he wouldn't fight her on. Not to mention, without a job, it gave her something to do.

As she headed past the living room, she scanned the area. She always did. She wouldn't admit it aloud, but she was looking for Jace.

Since they'd returned from New York, she hadn't seen him once. As ludicrous as it sounded, it made her think he was avoiding her. She didn't know why she felt that way, but she did. She'd hoped after he willingly comforted her something had changed between them. Maybe it was just her wanting to get along with the angry biker who wanted nothing to do with her. Maybe it was the inexplicable magnetic attraction she felt. Maybe it was all of the above.

"Hey, Classy."

She turned, spotted Dash behind her, and smiled. "Hey, Dash."

He wore his cut, a leather vest with the club's insignia on it. Tyler recently explained what a cut was. According to Ty, they all had one and wore them. Besides that, they all had tattoos with the insignia, a set of angel wings in flames with a skull in the middle. Under it read, Hell Ryders.

Dash usually wore his cut without an undershirt, revealing not only his tatted arms, but several other tats on his chest, including the club's insignia. "You makin' dinner tonight?"

"I am."

He rubbed his stomach. "Mind makin' me some?"

She crossed her arms over her chest. "Getting tired of take-out?"

He smiled. "Nothin' like a home-cooked meal."

She caught sight of Cuss moving toward her. The first thing she noticed, as usual, were his eyes. Right then, it wasn't just the sapphire color, but the mischief she read in them. "You cookin' again?"

"That was the plan."

He grinned, turning on the charm. "Classy, I'll give you a ride on my bike if you make me some extra."

She laughed.

"She won't be riding on anyone's bike." Tyler's voice boomed.

Turning, she spotted him at the end of the hall taking long-legged strides toward them. "It's okay, Ty. I hadn't planned on taking him up on his offer, and before you say it, I don't mind cooking for a house full of bikers." She faced Cuss and Dash, smiling. "But I'll warn you, once I find a job, you'll have to find someone else to make you home-cooked meals."

Cuss lifted a brow. "How's that comin' along?"

"Um, well…unfortunately, I haven't had any luck."

"I know the daycare center off of Main Street's hiring. Don't know if that's your thing." Cuss shrugged.

Her eyes widened. "Really?"

"Yeah, know one of the girls there. I can talk to her if you want."

It would be a great opportunity. She'd probably love it too. She always wanted to teach and work with kids, but she didn't have experience. "I don't have experience."

"You gotta record?"

She shook her head. "No."

"Think you're good then."

She smiled. She couldn't believe her luck. Moments ago, she'd been worried about a job. Now, not only was there a chance she'd get a job, but that job would be something she would enjoy. "If you talk to your friend, I'll make you dinner every night for a week," she promised.

"I'd do it for free, Classy, but I'll take you up on that offer 'cause you're a good cook, and I like home-cooked meals."

Smiling widely, she wrapped her arms around his waist, hugging him tight. He hesitated, but she didn't care. She was a hugger, her way of expressing gratitude. "Thank you. Thank you. Thank you," she whispered.

He patted her back awkwardly. "Don't start cryin' on me."

She drew away from the embrace. "I'll hold my tears, promise."

Grinning, he pulled his phone out of his back pocket, then made the call.

****

Allie in another man's arms, in his brother's arms. Lucky fucking bastard.

First time he sees her in days, and she's hugging Cuss like he just handed her the world. Cuss patted her back like an idiot because he was too stupid to realize he held the world in his arms.

Damn Cuss. There was something about the brother every woman loved. He couldn't figure it out, but apparently Allie wasn't immune.

She never hugged him, and he'd roughed up her ex. He'd held *her* when she cried and tried to comfort her.

Worse, her brother, Army, was standing there chuckling like it was hilarious, like Cuss was worth her.

And lucky Trig, he witnessed it. It hurt worse than the burning ache he felt every time he looked at her and remembered she'd never be his.

Trig needed to get the hell out of there before he did something he'd regret, like beat up Cuss or Army or both. He turned toward the wall, punched his fist through it, and walked away.

Chapter Ten

Mia took a sip of her drink. Her gaze narrowed on a brunette wearing a leather mini-skirt crop top, and clear stripper heels. The ensemble left little to the imagination. "She comes near my man again, and I'm going to slap the shit out of her."

Allie had only endured one Friday night at the compound before, but she'd began to refer to them as Friday Night Fiascos. A full house, everyone drinking, shooting pool, watching TV, listening to music, and trying to get lucky with the numerous half-dressed women strolling around.

Mia, Lynn, and she sat toward the back of the living room at the bar lined with stools.

Taking a pull of beer, Allie smiled, then turned her stool slightly to get a good look at the woman Mia referred to.

"Sweetie, didn't you see he wasn't interested," Lynn asked.

"Don't care if he's interested or not. I don't want her near him," Mia sniped.

Allie grabbed some chips and popped them in her mouth with the intention of hiding her smile.

Mia and Lynn were two old ladies part of Hell Ryders MC. Mia, a petite brunette with curves and spunk, often called "firecracker," had been part of the club for five years. Three of those, she'd been married to Stone. He barely spoke, barely moved unless he had to get Mia out of trouble, or so Allie heard. Lynn, a sweet blonde with pretty green eyes and a soft smile, recently married Wild, who never let her out of his sight.

A week and a half ago, Allie met them. She'd been in the kitchen, keeping her promise to make Cuss dinner, when they'd entered and introduced themselves. Since then, they'd become fast friends. Both women had taken her under their wing, invited her to the mall, dinners, movies, and so on. She confided in them, telling them her brother had the tendency to get up in the middle of the night, leave, and not return for hours. She'd never asked him why, primarily because she didn't want to butt into his life. He was almost thirty. Mia and Lynn told her it was club business and not to bother asking. He wouldn't tell.

"How's the job?" Lynn asked.

"I love it," she said, honestly. "The kids, my co-workers, everything…I love it so much, I feel bad only making seven meals for Cuss. You know he's the one who got me the job. He knows Tiffany, my co-worker. He talked to her. She called me that same night for an interview. The next day, I was hired on the spot."

"You can always make him extra meals. He won't complain."

"I thought about getting him soap to wash his mouth out. He really can't go an hour without cursing."

Lynn and Mia laughed out loud. She did, too.

Mia took a sip of her drink. "What I really want to know is what's the deal with you and Trig."

Nothing.

Absolutely nothing.

Before tonight, she hadn't seen him for days. The last time had been four days ago, and it had just been a glimpse. She'd seen him heading into his room, two doors away from her brother's. Before then, she'd seen him striding away after he punched a hole in the wall. Why? She had no clue. The loud thud of the drywall cracking sounded, and she turned. By then, he'd been toward the end of the hall. Cuss, who'd been on the phone at the time, and Dash hadn't reacted, as if it happened often. Ty called out his name, but he'd never turned.

Tonight was the first time since New York she had a good look at him. It didn't mean she hadn't thought of him, didn't mean her attraction had ebbed either. It meant he was avoiding her. The guys talked and when they did, he was mentioned, so she knew Jace hadn't disappeared. He went to the garage and hung out at the compound with the guys. He just never did it when she was there.

She sighed. "Nothing."

Lynn pressed her lips together. "That was a loaded nothing."

Mia smiled. "Is that why every time you sip on your beer he looks this way?"

Her cheeks heated. "No, he doesn't."

Lynn nodded. "Yeah, he does. I noticed, too."

"Maybe because he hates me," she mumbled under her breath. To their disbelieving looks, she added, "I'm serious. I think he does."

Mia lifted a brow. "Why do you think that?"

"Because…he…I think he's avoiding me."

"Yeah, I've kinda noticed," Lynn said, softly.

"Exactly, so—"

"He likes you. No other reason in the world why he'd avoid you," Mia said.

Lifting a brow, she asked, "What, are we in middle school?"

"No, but you're off limits. He probably thinks it's better to stay away. You know, so he won't be tempted."

"Um, I think you're both putting too much thought into this. Besides, if he really liked me, wouldn't he be trying…" She shrugged. "I don't know…to be nice or something."

Lynn shook her head. "You're off limits. Him going after you spells trouble between you and your brother, him and your brother, not to mention the club."

He avoided her because he liked her? She shook her head, trying to get rid of the thought. That sounded like something women told each other to make each other feel better instead of coming to terms with the fact the guy you crushed on had no interest in you. She wouldn't say this to them though. "I'm my own woman, and I chose who I date. My brother and the club have no say in it."

Mia popped a chip in her mouth. "Know you're new here, but there are rules. Remember I told you not to bother asking Army what he spends his nights doing?"

She nodded.

"This is like that. Army says you're off limits. Prez agreed, which means, babe, you're off limits. If Trig tried, he could get kicked out of the club."

"What?"

"It's as good as written in stone."

"But—"

Lynn leaned in and whispered, "I'm hearing you have feelings for Trig."

"I…" Her cheeks flamed, but she denied it. "I don't."

Lynn smiled, her eyes softening, then sipped her drink.

"Take this piece of advice from me," Mia said. "You two hit it off, before you announce it to the club make sure it's solid."

Lynn shifted, her gaze went behind Allie. She smiled. "Here come our men."

Allie spun and spotted both Wild and Stone headed for them. Time for her to go. "That's my cue." She slid off her stool. "See you guys soon." She smiled at them, then scanned the room. Her gaze gravitated toward the couch, the spot where Jace had been. He was gone. She waved at Dash and Bud, who'd finished downing shots, headed down the hall, and up the stairs toward her room.

A woman moaned.

Allie hadn't meant to look, but unwillingly, she turned her head. The door wide open, so inevitably, she caught sight of them. She stood there seeing, yet unbelieving, frozen with her eyes glued to an image she knew she'd never forget no matter how much she craved to.

Jace.

Shirtless sitting up on the edge of his bed, his head angled back, eyes closed, lips parted. A dark-haired woman draped over him, kissing his neck, her legs wrapped around him. Her black leather skirt hiked up to her waist, his hands cupping her bare ass.

Her heart clenched, squeezing in her chest so hard

it hurt. Deep and searing her from the inside out.

Jesus.

How it hurt.

And she didn't know why.

He wasn't hers. He was a biker who couldn't stand her. Single, free to screw however many scantily dressed women he wanted.

Her brother warned her bikers did it often, and still somewhere deep inside, she held hope Jace was different. He wasn't just a biker, he was the man who took his niece to dinner weekly, the man who'd roughed up her ex-fiancé, then held her while she cried.

It was more than that, too. She wanted to believe the man who affected her in a way no other man ever had, the man in whose arms she'd felt safe couldn't be anything like her brother described.

She hoped, a fruitless emotion, she knew now firsthand. In one, single, earth-shattering moment with a mere glimpse, her hope crashed and burned.

Her eyes brimmed with tears, helpless, hopeless, stupid tears she couldn't hold back.

He tensed, lifted his head, then his lids opened, and his dark eyes met hers. They widened briefly. For a second, she glimpsed something inside them, something she couldn't quite put into words that somehow mirrored what she felt stirring inside.

He had no right to show her, and she couldn't stand to see it, so she did what she should've done long before. She walked in the opposite direction of her room. With each step, her chest tightened so much she couldn't breathe. Bolting downstairs, she passed the living room, down the hall, and then into the garage and outside.

The cool air hit her face, arms, and legs. She took a deep breath. It did nothing to soothe the searing ache inside her chest. She needed to forget, erase the image from her mind, but it would be as fruitless and worthless as the hope she'd held.

She strode toward her brother's SUV and leaned against the side of it. Only then, did she let herself blink. Tears drifted out of her eyes and cascaded down her cheeks. She was a bigger idiot than she'd thought, crying for a man who'd never been hers.

"Babe?"

Frantically, she wiped her face, turned, and spotted the last person she'd wanted to see. No, the second to last. Just her luck, though she could argue she'd been lucky to have gone weeks without seeing him.

"Ripper." He stood six feet away. His gaze on her face, instead of sizing her like a piece of meat.

"Saw something you shouldn't have seen. Didn't Army warn you?"

How the hell did he know? She held his gaze, not speaking.

"I'll take that as a no." He shrugged. "It's club life, babe. Not every woman's like you. Some like bikers. Some like a lot of them. Some take whichever they can get their hands on. Some like others to watch and join in, so closing doors is optional."

Endless supply of sexually liberated women who wanted to be banged by multiple bikers a night? Yeah, Tyler should've mentioned it, especially given their open door policy. She would've been more careful. Had it been anyone else, she could've handled it. She just couldn't handle seeing Jace with another woman. Her own fault.

"See what I said is a surprise to you, babe, but that's life here." He took a step in her direction. "Think it's more, too. You wouldn't be out here in the dark cryin' unless you saw someone you cared about…" He leaned in to whisper. "And I don't mean your brother."

Shit. He read right through her. She swallowed.

"Know Army warned you 'bout us. Hell, if you were my sister, I wouldn't let you near this place." He nodded toward the garage. "Think you learned your lesson?"

"My lesson?"

"Don't fall for bad boys."

Fall? As in love? No, she barely knew Jace. Still, Ripper made a valid point. She let her attraction sway her, make her believe Jace was different.

"Is this you being nice?"

"I'm not nice. I'm a dick. Knew you were Army's sister, and hit on you to make you uncomfortable and piss off your brother."

Her eyes widened. "Why?"

"Told you, 'cause I'm a dick."

He'd been a dick then, but he wasn't a dick. A dick wouldn't go out of his way to talk to an emotional woman and warn her about bikers. Behind those dead eyes, there was a good man. No way in hell she'd tell him though.

"Besides, needed to break you in."

"What?"

"Classy girl like you, I needed to see how you'd handle it."

"A test? Did I pass?"

He smiled. "Yeah, babe, you passed."

She chuckled, thinking it ironic how she'd made

friends with the biker she'd avoided for weeks on the day she decided to get her own place.

Tyler wouldn't be happy, considering she agreed to stay with him until he finished remodeling his house, but now, she had no choice.

****

Allie.

Allie sat on his lap, her legs wrapped around his waist, her dark hair fanning his chest. The smell of her perfume around him, he cupped her ass. She pressed her lips to his neck and buried her hands in his hair.

Allie.

She moaned. No. Not Allie. A poor replacement because he couldn't have the woman he wanted.

Fuck.

He needed to forget Allie. Staying away from her hadn't helped, so he was being a guy, getting some tap who wasn't her in hopes he'd forget. It just wasn't working.

One look at the red-stained lips, leather mini skirt, and corset, and it hit him he wanted Allie, and he couldn't have her. All the taps dressed the same, wore the same lipstick, and said the same shit, too. None of them managed to turn him on wearing jeans, a blouse, and sandals because none of them were Allie.

But he'd had no choice.

For three hours, he sat in the compound's living room sipping a beer, watching Allie smile, and hearing her laugh, and he'd needed to fucking forget, so when he spotted the dark-haired tap striding his way giving him a fuck-me look, he'd taken her to his room. She took control, yanking his shirt off him, then climbing on his lap. He had to force himself not to push her away, and the only way he managed that was to imagine she was Allie.

Allie sat on his lap with her long, thick, dark hair fanning his chest, fantastic legs wrapped around his waist, and beautiful face buried in his neck.

But the bitch moaned again, and he lost focus along with the will to go through with this shit. Angling his head forward, he opened his eyes.

Shit.

Allie.

She stood just outside his open door, looking at him, eyes swimming in tears and unhidden pain marring her expression.

He felt it. The pain seared his chest, burning his insides alive.

It hurt.

It killed.

Damn it to hell, she wasn't even trying to hide it like she hid everything else. Why?

Fuck. She cared, cared about him enough she couldn't hide the hurt on her face or the emotion in her eyes.

And she'd never fucking care again, not after this. His fault. With his poor attempt to forget her, he ruined it. Had he been a smarter, better man he would've known, would've sensed it. If he hadn't been a coward, he would've tried. Maybe he could've had her for a night, a day, a single week. He lost her before ever having her. The knowledge of it kept him frozen in place for endless moments until she walked out of sight.

It forced him to react.

"Get up." His voice steeped in hurt.

The bitch moaned again.

He grabbed her shoulders and yanked her away. "Up. Off. Now."

She trailed her fingers down his chest. "But, baby—"

"Don't fuckin' touch me. Get the fuck off. Now."

She flinched, then moved up and off him.

He was being a dick, but he didn't care. The only thing he cared about had just walked away. He needed to get to her to explain, to see if anything could be salvaged.

"When I get back, be gone." He bolted out of the room, headed in the direction Allie had gone. He ran downstairs, nearly colliding with Bud and a tap. When he reached the living room, he scanned it. She wasn't there. He darted into the kitchen and found Mia sitting on the countertop with Stone standing between her legs.

He closed the distance between them. "Where is she?"

Mia's gaze shot to his. "Who?"

"You know who."

She shrugged. "I don't."

He fisted his hands. "Where is Allie?"

"Probably in her room."

He shook his head. "She came back down. You didn't see her?"

Her eyes narrowed. "No, why?"

Without answering, he strode away. Once in the living room, he scanned the area again then headed down the hall into the garage and searched there too. Parting the door to the outside, he found her, standing by her brother's SUV, her back leaning against the side of it. He sighed in relief, his steps slowing.

"Think you learned your lesson?"

Hearing the male voice, he stopped mid-stride. Ripper, the same brother who'd hit on her and made her uncomfortable weeks ago. He couldn't see him from where he stood, but recognized his voice.

"My lesson?" Her voice held no fear, no hesitation. Her body poised, yet relaxed.

"Don't fall for bad boys," Ripper warned.

He clenched his jaw, hating Ripper was being nice instead of his usual dickhead self.

"Is this you being nice?"

"I'm not nice. I'm a dick. Knew you were Army's sister, and I hit on you to make you uncomfortable and piss off your brother."

He'd known it, and still hearing Ripper admit it riled him. He fisted his hands.

"Why?"

"Told you, 'cause I'm a dick." Ripper hesitated then finally he said, "Besides, needed to break you in."

"What?"

"Classy girl like you, I needed to see how you'd handle it," Ripper replied.

"A test? Did I pass?"

"Yeah, babe, you passed." He heard the smile in Ripper's voice.

She laughed softly.

Trig hesitated, wondering what he should say, what he should do.

Before he realized what he was doing, he closed the distance between them, stopping six feet away, and called her name.

She tensed, straightened, and turned. The smile died, but she managed to hide the hurt he'd seen before. "Trigger." Her voice emotionless.

Fuck. Not good. She never called him Trigger. She always called him Jace.

Ripper strode up to her. "Catch you later." He gave him a chin lift, then left.

"I—" he began.

"You don't owe me an explanation, so don't bother."

Fuck. The brush-off hurt. "I do—"

"I saw something I shouldn't have seen. I didn't know about your open door policy, so I was shocked."

His brows lifted. "Open door policy?"

"Yeah, Ripper explained it to me."

He shook his head. "Not gettin' you."

"You leave doors open, so the other guys can join in or use your leftovers."

Shit. Fuck. She was right, and damn Ripper for telling her, but it wasn't the reason he left the door open. He'd simply been in too much of a rush to forget her.

He clenched his jaw. "Not why I left it open. I'm sorry—"

"Shouldn't you get back to your tap? I'm sure being out here is wasting her time," she said snidely. "She probably has a quota to meet tonight, and you're ruining it."

The tap probably did, but he hadn't ruined it. The only thing he'd ruined—what they could've been. His fault. He'd succeeded in killing whatever she felt for him. Her demeanor said it all. Her voice laced in sarcasm, her posture stiff. She wouldn't even let him explain.

"Allie—"

"I don't…"

Too late. She pissed him off with her icy tone and comments. Letting his anger best him, he took two menacing steps in her direction.

Her voice trailed off. Her eyes widened. She tilted her head up to meet his eyes.

Slowly, he leaned over her until he stood inches from her face. "You've had your say, Allie, so you're gonna let me talk now," he said firmly. "I didn't leave the door open on purpose. I never meant for anyone to see it, especially you. I'm fuckin' sorry you saw what you saw, but nothing's gonna change it now. I'll also point out I'm a biker, and I'm single, which means I can fuck whoever I wanna fuck whenever I want. Even men who aren't bikers have casual sex. This shouldn't be new information to you."

Her face paled, and she took a step away like he struck her. He supposed he had, with words. A low blow, but she made fucked up comments of her own, and they pissed him off. Still, it was fucked, and he shouldn't have said it, knowing it'd make a fucked up situation worse.

"If I'd wanted her so badly, I'd be in her now. Instead, I'm out here talking to you, trying to make sure you're okay, and you're giving me lip, not letting me fuckin' talk." He tried to explain, make it better, but the things he'd barked he couldn't take back.

She swallowed, looking resigned. "You're right. I'm sorry. Thank you for checking on me, but you shouldn't have. You didn't have to. I'm fine."

She waved her white flag, agreeing only to get away from him.

He took a step in her direction, but she took another step away. Sighing heavily, he ran his fingers through his hair. "Allie, I'm sorry. I shouldn't have—"

"It's fine."

He grinded his teeth and nodded, waving his own white flag. He couldn't trust himself to make anything better, not tonight. He tried and only made them worse. All he had left to do was pray to find a way to make it up to her.

Chapter Eleven

"How's the new apartment?"

Allie turned and spotted Tiffany, her co-worker, a gorgeous brunette and the friend of Cuss's who'd gotten her the interview. "Good. It's small, but it suits, and it was ready for move in, so…" She shrugged. "Can't complain."

Tiffany laughed. "But Tyler had plenty to complain about. Is he still giving you a hard time?"

Tyler. Her brother. Her protector. When she told him she found an apartment, he flipped. She expected it. He wanted her to move into his house. She hadn't been sold on the idea, considering they were both adults, and he liked to bring women home, but she told him she would consider it when he finished remodeling his house. She also agreed to stay at the compound during that time; except then, she had her run-in with Jace and his tap.

Staying had no longer been an option. She couldn't control her growing attraction, and it had already gotten her hurt. She reacted stupidly and felt guilty about the way she treated him. He had every right to react the way he did. She'd been a bitch, and he was right. He was a single man. He could sleep with whomever he wanted, when he wanted. She knew better than anyone men did this regularly, even some who were engaged and married.

She made a decision to avoid him at all costs. To do that, she had to move out, regardless of her brother's disapproval.

She smiled the fake smile she'd perfected. "Yeah."

"I love it."

She laughed. "Easy for you to say since he's not *your* brother."

"I think it's adorable. Wish I had a brother like that. Actually, I wish I had a sibling period."

Her phone vibrated. She plucked it out of her back pocket and read the caller ID. "Speaking of the devil," she mumbled under her breath, bringing the phone to her ear.

"Allie, need a favor."

At least, he wasn't calling to list the reasons she should move back in, which he had done several times. "Ty, don't know if you realize this, but I'm at work."

"Aren't you off in a half hour?"

She glanced at her watch, a half hour to four. "Guess you're right."

"You remember Della?"

Jace's niece, she wouldn't forget. "Yeah. Did something—"

"She's fine, but her mom didn't pick her up from school, and she isn't answering her phone. The school called Trig. Must be on his bike 'cause he isn't answering either, so the school called me to go get her, but I can't. Do you think you could?"

"Ty, I don't think they'll let me pick her up. I'm not related, and they don't know me—"

"I'm on her emergency contact card, and I told them you're my sister. All you need to do is show them your ID."

"Um, okay, but by the time I get out—"

"Don't matter, Allie. She's been there a while already."

"What school is it?"

He gave her the information. She jotted it down and hung up. Her gaze swung back to Tiff.

"What's up?"

"Jace's sister didn't pick up her daughter at school. They called Jace and couldn't get a hold of him. Then they called my brother and he can't, so he needs me to go when I get out."

"How old is she?"

"Five."

"You think something bad happened?"

She hadn't, but now…

Since the night she caught Jace with his tap, she'd avoided him by working overtime, then heading straight into her room and staying there. On her days off, she had plenty to do. Namely, getting her California driver's license, the plates for her car, and so on, it had been easy to avoid him. When she'd moved out, it became that much easier.

It was harder to avoid thinking about him, but she tried daily. Sometimes, thoughts crept in regardless of her attempts. Now, she was too worried about Della to even consider Jace, but Tiffany had a point. Something must've happened, if not to Jace, then possibly to his sister.

"She's been waiting for an hour. The poor girl's probably wondering if her mom forgot her. You should go now."

She wanted to go the moment she heard, too. "You think Betty will mind?" Betty, her boss, the best boss ever, had a special way with kids.

"I highly doubt it. You come in early and leave late every day."

She smiled and headed into her boss's office. The moment Allie entered, Betty, sitting behind her desk, greeted her. Allie explained the situation, and Betty immediately hurried her out.

Arriving at Della's school fifteen minutes later, she rushed inside, straight into the main office. When she parted the door, her eyes gravitated to the child wearing the school uniform, sitting silently, her head bowed.

"Della, sweetie?"

Della lifted her head. Her eyes, red and puffy, met hers. With a tightening chest, Allie strode to her and squatted so they were eye to eye.

"Hi, Allie."

She wiped Della's cheeks and whispered, "Hey."

"Do you t-think something bad h-happened?" Della's voice cracked, her little body trembled.

She wrapped her arms around Della, hugging her tightly. "I'm sure nothing bad happened," she whispered, then sent a silent prayer she hadn't lied.

"Ms. Holden?"

Drawing away, she focused on the secretary behind the desk.

"I need to see your ID, and then I need you to sign this," she said, pointing to a paper.

She smiled, and signed Della out of school. Together, she and Della walked to her car. Once there, she situated Della in the back seat, buckling her seatbelt.

"Thank you, Allie," Della whispered.

From the driver's seat, she turned and smiled.

"You don't need to thank me, Della." Wanting to make the beautiful, bright girl smile, she asked, "Are you in the mood for ice cream?"

Della smiled and nodded.

****

Trig pulled his phone from his front pocket. Noticing ten missed calls, his eyes widened. Riding, he hadn't heard it ring.

"Fuck." He scanned through the missed calls from Della's school and Army. Just then, another call came in. He answered it.

"Brother," Army greeted. "Where you been?"

"Riding."

"Don't know what's up with Tina, but she didn't get Della at school."

"You get her?"

"Couldn't man, on a guard."

He checked his watch. "Fuck, brother. It's four—"

"Allie got her."

No, it couldn't be. Allie hated him. She had reason to considering he'd hurt her, then been a dick. After that night, he'd wanted to make things right, but she hadn't given him the chance. She hid out in her room, and the first chance she got, she moved out, into some crappy apartment in a crappy apartment building too close to the wrong side of the tracks. Army, in his fashion, pitched a fit, but there'd been no way to convince her. He settled for installing a deadbolt.

"What?"

"Allie got her. School called Tina. When they couldn't get a hold of her, they called you. When they couldn't get a hold of you, they called me. I called Allie."

Allie. He'd been a dick to her, but beautiful Allie with her color-changing eyes had gone to pick up his niece.

"You there?"

"Yeah, yeah. I'm here." He swallowed. "Where're they now?"

"She called about half hour ago and said they were getting ice cream."

Allie. Fucking beautiful Allie with her fantastic legs and full lips hated him, but she'd taken his niece to get ice cream.

"Bro, you there?"

"Yeah, I'm here."

"'Kay, so you know what's up with Tina? You goin' to handle that before you head to the compound?"

"Probably should, but I'm not. Gonna make sure Della's good first. Then I'll handle whatever needs handling at home."

"Right, later."

He hung up, revved his bike then rode off.

Twenty-minutes later, he parked outside the garage and quickly strode inside. He found Bud and Blaze under the hood of a '76 Mustang. Both of them wearing white grease-stained shirts.

"Della and Allie?" he asked without stopping.

Blaze took a puff of his cigarette. "Livin' room watching cartoons or some shit."

Giving half-assed greetings along the way, he quickened his pace until they came into view.

Allie sat, her back against the couch. Her eyes cast downward, looking at Della whose head lay on her lap. Allie's fingers in Della's hair, Della giggled.

Beautiful Allie, smiling softly at his niece made her

much more beautiful. Made him think if he hadn't screwed up, he would've enjoyed the same picture several times a week.

The sight left him breathless, sparking a deep, fiery ache in the pit of his stomach. He couldn't do anything but stand there, watching them, waiting for the ache to dull.

"Trig!" Army shouted.

Allie turned and spotted him. Della sat up, then bolted off the couch, dashing toward him. Her body slammed against his legs, she wrapped her arms around him. He chuckled. Bending over, hands under her arms, he lifted her, pulling her against him for a hug. He then pressed a kiss to her forehead.

"How's my favorite girl?"

"Scared," she whispered.

He drew away to look into her eyes. They watered. "You remember what I told you, Del?"

She nodded.

"You don't need to be scared ever again. You call me, and I'll come and fix it."

"You think Mommy's okay?"

He hated this, hated his niece worried about her mom, hated his niece knew what it was to worry. At five-years old, she should be worried about dolls and school, not her parent. "I'm gonna check on her now. I wanted to make sure you were okay first."

"But Mommy—"

"Del, I'll take care of it, 'kay?"

Slight and small, but she nodded.

He set her on her feet. "You stay here with Army."

"Naw, bro, I'm with you." Army patted his back. "Allie can stay."

Allie's head shot up, her gaze darting to her brother.

"Don't mind. Right, Allie?"

She shook her head. "No, I don't mind."

Army rested his weight on one knee. "Del? You gonna say hi or what? Didn't miss me?"

She smiled widely, walked to him, and hugged him. "Hi, Ty."

Army released her, stood, then winked at her. A second later, he met his gaze. "Meet you at the bikes." He strode away.

He closed the distance between himself and Allie. "Thanks for getting her. Thanks for watching her, and thanks for staying."

She fidgeted, looking away from him. "It's no big deal."

He hated she couldn't stand to look at him, hated he'd made it that way. Pushing those thoughts aside, he concentrated on the positive. At least she was speaking to him. "It is to me, so thank you."

She smiled, a sad smile. "You're welcome."

He looked at Della. "Be back soon, Del." He then forced himself to walk away.

Outside, he hopped on his bike and headed for his sister's apartment, steeling himself for what he'd find.

His sister, Tina, had been a good, sweet kid. They'd lived in a trailer with an alcoholic mother and a drug-addicted father, so it'd fallen on him to care for her. He did, never minded it. When their dad left, it was a relief and a curse. They no longer had to worry about their father beating the shit out of them, but their mother hit the bottle night and day, more so than before. As the years passed, she only got worse.

By the time he was fifteen, his mother spent all her money on booze, so he'd gotten a part-time job after school because Tina needed to eat.

When he graduated from high school, he made the biggest decision of his life. He needed a job that paid better, his grades weren't getting him into college, and even if they could, he couldn't afford it. He joined the United States Army. He hated leaving his eleven-year-old sister with their mother, but it was his chance to get Tina out of a trailer and away from their mother for good. He spent four years in the military. He called and wrote her as often as he could. He sent her money, and he spent his leave with her. After his four years ended, the country was still at war. Tina seemed to be holding her own with his monetary help, so he reenlisted, two additional years.

While away, Tina met a boy and got pregnant at sixteen. By the time Trig got back two years later, the father was long gone. Tina was seventeen with a five-month-old and hitting the bottle. He did what he could—got her out of the shithole trailer, helped her with Della, and made sure she got the help she needed.

She'd relapsed twice, and Della had borne witness to it once. It was never pretty. It tore his heart in two. She was his baby sister, and he knew, in a way, he was to blame.

Arriving outside the apartment building in ten minutes, he parked his bike, headed upstairs, and then opened the door with his key. The living room was small, a couch, a TV. Everything impeccably clean, so unlike the times she was on a binge, a good sign. He walked past the living room and into the kitchen. It, too, was clean, and there were no empty bottles. Another good sign.

He headed into her room, parted the door, and peeked inside. There, he found her, sleeping soundlessly, her dark hair sprawled across the pillow where her head lay. Dark circles underneath her eyes. Her phone beside her. He neared the bed, grabbed her phone. On silent. No wonder.

Instantly, relief mingled with guilt. He thought the worst, thought she'd gone back to her old ways when she'd just overslept. Anyone who knew her would get that. She worked full-time and attended college part-time. With a five-year-old, it meant she practically never slept.

He sighed heavily, running his fingers through his hair, and pressed a kiss to her forehead. She blinked, then shot up in bed. He managed to pull away before her head collided with his.

"Oh, shit! What time—"

He placed his hands on her shoulders to still her. "Got Della. She's good."

She glanced at the clock on her bedside table. Her face fell; her eyes watered. "I'm a horrible mother."

"You aren't a horrible mother. You overslept, and you overslept 'cause you're overworked, and fuckin' exhausted."

She shook her head. "I bet you thought I'd started drinking again."

He exhaled. "Terrified you were, but it doesn't matter. You aren't."

Tears effortlessly spilled down her cheeks. "Della's probably scared, too," she whispered.

The sight pained him. He rubbed the tears away. "It was more than a year ago."

"Yeah, J, but she remembers. I know she does. The way she looks at me sometimes, I k-know." Her voice cracked.

"You had a problem. You toughed it out—"

"I've relapsed before. You know—"

"It's in the past, Tina. You can't think about it. You can't think about the mistakes. It'll only lead you where you don't wanna go."

She nodded. "Where is she? Is she upset?"

"She's with Allie."

"Allie?"

"Yeah, Army's sister."

"Right, I remember. Del mentioned her. Said she's very pretty."

No, she was fucking beautiful, but he couldn't admit that.

She wiped her face and stood. "I should go get her."

Army appeared at the threshold to the room. "Naw, called Allie. She's on her way."

Tina's gaze shot to Army. She flushed. "Hi, Army, sorry to have inconvenienced you and Allie."

"Not an inconvenience. Allie loves kids."

She shrugged. "Well, thanks."

"Listen, you need me to watch Della a couple more times a week?"

His sister looked at him, shaking her head. "J, please, don't. I'm her mother. She's my responsibility, and you already do—"

"Tina," he said in a tone she wouldn't take lightly. "She's my niece. I love her. I'm the only male figure she's got—"

"J, don't fucking start with this shit," she snapped.

"I appreciate everything you do, but she's not your kid. I know I'm a fuck up, but taking her away—"

"Fuck, Tina." He threw his hands up in the air. "Will you just fuckin' listen to me? You're *not* a fuck-up. I'd never take her away from you. I admire you. You've never taken the easy way out. You could've had an abortion. You could've put her up for adoption. Yet you fuckin' kept her, you fuckin' care for her and love her. You're overworking yourself to pay for school and working overtime to get it done. Why can't you fuckin' let me help you?"

She reared back, her eyes widening. "You pay half my rent and leave money in my wallet. You take Della almost every Saturday while I'm at work, and during the week you drop by at least three times, often, with groceries. Please explain to me how I'm not letting you help me?"

"I pay half your rent 'cause you refuse to live with *me*. For the same fuckin' reason, I drop by three times a fuckin' week and buy groceries."

"J—"

His eyes narrowed. "Don't fuckin' give me any more lip, Tina. You know that shit pisses me off."

Looking away from him, she pinched the bridge of her nose. "I love you, J. You've always taken care of me, but it's time for me to grow up, handle things myself. You do plenty, and I thank God every night for you, but you can't do more than you already are. She isn't your kid."

He had enough of this conversation. "You've been a grown up for six years, Tina, and you're only twenty-one. You should be partying with friends, living on a college campus somewhere, going out on dates and living life, yet you're raising a kid by yourself, working two jobs, taking courses online. I'm twenty-nine, and I'm a man, and I'm your fuckin' brother, so you're gonna take the help I give you, and you aren't gonna give me lip about how she isn't my kid."

"They're my mistakes, J. I don't regret them. They gave me Della, and she's my baby. I love her, but she's a kid and kids are hard work. This is my burden," she whispered, her eyes trailing away from his.

Shit. He hated that's what she thought, so fucking far from the truth. *His* fault. If only he'd been there, if he'd never left…

He lifted her chin with his finger until her eyes met his. Shaking his head, he corrected, "My mistakes. Should've been here."

Her eyes widened and welled. He hugged her before they trailed down her face. "You've been here. Always."

His heart clenched. He kissed the top of her head. "Love you, too, kid."

****

Allie arrived at the apartment building, a ten-minute drive from the compound and parked in an empty guest spot. She helped Della out of the back of her black Camaro, relieving her of her book bag, and took a deep breath, bracing to see Jace again. She hadn't been prepared the first time, so she had little hope she'd be prepared this time, but a girl could hope.

After days without a glimpse, she'd forgotten what the flutter in her stomach felt like, how it intensified with every passing second. She'd forgotten how handsome he was. His broad shoulders and muscled arms, his so rugged, striking, and pronounced features.

She'd forgotten his rough voice and her reaction to it.

Walking into the elevators, she pressed the third floor. Della led her to the apartment. They knocked and waited. A moment later, an older version of Della parted the door. Her gaze glued to Della. The woman, who had to be Jace's sister and Della's mother, was younger than her and beautiful like Della, same dark hair, eyes, and soft smile.

The brunette kneeled and embraced Della. "Baby, I missed you so much."

"I missed you too, Mommy."

"So sorry, sweetie. I overslept."

The brunette, still holding Della close, stood and met her gaze. "Hi." She held out her hand. "I'm Tina. J's sister."

She shook her hand and smiled. "I'm Allie, Tyler's sister."

"It's nice to meet you. Della's told me nice things about you. Please come in." Tina took several steps away from the door allowing her in.

"Oh, I…I should—"

"Allie, come in," Tyler shouted from inside. Not a second later, he walked into the living room and met her gaze. "Ordered pizza."

She cursed, silently. She didn't want to see Jace, really didn't want to share dinner with him either, but from her brother's tone, it wasn't a request. She didn't want to fight him in front of Della and Tina. Having no other choice, she nodded and headed inside.

"Thanks so much for picking up Della. I fell asleep. My phone was on silent, and well…I'm sorry to have inconvenienced you. I don't—"

Allie placed her hand on her arm. "It's okay. Della

and I had a great time. I may have spoiled her appetite though. Took her for some ice cream after school."

Tina laughed softly, shrugging. "That's okay. J does it all the time. Please have a seat."

She looked around the small living room that led into a dining room and kitchen. It was nicely decorated, not expensively but homey. She took a seat on the couch, placed Della's book bag at her feet, and rested her folded hands on her lap.

Tina sat across from her in a chair and hauled Della on her lap, hugging her. "It's time for homework."

"I already did it. Allie helped me. I need you to sign it."

Tina looked at Allie, smiling. "Thank you." She turned her attention to Della. "Let me have a look."

Della reached for her book bag, pulled out her homework assignment, and handed it to her mother.

Tina scanned the assignment then signed it. "So, you recently moved here?" She handed Della her homework. Della placed it in her book bag, then rushed out of the room.

"Yeah, from New York."

"Big city, never been. Is it like the movies?"

She laughed. "I suppose."

"Always wondered what it'd be like," Tina replied. "You know…you look familiar. I guess you just have one of those faces."

She flushed. Feeling the heat of her brother's eyes, she ignored him. "That's probably because you saw me on the news."

Tina's eyes widened.

She shrugged. "It's kind of a long story, but when I left, my former fiancé reported me missing, so…"

"Oh…sorry, I didn't mean to pry or…"

She smiled. "No need to apologize. I volunteered the information."

Jace walked into the room. She couldn't help it. She looked in his direction. His eyes met hers and held for a moment before she forced herself to look away.

"So what do you do, Allie?"

Thankful for the distraction, she said, "I work at the daycare center off Main Street."

"Oh, so you know Tiffany?"

She smiled. "Yes."

"We went to school together. We were pretty close in high school, but since then we've drifted apart. With a kid, you know, doesn't leave much time to hang out with friends, priorities change and well…We're still friends. We just don't hang out like we used to."

"Well, if you ever need a sitter, I'm available. I love kids, and Della's a great kid."

Tina smiled. "Thanks."

"Food'll be here in a few." Her brother headed into the dining room and took a seat. Jace followed suit.

"Are you going to the cookout? It'd be nice to know another person there who's unattached."

"The cookout?"

"Yeah, she's coming," Tyler said.

She looked at her brother, narrowing her eyes. "It's funny you should say that considering this is the first I hear about a cookout."

Tina's eyes twinkled with amusement.

"I was gonna pick you up on Sunday and take you," Tyler said, nonchalantly.

She schooled her features and forced herself to soften her voice. "What if I have plans?"

Tyler, looking confounded, stood. "What's the big deal?"

The big deal? She didn't want to go anywhere Jace would be. More than likely, the cookout was a club event. If this cookout was like their Friday Night Fiascos, she could potentially catch Jace, who she wanted to avoid, in the act again.

"Ty, I don't even know what the cookout is."

"The club has a cookout once a month. It's Sunday, and you're coming 'cause I'm picking you up."

She'd been right. A club event, which meant Jace would be there. She didn't want to go. "What if I have plans?"

He lifted a brow and crossed his arms over his chest. "Do you?"

"That's not really the point."

"Don't matter—"

"Tyler—"

"Allie, why are you riling me?" He had the nerve to look abashed.

"Why are *you* riling *me*?"

Tina's laughter filled the room.

She glanced at her and couldn't help but smile. "Does he boss you around like this, too?"

"No, but I have a stubborn brother, too. I'm quite familiar with these arguments. I have to admit it's funny when someone else is being bossed, not me."

She could see that, so she smiled. "Jace does this to you often?"

"Yeah, and there's no use fighting it. These stubborn men always get their way."

"Why are you talking about us like we're not here?" Ty asked.

Allie's gaze shot to her brother. Mocking anger, she smirked. "Because we're ignoring you."

He let out an exasperated sigh, threw his hands in the air then took a seat. "Don't get what the big deal is."

"The big deal is you can't... Never mind." Tina had a point. No matter how many times she explained, he wouldn't understand. Still, it peeved her. "I may decide to go on a road trip Sunday."

Tyler shot out of his chair. "I won't let you leave."

Jace's gaze shot to Ty. He tensed.

"Oh, yeah? How do you plan to do that?"

"Easy. I'll sleep on your couch."

Damn. He could even if she didn't let him in. When she moved in, she gave him a key. "I'll change the locks."

His hands turned to fists. He clenched his jaw. She grinned.

"*Allie.*" He pronounced each syllable, his tone firm.

"Fine, I'll go, but I'm not going because you want me to. I'm going for Tina." His narrowed eyes didn't soften, so she smiled and added, "There's a big teddy bear underneath that temper."

He fought a smile for several moments, and suddenly, he burst out laughing. "Don't say that in front of the guys."

She turned to Tina, whose mouth hung open. Tina shook her head. "Can't believe it. Never seen that..." Her eyes filled with glee. "You're amazing, and you *have* to teach me how to do that."

"Shit," Jace muttered under his breath.

Her smile widened. "I'll teach you everything I know."

Chapter Twelve

Allie dreaded the cookout for no apparent reason. Jace would be there, but apparently the sexually liberated women wouldn't, or so she heard from Mia and Lynn. Despite having moved, they remained her allies.

She hadn't told them about her encounter with Jace, but they knew something happened. Mia told her the next day Jace had been looking for her. Mia, smart and borderline psychic, knew something happened. Luckily, she hadn't pushed for details. Luckily, because Allie couldn't force herself to repeat it.

When Tyler showed up at her apartment Sunday, she attempted to hide her nerves, the best she could. Of course, though, her brother, being smart and in tune to her, sensed it.

"Allie, you gonna tell me what's up?"

She walked past him. "Nothing."

He gripped her elbow, tugging her around. "I'm not stupid, Allie. I notice shit, and I sense shit, too, probably the reason I'm still alive. So I know some shit's going on, and I wanna know what it is. One of the guys make you feel uncomfortable?"

She hated lying to brother, hated being put in the position to lie to him, but she would. Tyler and Jace were close, closer than he was with any of the other guys. It had something to do with them serving together, and she wasn't willing to risk their friendship because of her.

She was extremely, utterly, and undeniably attracted to Jace, and it wasn't either of their faults, but her brother would kill for her. One slip and she could destroy the relationship they'd build over the course of seven years; years she hadn't been around. While she lived in New York, living lies, Ty built a life for himself. She wouldn't destroy it, even if Jace deserved it. He didn't, not in her eyes.

"Don't tell me if you don't want to. I'm not gonna be Dad. I'm not gonna force you to do shit you don't want to do. So if you don't wanna come, then don't. But I know some shit happened, and I wanna know what it was. But again, I'm not gonna force you to tell me 'cause I know you.

"I know you love me, and I know you don't wanna fuck up shit between me and my brothers, but *you're* important. You're more important to me than any of this shit. In a fuckin' second, I'd throw this away for you, Allie, only for you, 'cause you're my blood and my sister and 'cause I know how my brothers are. You gotta tell me, and I can make it better. If I can't, I'll fuckin' leave this shit behind, and we'll go. You and me. It doesn't mean I don't fuckin' love them, the club, and this life I've built. It just means I love you more."

Her heart clenched. Why was he so good to her? She couldn't understand how her brother had become this amazing man when their father was such a dick.

She shook her head. "Ty, I'm fine. I promise."

His eyes scanned her face, and then he released a breath. "When you're ready to talk about it, come to me. We'll talk. Just don't lie, Allie. Right now, you're lying."

"Did you ever think maybe I want to build my own life, Ty? The club is your life. I moved here…after everything…to be close to you, but I have to find my own way like you did."

He paused for a second. The tension in his shoulders dissipated, and he nodded. "I get it, just wish you'd figure that shit out under my roof."

She smiled then bit the side of her lip. "Let's go or we'll be late."

Ty drove his SUV to the compound and parked around back beside the slew of bikes and cars. She pulled herself out, and they walked the distance to the back gate. It was sunny and hot, and she wore a pair of shorts and a white shirt. He opened the gate for her, and she strode through, finally summoning the courage to look up. Her eyes gravitated to him.

Jace looked good, wearing a pair of faded jeans and his cut. He stood beside the large grill with a beer in hand, talking to Stone, who manned the grill. She forced her eyes away and spotted Tina and Della walking toward her. She smiled.

"Hi, Allie," Della said, giving her a hug.

"Hi, Della."

Della turned to Ty. "Hi, Ty."

Tyler kneeled in front of her and opened his arms. "What? I don't get a hug?"

Smiling, Della wrapped her arms around Ty, embracing him, too.

She shifted her attention to Tina. "Hi."

"Hi, glad you could make it."

She rolled her eyes playfully and spared a glance at her brother. "Like I had a choice."

Tina laughed.

They took seats on a picnic table. She perused her surroundings. Besides Stone, Jace, and Blaze, she didn't see anyone else. The double doors in the back of the building opened. Several others drifted out including Mia, Lynn, and much to her surprise, Tiffany, headed for them. Lynn took a seat across from her. Mia sat beside her. Tiffany took a seat next to Tina. They chatted for a while, Allie fighting the urge to look in Jace's direction.

Stone whistled, then nodded to Mia. She stood. "My cue. Gotta get the sides."

"I'll help." She wanted to get away from the heat and Jace.

They headed inside to the kitchen, bumping into Dash and Cuss who were headed outside. Each of them grabbed a side. They had it all: macaroni salad, bean casserole, roasted potatoes, mac and cheese, and cole slaw. Outside, they set the sides and buns on the picnic table beside the grill and cooler, and then Stone began assembling the burgers and hotdogs.

Everyone crowded the area. Allie decided to wait and headed back to the table where they'd been sitting. She spotted Cuss sipping a beer, his eyes intense and focused behind her. She turned and spotted the object of his affection—Tiffany. Warmth settled in her chest. He looked at her the way every woman wanted to be looked at, like he lived and breathed for her and her alone.

She took a seat next to him, grabbing the beer she left on the table that had since gone warm.

He spared a glance at her. "Hey, Classy. How you been?"

She shrugged. "Good, and you?"

His gaze still intense and on Tiffany. "Good."

"All you have to do is look at her."

He straightened, his upper body turning to her, and then his sapphire gaze pierced hers. "Come again?"

"Tiffany. All you have to do is look at her."

His eyes widened, but he didn't say a word.

"Don't look at me like that. You know what I mean."

Shaking his head, he chuckled. "No, I don't."

"Are you fishing for a compliment?"

He gave her a level stare. "Really don't know what you're gettin' at, Classy."

"Okay, well…all you have to do is look at her. If she's looking at your eyes, she won't be able to look away."

He drew away slightly, his eyes scanning her face, and then he smiled. "Can't believe you just said that."

She took a sip of her warm beer. "I'm not telling you anything you shouldn't already know."

His eyes darkened. "Bikers got reps, and she's like you. She—"

Her brows furrowed. "What's that supposed to mean?"

"She's class like you. Her parents got money. She went to college, graduated top of her class. I barely graduated from high school, didn't go to college, and I gotta record. I ain't worth two looks from her. She dates clean-cut, pretty boys with college degrees who don't fuckin' curse."

Her chest clenched. "Cuss…" Having no idea what to say to that, she hesitated. Her eyes instinctually gravitated to Jace, who handed Della a hamburger. She then managed to tell a truth. "All a woman wants is to be loved, really loved. If you think you can love her, treat her with respect, and not cheat, she'd be a fool not to take you up on the offer."

He hesitated. The whole time, his gaze on her. Finally, he shook his head. "You're somethin' else, Classy. Don't even want to call you Classy. Feel like it should've been somethin' else, somethin' that means more, 'cause, babe, you ain't nothin' like you appear to be."

She smiled.

"It's a fuckin' sweet thing to say. The sweetest thing a woman like you can say to a man like me, but I don't believe that shit for a second."

He looked away from her, then went to take a pull of his beer. She placed her hand over his arm, stopping him. He turned his head, and his eyes hit hers.

"I didn't say it because it's sweet, Cuss. I said it because it's the truth. I'm not going to lie to you. Yes, there are women who want a man with a college degree, money, and whatever else, just like there are women who'll spread their legs just because you wear a cut. I won't pretend I know Tiffany well because I don't, but from what I know about her…the way she acts and talks, the fact she works at a daycare, and is here means she's not one of those women. There's also a reason she's single, why it hasn't worked out with any of those college, pretty boys. Are you going to let her get away?"

He swallowed, holding her stare. "You don't know the whole story. It's fuckin' complicated."

"You're right. I don't, but I saw you looking at her. Every woman wants to be looked at like that."

His jaw clenched, eyes narrowed. "Fuck," he hissed.

She supposed a biker didn't like to hear he'd been staring at a girl with his heart in his eyes.

She jerked her hand away from his arm. "I shouldn't have said anything. I'm sorry. It's none of my business."

"Fuck, Classy."

She began to shift away. "I'm sorry—"

He grabbed her wrist firmly, holding her still. "How was I lookin' at her?"

She swallowed, unsure if she should tell him. "It may make you angrier."

"Tell me."

"You looked at her like…" She meant to say like he loved her, but felt it may be too much for him to handle. Instead, she borrowed Jace's words. "…like the sun rises and sets on her."

"How do you know?"

"Because I saw it—"

He shook his head. "How do you know every woman wants to be looked at like that?"

She hesitated. Looking away from him, she whispered, "Because that's how I want to be looked at."

His eyes widened. They held each other's gazes for a long moment.

"Cuss? What the fuck?"

God, her brother sure knew how to pick the best moments.

Cuss released her and stood, facing Ty. "Nothin', brother. Just talkin'."

"We're having a conversation, Ty," she said, simultaneously.

Tyler fisted his hands, and then his eyes sliced to her. "Yeah, so why do you look like someone killed your puppy?"

Her eyes narrowed. She stood, closing the distance between her and her brother. "Never had a puppy, Ty."

The muscle in his jaw jumped.

"Cuss has been nothing but nice to me. If you pick a fight with him, I'm not talking to you."

His lips twitched, fighting a smile, and then he chuckled. Why this amused him, she didn't know. She stared at him blankly.

Once he sobered, he said, "You can't go a week without talking to me, Allie. Stop fooling yourself."

Damn. He was right. When he'd been in the military, the longest they'd gone without speaking was a month, and those months were the worst. She worried constantly. When he got out, they talked two to three times a week.

She smirked. "Try me."

"I'll try not to. Now, go get food."

She smiled and walked away.

"Miracle."

She spun and met Cuss's gaze.

"That's what I'm gonna call you."

Her smile widened.

Chapter Thirteen

True to custom, Trig spent Saturday with Della. He took her to the park, and then they watched a movie. Now, they were headed to dinner at Anthony's.

Arriving at the restaurant, he parked, helped Della out, and headed to the entrance. They walked inside, hand in hand, and he instinctually scanned the restaurant, stopping dead when he spotted her.

Allie. She sat in the far corner, facing the entrance. Her hair loose around her shoulders and styled in curls. Wearing a blue top, a genuine smile spread across her lips.

Without thought, he took a step in her direction. She stood, and he realized it wasn't a top, but a dress that fit snugly against her frame.

His view of her was blocked a second later when a blond-haired man sitting across the booth from her stood.

His chest tightening and stomach knotting, Trig stopped dead in his tracks. Fuck. She was on a date with a pretty boy with class, like her. He didn't need to see the man's face to know it.

Jealousy flooding him, his whole body tensed. He tore his gaze away, wondering if this was how she felt when she caught him with a tap.

No, it felt worse, much worse. He hadn't caught her sitting on the guy's lap with his hands on her ass.

Still, he'd paid double. It hadn't been enough to see her at the cookout in tiny shorts sitting close to Cuss with her hand on his arm. He meant to talk to her, but after seeing that, he lost the will along with the courage. She made it perfectly clear she wanted nothing to do with him. She hadn't even glanced his way. Now, he caught her on a date, and still, it fucking hurt.

Damn it to hell, he didn't know what hurt more. The knowledge she moved on and he missed his shot or the knowledge the pretty boy with class was better for her than him.

"Fuck," he muttered under his breath.

"J?"

His gaze snapped to Della, his beautiful niece, standing right there, and he'd just cursed. Beautiful Allie had the ability to shred his insides apart, making him forget where he was and who he was with.

"Sorry, Della. Don't repeat what I said."

She nodded, her eyes softening. The kid was too smart. She sensed something was up.

He put his hands under her arms, lifting her, and tucked her against him. Then he whispered, "Gonna get food somewhere else. This place is too crowded."

"Okay." She rested her cheek against his chest.

It made him feel a little better.

****

Allie closed the door behind her and locked it. When her cell phone rang, she dug into her purse to find it. Several rings later, she answered.

"How'd it go?" Tiffany asked.

She shrugged.

She'd just been on her first date post-split Wyatt. Keith, blond, blue-eyed, and handsome, was an attorney and a single dad to a two-year-old boy, Henry. Allie saw him every morning when he dropped off his son at daycare, but she'd never spoken to him until recently, until Tiffany told him she was single. He asked her out. She said yes.

Turned out, he appeared completely perfect. He was not only handsome, but a gentleman, opening doors, standing when she went to the rest room, and a good conversationalist, too. He'd talked about his son with pure adoration and his work like he loved it. He asked her questions, nothing too personal, got her talking and feeling comfortable.

The date had been great, but nothing about him, as perfect as he appeared, made her want to start a romantic relationship. No chemistry, as simple as that. She wanted to believe her last relationship held her back, but it wasn't the case. As perfect as Keith appeared, the entire night her mind drifted, and when it drifted, it settled on Jace.

"It went well."

"Great. Are you going to see him again? Did he ask you out?"

She dropped her purse on the couch, then headed into her room. "He has my number."

"You don't sound too excited."

Slumping on her bed, she began removing her shoes. "I don't know what's wrong with me, Tiff. I mean the guy seems perfect. He's sweet and kind, but something's missing."

For several moments, silence hung in the air. "You're still in love with him?"

This took Allie by surprise. She'd never mentioned Wyatt to Tiff. "I…"

"It's normal. I mean you were with him for a long time."

No, whatever she'd felt for Wyatt had since been buried. Jace was the reason, but she couldn't admit that. "Wyatt killed any love I had for him. It's just—"

"Trust."

Her brows drew together. "What?"

"It's hard to trust after…" Her voice trailed off. "I'm sorry. It's none of my business. It just occurred to me you never told me the story. Cuss mentioned something, and I…well…it's none of my business."

"Cuss mentioned Wyatt?"

Tiffany sighed. "Please don't be mad at him. We're really good friends, and well…I saw you on the news, and I asked, and he said your ex cheated so…"

"I'm not mad. Cuss is a great guy, and because of him, I have this great job, so—"

"I think so, too."

Her ears perked up. She waited, hoping Tiff would say something else about Cuss.

"Listen, I'm sorry I told Keith to ask you out. I never meant—"

"Tiff, it's not a big deal. I had a great time. It's just…maybe it's exactly what you said. Maybe it is hard for me to trust after Wyatt. The thing is, I had reservations about Wyatt when we met, and then he cheated. I don't want to make the same mistakes. I'm not saying Keith is like that. I don't know him, but there's no chemistry, and I don't want to settle. Last time I did, I got hurt."

"I understand." Tiffany paused. "Look on the bright side. You said he's sweet and kind. It never hurts to have an extra friend, especially one who's an attorney."

She chuckled. "So true. Never know what kind of trouble I'll get into working at a daycare."

They talked for several minutes while she changed into a pair of jaw-string shorts and spaghetti strap shirt, and then she hung up. She connected her phone to the charger, plugged it beside her nightstand, and lay in bed.

Not a moment later, a knock sounded on her front door. She tensed, got out of bed, pulled on a robe, and headed for the door. Looking through the peephole, she caught sight of Tyler. His head angled to the left. She could only see the right side of his face. She swung the door open. He faced her. His left eye was bruised and swollen almost shut.

"Ty? What the—"

"I'm fine," he cut her off, walking past her, and inside. He took off his cut, set it on her couch, and took a seat.

She closed the door, locked it then turned to him. "What happened?"

"Allie, I'm fine," he repeated. "Come sit. Let's watch some TV."

She crossed her arms over her chest. "Not until you tell me why you have a black eye."

He hesitated. His eyes softened, and he admitted, "Got in a fight. I'm fine."

Got in a fight? Did he think she would settle for that answer? "With who?"

"Some guy."

"Why?"

"Allie, it's club shit. Don't worry about it."

Club shit? What the hell was the club doing that

got her brother a black eye, and why was the damned club so secretive? When she lived at the compound and shared a room with him, she'd seen him take off in the middle of the night. Other times, he'd be gone all night and wouldn't return until morning.

Allegedly, he worked at the garage, but what he did, she had no idea. She'd never seen him work on a car or bike beside his own. She also often overheard him say he was going on a "run" or he had a "guard," but she had no idea what it meant. Mia and Lynn told her not to ask questions, that it was club business. She hadn't. But now that he had a black eye because of club business, she would ask.

"I will worry about it, Ty. I'll worry because you're my brother. What the hell is the club doing that got you a black eye?"

He didn't answer, just stared at her blankly.

Then, it occurred to her. She felt like an idiot not realizing it before. "It's something illegal. Is it drugs? Don't tell me it's prostitution or—"

"It's not drugs, and it isn't prostitution."

"But it's illegal."

When he didn't respond, she dropped her head, pinched the bridge of her nose, and cursed.

He stood, closing the distance between them and grasped her shoulders. "It's not illegal. It's not exactly legal either."

Her head snapped up and met his eyes. "If it's not legal, it means it is *illegal*, Ty. Whatever it is got you in a fight, got you hurt, which means it's dangerous, which means it could get you killed, which means nothing has changed. It's like you're back in the Army, and I'm going to constantly wonder if I'll ever see you again."

His eyes softened. "Allie, it isn't like that—"

"Tell me what it's like then?"

He clenched his jaw. Shaking his head, he looked away from her. "Can't."

He wouldn't say. Nothing could break him. Why was he always putting himself in danger? The thought of losing her brother made her sick to her stomach, and she couldn't do anything about it. He was an adult. It was his life, his choice. Resigned, she released a breath. "Let me get you some ice."

In her kitchen, she grabbed a plastic bag, put ice into it, and zipped it shut. She handed it to him. He followed her and sat on a stool in front of the counter.

"Want a beer?"

He smiled. She grabbed two beers, flipped the tops off, and handed him one.

"So what's new, baby sister?"

Leaning against the counter, she sipped her beer. "Went on a date."

He lifted a brow. Ice bag in hand, he held it against his eye. "Yeah, anyone I know?"

She shrugged. "It's a small town. You may know him. His name's Keith. He's an attorney."

"Don't know anyone by that name. How'd it go?"

"It went well, but…"

"But…" he prodded.

"There's no chemistry."

He shook his head, chuckling. "You believe in that chemistry bullshit?"

"You know what I mean."

"Naw, Allie, I don't."

"Fine. I'll say it. I'm not physically attracted to

him."

"That stuff fades anyway."

He made a good point, but he was forgetting something, something she wasn't sure he knew since he'd never had a steady woman. There were people you could fall for and people you couldn't. Only you knew this. Only you felt it.

"You've never met someone and from one look knew you could fall in love with them?"

He dropped the ice bag and threw the question back at her. "Have you?"

She hadn't expected that, and she didn't want to answer it. "Yes."

"You're confusing love with lust."

"I'm not." She took another sip of beer. "I'm not talking about love at first sight. I'm talking about being drawn to someone you barely know for reasons you can't explain. You get this feeling in your gut every time you see them that tells you, if you let yourself, you'll fall, hard and fast."

She'd known from the minute she met Jace. The unsettling flutter in the pit of her stomach said it all. She hadn't known what it was then, but knew now with certainty. She could fall hard and fast with Jace. It had never happened to her before, not until Jace, and it hadn't yet faded.

Ty understood. He'd felt it, too. His face softened. Emotion shone from his eyes. "Who is it, Allie?"

"Who is she, Ty?"

He didn't respond, but then again, she hadn't expected him to.

Chapter Fourteen

Trig rode by her work, parked out of sight, and waited. He didn't put much thought into it. By now, he did it subconsciously because before today he'd done it so many times, he'd lost count.

The first time, he convinced himself he'd done it for Army, his brother. The next day, he did it again fooling himself with the same excuse. Two weeks later, he tried to go straight home and couldn't. He couldn't lie to himself after that. It wasn't for Army. It was for him. He wanted to know about her life. If she was still dating the man he'd seen her with, if she was happy, so he continued to do it.

By this point, he couldn't drive by and not stop. He couldn't drive straight home without driving by, waiting for her to get into her Camaro, and drive off either.

An obsession of the worst kind because the object of his obsession would never be his, but he couldn't help himself.

He stopped.

He parked.

He waited.

He watched.

He was addicted. He kept feeding his obsession, and he didn't care.

No one knew. Though several of his brothers

noticed him taking off at the same time every day, none asked. They were men, and especially, they were brothers and trusted each other.

At this point, he didn't care who knew. In fact, he prayed someone would find out, so they'd bust his balls, and maybe then, he'd find the strength to quit her, and silence the addiction.

The doors leading inside the daycare swung open, and she strode out looking like a million bucks in a pair of dark-wash jeans and blue blouse with her hair spilling around her shoulders. She smiled, yet her eyes were soft, looking sad to leave. She clutched her bag against her chest, then headed toward her car. Thanks to the SUV parked beside her, he lost sight of her. He waited for her engine to rev. The seconds turned to minutes, and still, her car hadn't started.

A troubling feeling settled in the pit of his stomach. Following his instincts, he hopped off his bike and headed in her direction. He caught sight of her, leaning against the driver's side door of her car. Eyes wide, brows drawn, her bottom lip trembled. A man stood too close holding her arms at her sides, his fingers digging into her skin.

He would intervene. She'd see him, but he didn't care. Nothing could stop him. Before he moved, the unimaginable happened. The man released one of her arms, raised his hand, and slapped her hard across the face, the sound resonating in Trig's chest.

He saw red. Adrenaline pumping, he launched himself at him. His body slammed into the man, knocking him to the floor. Landing on the man's back, he stood. Hovering over him, he grabbed his head and slammed it hard against the ground. A thud echoed. The man groaned, but he didn't stop. He couldn't. He grabbed the man's arm and twisted it backward until it snapped. A wail pierced the air.

"Jace!"

In the haze of rage, he heard her voice. Breathing heavily, he straightened and faced her. She trembled. Her face a mask of fear. Her eyes filled with unshed tears, her cheek swelling with the imprint of the man's hand.

Her beautiful face marred.

Fuck.

He wanted to break the bastard's arm again, then break every other limb.

He fisted his hands tightly, letting out a deep growl attempting to control the anger coursing through him. Losing the battle, he turned to the man and kicked him on his side, turning him over.

Fuck. Her ex! The bastard lucky enough to have had her! He cheated on Allie, who hadn't deserved it.

The guy had enough, but realizing who he was, Trig couldn't help but kick him again, hard.

"Jace!"

Shit. He promised he would never beat a man in front of a woman. He swore he would never lose control again, but he had, and at that moment, he didn't fucking care. She hated him anyway. Now, she'd fear him, but it couldn't be helped. Bastard crossed a line, and now Trig knew with certainty what he feared was true.

She'd been running, running from a man who fucking beat her.

"Jace, please…"

He turned. Tears streamed down her pale cheeks,

her trembling fingers pressed against her stomach.

He wanted to hold her, console her, do whatever he could to make her better. He couldn't. He was too angry, and she was too terrified, terrified of him, of what he'd done, of what he was capable of.

"I d-don't...want y-you..." Her voice cracked.

He took a menacing step in her direction. "You don't want me to fuck him up?" His voice a low rumble.

Her eyes widened. She swallowed. "I...d-don't want you to...g-get in trouble..."

Fuck. Allie trying to look out for him? He heaved a sigh. Without further thought, he closed the distance between them. Wrapping one arm around her waist, he cupped the back of her head with the other and hauled her against him. She went willingly, clutching his cut tightly. Just like that, the anger faded. Allie. Safe. In his arms.

"Won't get in trouble," he whispered against her hair.

She pulled away from him then tilted her head up to look into his eyes. "You don't know how powerful he is. We can call the cops. I promise I'll—"

He shook his head. "You should've called the cops the first time, Allie. Now, it's in my hands."

A small gasp escaped her lips. Her fingers clutched his chest moments before she jerked away.

He let her go.

Several moments of silence drifted. Her mind, he knew, working, trying to figure out how he knew.

He yanked his phone out of his pocket, dialed, and brought it to his ear.

Her eyes widened. "Who are you calling? You

can't tell Ty." She shook her head. "He'll kill him. Please…Jace. This is my problem. I'll—"

Ignoring her pleas, Army answered the phone. "Problem. Allie's ex. Daycare. Bring SUV, a couple of the brothers, and Mia or Lynn." Without waiting for a response, he hung up.

His gaze went to her. "Get in your car."

"Jace…you can't… I can handle this—"

His eyes narrowed. He leaned into her then said in a quiet, deadpan voice, "You had your chance to handle this. You didn't, so now I'm handling it. Now. Get. In. The. Car."

"But—"

He got in her face, so close with each tremble her body grazed his. "Don't fuckin' care if you wanna involve cops. Don't fuckin' care if you don't want your brother to know. Don't fuckin' care how powerful the bastard is. He fuckin' hit you, and it wasn't the first time. The only thing I fuckin' care about is keeping you safe. I'm gonna keep you safe. Don't fuckin' care if you hate me for doing it. Now. Get in the fuckin' car."

"Please, Jace, I know you're only doing this for my brother, but you'll end up hurting him because he's going to lose it when he finds out, and he'll go to jail."

If only she knew he hadn't been able to stop thinking about her since the day he met her. If only she knew, even standing there, her face marred with tears, the imprint of that bastard's hand on her cheek, and swollen eyes, he still thought she was the most beautiful woman he'd ever laid eyes on.

She didn't know all of these things, and he couldn't tell her, so although he shouldn't have, he snapped. "You don't know shit, so don't pretend to know anything about why I'm fuckin' doing this. You want to believe it's for Army, then fuckin' believe it."

The roar of a bike sounded. He looked away from her, spotting Army's SUV, and Stone and Mia following behind on a bike.

Army parked behind Allie's car blocking her in, then jumped off. His eyes glued to his sister. One look at her cheek, and his whole body strung tight. He took powerful steps, closing the distance between he and Allie.

Army, so pissed, looked so out of control. Trig feared for her. Instinctually, he put his hand over Army's chest. "Cool it, brother."

Army's gaze sliced to his. "Cool it? Don't tell me to fuckin' cool it."

He got in his face. "Know you're pissed. You have every fuckin' right to be. I'm pissed, and she isn't my sister, but she just got hit by a man. She's fuckin' terrified and trembling, so yeah, cool it. Hold it together for a minute till we get her outta here."

Army sighed, clenching his jaw. His gaze, still hard, went back to Allie's. "You lied to me. I knew you fuckin' lied. I just didn't want to believe it. 'Cause you lied, I couldn't protect you."

She further paled. Her knees buckled beneath her.

Wrapping one arm around her waist, the other behind her knees, Trig caught her before she hit the ground. She leaned against his chest easily, covering her face with her hands. He shot Army a nasty glare then carried her to the passenger side of her car, opened the door, and set her inside.

Because Army had been a dick, because he had been and the guilt choked him, because he had to do something to comfort her, as he hovered over her, he whispered, "Everything's gonna be okay, Allie. Don't worry." He buckled her seatbelt and closed the door.

He nodded to Mia. "Purse's on the floor. Take her home. Stay there."

Stone and Army had already carried Wyatt to the back seat of the SUV. Army sat in the driver's seat. Stone hopped on his bike and revved the engine. Mia started Allie's Camaro too, so he headed to his bike, hopped on, and drove to the compound.

Once there, he, Stone, and Army carried a groaning Wyatt into the garage. Their brothers followed behind.

"What the fuck?" Cuss asked from behind them.

Rake chuckled. "Looks like we're pickin' up randoms and beating them to a pulp."

They walked down the hall, into one of the unoccupied rooms, and unceremoniously dropped Wyatt on the floor.

He turned and spotted Prez, looking feral. His eyes hard, his posture stiff. "Conference room. Now."

Army locked the door from the outside on their way out. Trig waited for him, and together, they strode the short distance to the meeting room, where they held church, their club meetings. Large enough to fit sixty brothers, a long rectangular table sat in the middle of the room with chairs, not that they ever used them. Usually, the brothers stood around, some leaning against the walls, others standing behind the chairs. Like then, two-thirds of the club stood surrounding the large table.

Prez crossed his arms over his chest. "Any one of you gonna fill us in?"

Army wasn't too happy about having to answer to

anyone, probably for the same reason he wasn't too happy about it either. They had a situation that needed taking care of, and then, they needed to make sure Allie was okay.

He wanted to get this conversation over with, and Army was in no condition to do it. Livid, Army had taken it out on Allie, his sister, a woman he loved to death. Trig couldn't imagine how much worse he'd be with his brothers, who were men. Trig spoke up. "Asshole's name is Wyatt. He's Allie's ex-fiancé, and he put his hands on her. Caught him in the act, beat his ass, and called Army for backup."

"A little overkill, don't you think. Guy's arm's broke. He has a nasty gash on his—"

Rake's voice died off when Army grabbed him by the neck and slammed him against the wall. It happened so fast none of them had been able to stop it. Not that Trig could blame Army, he wanted to do the same thing.

Wild and Pound hauled Army away, allowing Trig to get face to face with Rake. "Not overkill, brother, not even close. He slapped her so fuckin' hard the sound echoed in my chest, so no, it ain't overkill."

Rake cursed, running his fingers through his hair. "My bad, brother. You said he put his hands on her. You didn't say he hit her."

Cuss, leaning against the wall, pushed himself off, his jaw hard. "I wanna fuckin' piece of him."

Damn Cuss. It made him wonder if he liked her as more than Army's sister.

"Got third," Bud.

"Fourth," Dash.

"Fifth," Blaze and Ripper said simultaneously.

Army pushed Wild and Pound off of him. "He's fuckin' mine. All mine."

Damn Allie. Beautiful, classy Allie found a way to wedge herself into the hearts of his brothers. No doubt about it. His brothers wanted a piece of the man who hurt her without so much as thinking of the repercussions, the fact he beat a man in public, that the ex had connections and money, and came from a prominent family. He could cause them plenty of trouble. Not to mention, Prez still looked pissed.

"Guy's already fucked. Don't think any one's gonna get much of anything," Trick pointed out.

Army turned his glare to Trick, then met Trig's gaze. "Yeah, thanks for that, Trig." His voice laced in sarcasm.

Anger coursed through him so powerfully he thought he'd lose it again. True, he should've stopped after he knocked Wyatt unconscious and let Army handle the rest. But he couldn't have stopped himself, even if he tried. He needed to avenge her. More than that, he wanted to be the one who avenged her.

Jaw clenched, he took two steps in his direction and shot back, "Go fuck yourself."

Army lunged forward, only to be dragged back by Pound and Wild beside him.

He lifted his chin. "What're you gonna do? Beat my ass for savin' your sister? You gonna take it out on me like you took it out on her? Fine. Take your best shot."

Army attempted to yank himself out of Pound and Wild's grasp. "I didn't—"

"The prick just hit her. I warned you, but you didn't fuckin' listen. You were a dick, and she was trying to protect your ass. I were you, I'd be thankful one of my brothers was there, stepped in, and beat the shit outta that prick in broad daylight. So yeah, brother, *fuck* you."

Looking remorseful, Army defended. "I was pissed. She lied to me."

"You're ten shots past pissed, and again, she was trying to protect you. She doesn't know what we do."

Army dropped his head and cursed. After several minutes, Army met his stare, remorse filling it. Army finally understood. "Let's get this shit over with."

"Need to vote," Prez announced.

Vote? What the hell was there to vote about?

"You should know the facts. Wyatt Morris isn't your typical asshole. He's a very prominent defense attorney asshole whose family's got more money than Bill Gates. This blows back on us, it means trouble."

Then again, Prez made a valid point. Maybe it would change the vote of some of his brothers, but not him and not Army, and he was certain not Cuss, Bud, Dash, or Ripper.

Army's gaze sliced to Prez, who shrugged. "I look out for my club. It means anyone who comes in, I look into."

"If it blows back, it won't blow back on the club. It'll blow back on me. I was the one who beat the lights outta him. I'll take the heat," he said, instantly.

Army shook his head. "Fuck, no. She's my sister. Anyone's taking the heat, it's me."

He let out a frustrated sigh. "She doesn't want you going down, Army. I was the one—"

Cuss shook his head. "This argument's fuckin' pointless. One goes down, we all go down. It's why we vote. 'Sides, in this town, no one's gonna rat any of us out."

Blaze, secretary of the club, scanned the room. "Right. Not everyone's here."

"We got majority, so let's vote. Now." Army glanced around. "Doesn't make much of a difference to me."

Everyone understood the unspoken words. Army didn't have to say it. Vote or not, he planned on taking revenge, and if it cost him his cut, then so be it. Trig couldn't agree more.

"In favor of beat down," Prez asked.

Everyone nodded, everyone was in favor.

Because everyone cared about Allie.

There was no way, knowing Allie, you wouldn't.

Army didn't wait for Prez to speak. He strode out the room and down the hall. Unlocking the door, he walked inside, leaving the door parted. Trig walked in behind. The ex lay on the floor, in the same spot where they'd dropped him.

Cuss grabbed a chair, and then he and Bud grabbed the asshole and set him on it. Wyatt groaned in pain.

Army closed the distance between him and Wyatt. "Head up."

Wyatt lifted his head slightly, blood from his head wound dripped down his face and neck, soaking his shirt.

"You know who I am?" When Wyatt didn't answer, Army punched him in the gut.

Wyatt bent over, groaning. "Fuck."

"Gonna ask you one more time. You know who I am?"

Army didn't wait for a response. He grabbed his

broken arm and popped his wrist out of place. Wyatt's eyes widened. His face was a mask of pain. His scream pierced the air.

"You look at me when I'm talkin' to you."

Wyatt lifted his head, looking Army in the eye, and shook his head. "I...don't...know."

"I'm Allie's brother, fuckwad, so you understand why I'm pissed. No one fucks with my sister. No one cheats on my sister. No one touches my sister. No one hits my sister, and no one beats my sister. You've done it all. For that shit, you will pay."

"Please...don't...I'm—"

Army punched him in the face. Wyatt's head flew back, his eye swelling immediately.

"You don't seem to understand warnings very well, do you? I think Trig warned you in New York. You stay away from my sister. You don't touch my sister, but you didn't listen. Wasted some of your cash on a flight, then *hit* my sister." Army punched him again right in the nose.

The impact caused a loud crack and sent Wyatt flying off the chair, blood spurting from his face, staining the floor.

"You wanna hit someone, you hit a man, you son of a bitch, not a woman, not my sister!" Army lost it, kicking and punching him, repeatedly. He didn't stop until Bud and Cuss carted him away.

Trig took several steps forward, standing face to face with Army. "He's had enough. Allie needs you."

Army shoved Bud and Cuss aside, and then hovering over Wyatt, his voice steeped in venom. "You get the fuck outta here and stay the fuck away from her. Next time, I promise you, I'll get you alone. I'll cut off your fuckin' arms, so you never hit another woman. Then I'll cut off your fuckin' dick, so you never fuck over another woman. Then who knows what'll happen 'cause no one's gonna be there to stop me from doing anything else I think of." With that threat, Army strode away.

Trig followed hot on his heels.

Because he had to.

Because he needed to check on Allie.

Chapter Fifteen

Her whole body shook. Allie couldn't help it. Sitting in the corner of her couch, cradling her legs against her chest, she felt the prick of tears in her eyes renew.

"Oh, Allie…" Mia whispered, wrapping her arm around her back. "You have to trust them."

Tears streaming down her face, she let out a sob. Her fault. She should've gone somewhere else, far away from Tyler and the club. She'd brought her fucked up life to them. Now, her brother and the club were dealing with her mess, a mess she should've taken care of herself. If she'd been braver and smarter, she would've gone to the police.

At the time, she felt not reporting it was the right thing to do. Wyatt being a star defense attorney from a well-known and prominent family, the accusation would've made news. With his political and social clout, she would've been vilified, and her father's business negatively impacted. She hadn't wanted to ruin what her father worked so hard for his entire life, despite what he'd done to her. Never had she thought Wyatt would come after her, and Ty would've discovered the truth, the real reason she'd left, the real reason she waited a week before flying across the country.

"Allie, sweetie, you have to calm down. Army

141

walks in here and you're like this—"

"This is my fault." She sobbed. "I should've…n-never come here. I…s-should've…"

The deadbolt unlocked. Her head snapped up. Quickly, she wiped the tears streaming down her face. The door swung open. Ty took one step, one look at her, and stilled. His eyes softened in a way she'd never seen before, and then he dropped his head and stared at the ground.

"Mia, Stone's downstairs."

Allie looked behind her brother, toward the voice that affected her so much. Though he spoke to Mia, his gaze was on her, scanning her. Why was he there? She was a complete wreck. She didn't want anyone to see her like this.

Ty lifted his head. His eyes were misted, fighting tears. Her brother didn't cry. He didn't get emotional, ever. She jumped off the couch, closed the distance between them, and wrapped her arms around his waist. He hugged her tight. A sob tore from her throat.

"Shh…Allie. It's okay."

Her body shook. She held on tighter, thinking any minute the cops would come, take the only family she had left, the only man who ever truly loved her, away.

"I didn't kill him, Allie. Hit him a couple of times. He's not gonna bother you anymore. I promise."

She drew away quickly.

He let her go and tensed. A disbelieving expression clouded his face.

"You think that's what I care about? Do you think I'd care about him leaving me alone if I'm alone in the world?"

"Allie, he isn't gonna cause problems. Trust me."

"Trust you? I don't even know where you work, Ty. You won't tell me. All I know is Wyatt is a high-profile defense attorney with a lot of friends in high places and money. He can make your life and the club's life hell. He's used to getting what he wants, and he does, always.

"Why do you think he can't let me go? You think it's because he loves me? You think it's because he had some sort of revelation and realized he can't live without me?"

She shook her head. "It's because he gets what he wants, and now he'll be out for blood, for yours and the club's, and it's my fault." Her voice cracked. "Because I came here. I shouldn't've come here. I should've…" Looking away from him, she whispered, "…disappeared."

He grabbed her chin and lifted it. Her eyes landed on his. "No, Allie. You come to me. Always. He's not gonna go to the cops. He's not gonna bother you again. Trust me on this." He leaned into her and whispered, "This is what we do."

Her eyes widened. "What?"

He shook his head. "This isn't your fault. It's mine. I knew. I knew, and I let you move out, and I didn't put the guys on you."

Her brows furrowed. "What?"

He smiled. "Should've had the guys watching you."

"I don't need…" Her voice trailed off. She had needed them. If Jace hadn't been there, she would have more than a sore cheek. She shuddered.

"Need a drink," he said, snapping her out of her bleak thoughts.

She headed into the kitchen. Ty, trailing behind her, took a seat on the stool. She poured Ty whiskey. "Is Jace coming in or is he standing guard outside?"

Her brother chuckled. "Trig!"

Jace strode inside, closed and locked the door behind himself, and took a seat beside Tyler.

"Want a drink?" she asked, avoiding his eyes and ignoring the heat of his on her.

He nodded.

"Whiskey? Vodka? Or beer?"

"Whiskey, thanks."

She poured him whiskey, then grabbed a beer from the fridge for herself. "Have you eaten? I planned on making steaks tonight."

"Relax, Allie. I'll order some food."

Her gaze darted to her brother's bloodied knuckles then back to his face. She turned and grabbed a wash cloth, soaked it in warm water, and handed it to him.

He wiped his face and hands. "Been on any dates lately?"

Jace's hands tightened on his glass. Hardly noticeable, but she noticed.

She hopped on the counter and took a sip of her beer. "No, I haven't."

"What about that attorney? What's his name?"

He was trying to get her mind off Wyatt, but she hated his choice of topic. "Keith," she whispered.

"So? He hasn't called?"

"Yeah, he invited me to go to a movie with him and his son. I declined."

His lifted a brow. "Why?"

She rolled her eyes, playfully. "I told you why."

Jace took a gulp of whiskey and set the cup on the

counter with a thud. She spared a glance in his direction. His eyes, narrowed, glued to his drink.

"Yeah, but Allie, you gotta move on and I looked into the guy. He seems—"

Her eyes widened. "You what?"

"I looked into the guy. No record, comes from good family, wife left him, has a two-year-old he's raising on his own, co-workers like him."

She wasn't in the mood to explain he had no business looking into a man she dated once, but it was pointless. "Yeah, Ty, I know, but it doesn't change the fact I'm not interested."

"Feelings can grow."

Maybe, but maybe not. "Not interested."

"You said he was nice. You could be friends," he persisted.

From the corner of her eye, she saw Jace's jaw clench. "Ty, if I'm not interested in the guy romantically, there's no point in seeing him again. I don't know if I'll ever be interested in him romantically, and he's inviting me into his son's life. What if his son gets attached to me, and it doesn't work out? He'll be hurt, and I'm not willing to hurt a kid on the off chance I might fall for his dad."

Ty shrugged. "Makes sense."

She smirked. "I know it does." She sighed then announced, "What do you guys want me to order? I'll—"

Ty finished his drink. "You aren't doing shit, but taking a shower and relaxing. I'll order food and go pick it up."

Drained, she wasn't going to argue.

Ty smiled. "Been dying to drive your Camaro."

She shook her head, then headed for the shower. In her room, she picked out a pair of shorts, loose fitted top, undies, and a sports bra then went into the bathroom. She closed the door behind her, spared a glance in the mirror, and cringed. She looked like she felt, a walking disaster. Her eyes swollen and red-rimmed, her face blotchy, and a light bruise had started to show on her cheek. Tying her hair in a knot on the top of her head, she took a long hot shower, dried, and dressed. She walked out of the bathroom, steam filed out. In her living room, she spotted Jace, sitting on the couch remote in hand. His gaze snapped to her, scanning her the way he'd done before. Since he was empty handed, she offered him another drink.

"Wouldn't mind a beer, but I can get it." He stood and headed into her kitchen.

She followed behind.

He opened the fridge. "See you have tons of beer." His voice tight. He pulled out two beers and uncapped them, then handed her one.

"Keep it stocked for Ty. He stays here on occasion."

He nodded. She watched the corded muscles in his neck as he took a deep swallow of beer. He then angled his head to her, so she took the chance to say, "Thank you…for what you did."

For some reason, his eyes hardened, the hand around his beer tightening until his knuckles were white.

She took a step away.

He closed the distance she'd forced, crowding her. "Scared of me, Allie?"

No, but it wasn't wise to get too close to someone

who was angry. "No."

He leaned into her. "You sure?"

She smelled the whiskey and beer on his breath. Her gaze helplessly drifted to his lips. She was tempted, so tempted to press her lips against his. Why, when he was clearly unhappy with her, she had no clue.

"Allie."

She loved it when he said her name. She loved it more when his voice came out husky like it'd been then.

Her gaze snapped to his eyes. While she'd been daydreaming, he'd grown ten times angrier. She couldn't remember what he'd asked. "What?"

His jaw clenched, his shoulders tensing. Through gritted teeth, he said, "You're killing me."

Killing him? How the hell? She'd expressed gratitude. "You're annoying me," she retorted with little force. He still stood too close.

He fought a smile. "What?"

Her eyes narrowed. "You heard me. You annoy me." She couldn't understand him. One minute he saved her from her ex-fiancé, the next he was angry because she thanked him?

Lifting a brow, he grinned. "Why?"

She wouldn't answer. Primarily, she had a question of her own, and he was grinning that beautiful grin. She had to ask before the inevitable happened, before she got lost in his smile and forgot the question. "Why were you angry, Trig?"

His grin faded, instantly. "Not angry."

"You were. I can tell. All you bikers do the same thing when you're angry."

He chuckled, his body shaking from the force. The

sight of him standing in her kitchen an inch away, laughing was just too beautiful. As she'd feared, she got lost in him, forgetting what she'd said.

Once he sobered, he crossed his arms over his chest. "What is it we bikers do?"

Right, that's what they'd been talking about. "Your eyes get mean, and then there's the jaw twitch thing. Your posture changes too and, of course, can't forget fisting your hands."

He laughed loud. She laughed too. She couldn't help it.

Seemingly without thought, still laughing, his eyes dead on hers, he said, "You're fuckin' amazing."

He didn't mean it in the way her heart wished, but the reaction was the same. She stilled. The smile died on her lips. Like the wind had been knocked out of her, she couldn't breathe.

His smile died too, and he tensed.

"Don't worry. I know what you meant." She forced a smile. "I won't go crazy stalker girl on you."

His brows furrowed. "What?"

"You know, those women who take everything a guy says to mean something it's not and chase them?" She didn't chase men. Ever. A rule, something her mother told her when she was sixteen, that stuck.

He shook his head then changed the subject. "You sure you aren't scared of me?"

"Yes, I'm sure."

His eyes scanned her face, searching for what, she didn't know. "Seein' what I did, what I'm capable of didn't scare you?"

"No."

His eyes widened. "Why?"

"He deserved it, and I know you wouldn't hurt a woman."

"How can you possibly know that?"

She knew because he took care of his niece and his sister. She knew because he'd roughed up her ex for touching her and beat him up for slapping her, because he'd held her against him when she cried, and because sometimes he said things that proved it. Still, she wouldn't say those things, not aloud and not to him.

"I know you wouldn't hurt a woman," she said more adamantly.

"You don't."

Not in the mood to argue with a biker, her voice laced in sarcasm when she said, "You're right. I don't."

"I hate it when you do that."

He said it like he'd known her for years. Unsettling, since he didn't. He barely knew her, and he didn't even like her. "Do what?"

"Wave a fuckin' white flag."

"I…" The denial died on her lips. She had done it, and, she'd done it once before too. "There's no point in arguing with someone who's as hardheaded and stubborn as you are."

"I'm not—"

"Have you ever hit a woman?"

He hesitated, then finally shook his head.

"Oh," she said, sarcastically. "So I was right, but you're arguing with me about it. See what I mean? Annoying."

His eyes softened. In a tender voice, he said, "Yeah, Allie, you were."

His gaze snapped to her cheek. "Did you ice it?"

She shook her head. "I'm fine. He didn't hit me too

hard."

His eyes flared. "You mean it wasn't as hard as the last time?"

She took a step away, looking away from him.

"Tell me, Allie."

No, she wouldn't, and nothing he said would make her. She could be as stubborn and as hardheaded as him, too. What happened to her was in the past, and in the past, it would stay. She refused to open that door. It'd only cause more heartache. Besides, he'd beat the crap out of Wyatt for slapping her. If he knew the truth, there was a chance he'd kill him or tell her brother who'd do worse.

"Allie?"

Her gaze shot to his. "It was just a slap—"

He flinched, muscles bulging. "I was there. It was hard, so fuckin' hard the sound still echoes in my ears."

He had a point, but he was also angry, angry enough to take off and beat the shit out of Wyatt again. She didn't want that, and so she caved. "I don't know why you were there. I'm just glad you were. If you care about my brother at all, then what I tell you will stay between us."

He didn't say a word, but he nodded.

"He hit me before. Once. It's the real reason I left."

He fisted his hands, looking away from her then met her stare again. "He hit you one other time, but that other time, he didn't just slap you." He leaned into her and whispered, "He beat the shit outta you, beat you hard enough to leave marks. You had to wait for the bruises to fade before you got on a plane and headed here." Pure disdain in his voice.

She thought it would hurt to say it aloud. Turns

out, it hurt to hear it, too.

His eyes darkened. "And your dickhead father probably told you, you deserved what you got for disobeying your fiancé, and then he gave you several days off, so you wouldn't show up to work bruised."

She swallowed. How he knew, she didn't know.

He lifted his hand and softly grazed his fingers over her sore, bruised cheek. "You let us, we'll protect you. You don't want to tell your brother, then don't, but give him that, let us protect you. We can."

He paused, then blew her mind. "You deserve so much more than life handed you, Allie, so fuckin' much more." His voice ragged and yet tender.

Her eyes misted. It was him, what he said, the way he said it, while tenderly caressing her sore cheek. All of it made her think he meant it, made her want to believe it, and again, made her think he cared.

The deadbolt unlocked. Jace drew away. She turned. Ty strode in, carrying two pizzas. "Camaro is sweet, Allie. May need to get me one."

Still unsettled by the only man who could do that to her to such a degree her baby being praised didn't affect her, she smiled a fake smile.

Chapter Sixteen

Allie dropped her purse on the couch and strode into her kitchen, wondering what the hell she'd make for dinner. Outside, the roar of a bike sounded. It only meant one thing. Ty had come to pay her a visit.

Yesterday, he'd stopped by her work during lunch hour and taken her out to eat. She'd been in Wadden for close to two months and never had he done this. It gave her the impression he used lunch as an excuse to check on her. She didn't mind, considering the Wyatt encounter left her shaky, nervous, and afraid.

Ty ensured her he'd handled it. Jace told her as much too, but it didn't stop her worry. Wyatt Morris was the type of man who set his mind to something and got it, the type who never went down without a fight. He cheated while they'd been together, but now, he wanted to fight for her. Go figure. Every time she thought about it, guilt clogged her throat, a nagging nervous energy strengthened.

She headed for the door to greet Ty, parted it expecting to spot him coming up the stairs, but he never did. Turning, she grabbed her keys, headed out, and downstairs. She spotted a Harley with Cuss sitting astride it. He looked to her and smiled. Returning the smile, she closed the distance between them. "Hey, Cuss."

"Hey, Miracle." His eyes softened. "How you

been?"

She hated she'd become a victim again, hated people treating her with kid gloves. Still, it showed they cared, and so, she dealt with it by ignoring it. She shrugged then looked away from his eyes and lied. "Okay."

He didn't say anything else, but his eyes scanned her warily.

Hating that too, she broke the silence. "So you're going to sit out here or are you coming in for a visit?"

"Just doin' my job," he replied, easily.

"What?" She didn't understand. What job did he have sitting outside her apartment building?

Oh, God. Her brother had done what he'd said. He'd put the guys on her. Ty stayed the night two days ago, which meant someone from the club had been parked outside and watched her apartment the night before. Because of her. Because she'd brought her mess to California, to her brother, to the club.

The now too familiar guilt resurfaced.

Well, this wasn't her fault completely. Ty could definitely take part of the blame for having them sit outside her apartment when she had a perfectly good couch.

Suddenly angry, she demanded, "Inside, Cuss. Don't argue, and I'll make you dinner."

His lips twitched, hiding a smile. He hopped off his bike and followed her up the stairs and into her apartment. She unlocked the door, swung it open, allowing him in.

"Take a seat, watch TV, and relax. I'll get you a beer, unless you prefer something stronger."

He grinned. "You're gonna make some lucky

bastard a fan-fuckin-tastic wife." Then he added, "Beer's good, Allie. Thanks."

Damn, so sweet. Tiffany was a lucky girl. She made the decision then and there to intervene. "Because you said that and didn't argue, I'll make you filet and mac and cheese."

His grin widened. He got comfortable on her couch and turned on the TV.

****

Trig and Army had a run, their turn to scrounge the streets, making sure druggies, gang bangers, prostitutes, and old enemies were out of Wadden.

Hell Ryders had once been heavily involved in criminal activity, primarily running drugs and guns. It made their small, quiet town a hub for gangs and violence, and the residents suffered in its wake. Six years ago, the club voted, agreed to leave the drugs, guns, and the shit it came with behind, but the president at the time had gotten too greedy. He continued to run drugs and guns with the help of three other brothers.

The rest of the club had been oblivious to it. It went on for a year and ended one night in the woods. That's where they'd found their bodies. Marcus, their current president, had been vice president at the time. He'd taken the reins and vowed it was the end. It had been. Around that time, he and Army joined the club.

Now their runs consisted of ensuring drugs stayed off the streets of their town and ensuring other clubs and gangs didn't encroach their territory. For a long time now, they hadn't had any trouble. There was always the threat. One in particular, another motorcycle club they'd severed ties with, Chained MC, who hadn't been thrilled they'd lost Wadden as a route.

Hell Ryders lived off the garage and their guard services, which wasn't entirely legal, since often they were paid for extras, namely roughing up assholes. They were always assholes who deserved it. They made sure of it.

On their runs, they went in teams. Trig and Army were usually teamed together.

"Yo," Army shouted.

Trig turned to look in his direction and nodded.

Army closed the distance, hopped on his bike parked next to his. "Wanna pass by Allie's to make sure Cuss is there."

He nodded, revved his bike, and drove off headed to Allie's place. Once there, he spotted Cuss's bike but no Cuss. Army wasted no time parking, hopping off, and heading to her door. He followed close behind, waited while Army knocked.

Through the door, he heard the sound of the TV blaring. Not a second later, her laugh filled the air. She parted the door, still laughing, and barely fucking dressed, barefoot and wearing a pair of too short shorts and a tight spaghetti strap shirt.

"Hi."

Army strode past her then tensed. He followed behind and spotted Cuss sitting on Allie's couch, a beer set on the coffee table and a plate of food. Cuss had his own plate in his hand and had just shoved a large piece of meat in his mouth.

"What the *fuck*?" Army asked.

Exactly his fucking thought. They looked like a damned couple, enjoying dinner and beers, watching TV, and laughing.

Shit. Cuss and Allie. He had to worry about them

again, about Allie liking Cuss instead of him, about Cuss making a fucking move. It'd be so fucking easy. They were alone. She was barely fucking dressed. The fucking thought killed. Jealousy knotted his gut and turned his stomach.

Cuss's gaze shot to them. "Hey, Army, Trig." Barely audible, he still had a piece of steak in his mouth.

The door slammed behind them, and then, Allie stood barefoot in front of Army in her little damned shorts, showing off those fantastic legs, and perfectly manicured toes.

Fuck.

He looked at Cuss shoving a forkful of good-smelling mac and cheese into his mouth, who thank God wasn't checking out her ass because God help him he would fucking tear Cuss's eyes out of their sockets.

He heaved a sigh.

"Um, hi to you, too." Her voice laced in sarcasm.

"What the fuck is going on here?" Army asked.

A stupid question. Seriously. They were playing house. Allie comfortable in a pair of too-fucking-short shorts and a tight camisole, Cuss sitting comfy on her couch. Trig'd bet his life she'd gotten him that beer, and she'd cooked for Cuss, again. She'd never, not once, cooked for him. She was a good cook. When she'd lived at the compound, she cooked for some of the guys, and it was all they talked about. He'd roughed up her ex, beat up her ex, held her when she cried, but she'd never cooked for him. One more reason to be jealous.

Shit. He really wanted to hit Cuss. Hard.

"Obviously, Ty, we're having dinner."

Army ignored Allie, heaving a frustrated sigh. He moved past her and took two menacing steps in Cuss's direction. "Cuss, what the fuck?"

Cuss's brows drew together, and because he was a fucking idiot, he looked baffled. He dropped his fork and set his plate on the table. "What?"

"What do you mean 'what'? You got a job to do, and that job is looking out for my sister. You do that by watching guard outside, not fuckin' drinking beers, eating, and relaxing in front of my sister's TV."

Cuss stood, squaring his shoulders. "Brother, I can watch her better from inside her apartment, and she offered to cook for me. I'd be a fuckin' idiot not to take her up on the offer."

Army took another step in Cuss's direction and barked, "Outside. Now."

Allie stepped in between the two, tilting her head to look at Cuss. "Sit. Finish your food. Drink your beer and relax." Her attention then returned to her brother. "Leave. Now."

Army fisted his hands. "Allie," he said in a dead serious tone.

"Tyler Alexander Holden, I'm going to tell you this once then you and Jace are leaving."

She took a deep breath. "I didn't say anything when you announced you and Jace were going to New York with me. I didn't say anything when you insisted I bring all my stuff from New York, stuff, need I remind you, that I didn't need. I didn't say anything when you looked into a guy I dated once.

"Until recently, I hadn't asked you about the club and the club's business. When I did, it was only because you showed up here with a black eye and made it my business. And I didn't say anything when I realized you put the guys on me.

"Now I'm going to say something, and not only are you going to listen, you're going to do what *I* want and you're not going to give me shit about it.

"Cuss and whoever else you put on helpless Alyssa guard isn't sleeping outside sitting astride a Harley or in a truck or any other car. Whoever is on helpless Alyssa guard is coming into my apartment. I'm going to make him a meal, give him a couple of beers, and let him watch whatever he wants to watch on TV, and then he's going to sleep on my couch—"

Army threw his hands in the air. "But—"

"I'm not done." Her face flushed in anger. "Cooking them a meal, getting them a beer, letting them watch TV, and crash on my couch is the least I can do for coming here and dumping all this on the club's lap, so I'm going to do it, and you are going to let me."

"Cuss needs to keep an eye out—"

"For me? Yeah, I get that. It's why it's better if he's a room away instead of downstairs."

Damn, she had a point. Cuss made the same point, but still, a biker sleeping on her couch, that biker being Cuss, who looked at a woman and she spread her legs, it didn't sit well with him.

"Now, thanks for the visit, but you need to go."

His gaze shot to Army, begging him to say something, do something. Any-fucking-thing.

Army looked at Cuss. Before he opened his mouth, Allie said, "If you say 'off limits,' I swear I'm taking off, and I'm not telling you where I'm going."

Army looked to his boots then ran his hand through

his hair. "Fuck."

Allie then turned to Cuss. "I told you to sit." She took Cuss's plate and headed into the kitchen.

Trig stood frozen, hearing the sound of the microwave opening and closing, turning on, then shutting off with a loud beep. A moment later, she reentered with the plate of steaming food and handed it to Cuss, who finally sat and began to eat.

She'd reheated Cuss's food after it'd only sat out for a minute.

Fuck.

Army stared blankly, stumped. She'd stumped him. Trig was stumped, too, except he knew what he would do if he could.

Army turned, facing him.

"Lock the door on your way out, and let me know who's on helpless Alyssa guard tomorrow," Allie called out.

They left. Army locked the door. As they headed downstairs, Army cut into his thoughts. "Need a favor, Trig."

Trig spared a look in his direction but didn't speak. He couldn't. The bitter taste of jealousy lingered.

"Need you on Allie for the next week. I got a guard out of town. I know it's a big favor considering tomorrow's Friday, but…" Army's voice trailed off.

One week with Allie making him meals in short shorts, watching her walk and smile, and hearing her talk and laugh. Shit. He was the luckiest trailer trash on earth.

"Don't trust Cuss with Allie. Don't think he'd do anything but…Shit, there's something about him women can't help but drool over. Don't want Allie to fall victim."

Trig didn't know if he could successfully pull off hiding how he felt much longer, especially if Allie wore those shorts, made him dinner, and slept a room away, so he knew he should make up some excuse, say he couldn't watch her. But he couldn't. He didn't care if it made him selfish. He wanted to play house with her. He may never have her, but for a week, he'd pretend she was his.

He nodded.

"I know you got Della on Saturday, so I'll arrange for one of the other guys to watch her during the day."

He nodded again, thanking God small miracles were granted to trailer trash like him.

****

Walking into her apartment, Allie dropped her purse on her couch and headed into the kitchen, listening intently for the roar of a bike.

Tyler called her that morning and told her he had to go out of town for the next week on "club business." At this point, asking was pointless, so she didn't. After he promised to call her and check in, she told him to be safe and hung up. She'd completely forgotten to ask him who would guard her. During lunch, she called him, but he never answered. She supposed it didn't matter. She knew all the guys. Of course, she was friendlier with some than others. As long as it wasn't...

Her thought faded when she heard the roar of a bike. She didn't have to meet anyone downstairs but figured, Ty probably hadn't told whoever it was to come upstairs. She headed to her door, slung it open, and froze.

Shit.

There, as handsome and rugged as ever, stood Jace, wearing a black T-shirt tight across his chiseled chest, his cut, and well-worn faded jeans. His arm raised like he'd been about to knock.

She must've stood there staring at him blankly for a while because he lifted a brow. "Gonna invite me in, give me a beer, make me dinner, and let me crash on your couch or does that apply to everyone but me?"

He sounded peeved, not quite pissed, yet. A good sign, except it didn't bode well for the rest of the night.

Truth told, she didn't want him in her apartment. She didn't want to get him a beer or cook him dinner, and she really didn't want him sleeping on her couch. It would be too easy to pretend they were more than acquaintances. But, she couldn't be rude to the man who'd saved her twice just because she couldn't think, much less cook, or sleep with him in the next room.

Her cheeks flamed. "Yeah, sorry, I just...wasn't expecting you."

He parted his mouth, then shut it, clenching his jaw. Yep, she'd done it. Definitely pissed now.

She stood aside, and he strode through, his presence filling the room. He didn't sit. Instead, he turned to face her and crossed his arms over his chest.

She closed the door and locked it. "Do you want a beer or something stronger?"

"Beer."

She nodded. "I planned to make chicken parmesan with spaghetti unless you wanted something else."

He dropped his arms and looked away from her. "You don't have to go through the trouble of making me dinner. I can order something for us."

Of course, he'd say that. He was the only member

of the club who'd never eaten her food. Why? Probably because he hated her. When she lived at the compound, she cooked all the time and made plenty for everyone. He'd look at her in his angry biker way and walk away. She couldn't help but feel insulted then and now though she knew she was a good cook, even smug Wyatt told her so. "Are you scared I'll poison you or something?"

Apparently, this amused him, he grinned. "No, Allie."

"Then?"

"You don't want me here, so I don't want to inconvenience you."

She didn't, but he didn't want to be there anyway. "You don't want to be here."

His eyes darkened. "If I didn't want to be here, I wouldn't be here."

What did that mean? He rather be with her than at Friday Night Fiasco at the compound? Her heart fluttered with hope. She fought to ignore it then released a breath. "I'm making dinner for myself. I don't mind making a little extra for you. Besides, I think I owe you several home-cooked meals considering…"

He took a step, and her voice faded away. "You don't owe me anything." His tone rough.

She held his gaze. "Okay." What else was there to say? "I'll start dinner then…or no, I'll get you a beer first, then start dinner."

"Don't you wanna change?"

She glanced down at herself, still wearing jeans and a blouse, the same clothes she'd worn to work. She always changed after work, putting on a pair of shorts and T-shirt, something comfy. But he was there, looking hot and angry, standing too close, and staring down at her intensely, and it made her forget everything. Why couldn't he be normal like Cuss, sit down, watch a game, and drink a beer? Why did she have to be so attracted to him?

She looked back at him then nodded weakly. Still, she turned, headed for the kitchen. He grasped her wrist, holding her still. Heat shot up her arm. She angled her face to his.

"You gonna change?"

"I was going to get you a beer first."

He nodded and released her. She walked the rest of the distance to the kitchen, opened the refrigerator, and stared into it, not seeing anything. With the cool air hitting her face, she took a deep breath, grabbed a beer, and turned, almost bumping into Jace. A small gasp escaped her lips. How long had he been there? How was it possible a man as tall and wide as him moved soundlessly? And why was he in her space?

She sidestepped, reached into a drawer for the bottle opener, uncapped the beer, and handed it to him. "Going to change," she announced. "You should…relax and watch TV. I'll get dinner started soon."

She fled as quickly as her legs could take her.

Chapter Seventeen

Allie strode away. He watched her go, took a long gulp of beer, and headed into the living room. She came out a moment later, wearing shorts and a top that exposed some of her shoulder.

Damn, she was beautiful, so beautiful.

She headed to the coffee table, picked up the remote, and handed it to him. "You can watch whatever you like."

"What do you like?" She seemed baffled by his question, so he rephrased, "What do you wanna watch?"

"I'll be cooking."

"You won't be cooking all night, Allie. We can watch a movie or two. It's Friday. You don't have to get up for work tomorrow."

She swallowed. "You're the guest, why don't you pick something out?"

He didn't want to pick anything out. It's not like he could pay attention with her sitting next to him anyway. "I wanna watch what you wanna watch."

A soft smile spread across her lips. "I'll think about it."

He watched her as she headed into the kitchen, and then he turned on the TV and flipped through the channels aimlessly, waiting for her.

An hour later, Allie strode into the living room,

carrying two plates of food. He stood, freed her of the plates, and set them on the coffee table.

"Um…thanks," she mumbled then disappeared into the kitchen, saying over her shoulder, "Let me get the utensils."

A moment later, she walked in, set the knives and forks beside each plate, and sat in the far corner of the couch, as far away from him as possible.

"Are you guys volunteering for helpless Alyssa guard or is Ty making you?"

His gaze shot to her, but he didn't say anything for a while, not until she met his eyes. "You aren't helpless."

She shrugged. "Now, are you going to answer my question?"

"I watched you Wednesday night. Cuss volunteered Thursday. After we left last night, Army asked me to watch you."

"Why?"

He didn't want to say too much, but he didn't want to lie either. "Cuss has a way with women." He took a sip of his beer.

Her eyes widened, and she smiled. "Yeah, I know."

He tensed, anger and jealousy igniting. "He try something?"

"My brother has good instincts. Sometimes he knows things without me telling him, but other times those instincts fail him. Case in point: Cuss."

He lifted a brow. "Care to explain?"

"My brother's right about Cuss. He does have a way with women. Being a woman, I know. It's his eyes."

Shit. He didn't want to hear this, didn't want to

hear she liked anything about any man. His hands curled into fists. He fought the urge to make any sudden movements, show any hint of the emotion flooding him.

"But my brother's also wrong. I'm not interested in Cuss, and even if I was, he's taken."

He exhaled, relieved. "He isn't taken."

Her eyes met his and softened. "Maybe not in the literal sense, but trust me when I say, he's taken."

She was so adamant about it he couldn't help but ask. "How do you know? He tell you?"

"I saw it."

"Elaborate, Allie."

"I noticed him looking at someone."

What? Because Cuss looked at a woman didn't mean he was interested in her for more than a night, and it especially didn't mean he was taken. "That it?"

"Jace, trust me. I'm telling you I saw him. He looked at her like…" She shook her head. "Never mind."

Now, he was intrigued. Besides, she was talking freely to him. He wanted that more than he cared to know about Cuss. "You brought it up, now you gotta tell me."

"Right or else I get hardheaded, angry Jace?" She laughed softly. "I saw him look at her the way every woman wants to be looked at. I asked him about it. He didn't confirm it, but he didn't deny it. Honestly, even if he denied it, it wouldn't make a difference. I saw it. He's taken."

Could she tell that from one look? If she could, then she knew how much he wanted her, too.

She cut into his thoughts. "Are you planning on trying my food?"

He refocused his attention on the spaghetti and chicken parmesan in front of him, cut a piece, and popped it in his mouth. Damn. So good, no, fantastic. The favors melded perfectly in his mouth. No surprise there, considering all the guys raved about her skills.

He swallowed. "Fuckin' amazing, Allie."

Her fork had been halfway to her mouth, but hearing his declaration, she paused and smiled wide. "Thanks."

"Ever think about being a chef?"

She took a bite, swallowed, and shrugged. "I figured I'd get enough cooking done for my husband and kids, so no. I guess looking back now..." Her words trailed off, a sadness enveloping her features.

"Allie?"

"Sorry...Nothing."

A loaded nothing. It wasn't any of his business, but he wanted to ask. He hated seeing that sadness in her eyes, her face. He wanted to make it better, so he tried. "What is it?"

Her eyes met his. "Funny, how things work out sometimes..."

He held his breath, waiting for her to explain.

"When I was a kid, I thought by this time in my life I'd be married, planning a family. Instead, I'm starting over."

"You're young, twenty-five. You've got plenty of time for a family."

"Maybe." She didn't sound convinced. She glanced at his plate, then met his eyes. "Let me reheat it for you." She reached for his plate.

Damn, she wanted to reheat his food because it sat out for two minutes without him touching it? Smart, sweet, beautiful, and attentive on top of that. How wasn't she married with three plus kids?

He grabbed her wrist. "It's still hot. You eat."

She nodded.

He took a bite of spaghetti. "You'd make a great wife."

She chuckled. "Ahh…if it were only that easy."

He didn't get why it amused her. It wasn't funny. It killed knowing she was perfect and could never be his. "It *is* that easy, Allie. You're beautiful, smart, and sweet. You can cook, and you keep a clean house. That isn't enough, you drive a muscle car, drink beer, and manage to look classy doing it. You fit in here with the club, and I know you just as easily fit in with your old life in New York, living in a penthouse with a doorman."

Fuck. Had he said that?

Her jaw dropped.

He didn't know why the truth surprised her.

"Thanks…I think."

He smiled. "You think?"

She flushed. "Yeah, I'm not sure it was a compliment."

He lifted a brow. "How're you not sure it's a compliment, Allie?"

"Um…well…you sounded kind of mad when you said it."

She hit the nail on the head. He wasn't pissed she was all those things, but he was pissed he could never have her. Still, he laughed because he was with her. She made him a fantastic meal. They were talking and sharing, and he'd enjoy this for six more days.

Luckiest trailer trash on earth.

"Yeah, kinda." He held her stare for several moments. When she looked away, he resumed eating.

He finished his meal. Allie being sweet, beautiful, perfect Allie asked if he wanted seconds. He didn't need the extra carbs, but he would eat all she offered only because she offered.

She headed into the kitchen then walked out minutes later carrying a steaming plate of food. Setting it on the coffee table, she sat beside him.

"Decided what you wanna watch?"

She smiled. "How about *Friends*?"

He nodded and took a bite of his food. She slid a DVD into the player. They watched two episodes while he finished. He'd never watched *Friends*, but he was glad she'd picked it out. He got to hear her laugh, a lot, and she had a beautiful laugh.

When he finished, she grabbed his plate and headed into the kitchen. He followed behind. "I'll do the dishes." She'd cooked; he'd clean.

She turned and quirked a brow. "No one does the dishes. I have a dishwasher."

"Then I'll rinse and put them in the dishwasher."

She smiled, made way for him. "Suit yourself."

He rinsed the dishes, set them in the dishwasher, and ran the load. They headed back into the living room with two fresh beers and watched four more episodes. He got to hear her laugh some more, the entire time trying his hardest not to look her way. After, she bid goodnight and headed into her room.

He did what he always did.

He watched her go.

****

A loud crash woke her. Allie jolted up in bed, her

eyes gravitating toward where the sound came from, her bedroom window. Another loud thud sounded. This time, a rock struck the glass. She watched her window crack. She jerked at the sound. Her heart beating a thousand miles a minute, she scrambled out of bed and fell in a heap on the floor. Not a moment later, her bedroom door slammed open. A figure came to view. She gasped, placed her hand over her mouth, and scooted away.

"Allie?"

Jace. She recognized his voice though she couldn't see his face. Thank God for Jace.

He rushed toward her, kneeling in front of her, and picked her off the floor. He opened the closet door and set her inside. "Stay in here."

He didn't give her time to respond. He left quickly, closing her closet door and her bedroom door. A second later, she heard the front door, opening and closing, and the lock.

With her heart pounding so loudly in her ears and her breaths coming out in feverish gasps, she cradled her legs against her chest. Somewhere subconsciously she knew it wasn't a prank. This was something else, and it had Wyatt written all over it. She knew in her bones he'd take pleasure in terrifying her. She'd seen the gleam in his eyes the night he'd beat her. For him, it'd been a high, and though she wanted to believe he would leave her alone, she knew better. If there was a will, there was a way, and Wyatt always got his way.

Jace. Stupid, macho, biker Jace. He left her alone to investigate instead of staying inside the house. She should've never let him go. What if something happened to him because of her?

Her stomach turned. Her eyes welling with tears she fought to hold at bay. She couldn't make any noise. She listened for any sounds coming from outside.

Just then, she heard the front door unlocking. Her panic overwhelming her, tears choked her. The door to her apartment opened then closed. Light footsteps sounded, coming closer and closer until the door to her room squeaked open.

"Allie, it's me."

She heaved a sigh of relief, and tears spilled from her eyes.

He parted the closet door, knelt, wrapped his arms around her, and easily lifted her. The heat of his body permeated her skin, soothing her shattered nerves.

Nestled against his large frame, he carried her, and sat on the bed, her on his lap. One hand cupped the back of her head, the other tight around her back, holding her against his chest. "Don't be scared, Allie. I'm here," he whispered. He kissed the top of her head, the action so tender her heart clenched.

Gripping his shirt, she tilted her head to look up at him. Close enough to kiss him, she whispered, "You left me. You crazy, stupid biker. What if something happened to you?"

He had the gall to smile. "Nothing happened to me."

"It could've."

"You'd'd've been safe."

What? He was *crazy*. "I was worried about you."

"Needed to keep you safe. The only way to do that was look for the ass who's terrified you."

She swallowed. "Did you find him?"

He shook his head. "Got to call the cops."

Was he serious? Badass biker wanted to call the cops for a cracked window, but not when Wyatt slapped her?

He must've read her thoughts in her expression. The next second, he said, "You need a report to get the window replaced by the insurance."

"I don't have insurance."

His brows drew together. "You don't have renter's insurance?"

She shook her head.

"You should have renter's insurance, Allie." He sighed heavily like her having renter's insurance mattered so much now. "Still gonna call the cops. Management needs to know what happened."

She nodded, then straightened, intent on moving away.

His arm tightened around her. A breath away from her, he whispered, "Stay, Allie. You're shaking."

She didn't argue. She'd been trembling since she'd woken startled and scared, and it hadn't stopped. For some insane reason, it comforted her to have his arms around her and his scent filling her.

He shifted her slightly to pluck his phone out of his pocket then called 911. Ten minutes later, a knock sounded on the front door. He stood, the arm around her waist holding her up, then softly set her on her feet in front of him. His arm pressed against her back, his lips pressed against her forehead, he whispered, "It's gonna be okay, Allie."

When he drew away, his gaze trailed down her frame. She wore her PJ's, a spaghetti strap shirt and jaw-string shorts. He inhaled visibly, grabbed the blanket off the bed, and wrapped it around her shoulders. Grabbing her hand, he walked her to the couch where he told her to sit. He then headed for the door.

It took close to an hour for the cops to interview both of them, take pictures of the cracked window from the inside and out. Allie watched in a haze, riddled with nerves, still shivering. By the time, the cops left, all she wanted was sleep, so she could forget or try to.

The officers moved to the door, and then one of them turned to Jace. "Take care of your woman. She doesn't look good."

She waited for Jace to correct him. Instead he said, "Plan on it."

The cops exited her apartment. Without removing his gaze from her, Jace closed and locked the door then closed the distance between them. Sitting beside her, he tugged her against him until she sat on his lap, pressed against his chest.

"Still shakin', Allie."

She buried her face in his neck and inhaled. "Wonder why people assume we're together. If they only knew, I'm just a favor for a friend."

He cupped her face and drew it to his. His jaw clenched, but his eyes spoke volumes. A deep ache reflected in them. She didn't know why and hated seeing it. She hated more that a man like him, so strong and brave, could feel pain and express it so easily. He was supposed to be an angry biker, and yet he wasn't, or at least it wasn't all of who he was.

Because she didn't want to see it anymore, because she was scared, and because he'd saved her again, she closed her eyes and pressed her lips against his.

It was wrong and stupid, too, but at the moment,

she didn't care because his lips were soft and full and pressed against hers.

Feeling heat creep up her cheeks, she pulled away then hesitantly opened her eyes.

Shit.

He looked pissed. He *was* pissed. "You're killing me," he said through clenched teeth.

What should she say? Sorry?

She jerked away from him but couldn't put distance between them. His hold on her waist tightened, his fingers digging into her skin. Then he shoved her against his hard chest. Gripping the back of her neck, he kissed her.

He kissed her hard and rough, delving his tongue into her mouth with such brutal force it daunted her. As he explored every inch of it, she got lost, so lost she couldn't remember where she was, what she'd been doing. What she knew—Jace was kissing her like he'd been starving for her, and it felt fantastic. A kiss was all she wanted for months.

He didn't stop, not for a long while.

Finally, he trailed his mouth down her cheek then neck. She gasped for breath. Sensations rippled through her, making her quiver. Her arms went around his neck, and she dug her hands in his hair, moaning. His hands reached under her shirt, grasped her skin on the side of her stomach tightly and pressed her against the length of him.

God, he was big, even over his jeans and her shorts she felt how big. It didn't scare her.

She kissed his temple, then tasted his skin with her tongue. He made a deep, guttural sound in the back of his throat and shifted her until each one of her legs was at his sides, and she straddled him.

He tugged her shirt off her head the next moment. His eyes fixated on her chest like he wanted to devour her, and God help her, but she wanted him to.

He groaned. "Fuckin' beautiful." Then he captured her nipple in his mouth. He flicked his tongue against it, grasped it between his teeth, and sucked hard. It felt amazing, so amazing, her eyes rolled to the back of her head, a gasp escaping her lips.

He snaked his arm around her waist, then trailed it up her spine, stopping only when he gripped her neck and brought her face millimeters from his. His hooded, dark eyes snared hers. "You're fuckin' beautiful, baby." His voice dripped with emotion. He crushed his lips against hers, pressing her chest against his until her nipples hardened and puckered against every ridge of muscle lining it.

With his tongue tormenting her mouth, she gripped the hem of his shirt and lifted it over his head. Having to break away from his lips, her eyes feasted his chest.

She'd been right. He was carved from stone. Bulging muscles lined every inch of him. His shoulders were big, wide, and strong, his pecs firm, the muscles on his back that protruded his sides clearly visible from where she sat on his lap. And his abs, Jesus, his abs were sculpted, even sitting up they were defined. Near his hips was the sexiest muscle on a male body, the pelvic muscle near the waist, shaped in a V. On his left side, under his arm, he had a large tattoo that stretched from under his arm to his waist. She couldn't see it clearly, but she wanted to know what it was and what it meant.

He was perfect, so she couldn't help trail her

fingers down his chest, tracing the outline of his abs, and pelvic muscle. She pressed her lips against his chest and licked her way to his abs.

He dug his fingers in her hair and trailed them down until he gripped her under the arms and roughly hauled her up, her face inches from his, his expression ravished with lust. "Killing me."

The breath rushed out of her. Oh, God. Was that what he meant every time he said those words?

He didn't give her a chance to think about it for long. His hand pressed to her neck, pulling her lips against his again for another searing kiss that left her trembling. Running his hand up the inside of her thigh, he reached her core and rubbed her through the thin cotton of her shorts. She shuddered, moaning loudly.

His cock jerked under her. "You're so fuckin' wet."

His words egging her on, her body pulsed. She panted, silently begging him to take her.

He threaded his fingers inside her jaw-string shorts, and then he pushed her underwear aside. His thumb stroked the length of her core. Her hips bucked. Her back arched, her nails digging into his shoulders.

"Like it, Allie?"

She couldn't talk, so she nodded.

Jace buried his face in her neck, sucking and licking the sensitive flesh. He rubbed her clit once then twice. Her hips bucked each time, grinding against his fingers.

He groaned, then his mouth was on hers again, teasing and taunting, and then he bit her bottom lip. "I'm going to make you come, and when you come, you're gonna scream my name."

She wanted that too, but she couldn't speak. Again, all she managed to do was nod.

Suddenly, he stood. Her legs wrapped around him as he walked toward her room. In one swift movement, he released her legs. One arm around her waist holding her, he ripped her shorts and thong off, with the other. He then laid her on the bed, his lips glued to hers, his hand at her core.

Then he was gone. The heat of his lips still on her mouth, but he was gone, working his way down her body. Heat lingered on each spot his lips touched, neck, breasts, stomach, hips, but then it too—gone.

Gripping her hips, he roughly pulled her. Her heated flesh met his mouth. A startled gasp escaped her, pleasure pulsing through every pore. Her legs closed on his head instinctively. He reached under her legs, grasped her inner thighs, and pulled them apart. Holding her in place, he delved in, sucking, licking, devouring her.

He was skilled, beyond skilled. It was hard and rough, and had her screaming in seconds. She couldn't see, couldn't think but knew Jace gave her that intense pleasure, and she never wanted him to stop.

She dug her fingers into his hair and ground against his mouth. He lightly bit her clit, shoved his finger inside her, and then she was gone, arching her back and screaming his name.

When the high faded, he licked her one last time from top to bottom, savoring her taste. She gripped his hair, hauled him toward her until her lips met his. She tasted herself in his mouth and loved it, loved it so much she knew she'd be happy to taste it every day for the rest of her life.

She reached for his belt, unbuckled it, then drew away from his lips to whisper, "Take me."

His dark eyes, locked on hers, softened so much it ignited a searing ache inside her—the same ache she read in his eyes. She didn't know what it meant, but she knew he couldn't help it.

Then he did something else, something she never imagined. He trailed his fingers down her face in a soft, tender caress. He stayed there for endless moments. Then he got off her. Standing, he pulled a condom from his wallet, removed his jeans and boxers, and let her take her fill.

Beautiful, all of him. His shaft standing at attention, he wasn't big. He was huge, so huge she didn't know if he'd fit her.

She met his eyes. "I don't know if it'll fit." Her cheeks flamed.

He smiled his amazing smile. "It'll fit, baby. It'll fit perfectly."

Ripping the condom wrapper open with his teeth, he rolled it on. Not a moment later, his body was poised over hers, his gaze holding hers hostage.

In that single moment of time, the panic set in. She wanted him. She'd wanted him since the moment she met him but knew nothing would ever come of them. Her brother warned her about bikers, and still, she couldn't find the strength to say no. As reckless as it was, even if just for one night, she wanted him.

But he hesitated, so she said, "It's okay. I know it doesn't mean anything. You don't have to warn me."

His eyes darkened, the same ache shining through when he whispered, "It means something to me, Allie."

He said it so tenderly, her heart tightened.

Hopelessly and maybe foolishly, she believed him.

His lips claimed her. Soft and thoroughly, he kissed her. One hand buried in her hair, the other wrapped around his shaft. The kiss intensified. He pushed himself against her core, filling her slowly until completely immersed in her.

He was right.

He fit.

He fit her, perfectly.

Chapter Eighteen

Hovering over her, his eyes locked on hers, his dick buried in her tightness, he fucking knew he'd been right. He'd been so right about her, about everything about her.

From one look, he'd known, and the knowledge of it ravished him because he'd never have her fully, completely.

For her, this was one night.

For him, it was forever.

He knew, like he knew from one look he'd never meet a woman who compared. He'd never forget either. This moment would be seared in his mind for the rest of his life.

He knew it, felt it. So he knew he should stop, knew he shouldn't let himself feel any more of it, knowing he'd never be able to fuck a tap to blow off steam. She'd damaged him for good, soiling every other woman on the face of the earth, but he didn't care. If he got a piece of her, one night of feeling this, he would take it.

With her lying pliant and willing under him, he pulled out, then thrust into her slowly, allowing her to grow accustomed to the feel of him. Her walls clenching him, she moaned the sweetest moan. The entire time, her beautiful, color-changing eyes never left his. He let himself believe it was because she wanted to memorize him above her, inside, stretching, and owning her. He let himself believe it because he wanted that, too.

She wrapped her trembling legs around his waist, pressing her heels against his lower back pushing herself into him. One hand buried in his hair, and the other wrapped around his shoulders.

He slammed his lips against hers, delving into her mouth in a frenzy, then thrust into her again, and she moaned in his mouth.

He continued his pace, soft, slow, and deep. It took all the restraint he had to make love to her, but he did it. He wanted to give her what she deserved, and she deserved to be loved.

To him, it didn't matter. Even if he fucked her senseless, showing her what she'd be missing from that day forward, it'd always mean more than a casual fuck.

"Harder, Jace," she whispered against his lips.

He drew away to stare into her eyes. Then he gave her what she wanted, hard and fast.

Totally worth it. With each pound, her arms and legs tightened like a vise grip around him, like she'd never let go, moaning and whimpering.

Holding back the need to spill, he reached for her clit and rubbed it roughly. She spasmed. Her hips bucked wildly.

It did him in. He lost control. Groaning, his eyes on hers, hers on him, he came, hard.

Then she cried out his name.

His name.

The sound resonated inside his chest long after his release, the most powerful, mind-blowing release of his life. He'd expected nothing less because he'd been so right about her it fucking hurt.

His chest tightening, a deep ache seared him. Unable to move and unwilling to try, he wanted to stay.

But it was over. He knew he'd lose her, knew he couldn't prevent it. So, still buried inside, while he caught his breath, he relished the moment as best he could. Endless moments later, he cupped her cheek and rested his forehead against hers. "I was fuckin' right, baby. You taste and feel like heaven."

Her eyes, misted with her release, watered.

It cut him deep. He'd either hurt her or she already felt the shame of fucking trash like him. He would've apologized, but guilt clogged his throat.

Her arms tightened around him. A tear slipped out of her eye. "That's the most beautiful thing anyone's ever said to me."

It knocked the wind out of him. Letting the feeling sink in, he wiped the tear from her face.

Still, he didn't want it to end, so he kissed her long and hard. Her tongue darted into his mouth and entwined perfectly with his, like she didn't want him to leave.

Shit. He was getting hard again, and he still had on the old condom. He had to find the will to pull away and out of her. Wanting to relish it, he slowly pulled out. She tensed and unwrapped her arms and legs from him, then looked away. A sadness took hold of her expression. It pleased him so much the ache in his chest lessened. Then and there, he decided to do what he had never done before, cuddle. If he had just one night with her, he would take that night, and the night wasn't over.

Smiling, he stood and walked toward her bathroom, removed the condom, and flushed it. He stepped back into her room and found her curled into a ball with her back toward him. Without thought, he climbed into her bed.

She sat up, turning to face him. Her brows drew together. He read the question in her eyes, but he let his actions speak.

Wrapping an arm around her waist, he pulled her against him until she was sprawled on his chest. He ran his fingers through her hair, then pressed a kiss to the top of her head. "Sleep, baby."

She lifted her head to meet his eyes. "I don't have much experience...with...um...sex." Her cheeks flushed. "I know you do, and I'm sure you hear it a lot...but that was...amazing."

He tugged her up and over him, her face inches from his. He trailed his fingers down her face. "That's 'cause you're amazing, Allie."

"You don't have to say nice things to get me into bed. You already did."

"I wouldn't mind having you in my bed every night."

He meant it. She let him in, even if for just one night, and it meant he had a taste, and God help him, but he would fight for more because one night wasn't enough.

She smiled, then rested her head against his chest. In minutes, she fell asleep.

****

Morning dawned, the alarm clock on the side of Allie's bed blinked eight a.m. Trig hated the night had gone so quickly. He had nodded off twice. He didn't need much sleep and with her cuddled against him reality was, for once, sweeter than a dream.

But it was Saturday morning. He looked forward to Saturdays and spending the day with his niece all week. Right then, he wanted it to be any other day. He didn't want to leave Allie.

She slept, soundlessly, breathing deeply. Her head on his shoulder, facing him, her leg tangled with his, and her dark, long hair sprawled against his arm. Even sleeping, without a shred of makeup, she was beautiful.

He hated waking her. Not just because she looked so peaceful and so beautiful, but because after last night he didn't know how she'd react, how she'd feel about what they'd done, what they'd shared. And if last night was all he had, he didn't want to leave. He wanted to hold on to that moment as long as he could, wanted to stay there and stare at her. But he couldn't do that either; he had to get Della.

He pressed his lips against her forehead, kissing her lightly. He'd done it so many times throughout the night he'd lost count. Disentangling himself from her slowly, he shifted until her head rested against the pillow. After dressing, he took a deep breath, and then he did what he could come to regret.

Sitting on the edge of the bed, he kissed her lips ever so softly, then whispered, "Baby?" He ran his fingers through her hair.

She mumbled incoherently.

He kissed her again. "Allie, baby?"

Her lids fluttered open briefly, then closed.

He rubbed his fingers across her cheek. "You look beautiful."

She smiled and pressed her chest against his thigh.

"Gotta get Della. One of the guys will watch you today. Be back later."

She smiled and whispered softly, "Okay."

Like she wanted him to come back.

He grinned. He probably looked like an idiot grinning to himself, but he didn't fucking care. She wanted him back.

Yeah, he was the luckiest trailer trash on earth.

****

Allie buried her face in the pillow, seeking more of the intoxicating scent she'd dreamed about, the scent she usually avoided. In the haze of sleep, she didn't realize who it belonged to, but as the seconds turned to minutes, it hit her.

She shot up in bed, clutching the blanket against her, her eyes frantically scanning her room.

It hadn't been a dream. It had been real, and now, he was gone.

In the pit of her stomach, she knew who he was, and she'd been warned. So she knew without searching the rest of her apartment, he was gone. She hated she'd stupidly let herself believe everything he said, hated she thought for even a split second what they'd done meant something to him.

Sitting there on her bed, naked and deliciously satisfied, she held back tears, knowing she deserved the throbbing ache in the middle of her chest.

It wasn't his fault. She'd done this to herself.

She had to face facts now. Better now than later. She'd initiated it. She'd kissed him, and then, she let him kiss her and touch her and fuck her. To him, that was all it had been, an easy fuck, a one-night stand, no better than the taps he got off on.

Shame didn't even begin to describe how she felt. She'd never had a one-night stand, never had a sex-buddy. Never had she been so stupid and reckless with her body and her heart.

She was an idiot.

Allie sat there, immobile for moments too long. Then she squared her shoulders, lifted her chin, and got out of bed. Pulling on a robe, she parted her bedroom door and headed into the living room where she spotted Blaze on her couch.

"Hey, Classy."

She hadn't expected Blaze. In fact, she'd hoped she wouldn't see anyone from the club today. She should've guessed. Jace would fuck her and leave her, but he'd never leave her without a guard not because he cared, but because of Ty and the club.

She pulled her robe tighter. "H-Hi."

"Look surprised. Thought you knew the club was watchin' you."

"Yeah, sorry…I forgot for a second."

He scanned her face. Her clue he'd caught on she wasn't okay. She forced herself to look away. "Do you want coffee, some breakfast?"

He smiled. "Won't say no to food, especially not anything you make."

She gave him her best fake smile, then busied herself making pancakes and brewing a pot of coffee.

A knock sounded on her door, her heart skipped a beat. Blaze parted it. Cuss strode through, smiling.

She released a breath. "Hi, Cuss."

"Miracle, you makin' me breakfast?"

She smiled. "Actually, I was making Blaze breakfast. He didn't tell me you were coming."

Cuss's face fell. He then shot a glare in Blaze's direction, who laughed.

"Don't worry, there's enough for you."

Cuss's gaze met hers. He grinned.

They ate together on her small dining room table, and after, she made calls to Mia, Lynn, and Tiffany, and made plans to get out of her apartment. It reminded her of him, of her mistake.

Chapter Nineteen

Trig called her four times. Four. Fucking. Times. She hadn't picked up a single one of his calls. Not one.

He didn't know how late she usually slept, so he'd called her at noon. She hadn't answered. Around that time, he'd taken Della to the park. He'd glanced at his phone every half hour. Like a fucking wuss waiting for her call.

Two hours later, she hadn't responded. He called her again. And again, she didn't answer. He left her a message, simple and to the point, telling her to call him back. Like a pussy-whipped idiot, he checked his phone every fifteen minutes.

Three hours later, she still hadn't called. He called again, and again, she didn't answer. He then caved and called Blaze, who told him he had a guard and Cuss volunteered to watch her.

Cuss. Damn fucking Cuss. What was it she'd said? Cuss had a way with women, and she knew because she was a woman.

Jealousy knotting his gut, he swallowed his pride and called Cuss, who informed him Allie and Tiffany were at the mall, shopping.

Shopping and she couldn't bother to pick up his fucking calls? Giving him the brush-off, the fucking brush-off! He deserved it, too. She had class, and he was trash, but shit, it hurt. Allie wasn't just any woman.

She was beautiful and sweet Allie with her pretty color-changing eyes and fantastic legs. She'd kissed him, and they'd had sex, and now, she'd brushed him off.

He'd been afraid she'd regret what they'd done. After that morning, he thought she wouldn't, but, damn, he'd been wrong. As clear as day, and still, he didn't want to believe it.

Three hours later, after eating dinner with Della and dropping her off at home, he'd called Allie again. It rang once, twice, then he lost count, and her voice message came on. He'd already memorized it, and hearing her voice killed him, so he threw his phone across his dashboard and headed to the compound to change and pick up his bike.

At the compound, he changed into a faded black shirt, his cut, and strode to his bike, ignoring his brothers along the way.

Ten minutes later, he arrived at her place. Spotting her car parked, he headed up the stairs and knocked on her door. No answer. No surprise there. He knocked harder. Still, no answer. Pulling out his phone, he dialed Cuss.

Over blaring music, Cuss answered. "Brother."

"Where the fuck are you?" he barked.

"Was about to call you. Mia, Lynn, Tiff, and Allie are at the bar."

The bar? He'd kill Cuss. He'd rip his arms from his body. Fucking idiot Cuss allowed Allie to go there. "What the fuck is Allie doin' there?"

"What's the big fuckin' deal, Trig? They're havin' some drinks and dancing."

The big deal—he had Allie last night, and the taste of her was still in his mouth. The big deal—he couldn't stand the thought of her in a bar with bikers and drunks hitting on her. Even thinking of some ass clown dancing with Allie made him want to rip someone's head off.

"I'm on my fuckin' way. *Don't* tell her I'm coming."

****

"Allie? Hello, earth to Allie?"

She blinked, then looked at Mia and smiled her best fake smile.

"Something happened, and something big."

"I—"

"You can't deny it," Lynn cut her off. "You've been a zombie for the last hour, and barely touched your beer."

Tiff took a sip of wine. "Actually, she's been a zombie all day."

True, and as if last night hadn't been enough, she had another reason too. Jace called. He'd called four times. Four times she'd hit ignore and felt her heart breaking a little more. She wanted to hear his voice. Hell, she wanted more than that, and it's why she had no choice but to ignore his calls. What could he possibly say when he'd said enough by leaving? But more than that too, she couldn't let on how much he hurt her, and she didn't think she could hold it together.

"I need something stronger tonight, ladies."

Their eyes widened, but before they asked any questions, she motioned for the waitress and ordered four shots of tequila.

Hoping to take the heat off her, she asked Lynn, "How did you manage to get away from Wild?"

Lynn laughed cheekily, flipping her blonde hair

behind her. "He knows Cuss is here, so…" She shrugged.

The waitress returned with their shots and set them in the middle of the high top.

Tiffany raised her shot glass. "Cheers. To more girls' nights."

Allie lifted her glass, tipped it against the others, and shot it back, feeling the burn at the back of her throat. It felt good, so she ordered another round. The round came, and together, they shot them back.

Spotting Cuss drawing near, she smiled. "Cuss, you've come to join us?"

He finished closing the distance between them and lifted a brow. "Come to tell you guys to slow down on the shots, Miracle."

Mia glared. "Why should we?"

He sighed. "There's one of me and four of you. Can't fuckin' look out for four of you if you're all drunk and start disappearing."

Tiffany chuckled, softly. "Why do you assume we'd disappear?"

"'Cause you women all do. Head to the fuckin' bathroom for fuckin' hours doing I don't know what the fuck."

Allie threw her head back and laughed, laughed loud. Cuss was all badass biker, and yet he could be so dense it was adorable. "I'll let you in on a secret," she told Cuss. "We spent so much time in the bathroom because we're talking about you."

His eyes widened. "No shit?"

The shots had their desired effect, she smiled a genuine smile. "Yep."

"Oh, look to your left." Lynn tapped her arm. "Not

right now, in a little. There's a man with blond hair who's been looking at you for like ten minutes."

She didn't want to look, knowing she wouldn't be interested in him even if he was Brad Pitt.

"Yeah, I noticed him looking at you like five minutes ago," Mia added.

She ignored them, searching for a way to distract them.

"Oh, he's coming this way." Lynn's eyes widened.

Great.

"Allie?"

Shit. She recognized that voice. She turned and smiled. "Hi, Keith."

He smiled. "Thought it was you." He shifted his gaze to Tiff and greeted her.

She made introductions. He politely greeted them, then asked her to dance. She spared a glance at Mia and Lynn who were smiling like idiots. Then she turned her gaze to Keith.

"She'd love to dance," Lynn answered for her.

She would scream at Lynn later. Lynn had good intentions, but she didn't want to dance with Keith. It'd only serve to remind her he wasn't Jace. Still, she couldn't be rude to the guy. He did nothing to deserve it. Having no choice, she stood and headed for the dance floor.

****

Trig strode in, his eyes scanning the bar. The place was big, considering the small town of Wadden. Decked out in beer bottles, domestic, imports, some he'd never even heard of. Booths lined each wall. In the back end, several pool tables were assembled. The bar lay in the center of the room and wrapped around, circled by high-top tables, dozens of them, except for a section on the right side where there was a dance floor.

Immediately, he spotted Cuss who sat with Tiffany, Mia, and Lynn at a high top near the bar. Cuss's back facing the door, a beer in hand. No sign of Allie. His anger grew to new heights.

He fisted his hands and took ten long strides to reach him. "Where the fuck is Allie?" he barked to his back.

Cuss stood and turned, hardened his gaze, then snapped back, "Brother, get you're in a pissy mood 'cause you're usually in a pissy mood, but I ain't in the fuckin' mood to put up with your shit."

"Where the fuck is she?"

Cuss nodded toward the dance floor. His gaze shot to the right.

There she was.

Allie. Allie with her beautiful face and fantastic legs. He had a great view of those fantastic legs that went on for miles because she wore a short jean skirt and "fuck me" heels, one of the pairs with the red bottoms he'd seen in her enormous closet in New York, one of the pairs he'd told her to bring.

She was dancing with the college boy with class he'd seen her with at Anthony's, the one she claimed she wasn't interested in. The lucky bastard spun her. Her dark, thick, silky hair swirled around her, hitting him in the chest. She stumbled and fell on him. The man's arm snaked around her waist holding her against him. She laughed, loud.

"Fuck."

She fucking ditched him for the college boy with class. She knew he was trash, and a woman like her didn't fuck a man like him. If a woman like her managed to fuck up and fuck a man like him, she never went back for seconds. She gave him the brush-off and hooked up with a college boy worth her.

He knew this, and still, it didn't lessen the envy tightening his gut, didn't lessen the searing pang throbbing in his chest and burning its way up his throat. He did nothing but stand there enduring the awful aches, watching her dance with the college boy when not a day before she'd given herself to him. He watched and watched, and then something inside him snapped. Before he realized what he was doing, he was standing behind her, close enough he smelled that fantastic perfume she always wore.

"Outside. Now."

Chapter Twenty

"Outside. Now."

A chill shot up her back. She stiffened then turned and tilted her head up to meet his eyes. Her breath left her.

Jace, but he looked different. A five-o'clock shadow marred his face, his hair disheveled. His jaw set in anger. It wasn't the reason he looked different. His expression, something about it seemed ravished.

Keith grabbed her hand and pulled her away from Jace. "Can I help you?"

Bad idea. A really bad idea. Jace was beyond angry, so angry a vein in his neck pulsed. She turned to Keith. "It's okay. I know him. Thanks for the dance. See you around?"

Keith spared a glance at Jace, then reluctantly released her hand and nodded.

Allie watched him go then turned and shot daggers at Jace. She crossed her arms over her chest so he couldn't see her shaking hands. "Can I help you?"

His eyes narrowed. He took a step in her direction. "Outside. Now."

She took a deep breath and lifted her chin. "No."

He leaned into her until nose to nose. "Don't try me, Allie."

"I'm not going anywhere with you, Trig."

His jaw twitched; then in one swift movement, he

wrapped an arm around her waist, pressing her against the length of him and lifted her off the floor. Her stupid body molded against his, willingly. Still, she fought, pushing at his chest and wiggling in his grasp.

He leaned into her ear and menacingly whispered, "Stop fightin' me. Your skirt's riding up and if any of the assholes in here get a peek, I'll slam their fuckin' heads into a brick wall."

His breath at her ear, she shuddered. She sent up a silent prayer hoping he hadn't felt it, hoping he couldn't hear the sound of her heart pounding. She took a deep breath, then whispered in a soft voice, "Okay, but I can walk."

"Sorry, Allie, lost that privilege. Now, I carry you."

He walked out of the bar, her body tightly pressed against his, feeling every muscle across the expanse of his chest contract as he moved. When they reached outside, her skirt had ridden up.

"Stop."

He stiffened. "Been through this—"

"My skirt."

With his free hand, he tugged her skirt down, his fingers grazing her thigh, pooling heat in her middle. She closed her eyes and took a deep breath, fighting to ignore her body's reaction.

"Good?" he asked in a soft tone.

She nodded.

He released her slowly, allowing her body to slide down his. She shuddered, like every other time she couldn't help herself. As soon as her feet hit the ground, she scrambled away.

"Get on the bike," he said between clenched teeth.

She wanted to say "Hell no," but he was back to

angry, so she tried to appease him by staying calm. "No."

His eyes narrowed. "Get. On. The. Bike."

She should've known better, bikers didn't take no for an answer, no matter how nice she said it. Her eyes narrowed. "No way in hell am I getting on the back of your bike."

He fisted his palms. "You're gonna fuckin' do it, or I'll do it for you."

She lifted her chin defiantly. "No."

"Tryin' my temper, Allie."

"Not getting on the back of your bike, Trig."

He closed the distance between them, leaned into her. An inch away from her lips, he said, "You want me to touch you again? You want me to feel your tight little body against mine again? I'll tell you it fuckin' turns me on. Way the fuck on. I know you like it too, so if that's your game, I'm down for it, *baby*."

He was being a dick. He'd never been a dick to her before. She was so ashamed of what happened, so ashamed she let herself believe he cared, and now he'd reminded her of her mistake, calling her "baby" and saying it cruelly, tainting how he'd said it the night before.

Her face flamed. She felt the rush of tears coming and swallowed. "You're an asshole." She meant to say it with force, with the anger burning her throat, but it came out weak and trembling.

"I'm an asshole who's lookin' out for you. You've had too much to drink, and every-fuckin'-one of those men in there...." He pointed toward the bar. "...are waiting for the smallest signal to get up your skirt. I'm not having it."

Did he think she'd fall for that crap? "Don't know if you've fucking noticed, but I'm twenty-five, and I can fuck whoever I want."

His eyes widened, shock flashing across his face. His jaw twitched. "You won't be fuckin' anyone. Not on my watch. Not ever."

"What are you so afraid of?" she asked in a mocking tone. "That they'll fuck me and leave me like you did last night?" She shouldn't have said it. It would only prove how much he hurt her.

His eyes widened further. In a tight voice, he said, "I didn't—"

She cut him off, unwilling to hear any of his lousy excuses. "You're not my father, and you're not my brother. Even if you were, you have no say in who I fuck."

His eyes hardened to slits. "You're not a tap."

No, she was not sexually liberated. She didn't have it in her, couldn't give herself to someone she didn't care about. "It didn't stop you from fucking me." She hated she felt guilty for bringing it up again. It wouldn't change anything, wouldn't make him feel bad for taking what she'd freely offered.

"I didn't fuck you, Allie. I fuck taps. I don't fuck you."

He could deny it all he wanted, but he fucked her because she'd been there and willing.

"You're *not* a tap."

He said it to make her feel better. She didn't believe it for a second, but arguing with him, wouldn't get her anywhere. "Okay."

"Don't fuckin' do that shit. You know I hate it when you wave a white flag."

"I don't know what you're doing here, Trig. I'm fine with Cuss. He drove us here, and he can drive me back."

"You aren't going anywhere with fuckin' Cuss. Now. Get. On. The. Fucking. Bike."

"I'm not getting on your bike." She turned away from him toward the bar.

Before she could take a step, he wrapped his arm around her waist and pressed her back against the length of him. Against her ear, he whispered in a menacing tone, "I'm *not* fuckin' playing games, Allie. I will fuckin' make you get on the bike if you don't do it yourself."

She glared at no one in particular since she was still in his grip turned away from him. "Don't know if you've noticed, but I'm wearing a skirt. Even if I wanted to, I can't get on your bike."

He sighed heavily and released her. "You fuckin' walk away from me, there will be consequences, Allie."

Resigned, she turned to face him. He removed his cut then handed it to her. "Wrap it around your waist then get on the fuckin' bike."

Allie wrapped it around, turned to his bike, and stared at it for several minutes wondering how she'd manage to get on it without flashing him and everyone else in the parking lot. She took a deep breath and walked to the bike. Before she made an attempt, he threw his leg over it. Sitting astride, he offered her his hand.

"No one's lookin'. Put your foot on the peg then throw your leg over."

Putting her hand in his, she put her heel on the peg and lifted herself. A second later, she slipped, probably a combination of the six-inch heels she wore and inexperience. He twisted his upper body, wrapped his arm around her waist, catching her. Her body hit his, and the breath rushed out of her.

His mouth at her ear, he said, "Got you. Now lift your leg."

She did.

"Good, baby."

He said it in the softest voice, like the night before. Her stomach fluttered.

Releasing her slowly until her butt landed on the seat, he turned, grabbed her legs, and unexpectedly pulled her toward him. Her hands gripped his shoulders to steady herself. Tucked against his back, he tightened his cut around her legs, grabbed her arms, and wrapped them around his waist.

He shifted his head to look at her. "Keep your hands tight round my waist. Keep your feet on the pegs. Try not to move them. Don't want you getting burned on the exhaust."

She nodded though she wasn't sure how to manage any of the things he said considering she was terrified. She'd never been on a bike before, not even Tyler's.

Jace started his bike. It was loud, so loud even if she screamed, no one would hear her. The vibrations on the motor rumbled between her legs. She would blame the bike for the burning desire in her stomach, heating her center, but she knew better. It wasn't the bike. It was Jace. Crushed against him, her cheek against the muscles on his back, her arms tight around his waist, she felt his abs.

They moved. She jolted against him, her fingers gripping the skin on his stomach. His hand was over hers a second later. His fingers grazed hers, caressing her, almost like telling her it would be okay.

No wonder she let herself believe he was different. He constantly did things like that. If she wasn't so terrified, she'd be angry.

They continued moving, out of the parking lot and onto the street, not fast but not slow either. When the air hit her face, she relaxed. She finally got it, the appeal of riding.

The wind in your face.

The rush of adrenaline.

Freedom.

At twenty-five, almost twenty-six, she'd never felt that free. Not once, not ever, but knew she *needed* to feel that every day.

In no time, they pulled up to her apartment building. Jace parked in the space beside her Camaro and turned off his bike. He grabbed her hands at his waist before she could release him, and gave them a squeeze. She jerked away, then attempted to get off the bike. Her leg hit the hot chrome exhaust. She winced.

"Fuck," he cursed. At hyper speed, he hopped off, put his arms under her swiftly, picked her up off the bike, and carried her up the stairs to her apartment. "Keys."

She reached into her pocket and handed it to him. He opened the door, walked inside, and set her on the countertop. His gaze met hers, and then he barked, "Don't. Move."

He closed and locked the door. She unwrapped his cut from her waist. The next instant, he was beside her, lifting her leg to analyze the burn. The mark was red and already swelling. He let out a string of curses and then met her gaze. "First aid kit?"

"In the bathroom under the sink."

In seconds, Jace returned, set the kit on the counter, and opened it. He rifled through the contents until he found burn ointment. He spread it lightly over the swelling and bandaged it. His narrowed, pissed-off eyes then met hers. "If you wouldn't've been in such a fuckin' rush to get away from me, it wouldn't've happened."

Like he could blame her for wanting to get away from him. One minute he did and said the sweetest things, and the next he was pissed off and being an asshole. "Leave. Cuss is supposed to watch me, not you."

He slammed his fists against the counter beside her so hard it trembled under her. "I'm supposed to watch you for the next week. Your brother's orders."

Shit. Shit. Shit. She had to look at him and smell him for an entire week and pretend she wasn't hurt, pretend he hadn't used her?

A flood of tears hit her eyes. She held them back and looked away from him. "I think Ty won't mind considering what happened last night."

He lifted her chin with his index finger, forcing her to look at him. "You gonna tell him?"

"It doesn't serve any purpose except get you in hot water with Ty and the club. I wouldn't do that, but you have to understand I can't and I won't fucking look at you after what happened."

"Don't give a fuck. I gave your brother my word, and I'm keepin' it."

Tears she held drifted down her cheeks. "Why are you doing this to me? Why do you want to hurt me?

Does it thrill you to know you fucked me and left? Do you want to relive your conquest that badly?"

He flinched. "I didn't fuck you, and I didn't fuckin' leave you. I fuck taps. I don't fuck you."

Exhausted, drained, and in no mood to argue, she wiped her tears and hopped off the counter. He grabbed her waist, lifted her, and set her back on it, positioning himself between her legs against the counter. Her skirt hiked up. She made a futile attempt to pull it down as much as possible, then fought the urge to push at him. No point. He wouldn't bulge.

"When I fuck, I don't eat her out. When I fuck, I don't go fuckin' slow, and after I fuck, I don't cuddle."

"Whatever you say, Trig," she snapped. "I was fucked, so I know."

"Stop cursing. It isn't you."

"I have to because it seems there's no other way for you to understand me!"

He grasped her hands tightly and held them at her sides. "I understand you just fine. Everything that comes out of your mouth I hear 'cause I listen 'cause I can't do anything but listen. Everything you've ever said, I've memorized 'cause I hear it over and over again. It's like your voice is on instant replay inside me. You're all I fuckin' hear, all I fuckin' think about. I close my fuckin' eyes, and it's you I see. You're all up in my shit, and you won't fuckin' go away no matter what I do, no matter how hard I try. It's like you've fuckin' seared yourself into me. So yeah, I fuckin' listen, and you aren't fuckin' anyone but me. Had a taste, and I'm *not* letting you go 'cause I want more. I've decided I'm gonna fight for more. I want all of it, all of *you*, and it means you don't go to bars and dance with anyone but me 'cause you aren't fuckin' anyone else. Get me?"

Her jaw dropped. She felt like she'd been punched in the stomach, unable to wrap her mind around everything he'd said. He wanted her again? Why? She looked down at her legs to gather her thoughts. Part of her was thrilled, but the rational side of her knew she shouldn't be. It was too unbelievable, didn't make sense. He'd left. He didn't leave a note or wake her. He'd just left.

"It didn't mean anything. I—"

He tensed. "Did you not just hear what I said?"

"You're doing this for Ty."

"I was doing anything for Army, who'd saved my ass one too many times, it'd be me not thinking about his baby sister's legs, ass, tits, and beautiful fuckin' face, a sister's who's off fuckin' limits." He leaned into her, his lips grazed hers.

She shuddered.

"And I fuckin' tried, but then you kissed me, and I couldn't stop. You let me taste you, very inch of you, and I still taste you in my mouth, so I want more."

"You left." She heard the accusation in her voice.

"It's Saturday."

"I know what day of the week it is, Trig," she snapped.

"Had to get Della."

Shit. Della. That's why he'd left? To pick up his niece?

He leaned closer, eyes flashing. "I didn't want to leave, but I had to get Della. I didn't want to wake you because you were sleeping, and you looked like a fuckin' angel naked and cuddled up next to me, but I had to leave 'cause Della has no one else.

"So I woke you, knowing there was a good chance you'd fuckin' regret what we did, but I did it anyway. I told you, you looked beautiful. You fuckin' smiled at me and pressed up against my thigh, and then I told you I had to get Della, that I'd be back, and you fuckin' smiled again and said 'okay' like you wanted me to come back.

"I left here grinning like a fuckin' idiot because I thought you wanted me back. I called you at noon because I didn't wanna wake you, and you ignored my call. You ignored all my calls. Then I find out you're with Cuss at the bar. I show up, and I find you dancing with college boy. It couldn't be more clear, Alyssa. I get it, but don't fuckin' play the victim."

What? He woke her? Why couldn't she remember? She was a heavy sleeper, but she would've remembered Jace, except he'd said it play by play like it actually happened. Why would he lie? He just admitted he liked her, had for a while. Men didn't make declarations like that, not unless it was true, not unless he really wanted her, and he had called four times.

She believed him. The ache in her chest lessened. Her stupid, foolish heart made the decision, but she didn't care.

Remembering the last part of his rant, she asked, "Why would I play victim?"

He released her hands, pulled away from her, and leaned against the wall. The muscle in his jaw twitched. A pained look streaked his face. "'Cause I'm a biker and you're you. You regret being with a man like me, and feel guilty about it, so you chose to forget everything I said last night, everything I meant, and convince yourself you were just a tap I'd left."

It stung he thought so little of her. She looked away from him. "Can't believe you'd think that."

He took a step in her direction. "I could say the same, Allie."

Damn. He had a point. She had judged him. Never mind the fact she didn't remember him waking her, he called four times. She couldn't remember Wyatt ever calling her four times in one day. In fact, no man had ever called her four times in a single day.

Oh, God. She'd done this, judged him, made herself believe the worst because she was insecure and couldn't believe a man would want her because none wanted her for more than a trophy. All it did was lead to an argument and end whatever they could've been. No way a man, any man, would deal with what she dished out. He'd cut his losses while he could.

She buried her face in her hands and sighed heavily. "I don't remember you waking me. I didn't pick up your calls because I couldn't stand to hear your voice thinking that it didn't mean anything to you." She lifted her head and met his stare. "Last night, I believed you when you said it meant something, but then I woke up alone, and there was no note, and I couldn't remember you waking me. I still don't."

He held her stare for a long moment, then closed the distanced between them, positioning himself between her legs. Wrapping one arm around her waist, he cupped her cheek with the other and pressed his lips against her forehead. After a moment, he drew away slightly to meet her stare. "We're doing this. You and me. We're gonna do it right. We keep it quiet till we're ready, then we'll tell Army and the club."

With her heart in her throat, she nodded.

He waited a split second, his eyes scanning her face, and then he smiled his amazing smile, and claimed her lips. He kissed her long and hard.

One kiss was all it took. Before she knew it, she was panting against his mouth, pulling his shirt off, and unbuckling his jeans. He kissed her lips and trailed down her neck until he reached her breasts. Gripping her shirt, he yanked it off with such force it ripped, and then he buried his face in her chest. Her arms around his head, she wrapped her legs around his waist, pressing herself against his throbbing shaft.

With his hand firm on her lower back, he whispered, "Gonna be quick, baby."

He pulled a condom out of his pocket, slid his pants and boxers down his thighs, and rolled the condom on. He then tugged her panties off, wrapped one arm around her waist, pushed her into the length of him, filling her. He did all that right there, on the counter in her kitchen.

His eyes holding hers, she gasped, gripping his shoulders for support.

"Fuck, baby. Heaven."

She couldn't do anything but hold on to him as he moved out of her and into her again and again, the corded muscles in his neck tight. She moaned, and then he grabbed the back of her neck and tugged her against his lips.

He broke away from the kiss, gasping, staring straight into her eyes, thrusting inside her. "Come for me, baby. Let me hear you come."

The power he had over her, his words alone threw her over the edge.

Her body spasmed. Her walls clenching him, she came so hard the world melted away. Everything melted away but him. His dark eyes staring into hers, his body moving into hers, his shafted buried inside her. He was all she saw and all she felt.

"Damn fuckin' beautiful," he whispered, then groaned.

His cock pulsing inside her, a look of utter satisfaction flashed across his face. He yanked her against him, flattening her chest against his. His breath at her neck, his arms almost too tight around her, he held her for several moments. Both of them panting, and then he kissed her softly.

Pulling away from her lips and resting his forehead against hers, he let out a slew of curses. His jaw set, his eyes hard.

"W-what's wrong?" Her voice quiet and soft while she tried to catch her breath.

He cupped her cheeks. "Fucked up."

Her heart fell to the pit of her stomach.

"Shouldn't have done that."

Her stomach turned.

"I couldn't fuckin' help myself. You look so beautiful in that skirt and those fuckin' shoes, sitting on the fuckin' counter—"

"What?"

"Our second time, should've taken you in bed and—"

He thought she needed a bed? He couldn't be more wrong. "I loved it," she blurted. "I like a change of scenery, and I like it…hard and fast. It…makes me feel like you can't get enough."

He fought a smile. Then he ran his thumb across

her lips. "Give it to you whenever, wherever, and however you want it. That's a promise, baby."

She quirked a brow. "I want it in the shower. Now."

He laughed. The sound so rich and deep it sent shivers down her spine.

Jace lifted her and strode into her bathroom where he proceeded to give it to her, hard, fast, and in the shower.

****

Allie sprawled across his chest. Her hand lay firm over his heart, her head resting on his chest, her beautiful eyes on his, she smiled. He had one hand in her hair, the other under his head. He smiled, too.

He'd kept his promise, giving it to her in the shower. Against the wall, her legs wrapped around his waist, one hand on her hip, the other pressed against the wall as he buried himself inside her.

Amazing.

It had only been half an hour, and he could go again. He knew in his chest, he'd never tire like he'd never tire of the sight of her eyes on his, smiling like she was now.

He was in heaven. He had Allie. She wanted him, maybe not as much as he wanted her, but she did. She wanted to give them a try.

He hadn't meant to confront her in the bar, force her onto his bike, but seeing her with college boy, something inside him snapped. If he couldn't have her, no one would, so he'd carried her out, given her his cut, and taken her home on his bike.

She didn't understand the significance of it. A biker didn't give anyone his cut, not a woman he couldn't stop thinking about, not even his old lady. Bikers gave their old ladies their own cuts. Another thing bikers never did: they didn't put a woman on the back of their bike unless they were claiming her. He'd done both, then admitted so much. He hadn't meant to.

Thinking she'd ditched him, it was the last thing he wanted to do, but everything she said riled him. In those heated moments, logic and pride failed him and anger spoke. He acted like a fucking wuss. Then again, he'd acted like a wuss all day, glancing at his phone every ten minutes, waiting for her call. When everything had been said and done, he couldn't find the will to care because she was sprawled on him, looking at him, smiling.

Her gaze drifted away from his, and then her smile faded.

"Allie?"

Her gaze shot to his. She smiled weakly. Allie was like an open book, every thought showed on her face, so he surmised she thought of something she probably didn't want to talk about. This, them, meant something to him, so he'd push. She needed to be honest or it'd never work, and he wanted it to work. He needed it to work.

"What's wrong?"

"You're not going to be with anyone else, right?"

He shot up in bed, taking her with him, and shifting her until she straddled him. "Allie, I said we're doing this. It means I don't date anyone else. I don't sleep with anyone else. Means you're it."

When she didn't say anything else, he added, "The same applies for you. I don't share."

"You've shared—"

He shook his head. "Never shared a woman in my life. Some of the guys may be into fuckin' the same woman at the same time, but not me. Don't share."

She shrugged. "Yeah, but what about the women at—"

"That's casual sex. It wasn't exclusive. They knew it, and I knew it."

"But they're around, and no one will know we're together, so...won't you be tempted?"

"No," he said immediately. He couldn't blame her for asking. Bikers had reputations, and he'd had his share of women, but never a steady one. It wasn't just about him. It was about her, about the fact she'd been burned before. "Haven't had sex since I met you."

Her eyes widened. "What about the woman I caught you with?"

"Never had sex with her, and I only tried 'cause I wanted to forget you."

Her hands at his chest, she pushed away. "What...I..."

Maybe he shouldn't have said that. Maybe it was too much, too soon. In his defense, compared to everything else he'd admitted, this wasn't much news.

Instinctively, he tightened his arm around her waist holding her against him. "Told you this shit, Allie."

Her brows drew together. Shaking her head, she whispered, "You never—"

"Told you you're all I think about. Told you no matter what I do, I couldn't get you out of my head. Told you I caved when you kissed me 'cause I wanted you so bad."

"Yeah, but you didn't say when. I mean...that was like a month and a half ago. You make it sound like…all this time—"

He held her gaze. "Yeah, baby, all this time."

Her eyes softened and drifted from his. She trailed a finger along the scar on the side of his lip, then met his gaze again and smiled. "Me, too."

Those two simple words made his great night the best one ever. He smiled, kissed her, and then lay down, bringing her with him. She laid her cheek against his chest, her hair spilled around him. She closed her eyes. Before she did, he caught her smiling.

Maybe he was a fucking wuss, but he was also the luckiest trailer trash on earth.

Chapter Twenty-One

"Hey, Allie!" Mia yelled over the loud chaos that consumed the daycare during lunch time.

Allie spotted her and smiled.

Mia called her incessantly Sunday, demanding to know what happened between her and Jace. She hadn't answered the first five calls because she'd been too busy with Jace. They'd slept in, had a round of insanely hot sex, and she made lunch. They watched a movie and went for round two. Afterward, they fell asleep. When she woke, he lay on his side, his arm and leg thrown over her.

Needing to use the restroom, she wiggled herself away from him, and spotted the large tattoo on his back, the Hell Ryders' logo, a set of angel wings burning in flames, beautifully intricate, and lifelike. The wings went from his shoulders down to his lower back. In between, he had the skull and under that, near his lower back read, "Hell Ryders." Curious, she'd shifted, moving to his side to admire the tattoo there. A black portrait of six soldiers inscribed *Army Free: Lives Lost, Never Forgotten*. Waking a short time later, he caught her admiring his tattoos and grinned.

While she made dinner later that night, he left to get a change of clothes and returned half an hour later with a week's supply. They showered together and had round three. Before bed, round four. He was insatiable, and in regards to him, so was she. She hadn't been able to stop smiling all day.

In the back of her mind, she couldn't help but wonder how long it would last. She'd never felt for any one like she did for Jace. It scared her. It was too soon to feel how she felt, feelings that she hated to admit felt like the forever kind. Maybe, it was her inexperience. She'd only had two boyfriends, two lovers, and never slept with either of them in such a short period of time. Maybe it was just a physical thing, and her heart wanted it to be more.

Though she wasn't sure she believed that, it wasn't just about the way he looked, it was him, all of him. A tough, rough-around-the-edges biker with a big heart, a man who looked after his sister and his niece, a man her brother trusted, a man who'd defended and protected her. Still, she had to face the facts. She knew very little about him. He hadn't said much about himself, and she hadn't asked because he should be the one to share, but quite frankly, it was too soon to start sharing.

What scared her the most was, maybe for him, it was just physical. They'd spent most of the day having sex. They'd talked and laughed, but mostly they fooled around and had sex.

After round three, she finally got around to calling Mia. She'd insisted everything was fine, but Mia wanted to have lunch. She didn't mind, except Mia knew she omitted something. It could've been the way Jace stormed into the bar and carried her out, but she wasn't so sure. She and Jace agreed to keep quiet until they were ready. Mia told her they should too, but she knew Mia well enough to know Mia wanted details.

Needless to say, she was nervous about lunch with

Mia because she wasn't a good liar. Tyler often read through her lies, and Mia was a bulldog when she wanted dirt.

Still, she waved her over.

Mia neared, scanning her from top to bottom. "Love that blouse."

"Thanks."

"You ready?"

She nodded, told Tiffany she was headed for lunch, and then together they headed to a local sub shop. They ordered, paid, and sat to wait for their food.

"So...you going to tell me what happened Saturday?"

She flushed. "Nothing happened. He was angry, but when isn't he?"

Mia gave her a knowing smile. "That's it?"

"Yeah, apparently Ty told him to watch me while he's gone. I guess he was upset I wasn't at home and out with you guys."

"And?"

"And you know Jace...He carried me out, then took me home."

"In his car?"

"No, on his bike."

Mia's eyes widened, looking shocked. Odd considering nothing seemed to shock her, ever.

When Mia didn't respond, she added, "I was wearing a skirt, so he gave me his cut to wrap around my waist, and drove me home."

Mia's jaw dropped open. She stayed like that for several seconds, not saying a word. Odder. Mia couldn't go a minute without talking.

"Um...are you okay?"

Mia leaned into the table. In a quiet voice, she asked, "Allie, do you realize what any of what you told me means?"

Shit. Had she said something she shouldn't have? Yep. Why else would Mia stare at her dumbstruck and speechless? Her stomach turning, she shook her head.

Mia lowered her voice to a whisper. "Bikers don't put women on the back of their bikes unless they're claiming them—"

"W-what do you mean?"

"I mean...unless you're an old lady or a steady woman in his life who he's protecting, means the club's protecting her—"

"I am because of Ty—"

Mia shook her head. "You don't understand, Allie. Army ever put you on the back of his bike?"

"No, but—"

"Right, you're his sister. The club protects you as his sister. It also means you're off limits. After the whole Wyatt situation, the club's got your back more than ever. They voted to deal with it, and they are. Now, they're looking out for you. I know this because they vote on everything, not because Stone told me or because I was there." She shrugged. "You know club rules and all, but Army's never going to put you on the back of his bike because you aren't his woman."

Denial reared its head. "But...the first time I went to the garage Ripper offered me a ride, and Cuss has offered me a ride, too. He said if I cooked for him—"

Mia placed her hand on top of hers. "Heard about the Ripper thing from Stone. Why do you think Army was so angry that day?"

Ripper had been a dick, and her brother had been

protecting her or it's what she thought.

"Ripper tried to claim you. Army wasn't having it, so he beat his ass to prove a point. You're off limits. And as for Cuss, I know Cuss. He knew you'd say no. If on the off chance you agreed, he would've told you why he couldn't give you a ride."

Shit. She had said too much, way too much.

"As for him giving you his cut to wrap around your waist…" She let out a deep sigh. "Bikers don't give their cuts to anyone. Allie, I mean *no one*, not a steady girl, not an old lady, especially not to wrap around your waist because you're wearing a short skirt."

"You're telling me Stone has never let you wear his cut?"

"Oh, I've worn it. In the bedroom with nothing underneath." She winked. "But never in public and never to sit on, on the back of a bike."

Oh God. What did it mean? That he really liked her? It happened before their big talk, so it had to mean he *really* liked her. Right? Or, shit. She could barely think. Her thoughts rambled in fragments.

"I know what's going on," Mia said.

Luckily, it gave her mind something to focus on besides her chaotic thoughts.

"Even if you hadn't told me what you did. Lynn, Tiffany, and Cuss know, too. One look at Trig when he saw you with Keith and we knew."

She folded her trembling hands. "W-what do you mean?"

"I know Trig. I've known him for five years. He's had a rough life. Considering, he's a good man who takes care of his own. I've never seen that look on his face, not when his sister relapsed, not when his mother died—"

Bile rose in the back of her throat, she forced herself to swallow it. "His mother died? His sister relapsed from what? What about his father?"

Mia winced. "I can see I've said too much."

In too much shock to push, Allie didn't.

"My point is, if you don't see yourself being able to handle this life, I suggest you end things now. None of us want to see him hurt, and honest to God, I don't know how much more he can take."

Mia warned her off? A heaviness settled in the pit of her stomach. She looked away.

"This life isn't easy. I didn't come from money like you, and this life was still an adjustment, but I fell in love with Stone. I do it because I love him, and I can't picture my life without him."

She couldn't help but feel betrayed and offended. Maybe Mia was trying to protect her family, the club, it wasn't what offended her. It was more about what she'd implied. Did she think people with money didn't suffer? Did money imply you had an easy life? People were more than money and their pasts. She was so much more than designer bags and shoes like Jace was so much more than a biker.

She met Mia's stare. "And you're saying this to me because you think I'll miss the designer bags and shoes, or because you think I can't deal with this life because I came from money and money somehow implies my life was effortless?"

Looking hurt, Mia leaned back against the booth. "I didn't mean it like that, Allie."

"I know you're trying to protect your family, Mia, but I thought I was part of that family."

She left Mia speechless again.

Allie took a deep breath, trying to control her anger. "Let me tell you about the life I had with the designer bags and shoes. It was lonely. I wasn't a person. I was an object, an object my father controlled. He told me what to study, where to work, where to live, what to buy, and then, he told me who to date.

"I fell for the man I was told to date. He asked me to marry him, and I said yes. I wanted a small wedding, but my father insisted on a lavish one. I was planning this ludicrously extravagant wedding when I caught my fiancé cheating.

"I broke it off, and then I stupidly gave him another chance, and guess what? He cheated again with *three* different women. When I told him I was leaving him for good, he *beat* me. I had to wait for the bruises to fade before I flew out here to restart my life because I didn't want my brother going to jail for killing him. I flew out here because Ty's the only person who's ever cared enough about me, because my father wouldn't protect me.

"He said I deserved what I got because he wanted me to marry a man so his multimillion dollar company could make more money. Then he said all men cheated and admitted he'd had a mistress for thirty years. He said my mother knew. It isn't far-fetched to assume he beat her too, considering he didn't care my ex beat his only daughter.

"When I restarted my life here, I couldn't even get a job because my father forced his employees to badmouth me, which means I have a degree I can't use unless I want to start from scratch. I suppose it was a blessing in disguise. I'd rather do what I'm doing now, even if I'm not earning a six-figure pay check. Of course, then my ex shows up and slaps me in broad day light."

She released a loaded breath. "So, no, Mia, money doesn't necessarily mean my life's been perfect. It doesn't mean I can't handle club life. As a matter of fact, I think I've handled it well, considering all the designer handbags and shoes I own."

With those last words, she picked up her designer bag and left. The food hadn't arrived yet, but it didn't matter. She couldn't eat. If she tried to eat, she'd throw up.

Heading back into the daycare, Allie went on with her day as if nothing happened. Mia called her several times. She ignored the calls. Too angry and too hurt, she wasn't ready to talk just yet.

****

Something was wrong with Allie. Trig took one look at her Monday night, and he knew.

Shutting the door behind himself, he pulled her into his arms. "What's wrong?"

She smiled that fake smile. "Nothing. Just wound up. Need to go for a run."

No kiss, no asking about his day, she simply walked away. It pissed him off. He'd known something was wrong, but it was too soon to push.

Following her into her room, he found her standing in front of her closet in a lacy thong. The sight stirred his cock. It took him a moment to remember what he intended to do. When he did, he strode up behind her, wrapped his arms around her waist, buried his face in her neck, and feathered a kiss under her ear.

"Don't get a welcome home kiss, baby?"

Allie turned in his arms and gave him a kiss that had him wanting to throw her on the bed and bury himself into her. She pulled away smiling, a teasing glint in her eyes, and whispered, "Good enough?"

Her mood improved, but not by much. She smiled and laughed easily, her eyes less guarded, but something had happened.

They went for a run. He'd run that morning after she left for work, but he went anyway. He didn't want her running alone. They got back from their run, showered together, and she made him dinner. They ate on the couch watching TV. He did the dishes, and cleaned up the kitchen. Mainly because he wanted to take care of her, kind of like she took care of him by cooking. After, they made love and fell asleep cuddled close.

The next day had been more of the same. She laughed and talked to him easily, but he caught glimpses when she seemed lost in her thoughts, a sadness enveloping her features.

Now, as he pulled up to the compound, he couldn't help but wonder what it was again. He couldn't help but wonder if it had anything to do with him, if he'd moved too fast, told her too much too soon, and if it'd given her second thoughts about them. He hated to think so, but he didn't know what else it might be.

Striding into the garage, he greeted his brothers then headed down the hall and up the stairs to his room. Intent on getting a workout done before noon, he changed into a pair of athletic shorts and wife beater. As he walked out, Mia called his name. He turned.

"Hey."

Looking uncomfortable, she closed the distance

between them. "Hey, can you tell Allie to call me?"

His brows drew together. The request alone intrigued him. Mia and Allie were friends, so why she needed him to tell her, he had no idea.

"She…" Her gaze dropped to the floor. "I…may have said something…"

Shit. Maybe Mia had something to do with the change in Allie. If they'd gotten in an argument for some reason, it explained what had been bothering Allie, which meant it had nothing to do with him. He rather not get in the middle of it, but curiosity prompted him to ask. "You get in an argument or something?"

She flushed. "I think…" Mia shook her head. "I know I upset her. I've been trying to call her to apologize, but…"

Damn. She seemed nervous. He'd go as far as to say a little scared. "Mia, this have something to do with me?" He didn't know why he asked, probably those instincts he had that kept him alive for so long.

She nodded.

He fisted his hands. "What about me?"

She looked behind him then met his gaze. "We saw you on Saturday. We know."

He tried not to react, couldn't let on he knew what she meant. He didn't think he pulled it off. The moment he heard, his body tensed.

"I was looking out for you. I told her if she couldn't handle this life then…she shouldn't lead you on."

He couldn't believe it. Finally, he knew the reason his beautiful Allie had been stuck in her head for two days. He had one day enjoying all that was beautiful about Allie before Mia said some fucked shit to her, warning her away, as if he didn't have the odds already stacked against him.

Sabotage.

Betrayal.

And from his own family.

He clenched his jaw so hard the muscles hurt, seeing red. With that, logic and rationale fled. "What?" he screamed.

Looking repentant, but she held her ground. "I was looking out for you. I know you've been through a lot—"

"Don't fuckin' say shit, Mia. Don't wanna hear your fuckin' excuses." He shouldn't have said that or reacted that way. It only proved he cared about Allie, but Mia's betrayal hurt deep. He couldn't've helped it.

She paled, so much so he actually thought she'd faint. "I'm sorry. I just—"

"Don't wannna fuckin' hear it. You've fuckin' *betrayed* me. I'm supposed to be family, Mia. We don't betray our family. So I don't wanna talk to you, see you, or hear you. Wanna do me a favor? Make sure I don't."

He strode away and worked out his frustration at the gym. Two hours later, he was still livid, so he went for a ride.

****

Allie heard the familiar roar of Jace's bike and smiled. She just gotten home from work and changed into a pair of tights, tank top, and sneakers.

For the past two days, they'd been running together. She'd never run with a partner before, but she loved it because her partner was Jace. Jace ran in a pair of shorts and no shirt, which meant she got to watch sweat drip down his chest and abs, not to mention she loved eyeing his tattoos. A distraction, but so totally worth it.

The knock on the door startled her. It wasn't his usual tap, more like a bang. She walked to the door and slung it open. One look at him, and she knew why. His mouth tight, his jaw clenched.

"Hey, how was your day?" Stupid question, but she had to start somewhere.

He didn't answer. Instead, he closed the door with his booted foot, dropped his cut on the couch, and faced her. "Anything you wanna tell me, Allie?" His voice rose with each word.

Nothing she could think of, which didn't bode well for her. Obviously, he thought she needed to tell him something, something he'd found out.

She didn't know what to say, still wasn't sure why he was angry, and didn't want to ask knowing he'd tell her when he was ready. Pushing it could potentially get him in a worst mood.

He crossed his arms over his chest. "Talked to Mia today."

Oh, God. He found out she had a little meltdown. Mia offended her, and she'd reacted poorly, never denying she and Jace were an item, and by saying what she had, she'd implied it.

Flushing, she said, "I'm sorry."

The apology upset him more. The look in his eyes went feral. "What the fuck you apologizing for?"

"For what I told her. I…I was upset…"

He quirked a brow. "What *did* you tell her?"

"She said club life was hard, and I came from money, so if I couldn't handle it, then I shouldn't lead you on. I asked her if she told me that because she thought I'd miss the designer bags and shoes or if it was because she assumed since I came from money my life had been easy, and I couldn't handle club life."

This upset him more, to that degree where the vein in his neck began pulsing. "You fuckin' kidding me?" he shouted loud and suddenly.

She jumped, grasping her chest. "I'm sorry. I know I should've denied there was anything going on, but I...I was offended, and I lost my temper..." Her voice trailed off when he walked toward her, the anger hadn't abated, not a bit.

"Listen to me, Alyssa. You don't fuckin' apologize to me for feeling. I'm not your fuckin' father, and I'm not your fuckin' ex. You fuckin' apologize 'cause you should've told me this shit Monday."

Wait, he wasn't mad at her per se, he was mad at Mia? Feeling the need to defend Mia, she pointed out, "She was trying to protect you. I get—"

"Don't give me lip. Don't fuckin' make excuses for her. As far as I'm concerned, she doesn't exist."

God, he was so angry he was being irrational. "I think you're being irrational—"

He closed the distance between them and yelled, "She fuckin' betrayed me!"

"She doesn't want to see you get hurt."

"She fuckin' accomplished that shit on her own. She hurt me by hurting you."

Her jaw dropped. After all he'd said and done, she shouldn't be surprised. She couldn't help it though.

"Don't look so shocked. You think I didn't know some shit went down, that something was fuckin' with your head? I knew. I didn't wanna push you to tell me.

You've been walking around here stewing on that shit for two days 'cause of Mia."

Still, she felt the need to add, "I could've handled it, and you shouldn't get into a fight with your family for me."

His eyes spitting fire, he took a step in her direction. Mirroring him, she took one back. He took another. She did the same and bumped into the door behind her. He placed his hands against the door, on either side of her head locking her in.

"Listen to me, and listen to me good, Alyssa. No one fucks with what's mine, and she did."

She'd known since the day he'd roughed up her ex no one messed with his anything, but she could handle her problems on her own. She didn't need him to control her life. It's what her father had done, and she wouldn't put up with it.

Angry now, she shot back, "Listen to me, Trigger, and listen to me good. I can handle my problems. I don't need you to do anything for me."

"Like you handled your ex?"

Well, he had a point there, but it didn't mean she was helpless. "I've given the club plenty of problems, and I'm not keen on the idea you added another. Don't tell me I should've told you about a conversation I had with my friend. I don't owe you any information about my life when I know nothing about yours."

Eyes flashing, he shot back, "You're mine. It fuckin' means I handle everything for you."

"Maybe I shouldn't be then."

It struck a nerve, no denying it hurt him to hear it. He looked anguished, like she'd reached into his chest and ripped out his beating heart.

She regretted what she'd said instantly, would've without seeing that. She shouldn't have said it. Really, she hadn't meant it, not at all. She'd just been trying to make a point. She wanted him, cared about him. No, she more than cared.

His eyes never leaving hers, his voice rough when he said, "You still think Mia didn't hurt me by making you even think about leaving me?"

Her heart clenching, her eyes welled with tears. She shook her head. "No, I'm sorry. I didn't mean it. I…My father controlled my life. I can't live like that again. I can't."

He stood there staring at her for a long moment.

She pressed her palm over his heart. She didn't know why, maybe to make sure she hadn't ripped it out, to make sure it still beat. "I swear I didn't mean it, Jace."

Finally, he cupped her face and pressed his lips against her forehead then released a breath. "It won't be like that with me, baby. I promise."

She exhaled, wrapped her arms around his waist, and held him while he held her.

Pulling away from the embrace to stare into her eyes, he drew his fingers through her hair. "You're mine. I take care of you. It doesn't mean I control you. It means I handle shit. If it's club shit, I handle it and tell you about it later. Everything else, I'll talk to you about first, 'kay?"

She nodded.

They had their first fight. A big one, but it hadn't lasted long.

She smiled and buried her face in his chest, and then she bypassed her run for make-up sex.

Chapter Twenty-Two

"We gotta talk, Allie."

Her chest tightening, she met his stare.

Their last night together, they'd finished eating dinner. Tomorrow, her brother would be back. His return would change the relationship Jace and she had shared for the last week.

It had been amazing. She was happy, content, more so than she ever remembered. Jace was exactly the man she'd thought him to be, despite the fact he was a biker with a nasty temper, despite the fact the club was involved in illegal activities she didn't know the extent of.

Her brother insinuated they protected people, but what they did wasn't entirely legal. There had to be more to it, and she couldn't know. Still, she knew little about Jace's past, about him, but he was kind, caring, affectionate, and attentive.

Aside from when she was at work, they'd spent every waking hour together. Every night when he got home, he kissed her thoroughly then asked about her day. He didn't just hear her, he listened. She could see him thinking, analyzing as if she'd said something significant. Afterward, he ran with her and later showered. While she cooked, he sat on the counter, sipping a beer or drinking a shake, and talked with her.

When they sat on the couch to eat, he shifted her

until he'd nestled her as close as possible. He insisted on doing the dishes, and he wouldn't take no for an answer. They watched TV, he kept her close, running his hands through her hair or touching her in some way. He was always like that, trying to find ways to touch her, even innocently.

They went to bed, and he'd make love to her, soft and slow. Only when she begged or when she teased him and he lost control would he take her hard. Afterward, he'd press her close, and when she woke, she'd still be that way.

But with Ty's return, everything would change, and the fact he often showed up at her house unexpectedly didn't help. The guys would still watch her, which meant likely Ty would arrange for others to watch her. Meaning, Jace couldn't come and stay. Another one of his brothers would be there, and they were supposed to be at most friends.

More than likely, he wanted to talk about this, but the way he said it and what he said sounded so ominous. In her experience, that phrase was usually followed by "this isn't working out," and so, she held her breath and waited for him to speak.

"Baby, come here." Standing against the wall in her kitchen, he opened his arms wide.

She walked over to him and fell into his embrace.

He kissed her forehead, then cupped her cheeks, tilting her head up to meet his eyes. "Things are gonna change. Nothing we can do about it. Don't wanna hide this from your brother, from the club. Don't wanna hide you, but we gotta for a little while."

She nodded.

"I'll do what I can, Allie, to be with you every

chance I get, but I gotta get back to club business, and I gotta get back to Tina and Della, too."

"I know," she whispered.

He sighed heavily. "Fuckin' hate this shit."

She hated it, too. She wanted things to stay the same, wanted to wake beside him, make him dinner at night, and sleep beside him. Call her selfish, but she wanted to stay in the perfect bubble they'd created for themselves where there was no club business and no responsibilities beside the two of them.

She nodded.

"I'm gonna try to arrange to watch you as much as I can, and maybe one night or two a week you can go to Tina's. We can eat together or you can make dinner here, and I'll bring them over. Friday nights, we can meet at the club and try to sneak out."

She nodded.

He ran his thumb over her lips. "It's gonna be hard. Seeing you and not being able to touch you, but we'll do it until we're ready, 'kay?"

"Yeah." She looked away from him. "Do you think anyone will say anything?"

His eyebrows lifted in question. "About?"

"Mia said Cuss, Tiff, and Lynn knew about us. I didn't deny it, and if you were as angry at me as you were at her, you probably confirmed it too."

He shook his head. "Wasn't angry with you, Allie. Was just fuckin' angry." He paused for a moment, his gaze scanning her face. "Cuss won't say shit 'cause I'm his brother, and it isn't any of his business. Besides, he's a man. Men don't fuckin' gossip. He'll warn Tiff not to say anything, not that she's around the club much anyway. As far as Mia goes, think she knows better than to say shit after I talked to her, and she'll warn Lynn to stay out of it."

"Okay, honey." She'd never before called a man any form of endearment, but she was glad it slipped.

His eyes widened. He broke out in a wide grin and looked so beautiful smiling, staring down at her that she lost track of thought. Not the first time he'd smiled, but every time he did, she got lost.

"So glad you fuckin' kissed me. Totally worth it."

She didn't understand the last part of his statement, but too lost admiring his grin, she didn't bother to ask.

****

The door unlocked then opened. Tyler strode through, opened his arms wide. "Missed me?"

She smiled and nodded then gave him a big hug. Pulling away, she walked into the living room and sat on the couch. "How'd it go?"

He followed behind and sat beside her. "Work's work. Same shit. Different day." He shrugged. "How was your week, Allie?"

A tough question. She and Jace had sex, fought, became exclusive, fought again, and then made up. They'd spent the week living together and acting like a married couple. She'd also gotten in an argument with Mia, whom she still hadn't spoken to but needed to, sooner rather than later. None of this, she could admit.

"Good." Not a lie, the truth. Fights with Jace and Mia aside, it had been a great week. Still, she hoped Ty didn't sense how much she omitted.

"Trig was here all week?"

"Yep." The entire week there'd been traces of him everywhere. His boots and clothes in her room, his cut draped across her couch, his wallet and keys on the counter. He was messy, but she loved it. Every piece of Jace scattered around her apartment served as a reminder he was there. Now all gone. The only thing left was his faint scent and the memories. Everywhere they'd been, made love, kissed, and caressed.

"How'd it go?"

Oh, God. Really? "Good."

"I know he can be moody, just wondering."

He was always angry or so she'd thought before the last week. Now, she knew better. He was more temperamental than anything else. He got in nasty moods, but not as much as he smiled and laughed.

She shrugged, praying her brother would stop talking about Jace before she started flushing, thinking about all the places they had sex. "I guess, sometimes."

"So he was nice?"

Sighing heavily, she rolled her eyes. "If you were so worried about Jace being moody, then why'd you make him watch me for a week?"

"'Cause he's moody, and I knew he wouldn't fuckin' hit on you."

He had a point. Jace hadn't hit on her. She hit on him. That's how it started. "None of the other guys would hit on me either."

"They'd flirt though. Tellin' you how good you cook, offer you rides, and shit like that. Didn't want you to start getting ideas."

Ideas, ugh? Damn, her brother could be way off sometimes. She wasn't interested in any of them, never had been, except Jace. Not that she was complaining; she was glad he'd been wrong this time. Even if she and Jace didn't end up working out, she'd enjoyed a week of pure bliss.

"Why don't you want me dating any of the men in the club?" Perhaps she shouldn't have asked, but she needed to know. It would be useful when she told him the truth.

He quirked a brow. "Allie, don't start getting any ideas."

"Ty, I'm asking because it doesn't make sense for someone who's joined this club for life, who's always talking about the club being a family, being so against me dating any of them. It doesn't add up. If they're such good people, why aren't they good enough for me?"

He held her gaze then finally said, "Told you this, Allie. Outta thirty guys in the club, two got steady women. What does that tell you?

"Besides, you went to an Ivy League school, got a master's. You made six figures not too long ago. You're class. Not many of the guys went to college. Some of them didn't even graduate from high school. They aren't good enough for you. Not one of them."

She understood. But to her brother's standards, no one would ever be good enough for her. And she didn't think Ty, despite having the best intentions, fully understood sometimes those who didn't appear to have accomplished much at all had accomplished the most.

To most, she'd accomplished a lot, but in truth, she accomplished none of the things that really mattered. She went to an Ivy League school because she'd busted her butt studying and had the monetary means, but she'd studied what her father chose. It's the way her life had been. Until recently, she'd never stood up for herself, never stood up for what she wanted, what really mattered. She wasn't married and didn't have kids.

Those were the things she wanted, that mattered to her—to find someone who truly loved her and build a family and a life with him. If she died tomorrow, no one but Ty and, maybe, Jace would miss her.

Besides, her heart wanted Jace. She didn't care if he graduated from high school or if he had a college degree. Obviously, she didn't care he partook in questionable activities. The thought barely crossed her mind. All she knew was how she felt about him and how he made her feel. With him, she wasn't an object. She was a person, a woman who deserved to be loved. He accomplished this in the simplest of ways, the way he was with her, caring, attentive, and affectionate. No other man had ever been that for her.

"I get it, Ty," she whispered. "But I'm starting over. I don't earn six figures anymore because I don't want to. I want to work with kids, and it's what I'm doing. I don't get paid much, and I'm not complaining because I finally like what I do. I don't need a man with a degree or a man who makes six figures. I want what I've always wanted—someone who loves me."

He smiled then shook his head. "Don't want this life for you, Allie. It can be rough, and you don't deserve rough. You deserve easy."

She looked away from him. "Who's watching me tonight?"

"Me. Don't know if you realized, but it's Friday, means the guys are at the compound, partying and getting laid."

"And you're missing out because of me?"

"Yeah, didn't think you'd want to go."

He couldn't be more wrong. She wanted to go. She wanted to see Jace. It would be hard to stand in the same room and pretend nothing changed, but it was better than nothing at all. Even thinking of seeing him, her heart began racing, but she couldn't let on. She schooled her voice before she spoke. "I don't mind going, Ty. Wouldn't mind hanging out with Mia and Lynn."

Crossing his arms over his chest, he smiled. "You sure?"

"Yep, let me get dressed."

They rode to the compound in Ty's SUV. He parked. She hopped out and took a deep breath, forcing her nerves to settle. As soon as they strode in, blaring music greeted them. She folded her hands into each other, walking along the hallway beside Ty. When she stood under the threshold leading into the living room, she smiled. Her eyes scanned the room until she found him.

Her heart fluttering, the pounding so loud now she thought it might pop right out of her chest. Damn, he looked good, sitting on the couch, beer in hand, wearing his usual: jeans, black shirt tight around his chest, and his cut. He stared at her, as if he'd been waiting for her, as if he knew she'd arrived, but his eyes hardened, jaw clenched, and brows furrowed.

She couldn't help the doubts crossing her mind. Maybe he didn't want her there. Maybe he had a change of heart. Maybe she'd done something to upset him.

Trying to silence her rambling brain, she forced herself to look away and spotted Lynn rushing toward her.

"Hey," Lynn said, brightly.

She closed the distance between them. "Hey."

"Miracle." Cuss strode up to her, smiling.

She smiled at Cuss. "Hi, Cuss."

Lynn grabbed her hand and dragged her toward the kitchen. "Come, let's get you a drink."

The kitchen was empty except for Mia, who sat on the counter, a sad, apologetic look on her face. Not the fun-loving, quick-to-blab Mia. Allie bit the side of her lip, knowing she should've called Mia. She shouldn't have waited so long.

Closing the distance, she said, "I'm sorry."

Mia's eyes watered. "No, Allie, I'm sorry. I should've never said what I said. I didn't mean to imply—"

"I care about him, Mia, a lot, so I can't blame you for looking out for him because it's what I want for him." She hugged her tight.

"Thank you, Allie. You're a good person."

Pulling away from her, she smiled. "He'll come around."

Mia shook her head. "I've had a lot of time to think about it, Allie. I can't blame him if he doesn't, and I don't expect him to."

"You were only—"

She shook her head. "I didn't realize it at the time, but I forced you to doubt this life and in doing so, I forced you to doubt him, too. From what you've told me, and from knowing him, he's falling for you. I could've ruined it because of what I said."

She paled, then swallowed. Could he be falling for her? Was he playing angry as a ruse or had he been pretending that morning?

"Relationships are hard and take a lot of work. I added to an already complicated situation." Mia reached out, placing her hand over hers softly. "Just so you know…I'm rooting for you."

She smiled, shakily. "Thanks."

"Enough of this." Lynn jumped in, handing each of them cosmopolitans in martini glasses. "Drinks are ready."

"We're being fancy tonight," Mia quipped.

Lynn winked. "In your honor, of course."

Allie forced another smile and sipped her drink.

Chapter Twenty-Three

Trig hadn't laid eyes on her yet, but she was there. He felt it inside him. Sitting on the couch, nursing a beer, he forced his muscles to relax. His gaze gravitated to the threshold, knowing with every breath in his body she would appear.

Allie, so fucking beautiful, wearing a pair of tight jeans and a black blouse. One look and his heart started pounding so loud he swore it could be heard over the blaring music. His fist tightened around his beer, fighting the urge to close the distance between them, wrap his arms around her, and kiss her until she was weak in the knees.

That morning, he'd made love to her and came staring into her beautiful eyes. She made him pancakes. They ate together, and then he kissed her before she left for work. But it didn't feel like hours ago, it felt like days. Right then, seeing her, and not being able to do everything he wanted to do, stung.

For him, nothing ever came easy. This was more of the same. He'd finally found a woman he wanted for keeps, and she was his brother's sister, off limits. For the time being, they had to keep quiet.

He'd be a fool not to be worried. He'd admitted too much, too soon. She hadn't run, but no doubt it was too much for her. She'd recently gotten out of a nasty relationship. She needed time, time he wished would drift by in the blink of an eye. He wasn't sure if he could go a single day without her, not after he'd had her to himself for seven full days.

Her gaze met his, and she quickly looked away.

Like they hadn't spent the last week living and breathing together, making love, and playing house.

Like she didn't fucking know him.

It killed. His chest tightened. An ache took hold; he fought to keep it at bay.

She looked at Lynn, smiled, and greeted her. Her voice, another reminder of how much he wanted her, sitting on his lap with her tongue in his mouth.

Cuss strode up to her, smiling. "Miracle."

Trig clenched his jaw hard, battling the urge to punch Cuss in the face. He didn't like Cuss calling her "Miracle," and he wanted to know why. Not that he didn't agree, she was a miracle. She changed him, made him want shit he didn't deserve, made him laugh and smile, forget the past, and live for the moment, but she was *his* miracle, no one else's.

She smiled at Cuss. "Hi, Cuss."

All he wanted from her, a simple fucking greeting, and he never got it. It boiled his blood Cuss got it though he hadn't spent the week with her.

Pulse racing, ears pounding, he missed what Lynn said to her. Before he could do something he would regret, Lynn dragged her out of sight. He was left staring at the threshold leading into the kitchen, feeling nothing but a searing ache in his chest.

He didn't know what he expected, but it hadn't been to be completely ignored. They agreed to keep quiet about them, but he thought she'd at least fucking say hi. He'd been hopeful she'd find a way to sit by him or, damn, find a way to be alone together.

Tilting his head down, he glared at his beer contemplating whether he should take out his frustration on it and pitch it across to room. He chugged it instead.

Army took a seat beside him. "Brother, what up?"

He shrugged. "Nothin' much."

"Tina and Della okay?"

"Yeah, talked to Tina three times this week. Haven't seen them though."

"Sorry about that, Trig. I owe you."

Army was wrong. If anyone owed anyone, he owed Army for bringing Allie into his life, even if she'd since had a change of heart, even if she got wise and dumped his ass. The pain of losing her would kill. He knew this because it stung when she'd looked right through him, but it would be worth it. He'd gotten a glimpse of happiness even if it'd been for a fleeting week.

He met his stare, fighting the guilt rising. "Naw, you don't. You would've done the same for me."

Army shrugged. "Yeah, but still…Know you missed out here last Friday and seeing Della and Tina. Know Tina needs all the help she can get though she won't admit that shit and know you love seeing them and checking on them, so thanks."

He nodded.

"All you're having is beer tonight?"

"Yeah, gotta get Della in the morning, not so much fun when I'm hung over."

"You never were much of a drinker. Though as of late, seems you've slowed down on everything."

He looked away from his empty bottle and met Army's stare, unsure what he implied.

Army smiled, lifting a brow. "Haven't seen you with a tap for months, Trig. Looks like it's affecting your temper. We all need a little release some time."

He'd gotten plenty as of late, and he wanted more, but from only one woman.

"I'm good."

"You sure?" He nodded in the direction of the bar. "Tap's been lookin' at you since I got here."

He spared a glance and realized the tap Army referred to was the same tap he'd used to try to get his mind off Allie. She wore a denim skirt so short if she bent over a tad, he could see her ass. She also had a crop top, exposing her stomach, and six-inch stripper heels. He didn't even know her name, and he didn't fucking care to know.

"Not interested."

"She's good, Trig."

He had no plans to find out. He did know she'd fucked her way around the club at least thirty times already, except for Stone, Wild, and him. Probably the reason why she was giving him the look. She wanted to get fucked by the only biker she hadn't fucked yet. She was better suited for him than Allie with all her class, but he'd had Allie for a week, and there was no one like her. Even being as pissed as he was because Allie ignored him, he wasn't tempted.

"Don't fuckin' care."

Army shrugged. "Suit yourself." He took a deep drink of whiskey.

He'd been sitting there for close to two hours, talking senseless shit with Army and Blaze when he felt it. The pang in his chest deepened, and he knew Allie was back in the room. He heard her laugh and nearly

241

doubled over with yearning. Fighting the urge to look her way, he glared at the empty beer bottle in his hand, wrapping his fist around it until his knuckles were white.

"Lucky son of a bitch," Bud said.

He snapped his head up. The tap stood in front of him bent over. She had no underwear on, so not only did he have a clear view of her ass but her pussy, too.

Bile rose in the back of his throat. "Fuckin' shit." His gaze gravitated to Allie. Her eyes were wide, a mask of hurt marring her ashen face.

Fuck.

He hurt her. It hadn't been his fault. He hadn't asked the skank to bend over in his face, but she had, and it hurt his beautiful Allie.

He bolted off the couch, throwing his beer against the wall. It shattered and fell to the floor. The voices around him deadened. The tap straightened and turned to face him.

"Get you want me to fuck you 'cause you've fucked every one of my brothers, but I'm not fuckin' interested. Thought I'd made it clear last time."

She flinched, her face paling.

He felt the heat of his brothers' eyes on him. Beyond livid, he didn't care. "Apparently I didn't, so I'll fuckin' repeat. Don't want to fuck you. Don't want you bending over in my fuckin' face. Don't want you lookin' at me. Not fuckin' interested, so don't fuckin' come near me again."

"Fuck, bro, that was fuckin' harsh."

His gaze shot to Rake. He glared. "I'm sure she'd be down for you making it up to her."

Blaze stepped in front of him. "Brother, chill."

"You fuckin' chill. You wanna fuckin' tap chasing you when you aren't fuckin' interested?" Blaze's absent response was response enough. "Didn't fuckin' think so."

With those last words, he walked out of the room and into the kitchen, not sparing a glance in Allie's direction.

"Brother, you okay?"

Army. In a mood, no one else would follow.

He wasn't okay. He was fucking pissed at that fuckin' tap, livid with himself for even suggesting he and Allie meet here.

This was torture. Seeing her and not being able to hold her, touch her in any way, having her fucking ignore him, and then she'd seen the tap bend over, and he'd seen the look on her face.

Guilt for hurting her choking him, he lied, "Fine."

"Trig, don't know what the fuck's wrong with you, man, but you gotta see what you said was fucked. You humiliated her in front of the club and the women."

He turned and met Army's gaze. "She humiliated herself by bending over in my face. She humiliates herself every fuckin' night when she's fuckin' one of us."

"Brother, there's nothing wrong with that. She's a woman, and there's fucked double standards, but if she were a man would it fuckin' matter?"

No, it wouldn't, not to him. He'd just used it as an excuse to explain why he'd lashed out without saying the truth.

"Get you been burned by a tap before, but it was a long time ago, and that woman out there had nothing to do with it, so what you did was fucked."

It was much more than being burned by a tap before. His woman had been sitting across the room watching. He'd seen Allie's face blanch, seen that deep pain shine through her eyes. He had a point to make, not only to the tap, but to Allie too. The point was he didn't want a tap. He wanted Allie, only Allie.

Allie walked into the kitchen. Holding his breath, his gaze shot to hers.

"Ty?"

Army turned. "Yeah?"

"I'm going to call a cab."

"What? Why?"

"Mia and Lynn are busy with their men and well, I'd like to sleep in my own bed. I'll be fine."

Army shook his head. "No, I'll take you home, stay there for the night. Gotta keep an eye on you."

"I'll take her home. Don't mind," he volunteered.

Army faced him. "Appreciate it, man, but can't let you. You watched her the whole week—"

"I gotta get up early and pick up Della anyway. Don't mind. You stay here. You been gone all week. Deserve to get drunk and relax."

Army quirked a brow. "I'd say you need it more than me."

God, if he only knew. To relax, he needed Allie. With her, he was a different man, one who smiled, laughed, and enjoyed life. "Like I said, don't mind, gotta wake up early and get Della."

Army smiled. "If you insist." He then turned to Allie. "I'll be at your place early."

She smiled. "Or you can sleep in. I wouldn't mind spending some time with Della."

Army's gaze hit his.

He shrugged, playing it off like he didn't care either way. "Fine by me."

"Right then, I'll call you when I get up tomorrow." Army kissed Allie on the cheek, then walked away.

He looked to her, but she didn't meet his gaze.

Chapter Twenty-Four

The ride home was silent, partly her fault. Allie didn't know what to say or how to feel.

Seeing that woman bend over in front of Jace felt like someone had ripped her heart right out of her chest. He'd freaking lost it and said those horrible things. He had a point. No man wanted a woman chasing him, especially not a woman he didn't want, but he could've gone about it another way.

At first, she'd been relieved, but after, it got her thinking. Maybe when he was tired of her, he'd treat her the same. She began questioning the real reason he wanted to keep them a secret. So when he tired of her, he could get rid of her and no one would be the wiser?

After how much he claimed to care, it didn't make sense, but it wouldn't be the first time a man lied to her. She hated it, but she couldn't help her mind often drifted to the worst-case scenario. Her mood took a turn, and then she'd just wanted to go home.

As soon as he parked, she hopped off his SUV, headed up the stairs, unlocked her door, and entered. Still, she avoided looking at him but heard when he closed the door and locked it.

"Allie?"

She had no choice but to meet his gaze. Damn, in that moment, she hated how much she wanted to throw caution to the wind and kiss him, have him take her right there on the floor in her living room. She wanted to forget that one day she, too, could be at the end of his public, nasty, pain-filled remarks.

"Want to share why you aren't talking to me or lookin' at me?"

She swallowed, garnering the strength to ask what she had to. "I…"

His brows furrowed. "Allie?"

She folded her hands into each other. "Will you treat me like that when you're done with me?"

His eyes widened, his jaw clenched. He was silent for a long moment, holding her gaze. "I won't ever be done with you." His voice rough and filled with emotion.

The breath rushed out of her. He'd said and done so many things to show her he cared, but she couldn't wrap her mind around what he'd said then. It implied more than dating, implied long term and commitment. It was too soon for that. It had been a week since they'd first had sex, six days since they began dating.

She looked away from him, her mind scrambling.

"Allie?"

Her gaze shot to his.

"Now, you think I can do what I've wanted to do since you set foot at the compound?"

She hesitated, then finally nodded. Not a moment later, he pressed her against him, buried his fingers in her hair, slammed his lips to hers, and invaded her mouth.

How she'd missed it—his mouth, his hands, his warmth, all of him, and it hadn't even been a day.

Then and there, she knew. If she wasn't gone already, she was falling hard and fast. Maybe it was a mistake, but it was a mistake worth making, a mistake she wouldn't regret. No man, except her brother, had ever made her feel important, wanted, needed, and treasured, and Jace did that for her. Of course, he did it differently. Making her feel desired too, and he did it seemingly unknowing.

"Fuckin' missed you so much, baby," he whispered against her lips.

The words pierced through her chest. She shivered.

Totally a mistake worth making.

Delving into her mouth, he cupped her butt and lifted her off the floor. She wrapped her legs around his waist. He reached for her jeans, unbuckled, and unzipped them, then dug his fingers in under her thong until he touched her heat. He ran his fingers along the length of her. She moaned, her legs tightening around him.

"Always fuckin' ready for me. Always fuckin' wet." He growled and yanked her blouse down exposing her breasts. He dipped his head and swirled his tongue around her nipple, then sucked. His finger found her clit and rubbed.

She was so close already. "Please…" She moaned, digging her fingers into his back.

He chuckled, pressing himself against her, the length of his erection touching her. Not a moment later, he released her. Gasping for breath, her feet hit the floor. She wobbled.

A breath away from her, he demanded, "Pants off."

That one word, that one demand. A shudder ran through her. She removed her pants quickly.

His hooded eyes on her, he shook his head. "Thong too, Allie."

She removed her thong. Her body trembling, she held her breath, waiting.

"Couch."

On trembling knees, she walked to the couch and sat. Her eyes lifted to his.

He stood feet away, looking so damn sexy fully clothed. Desire clear in his eyes, he raked her from top to bottom. "Open your legs."

She parted her legs.

"Wider, Allie." His tone harsh.

He clenched his jaw then slowly strode to her, each step purposeful. Kneeling in front of her, he placed his hands on her thighs and spread her legs wider. He dove his tongue in her flesh.

She screamed, arching her back off the couch.

He didn't stop. He dove deeper, harder, faster. Then he sunk his fingers in her, and the world melted away.

Seeing stars, she didn't notice when he undressed. The next moment, he sank on the couch beside her, wrapped his arm under her, flipped her over him, and buried himself inside her.

"Ride me, Allie. Make yourself come again, baby."

With her hands on his chest, she rode him hard and fast. He helped her, each hand on her hip, pulling her up and down against his shaft.

"Fuckin' beautiful. Gonna come so fuckin' good, baby."

She was close again, so close. Every word out of his mouth got her hotter, fever-pitch hot.

"Now, baby, now. Come now. Come with me."

She came, threw her head back, and moaned. He grasped her by the back of the neck and pulled her face to his until her gaze met his. Then and there, staring into his eyes, hearing his rapid breaths, feeling him inside her after that mind blowing orgasm, she knew. She wasn't falling fast and hard.

She'd already fallen.

"Shit."

His arms snaked around her back. He hauled her against him, claiming her lips in a searing kiss. "Fuckin' amazing. Missed you so fuckin' much."

She buried her face in his neck and forced herself to ignore the pang in her chest, convincing herself she couldn't possibly love him. It had been only a week.

"Why me?" She didn't realize she said the words aloud until his body jerked. Even then, she wasn't sure if he understood her question.

Pulling her slightly away from him so his eyes captured hers, he cupped her face, tightened his other arm around her waist. "'Cause you're beautiful, smart, and sweet. You drink beer and drive a Camaro. You can cook. You keep a clean house, and you don't mind I don't. 'Cause I fuckin' love your eyes. They change color in the sun. It's all that you are, and it's the way you make me feel. I'm not fuckin' pissed at the world when I'm with you. I'm just fuckin' happy. It's not something I've ever been, Allie, not like this."

Shit. Fuck. Totally warranted. It felt like her heart melted inside her chest, and that pang became a full-blown ache. A good kind of ache, like when you realized maybe the someone you loved could love you back.

Jace pulled her against him. She went willingly, resting her face against the crook of his neck. He shifted, still buried inside her. Her back on the couch, he hovered over her, staring into her eyes. "It fuckin' killed when I saw you walk in today and ignored me."

"Um…I…I thought you were angry with me."

He lifted a brow. "Why?"

"You looked angry."

He shrugged and ran his fingers down her cheek. "Kinda was. I wanted to kiss you, but I couldn't."

She stilled. Maybe Mia was right. Maybe he was falling for her. She was already gone for him, and it happened so fast. "Jace," she whispered, her throat clogging.

His fingers slid over her lips. His gaze lingered there. "Yeah, baby?"

"I…I'm pretty tired. Can we go to bed?" It hadn't been what she'd been so close to admitting, but she was glad. She needed time to think. She couldn't grasp how she could possibly love him knowing so little about him.

He smiled. "Yeah, baby. We can go to bed."

****

The blaring alarm clock woke him. He blinked several times. Allie sprawled on top of him. Her head on his chest, her legs tangled in his. He smiled, shifted her until her head lay on the pillow and turned off the alarm. Snuggling beside her, he feathered kisses over her face. She stirred briefly but didn't wake. He trailed his lips down her neck and chest then lapped his tongue around her nipple. She arched her back, moaning softly, and whispered his name.

He grinned against her flesh, loving the game. The same game he played with her every morning for the past six days. She hadn't lied when she said she was a heavy sleeper.

He kissed her lips. She kissed him back. Finally, her eyes drifted open. A smile spread across her lips.

"Mornin', baby," he whispered.

"Morning, honey."

Every time she called him that, a warmth settled deep in the center of his chest. It replayed in his mind until that warmth spread to his gut.

They rode in his car to get Della and took her to the park, then ate lunch at Allie's. Since Army hadn't called her, they decided to head to a movie. After the movie, he drove them to his house.

In the same neighborhood as Army's house, his had more land, was fenced off, and isolated. It had been a wreck when he bought it. He'd since put a lot of hours, labor, and money into making it a home. It was worth it. He loved the piece of land. Pulling up the drive, he hit the remote to open the gate.

Allie turned to him. "Where are we?"

"J's house," Della responded.

Her eyes widened, briefly.

"J has a very pretty house. It's big. I stay here some times, so I have my own room," Della continued. "He wanted Mommy and me to live with him, but Mommy said no."

Looking through the rearview mirror, he met his niece's eyes. "It's not big."

"It is, too. It has five bedrooms, and it's two stories, and it has a pool."

The way Della said it made it sound like a mansion. He supposed to her it might be, but to Allie, who'd lived in a penthouse in New York, far from it.

He spared a look in Allie's direction. "It isn't big. A total wreck when I bought it, had only four bedrooms. Remodeled a lot, pretty much every room, and I added a garage and a master suite."

She nodded.

He pulled up the drive, waited for the gate to close behind him, then drove up to his house, and parked along the circular drive. It was a two-story brick home with an attached two-car garage surrounded by two large willow trees that shaded the area around it. He'd hung a tire swing on one of them for Della.

He hopped off the car, helped Della out, then walked up the steps to the porch where he'd hung a swing. Turning, his gaze hit Allie, taking everything in. "Allie? You coming?"

She nodded and neared.

He unlocked the door, opened it, letting Della and Allie in first. "Della, wanna get washed up for dinner while I show Allie around?"

She nodded and dashed up the stairs.

He faced Allie. Her eyes wide, she studied his home from the foyer. The layout was open concept. To the right, a small seating area with a brick fireplace. Straight ahead, the main sunk-in living room. It also had a brick fireplace. On the mantle, he had several framed pictures of Della and Tina. A large sectional sat in the middle. In front of it, a flat screen TV. A large window framed a clear view of the backyard, and beside it, a set of double French doors led outside to the back porch and yard.

To the left of the living room was the dining room. There, too, was a large window. A dark wood table positioned in the middle seated six. Between the dining room and kitchen was a hallway that led into a storage closet, bathroom accessible from the backyard, the laundry room, and garage.

The kitchen, twice the size of the dining room, he'd remodeled the most, installing new, stainless-steel appliances, dark-wood cabinets, and light-granite countertops that circled the entire area.

He scanned his home, and then his gaze darted to her. She stood in the middle of the dining room, her eyes on the mahogany wooden table.

She ran her fingers over it. As if sensing his eyes on her, she met his gaze. "This is a beautiful home, Jace."

She was just being nice. He smiled. "You haven't seen it all yet, Allie."

"Think I've seen plenty to know it is, but if you insist, lead the way."

He led her through the French doors outside to the porch and the backyard. The pool sat fifty feet away from the back doors surrounded by several lounge chairs and a patio table for four. He showed her his office, then led her upstairs to the four bedrooms. Last, he took her into his room. He had a four-poster bed, also dark wood, a dresser, armoire, and TV. Beside the TV, a walk-in closet he didn't think he'd ever be able to fill. To the other side, the en suite bathroom with tub and shower. At the back end of the room were two large windows. In between, a set of double doors leading onto the second-story balcony.

She went to the doors, parted them, and stepped outside. He followed her and found her resting her weight against the railing looking out into his backyard. He came up behind her, wrapped his arms round her waist, buried his face in her neck, and feathered a kiss under her ear.

She turned to face him and pressed her lips against his. "It's beautiful."

"Know it's not fancy or—"

She placed her fingers over his lips. "It's beautiful and homey. Perfect for a family." She lifted a brow, then teased, "...or a hot, angry, badass biker with a big heart who loves his sister and niece."

He hid his smile. "Did you just call me a hot, angry, badass biker?"

Allie flushed. She looked away from him. After a moment, she met his stare. "Before I knew your name, that's what I called you."

He chuckled, shaking his head. "Don't believe you."

"Why would I lie, honey?"

His heart squeezed. He loved when she called him that.

"I had names for some of the other guys, too."

The smile fell away from his lips. Knowing he could come to regret, he asked, "What were they?"

"Dash was Tatted Sleeves, Bud was Tatted Chest and..." She hesitated. "I actually feel guilty about this one, but it's kind of true."

Who the hell was it? What the hell was it? He shouldn't have asked. If she'd called any one of his brothers "hot" he'd definitely have to punch them in the face.

"Ripper was Dead Eyes."

Dead Eyes? Damn, not bad and true. Sometimes, he swore Ripper was dead inside. Then again, sometimes he showed another side of him, like the night he tried to comfort Allie. "Pretty good."

She smiled.

After dinner that night with Della, Allie, and Army, he dropped Della off at home and headed to his empty house. For the first time in more than a week, he lay on his bed. He thought about Allie until he drifted to sleep.

Chapter Twenty-Five

It had been a little over three weeks since Ty had come back, and it had taken getting used to. Mainly, she missed Jace. While Ty had been gone, she gotten used to having Jace around. Their relationship went from easy to hard, complicated, and sometimes outright frustrating. Not because they began arguing or fighting but because a number of other reasons.

Things changed drastically. Her brother and the club still didn't know she and Jace were an item, and Jace had to get back to his life with the club and with Della and Tina. He'd been going on "runs," which he didn't share with her because he couldn't, club business and all that. He had shared he and Ty usually went on runs together. When she worried, she worried about both of them. Two to three runs a week: Mondays, Tuesdays, and sometimes Thursdays. Those nights, she spent with either Cuss or Blaze. She preferred Cuss, not only because she had a soft spot for Cuss, but also Cuss knew about Jace and her. After Jace's runs, he'd come over and spend the night. Cuss would then leave. She had no idea where he went, but knew he didn't go back to the compound. Otherwise, it'd blow their cover. She paid him back by making him dinner on those days.

During one of those nights, Jace came over after his run, and she noticed he carried a gun. What type? She had no freaking clue. Quite frankly, she didn't want to know. She was terrified of guns. He caught her looking at it and told her not to worry. Right, well, it didn't quite work out like that. She then began worrying for not only Ty and Jace, but the rest of the guys too, much more than she had before.

Usually, she saw Jace three times a week: either Monday or Tuesday when Cuss watched her, Fridays when he watched her, and Saturdays when she spent the day with him and Della. She used Della as an excuse to spend an extra day with him telling her brother she wanted to see Della. True, she loved Della, but she also wanted to be with Jace even though they weren't free to act like a couple because they were often out in public, not to mention in front of Della. Though he often found ways to touch her or steal kisses, so it was worth it.

Apart from those days, it was impossible to see him. Ty spent Wednesdays, Sundays, and sometimes Thursdays with her, and Jace spent that time with Della and Tina. Once, she'd seen him on a Sunday at the club's cookout.

That day, they had their second argument.

She sat with Tiffany, Mia, and Lynn planning their next shopping trip when Cuss walked up to them. She hadn't seen him yet and smiled at him.

He nodded. "Hey, Miracle."

"Are you volunteering to take us shopping again?"

Cuss chuckled and nodded.

The next moment, Jace stood in front of her, the muscle in his jaw jumping. "Allie. Inside. Now."

She hadn't known what to think, but she went. He looked like he was about to lose it, so it wouldn't be good, not in front of the entire club. When she headed inside, he dragged her into an empty room and shut the door. He still had that angry look on his face, but he didn't say anything.

"Is everything okay?" Another one of her stupid questions, but the silence had been too unbearable.

"No, everything isn't okay," he snapped. "Don't want you goin' anywhere with Cuss."

Her eyes widened. It had been so absurd to hear that since Cuss often covered for them. "What? Why?"

He closed the distance between them and leaned into her. "'Cause I don't like him calling you 'Miracle.' It fuckin' pisses me off, and I'm fuckin' tired of hearing it."

What? If it wasn't for Cuss, she'd hardly ever see him. She wanted more time with him, not less. "Well, too bad." She knew the minute after she said it, she shouldn't have.

The vein in his neck began pulsing. He grabbed her arm and pulled her toward him. Snaking his other arm around her waist, he crushed her against him. She didn't bother fighting back. It would've been useless. Instead she let herself enjoy the moment, her body against his.

"Don't fuckin' play games with me, Allie."

Taking a deep steadying breath, she chose her words wisely. "He's taken."

He tightened his hold around her back, his eyes narrowing to slits. "You say he's fuckin' taken. Does that mean he wasn't, you'd be with him instead of me?"

"Are you jealous?"

"No fuckin' shit," he shot back, immediately.

Her jaw dropped. A warm feeling settled in the center of her chest. Maybe it was a little crazy, but it made her feel like he cared, a lot. Her anger melted. She softened against him. "I'm not interested in anyone but you. He calls me that because I can get Ty out of a bad mood…"

She tilted her head and explained, "He likes Tiff. A lot. I think he's liked her for a long time, but he says she's too good for him. I told him all a woman ever really wants is to be understood and loved, and if he thinks he can give her that, he should go for it."

She didn't know whether it was the way she'd melted or what she'd said, but that instant, his anger faded. He kissed her, and he didn't stop. It led to make-up sex where they'd had no choice but to be quiet.

By now, she was tired of lying to her brother, sneaking around, and pretending she didn't care about Jace when she knew she was head-over-heels in love with him.

She knew she was deeply in love because he hadn't changed, not one bit. He was still the same caring, attentive, and loving man he'd been the first week. If possible, he'd grown more attentive. He called her at least three times a day, in the mornings, at lunch, and in the evenings, if he wasn't with her. He also texted her randomly, to tell her he missed her, to tell her he was at the club or on a run. It seemed like he told her everything, except that wasn't really the case.

He hadn't opened up to her about his past. In fact, last week she asked him about his parents, and he'd shut her down. Not that she was one to talk; she didn't like rehashing the past, but they were an item. She should know more about him. She hadn't hid anything about her past. Besides her father and Mia, he was the only other person whom she'd told the truth about Wyatt. Well, she supposed he somewhat guessed, but she confirmed it instead of shutting him out.

This to her, especially after realizing she was in love with him, troubled her. It made her think maybe he did, in fact, see her as temporary in his life. She could be overanalyzing and overly insecure, but problem was, after the night he told her he'd never get tired of her, he hadn't talked about the future or about when they should consider telling her brother and the club. He didn't even seem bothered he saw her only two to three times a week.

They hadn't been together long. She shouldn't be concerned about this, but she was. She didn't know what to do. It's not like she could ask anyone for advice. No one was supposed to know, and it didn't feel right to let Tiffany, Mia, or Lynn know she was in love with Jace before she told him.

With these thoughts tumbling through her mind, she slung her purse over her shoulder and walked out to her car. A Friday afternoon meant the next two days she'd spend with Jace. Regardless of her many insecurities, this made her happy.

She reached her car, her eyes gravitating to the driver's side back tire of her Camaro. The rim of her car rested on the pavement. Cursing silently, she grabbed her phone out of her purse and called Triple A. Her brother worked at a garage but she called someone else for help because without a doubt, he wouldn't let her pay, and she wasn't totally useless. She had a savings account and a job. She could afford a new tire. She had to do it fast before Jace showed up. He often did Fridays.

"Triple A."

"Hi, I need a—fuck!"

Totally warranted. She caught sight of the front driver's side tire and it, too, was flat.

"Hello?" The voice drifted through the phone.

She barely heard, rushing to the other side of her car where she noticed those tires, too, were flat.

"Hello?"

Allie stared at the tires not seeing them, but feeling a weight settle on her chest. Her eyes welled with tears.

"Miss? Are you okay? Miss?"

The voice snapped her out of her innate state. "Yes, I'm fine. I won't need your services."

She hated what she was about to do, what she had to do, but there was no way around it. This wasn't a coincidence. This was Wyatt. She knew when the rock cracked her window in the middle of the night, but she'd pushed it out of her mind without ever discussing it with Jace or Ty.

She knew two weeks ago when she found a note on her car, yet convinced herself one of the guys had played a prank on her. Never mind deep down she knew neither one of them would try to scare her, especially not like that. She convinced herself because she wanted to pretend it wasn't true. And now, she couldn't ignore it anymore. She had to face the facts. Wyatt was messing with her life because he couldn't let go.

She was thankful neither Ty, Jace, or the club had been implicated in beating Wyatt, but now she had the sinking feeling she knew why Wyatt hadn't involved cops. He was seeking revenge another way.

Without further thought, she dialed Jace. Thankfully, he answered on the first ring.

"Got a problem, honey."

****

His phone rang. Trig rolled out from under the car and dug into his pocket. Reading Allie's name on the screen, he sat up, answered it quickly, and brought it to his ear.

"Got a problem, honey." Her voice shaky.

Gut turning, a sour taste in his mouth, he snapped, "Where are you?"

"I-I just got out of work."

Fuck. What time was it? He met her at the daycare every Friday. Call it being overprotective, but since he'd caught her dickhead ex there, he tried his hardest to meet her outside. The ex had been taken care of, and there hadn't been any blowback but still.

He glanced at the clock hung on the back wall of the garage. Fifteen past four.

"Talk to me."

"My t-tires are flat."

A cold chill blasted through him. He shot off his butt so quickly the creeper, a wooden board with wheels he'd been laying on under the car, rolled several feet away. "All of them?"

"Yeah, Jace, all of them," she whispered.

Fuck. Not good. First, the rock cracking her window and now this; it wasn't a coincidence. After that night, he'd been on hyper alert. Calling the cops every day for two weeks, but they convinced him it was a prank, and after nearly a month with nothing, he believed it.

Trig opened the door leading into the compound and dashed down the hall. "Go inside the daycare. Now. Stay with Tiffany. I'll be there in a few."

"Um…"

He stopped in the living room, rushing to pick his keys and wallet off the couch where he dropped them. "Allie. Don't fuckin' fight me. Do what I say. Get in the daycare. Now."

"Okay, honey," she whispered in the same small voice.

The line went dead.

Guilt clogged his throat. He'd been harsh, too harsh. She wasn't stupid. She knew who this was and what it meant. If her voice was anything to go by, she was fucking terrified, and he'd been a dick.

Army sat on the couch, several feet away, his phone in hand. "What happened?"

"Tires flat."

Army shot off the couch, his eyes hardening. "Why didn't she call me?"

A good question. He needed to think fast. "It's Friday. I watch her Fridays." He turned to Blaze. "Need you to finish the oil change and see about getting tires for Allie's Camaro, four of them." To Army, he said, "You comin'?"

Army nodded.

As they headed into the garage, he shouted orders to Trick, telling him to bring the flat truck to haul Allie's car. He then jumped into his SUV, Army hopping into the passenger side. Trig drove to the daycare in record time, illegally parked in front. Leaving the keys in the car, he rushed inside and spotted her immediately in the corner talking to Tiffany. Her beautiful, color-changing eyes big and gleaming, fighting tears. It fucking did him in. The guilt strengthened and compounded with anger. His chest would rip in two.

He headed toward her. Her gaze met his. She released a loaded breath. For a split second, he thought she'd put him out of his misery, run to him, and wrap her arms around him. Instead, her gaze darted behind him. She walked up to Army, who now stood at his side.

"Hi, Ty."

"You okay?"

She nodded.

"Should've called me," Army said.

He'd known Army a long time, and knew when Army asked the same question twice, he wasn't convinced. It meant Army knew something was up, and that meant Army would keep Allie close, not just because her tires were flat, probably slashed. The little Trig had of Allie he'd lose, unless they told Army they were together. Fucking sucked. He didn't think she was ready to tell her brother. She hadn't mentioned it and didn't even seem bothered by the fact they barely spent time together.

"I knew Jace was on his way to my house though. He watches me Fridays," she said smoothly.

Army spared a glance at him, then nodded. He wrapped his arm around Allie's shoulders. "Let's get to the compound where we can talk about this in private."

He didn't know if Army referred to them or the slashed tires, but he didn't let his worry show. He followed behind.

They arrived at the compound minutes later and headed into the garage's office to talk.

Army, wasting no time, cut to the chase. "Tell me what happened."

She sighed heavily, pulling her dark hair behind

her ear. "I guess I should start from the beginning… The first night you were gone, while Jace was with me, someone threw a rock at my bedroom window. It was loud enough it woke me, and then another rock was thrown hard enough, and it cracked the glass—"

Army's gaze sliced to his. "Why didn't you fuckin' tell me?"

"Considering two days before we'd beat the shit outta him, I didn't think he could've pulled it off. I went outside, checked it out. I found no one, so I called the cops. They filed a report. I called them every day for the next two weeks. They told me shit like this happens, kids playing stupid pranks. Nothing happened after that, so there was no need to tell anyone."

Army's gaze went to Allie. "Go on."

Her eyes watered. She pressed her shaking hands against her stomach. "Two weeks ago, I found a note on my car—"

"Fuck." He ground his teeth. His whole body tensed. He didn't give a flying fuck she didn't tell Army because Army always flew off the handle, but why hadn't she told him? He would've handled Army. He would've done it with pleasure because she was his. Instead she said nothing and waited for something bigger to happen, something she had to know would eventually happen, something that could've been much worse.

"What the fuck?" Army roared, taking a step in Allie's direction.

Without thought, he jumped between the two, facing Army. The heat of her hand at his lower back calmed him. In public, around people who didn't know about them, she found ways to touch him. He loved it.

Right then, he loved it more because he needed her touch. "We're not gonna do this shit again. Take a breath. She's fuckin' shaking and scared. Do *not* fuckin' make her lose it." He had to say it, knew it was bound to piss Army off more, but he couldn't handle watching Allie break down now. He'd want to hold her, and then and there, he couldn't.

Army took a deep breath. Only then did he move away. "Why didn't you tell me any of this, Allie?"

She blinked, and two thick tears streamed down her face. "I'm sorry…"

His heart clenching, his whole body ached, wanting so desperately to pull her against him and comfort her like she deserved.

She wiped the tears quickly. "Ty, it was meaningless. I mean the note was on a scrap piece of paper and said, 'I'm watching.' I didn't…" She shook her head. "No, I knew. I guess I didn't want to believe it."

Army grasped her around the back of her neck and tugged her against him, rubbing his hand against her back. "Should've told me. Should've fuckin' told me this shit when it happened." After a brief moment of silence, he said, "Need to move you into the compound."

Fuck. Army was right. It was the right thing to do. Nothing was more important than her safety, but it'd suck, big.

She drew away from Army. "No, I'm not going to let him rule my life, Ty. I can't—"

"Sleep on it, Allie," Army said, firmly. "You'll see it's the right thing to do."

"I have a lease and—"

"I'll get you out of the lease. I'll move your shit, too, like I did the first time."

"But—"

"Alyssa, don't fuckin' fight me. Not on this. I'm pissed as fuckin' hell with you. You didn't tell me any of this. Means now we're on defense. Don't like being on defense, especially not when it comes to you. You're moving in if I got to carry you kicking and screaming." Army shook his head. "Sleep on it, and tomorrow you'll realize I'm right."

Turning to him, Army instructed, "Take her home."

He did.

Chapter Twenty-Six

Jaw clenched, Trig tightened his hands around the steering wheel until his knuckles ached. He hadn't looked at her since she sat beside him, but the image of her tear-streaked face was burned in his mind. He didn't want to see it again. Still, he fought the urge to look. He wanted to make it better, wanted to make her better.

He sighed heavily, and then, despite his resolve, he spared a glance in her direction. She sat still like a fucking stone with her oversized purse on her lap. Her face pale, paler than it'd been when she'd been crying.

"Fuck."

Pulling off on the side of the road, he unfastened her seatbelt and hauled her against him until she was on his lap. Immediately, she wrapped her arms around his neck. He buried his face in her hair and feathered a kiss on her forehead.

He was pissed she hadn't listened to him, livid she hadn't told him, offended she hadn't confided in him. And still, because he was a fucking wuss when it came to her, he held her against him, ignoring how pissed he was because he needed to make her better.

After long moment, she pulled away, those color-changing eyes met his and she whispered, "Thank you, Jace."

What the fuck she thanked him for he had no fucking clue, but whatever. He waited until she moved to her seat and refastened her seat belt before he drove.

Minutes later, they walked into her house. He sat on her couch and motioned for her to sit on his lap.

She walked to him and sat on his thighs.

Snaking an arm around her waist, he tugged her until her hip pressed against his stomach. "I'm fuckin' pissed, Allie, real fuckin' pissed." He kept his tone low and calm.

"I know," she whispered.

"You know why?"

"Because I didn't tell you about the note."

"Why?"

"I told you. I didn't want to believe it."

He shook his head. "Why do you think that pisses me off?"

"Because you want to handle stuff for me?"

"I don't want to handle shit for you, Allie. I need to handle shit for you 'cause you're fuckin' mine. Remember, we had this conversation?"

"If you don't want to handle it for me, then don't."

His arm around her waist tightened, bringing her an inch from his face. "You tryin' to fuckin' rile me? You want me to fuckin' flip?" His voice rose with each word.

"No."

"Then don't get fuckin' smart."

Her eyes narrowed. "I'm not getting smart. I'm giving you advice. If you don't want to do something, then you shouldn't do it."

Fuck, she could frustrate a saint. "It's not about what I want, Allie. It's about what I *need*. I didn't want to want you. I wanted to respect your brother and the club by not fuckin' wanting you, but I didn't get a choice. So it doesn't make a difference what I want 'cause with you it isn't about wanting. It's about needing. I fuckin' *need* you."

"Well, I'm sorry about that, Jace. I'm really sorry you got stuck needing me." She pushed at his chest, hard.

He shifted her until she laid flat on her back with him pinning her. His chest against hers, resting most of his weight on his elbows. "Tell me how what I said offended to you, Allie. Fuckin' explain to me what the fuck goes on in your head, 'cause I think what I said was a compliment, but you aren't taking it that way, so please explain to me 'cause I'm tired of guessing."

Her eyes glimmering, she shot back, "Tell me how what you said isn't offensive, Trigger. In what world do you live in that saying you don't want me is a compliment? Oh, wait, I shouldn't be upset because I'm just some woman you're fucking, some woman no one knows about, who knows nothing about you because you won't tell me."

He flinched. He felt like she slapped him, like they were back to that night at the bar. He hated she believed that after all this time. "Never said I didn't want you, Allie. Never in my fuckin' life have I said I didn't want you, never even thought it 'cause I've wanted you since the moment I saw you—"

"You just said—"

"I fuckin' said I didn't want to want you 'cause you're Army's sister, means you're off limits, Allie. I didn't want to betray my fuckin' brother and the club. I served with your brother. We were prospects together. The club's family. I gotta a fuckin' home for the first time in my life partly 'cause of that family. I gotta a job that fuckin' pays well, so I can take care of Della and Tina 'cause of that family. Never fuckin' said I didn't want you. Said with you it's more than what I want 'cause it's out of my control. I can't fuckin' help how much I want you. I want you so much I *need* you."

Her eyes widened. Her face changed, looking like something dawned on her.

"You're not some woman I'm fuckin'. I'm not keeping you in secret for me. I'm doing it for you 'cause I'm not sure I'm what you really want. We been together for a little more than a month. Not three months ago, you were engaged to a dick who beat you, so I'm not sure if I'm just a rebound fuck, a way to rebel, or some other fucked shit like that. It were up to me, I'd sink myself inside you right now, then march over to the compound and announce I'm patching you."

Then and there, staring into her glimmering eyes, he made the decision, one he could come to regret, but he made it nonetheless. He would tell her everything. He wanted her to know him, all of him, not just pieces. If she ever loved him, then he'd know it was for the good and the bad, not the pieces he'd let her see.

It could backfire and blow up in his face. She'd cringe, shove him away, and ask him to leave. Then he'd never again feel the warmth of her body against his. A risk, but a risk he was willing to take. He would take the risk knowing he would separate himself from the dick ex by simply being honest.

It was all he had because he didn't deserve her. She deserved a man of her caliber. He knew and felt it in his bones. If his risk backfired, he'd console himself with the knowledge her leaving him was inevitable. Knowing that, wouldn't change the pain of losing her, but still.

"My dad was a drug addict, did whatever he could get his hands on. My mom was a drunk. I grew up in a trailer. Tina and me. I looked out for her 'cause she's my little sister and 'cause my dad could get abusive.

"When he left, I didn't have to worry about that shit, but it meant my mom hit the bottle every day and night, spent all her money on that shit. There were a lot of empty bottles of vodka but no food, so first chance I got, I got a job 'cause Tina needed to eat. After high school, I couldn't get into college with my grades, didn't have the money for it anyway, so I joined the Army 'cause more than anything, I needed money. I needed to get Tina out of that trailer, away from our drunk mother. I enlisted for four years, sent Tina money, went home when I could, wrote, and called.

"Tina was turning into a beautiful woman, though mom was still a drunk. When my four years were up, the country was still at war. I reenlisted. Tina said I should. She seemed fine. I figured in another two years, I'd've saved enough for a house and some. When I got back, Tina had a five-month-old and was drinking, heavily. She didn't mention it. Hadn't seen her for a year, so I had no clue.

"The father was long gone. I did what I could. Sent Tina to rehab, got an apartment, and took care of Della. Knew about the club, had thought about joining for a while. I told Army 'bout it, and we joined together. I moved Tina and Della into their apartment, bought my house around the time I started as a prospect. About nine months later, Army and I were patched. My mom died a year later. A year after that, finished remodeling my house. Tried to move Della and Tina in, and Tina refused, so I live alone."

He waited for her to push him away.

Instead she smiled, sadly. Tears welled in her eyes and spilled. "You aren't a rebound. You are exactly the man I thought you to be," she whispered, and then she pressed her lips against his, softly, just like the first time.

Chapter Twenty-Seven

Hovering over her, resting his weight on his elbows, Jace recounted his life. Allie stared at him wide-eyed, unable to believe everything he'd endured, everything he'd achieved. When he was done, his arms tightened around her almost as if afraid she would run. His face a mask of anguish, hidden sorrow in his eyes.

She knew then, one certain truth: sometimes the people who hadn't seemed to have accomplished much had accomplished the most.

Jace was one of those people, exactly the man she thought him to be.

No matter what happened between them, she'd never regret loving him. Despite the odds, he managed to make a man out of himself, make something of his life, for himself, but especially for his sister. He was the type of man who deserved to be loved and was worth loving.

Allie smiled. Tears glistened, then fell. "You aren't a rebound. You are exactly the man I thought you to be." She kissed him, pressing her lips lightly against his.

When she pulled away, his brows drew together. "I want to tell Ty tomorrow."

He shook his head and cupped her cheek. "Allie, baby, think you need some time—"

"No, I don't. I've missed you. A lot. I don't want to

lie to Ty anymore. I don't want to sneak around anymore. I just want to be…us."

He threaded his fingers through her hair. "I gotta agree with you, Allie. Hate fuckin' lying to Army, to my brothers, and I hate sneaking around, but you gotta be prepared. This isn't gonna go smooth with your brother. If he gets real pissed, I can get kicked out of the club—"

She'd completely forgotten that part. "Maybe we shouldn't then—"

"It happens, you're worth it. I'd give the club up for you in a heartbeat. I wanna do this, us. It's gonna happen sometime. The longer we sneak around, the harder it'll be to tell them, and the more pissed off they'll be."

Smiling, she nodded.

"You let me handle it—"

What? No way was that happening. Ty was her brother, her family. She knew him better than anyone, meaning she knew how to deal with him, and his moods better than anyone. "I'll handle my brother—"

"Allie." His voice low and firm. "It's club shit. I deal with club shit, remember?"

She shook her head. "He's my brother. I deal with my brother."

His eyes hardened. "Club business."

"It's family business, and I'm Ty's family."

"Alyssa, you're not in the position to rile me."

"What—"

He crushed his lips against hers, silencing her. He then delved his tongue into her mouth roughly, giving her a kiss that had her heated and wet in seconds.

Allie missed him. She missed him so damned

much. It had been so long, too long. Two whole days, and she needed him.

She shifted her hips, grinding against the length of his erection. He wrapped his arms around her, releasing his weight and trapping her so she couldn't move. The head of his shaft pressed between her legs. She squirmed, fighting to rub against him.

But he didn't bulge, not an inch. Instead he trailed his mouth down her neck. "You gonna let me handle it?"

His heated breath at her neck, she shivered, her nipples puckering against his chest. She lost track of thought except for the length of him against her. Him, she couldn't forget. "W-what?"

He nibbled on her ear, one hand running up her leg, lifting it, and resting it against his back, and then he ground into her.

She moaned.

"You gonna let me handle it, baby?"

Handle what? What had they been talking about? She couldn't focus.

He pressed into her again, his cock rubbing against her clit over her jeans.

She whimpered, but she remembered, sort of. "This is...not fair."

He chuckled.

The deep sound vibrated in her chest. Panting, she couldn't take anymore, so she begged. "Honey, pleaseee..."

His lips slammed down hard on hers. Brutal, like he was trying to punish her, but it only got her wetter.

"Know what you gotta say, baby." His hand trailing to her breast, he lowered her shirt, buried his face, and sucked her nipple.

She would lose her mind. "Yes…please."

He released her nipple. She whimpered at the loss.

His face inches from hers, he asked again, "You gonna let me handle it?"

"Yes, honey. Whatever you want, just please."

The heat of his body was gone but not for long. He removed her jeans and thong, then grabbed her around the waist, hoisting her up on her knees, and bent her over the couch. The next instant, he was behind her. One hand gripping her waist, the other he snaked around her stomach. He cupped her breast, hauled her back against him, and buried himself inside her.

She screamed, loud.

"Fuckin' heaven, baby," he whispered against her neck.

She shivered, her legs trembling. He pulled out of her, then pushed into her again and again. Hard and fast, like he knew she liked it, like he was rewarding her. He kept his pace, in and out of her quickly. Then his hand at her breast slid down her body agonizingly slow. Finally, he cupped her flesh and rubbed his fingers against her clit. "Come with me, baby."

She threw her head back because she came, hard. He didn't stop. He continued to move inside her, continued to rub her. Then the unimaginable happened, something she'd never experienced before, something she'd thought a myth. Moments after her release, the pleasure started again. It built and built and didn't stop building.

He wrapped his arm across her, gripping her shoulder, holding her still, and close against him. "I feel you…" He groaned, pumping inside her faster.

His words threw her over. Feeling his cock pulsate inside, she screamed. A second orgasm flooded her blood, her veins. She swore she felt it in her soul.

He growled, muttering an almost incoherent, "Fuckin' heaven."

When he stilled, his feverish breaths heated her neck, his arm still tight around her, holding her up. He shifted them until his back lay flat against the couch, and she was sprawled on top of him. One arm around her waist, the other buried in her hair.

They stayed like that for a while, catching their breaths.

Finally, he broke the silence. "Tina's off tomorrow. First thing, I talk to Army."

She tensed against him.

He rubbed his hand against her back soothingly then pressed his lips against her forehead. "Don't worry, baby, everything's gonna be fine."

She lifted her head to meet his eyes. "I want to be there with you."

He lifted his head, pressed a kiss to her lips. "Gotta talk to your brother alone."

"I know you two need to talk 'man to man' or whatever because you're both macho men bikers, but he needs to know how I feel about this." She hesitated. "You said you wouldn't control my life. If you leave without me, then you are. He's my brother, and I know my brother. He needs to know how I feel."

His eyes hardened, the way they did when he was angry, probably the "control" comment she made but it had to be done. There was no other way to get through to him, like she knew there was no way to get through to her brother unless she was there.

"Knew you were smart from one look. Didn't know you had it in you to bring up shit like that to try to get me to agree though."

She smiled. "Look who's talking, Mr. I-use-sex-to-get-what-I-want."

He fought a smile, and then he gave up. She had a point. He didn't seem to mind. "It's for your own good."

"It's for our own good."

****

"What. The. Fuck?"

The shriek woke her. The next instant, Jace grasped under her arms and shoved her behind him. Simultaneously, he threw a blanket over her.

A heavy sleeper meant all that movement and still she was half asleep trying to process everything when she heard another shriek.

"What the *fuck*?"

Oh, shit. She knew that voice. Her brother, of course. He had the worst timing, ever.

"Let me explain."

Jace. She could hear him but couldn't see his face considering he shoved her behind him. All she could see—the mass of muscles lining his back and the Hell Ryders tat. Trying to gather her thoughts with a sleep-hazed mind wasn't easy.

"Explain? What the fuck are you gonna explain? How you been fuckin' my sister behind my back?"

Shit. Shit. Shit. She was naked. Jace was naked, and her brother was in her room. She should've never given him a key.

Wrapping and tightening the blanket around herself, she peered over Jace's shoulder. Only caught a brief glimpse of Ty, before Jace felt her move and pushed her fully behind him.

"Allie's in the fuckin' room. Calm down, and we'll talk about this."

"You fuckin' kidding me? You're fuckin' my sister in her fuckin' house, and I'm supposed to be fuckin' calm? She's off fuckin' limits, and you're my fuckin' brother. Before the club, we were brothers. We served together. I trusted you. You fuckin' stabbed me in the back—"

Gripping the blanket firmly around herself, she moved away from Jace. He reached for her, wrapping his arm around her waist. Finally though, she caught a good glimpse of her brother. Nostrils flared, eyes glaring and deadpanned on Jace.

"Ty—" All she got out before Jace pushed her behind him.

"Stop it, Jace," she snapped.

"You touch her again. I'll fuckin' shoot you on the spot."

Oh, God. She'd made it worse. A lot worse.

Jace released her.

Blanket still firmly wrapped around her, she pulled herself beside Jace. Her eyes gravitating to the gun in Ty's hand, pointed toward the ground. His finger on the trigger.

The breath rushed out of her. She squeezed her eyes shut, shaking her head. "Don't, Ty. Don't hurt him." Her voice cracked.

"You've fuckin' scared her half to fuckin' death. Put that shit away." His voice low, but there was a menacing sound to it that hadn't been there before.

Ty put the gun on the back waistband of his jeans.

Only then did she meet Ty's gaze. "Ty…" Her voice came out shaky. "It's not what it looks like."

"Looks like he's been fuckin' you for a while, Allie, hiding you like you aren't worth being claimed. Looks like you been lying to me. Looks and sounds like you've fallen for a biker."

He'd made it sound so bad. If she wasn't so guilt-ridden, and insecure, she would've denied Jace was hiding her. She would've said something or done something like fight the tears spilling from her eyes.

"Fuckin' asshole," Jace snapped. "You wanna be a dick? Be a fuckin' dick to me. Don't be a fuckin' dick to her. She's your sister."

"Says the brother who's been fuckin' her," Ty shot back.

Jace jackknifed out of bed. In a split second, he faced off her brother, butt naked.

She managed then to find her voice. "Stop!"

Their gazes shot to her.

"You want to know the truth, Ty?"

His gaze on her, he jerked his head.

"The truth is I've wanted Jace since I met him. He made it hard because he was always mad. I thought he didn't like me. That would've turned me off except every now and then he did something sweet, like rough up my ex or let me cry when I needed it.

"Then you left, and you left him here, who I was trying to avoid because he was always so cold with me. The night the rock was thrown at my window I was freaked and again, he was here being sweet. I kissed him. Then we started dating, but it wasn't easy because I'm off limits. We didn't have another choice but to keep us a secret."

Clutching the blanket against her, she rose and rested her weight on her knees. "I'm sorry for lying to you, but you have to understand, Ty, this was harder for him and me than it was for you. You're my family. I lied, and it hurts. Jace has been lying too, and it hurts him too because you and the club are his family.

"Despite the fact Jace and I are consenting adults, you made it impossible for us not to hide. I get why you were protecting me, and I'm glad, but this is different. Before you start pointing fingers at us, please think about that."

She fell silent and waited for Ty to say something, anything.

After a long moment, his eyes scanning her face the entire time, he turned to Jace, his jaw set in anger. "Gotta talk to Allie. Alone."

Jace fisted his hands, and then reluctantly nodded. He strode to her, cupped the back of her head, tugged her against him, and kissed her forehead. He met her eyes. "Be outside."

She nodded. "Okay."

He pulled on his jeans, walked out of her room, and out of sight. Her front door opened, then closed. Only then did she meet her brother's eyes. He was still angry, really angry.

"You love him." It wasn't a question, but a statement.

She nodded. "Yes, Ty. I'm in love with him."

He sighed heavily, closed the distanced between them, and sat on the edge of her bed. Resting his elbows on his knees, he buried his face in his hands.

"Ty?"

He looked at her.

"I've never felt this way about anyone. He may not feel the same." She shrugged. "I don't know, but I know I love him. I loved him before I knew he didn't go to college, before I knew he grew up in a trailer. Now I'm certain because despite the odds, he's a good man. He made himself that man. I know he deserves to be loved like I love him…even if he doesn't love me." Her voice cracked.

Ty didn't speak. He didn't move either. Tears fell, staining her face, and still, he didn't move.

"He's so good to me, Ty. He's so good…to me. I've never felt so…" She hesitated, searching for the right word. "Alive. I feel alive. For the first time in my life, I'm not an object someone can control, I'm a person. So it doesn't matter if he loves me. I know how he makes me feel, and I can live with that."

He dropped his head, ran his fingers through his hair, shaking his head. He met her stare. "You deserve more, Allie. You deserve to be loved, too. Don't fuckin' settle. Don't ever fuckin' settle. Better than you is no one, nothing."

He stood. "Gotta talk to Jace."

"Promise me."

No hesitation. "I promise."

He knew what she meant. She hadn't needed to tell him. It's why he was her brother. He'd keep his promise, no matter what Jace said or didn't say.

Chapter Twenty-Eight

Trig waited and waited, and he wasn't patient about it either. He didn't want to leave Allie alone. She was safe with her brother, but it didn't mean she was okay. It didn't mean she wasn't upset or worst, fucking crying.

He hated when she cried. She was tough and strong and taught not to cry. When she cried, he knew she'd had too much, and knowing that made it worse.

Her brother loved her and would never hurt her, but in an instant, Army forgot shit like the fact Allie was sweet, beautiful Allie. Army let his anger get in the way of logic, let it blind him to the point he couldn't see Allie was a woman who needed to be comforted.

Trig understood his anger. He'd been pissed for not knowing Wyatt had put his hands on her and that she hadn't told them about the note, but still, she was Allie. She needed and deserved to be held and told everything would be all right even if it wasn't.

Army didn't get it. Like Army didn't get, you didn't pull out a gun in front of Allie. She'd spotted his one night, and she stared at it wide-eyed for a full ten minutes. He'd told her not to worry, explained the safety was on, but it hadn't helped. He told her they carried them for protection, not because they used them. That hadn't helped either. It wasn't until he put it out of sight she'd been able to fall asleep.

Yet Army had his gun firm in his grip, typical Army style. No bluff. If he'd dared touch Allie after Army's threat, he would have a hole somewhere. He got that, but shit, Allie was there. Army could've shot him later, in the back for all he cared, just not in front of Allie. She deserved hearts and flowers, not guns and death threats.

He heard footsteps nearing and turned toward the door a moment before Army swung it open. His accusing eyes snared him. That one deadly look from anyone else would've started a brawl, but Army had reason. He forced himself to relax.

Army closed the door behind him. "She's bet—"

"Don't fuckin' say it."

He didn't deserve her. He knew it, didn't need to hear it because he thought about it every second, minute, and hour of every day. But he wanted her, and if she wanted him, he'd keep her.

"Don't fuckin' say it. You know it. She knows it, and I sure as hell know it. Every time I look at her, I'm fuckin' reminded but don't fuckin' say it."

"'Cause I don't say it, doesn't change it."

"I know that better than anyone. My father's a drug-addicted deadbeat. Don't even know where the fuck he is, if he's even alive, and my mother was a fuckin' drunk. Trailer trash like me has two options: join a gang and end up dead or go to the Army and make some money if I don't end up dead.

"It was the only way out for me, the only way I could look out for my drunk mother and sister. Still, it killed me 'cause me leaving didn't stop my mother from drinking to care for my sister. She ended knocked up at sixteen, and that's on me. Couldn't do anything else with my fuckin' check but put a down payment for a house and help raise my niece."

"Know the story, Trig. What I don't know is why you fuckin' betrayed me and the club, why you're fuckin' my sister."

His jaw locked and hurt. He'd been clenching it too hard. "You can be a fuckin' asshole when you wanna be, know that?"

Army took a step in his direction. "You're the one fuckin' my sister, been fuckin' my sister behind my back for more than a month. If that isn't an asshole, don't know who is."

"It isn't like that, and you fuckin' know it. You know I've had your back for seven years. You know the club's my family. You know I still got your back, same applies for our brothers."

Army took another step, coming inches from his face. "No, I don't 'cause you been fuckin' my sister. Not only she my sister, but she's off limits to the brothers. That includes you, Trig. Don't give a fuck you saved my ass in Afghan. It applies to you too, and you fuckin' knew it, and you still crossed the line. I didn't wanna believe it. Been ignoring the signs, but yesterday you proved it, jumping outta the fuckin' car like you had a rocket up your ass. And before, you'd always be searching the compound for her. Prayed the whole way here I was fuckin' wrong, but guess what? I was right."

Army was livid, practically foaming at the mouth, and now in his face. No one got in his face. Army knew him well, so he knew this. Like Army knew from his actions not half an hour ago he cared about Allie. Army just didn't know how much. It's what he wanted to know, and yet he couldn't come out and ask. He wanted to fuck with him.

He couldn't blame him. Like Army had known about him and Allie, he'd known Army was getting wise about it. Still, he hadn't been cautious. Maybe subconsciously he wanted them to get caught, to end the bullshit of seeing her around and not being able to hold her, kiss her, or talk to her.

He said what Army wanted to hear because it was the truth, because he owed it to him, and to the club. "You want me to say it. I'll fuckin' say it. She's outta my league and deserves better than trash like me, and still, it doesn't change the fact that when she looks at me with her heart in her eyes I wanna rob a bank to give her everything she deserves. It doesn't change the fact *she picked me*, and I sure as hell ain't gonna let her go if she wants to stay. I don't even think I *could* let her go if she wanted to leave."

"You expect me to believe she's different from a tap to you? You, who's never fucked the same woman twice? Oh, wait. My bad, you did. Lilliam, right? But she got too fuckin' attached, so you threw her out on her ass, and Dodge fucked her and knocked her up."

A low blow. A part of him couldn't understand why Army'd brought it up. He deserved Army's wrath, but Army had now crossed the line by comparing sweet, beautiful Allie to a manipulative bitch like Lilliam, and it infuriated him.

Lilliam, one of the club's taps, had a hell of a body. Whenever he wanted some, he'd gone to her. It had been just sex. They hadn't even slept in the same bed. The problem: she'd gotten ideas. She stopped fucking his brothers, then told the old ladies he would patch her. When he heard, he'd ended it, whatever she thought they had. That same night, she'd jumped in the sack with Dodge, another one of his brothers. Three months later, she announced she was two months pregnant in front of the club. Dodge had done the honorable thing and married her. That was three years ago, and Dodge was still living in hell. Besides showing up to their meetings and cookouts and doing runs, he was hardly ever at the garage. He had a toddler to care for because Lilliam was not only a manipulative bitch but a bad mother who still acted and dressed like a tap, hitting on the brothers to rile Dodge.

Allie wasn't a tap. Allie wasn't a manipulative bitch either. She was sweet, smart, and beautiful Allie. It wasn't just sex. It was real. She was his woman, and he treated her like gold.

He moved so quickly, Army didn't have time to dodge his blow. His fist connected with Army's lip, cracking it. "Compare that fuckin' cunt to my Allie one more time, I'm gonna wipe the floor with you."

Army straightened, wiping the blood dripping down his lip with the back of his hand.

"You fuckin' deserved that. You fuckin' know Lilliam was a tap trying to get more. You just fuckin' caught me and Allie sleeping together. Her head was on my chest, her hand on my stomach, and her legs were tangled in mine. I was holding her close, means even in my sleep I treat her like she's mine, so you know *I know* Allie's different."

"No, I fuckin' don't 'cause you been hiding her. I'm thinking she meant something to you, you would've come to me."

"And tell you what?" His brows drew together. "That the fuckin' moment I saw her I wanted her? That from one look her face was seared in my mind? Never in my fuckin' wildest dream thought I'd have a chance. She's fuckin' class, and I'm trash. Like it'd make a damned fuckin' difference. If you'd known, you would've kept her as far away from me as possible."

Army swung, his fist connected with his jaw. It hurt. He deserved it, so he didn't fight back. Tasting blood in his mouth, he spit and straightened.

"Pissing me off on fuckin' purpose," Army sniped. "I know what she wants. She wants a man who loves her. If I thought you could love her, I would've never kept her away."

"You think I don't?"

Army fisted his hands, gritting his teeth.

He knew why. Because he still hadn't said what he wanted to hear, that he loved Allie.

"I know you're a good man, but you're in this life, and this life isn't easy. You can still end up dead, and if you do, it'll kill her."

He lifted his chin. "Same goes for you."

Army flinched, actually flinched. Army, like him, was hard-as-nails, carved from the same cloth—the United States Army, and men like them didn't react, not unless it was big. Trig had struck a nerve. He couldn't understand why. It was obvious to anyone who cared to look Allie adored her brother.

"It's different."

He shook his head. "It isn't. Your father's a dick. She always knew that deep down 'cause of what he did to you. Your mother was a pushover. Apparently the only thing she ever did for Allie was give her those letters you sent. You've been the only constant in her life, the only one who gives a shit enough to value her,

her choices, her opinion. That means *everything* to her."
All of this he knew. Allie told him. She told him
everything, and he listened.

He shook his head. "If something happens to you,
she'll never be the same. Ever."

Eyes flaring, finally, Army asked what he wanted
to. "Do you love her?"

He hesitated, shifting his weight from one foot to
the other yet never losing sight of his eyes.

"Simple question, Trig. You love her?"

"You know the answer, Army. You know I'd never
fuckin' betray you or the club. If I didn't love her, I
wouldn't have kissed her back when she kissed me, and
I sure as hell wouldn't have let it go further. Would've
stopped it." He sighed heavily, ran a hand through his
hair. "It's more than love, I fuckin' need her."

Army didn't move, not a muscle.

"Never been content in my life. I love Tina and
Della, and I lived for both of them, but I never felt
this…happy."

Army looked away from him. After a moment, he
met his stare again. "Why'd you hesitate when I asked
if you loved her?"

"Wanted to tell her first."

"If you love her, why hide her?"

"We were gonna tell you today. Her decision. Tell
you the truth, I wanted to wait, give her more time to
decide if I'm what she really wants 'cause not three
months ago, she was engaged to a dick. I don't know if
'cause of that dick she thinks she can't do better than
me. Don't know if I'm what she needs. I wanted to
wait, but it don't mean shit. I know how I feel 'cause I
feel it, been feeling it for a while, and I know she's

what I need. She's all I'll ever need."

He'd wanted to wait for more than that, too. Once they were public, she'd know more about the club, about club life. Club life wasn't for everyone. It could be a good life, but it could be rough. Showing her that life was a risk. She could reject it, reject him.

Army's unblinking eyes held his for a long moment, not saying anything, not moving either. Then his body loosened. "Don't rob a bank. You'll go to prison for nothing 'cause she left that life, brother, doesn't want it. Another piece of advice, tell her how you feel 'cause she doesn't know."

"She knows—"

Army shook his head. "She doesn't. She knows you care, but she thinks she cares more."

What the fuck? How could she possibly think that?

"Know what you're thinking. I know Allie. She's beautiful, but she doesn't know it. She's insecure probably 'cause she grew up with my dick of a father who never let her choose. Probably, too, 'cause she's been cheated on and beat."

He nodded, then he smiled. Army approved.

Chapter Twenty-Nine

Despite her shattered nerves and rambling brain, Allie found a pair of shorts and a top, dressed, then sat on her bed and waited impatiently for her brother and Jace to have their talk. She wanted to walk into her living room and press her ear against the door, but it'd probably just get her more worked up, and she couldn't handle that. A part of her, the part of her who knew they needed to have their man-to-man talk stopped her. She forced herself to sit still, staring blankly at her white wall, and wait.

When the front door opened, she bolted off her bed into the living room. There, she spotted Jace walking in, shirtless, in the pair of jeans he'd forgotten to buckle. Her breaths quickened. She ignored the desire that sparked and forced her eyes away from his chest to his face, zoning in on a red mark on his jaw. Her gaze darted to her brother and his broken lip. They'd both gotten their shots in, probably explained why they both seemed relaxed. A good sign, but she couldn't help feel peeved.

"You hit him?"

Ty's brows furrowed. Immediately, he shot back, "He hit me first."

Her jaw dropped. Really? Ty wouldn't lie, especially not when Jace stood right there and could easily deny the claim. Why would Jace hit Ty? If anything, her brother would've struck first. He'd been the one who'd caught them in bed and realized they'd been lying.

Her gaze snapped to Jace. "You hit him *first*?"

Jace crossed his arms over his chest. "He deserved it."

She didn't understand that either. What had Ty done to deserve a punch? She didn't know who she was more irritated with: Jace for hitting her brother or Ty for breaking his promise.

Narrowing her eyes at Jace, she then snapped them to Ty. "You promised."

He tilted his head. "Never said what I was promising."

Her eyes widened. Another thing she couldn't believe. "Care to inform me what you were promising?"

"That I wouldn't shoot him."

Her cheeks flamed. She took a deep breath, schooling her anger. Her brother knew what she'd meant when she'd asked him to promise. Neither seemed in the least bit sorry for what he'd done. It seemed they couldn't care less what she had to say about it.

She'd let them have their man-to-man talk, alone. She'd given them privacy thinking they'd respect the fact she was in the middle and didn't want them fighting, yet they'd both taken their shots to prove who knows what without considering her.

Not in the mood to deal with either of them, she turned on her heel, marched into her room, and locked the door behind her. Immature and childish, but at the moment, she didn't care.

"Allie?" Ty called her from the other side of the door. "Come out. I'm hungry."

Oh, the freaking gall of her brother. The heat on her cheeks crept down her neck.

"And we gotta get you moved out by three 'cause Trig and I gotta meet with the club."

"I'm not making you anything to eat, Ty. I'm not moving. I'm staying right here, far away from both of you."

"Alyssa, do not make me knock down this fuckin' door."

Damn. He would knock down her door. Typical Ty style—not because she was being immature but because he knew she'd taken that step, alienating herself from them, which meant she wasn't okay. Ty, being her brother, needed to make sure she was okay and would use breakfast as an excuse even if he knew that particular excuse would infuriate her.

Jace sighed, and then he asked softly, "Allie, baby, come on out, so we can talk."

"Alyssa." Ty's voice firm. "Open the..." His voice drifted off when he let out a huff. "Fuck, Trig."

"Let me fuckin' handle her." Jace's voice hardened.

Jace, the Jace she'd come to love, sweet Jace who never let her go to bed angry or let her "get in her head." Still, he hit her brother first, and she didn't know why, so she shot back, "I don't need any handling, Jace. What I need is to be left alone."

"Oh, way to go," Ty shot back, sarcastically. "Now, we'll fuckin' starve—"

"She isn't your fuckin' chef."

She rolled her eyes, and then fought a smile. They

may be bikers, who could act like children, but they were bikers she loved who cared about her. Wyatt being Wyatt would've let her stew. She heaved a frustrated sigh, parted the door, and met their gazes. "I'm not very happy with either of you."

Ty's eyes widened. "He hit me first, and I didn't shoot him."

She bit the sides of her mouth, so she wouldn't laugh like she wanted to. "You broke your promise and hurt Jace." Her gaze snapped to Jace. "And you hit my brother."

"He deserved it."

She rubbed her temples, thinking she'd never change their minds. She made a mature decision and let it go. They blocked her way out. "Are you going to let me through?"

Jace and Ty made way for her. She walked by them, intent on ignoring them, and headed into the kitchen. Once there, she searched for a bowl and the ingredients to make pancakes for breakfast. She organized them on the counter, her back to Jace and Ty who'd followed her into the kitchen, and then, she mixed the batter.

Mid-way done, she felt the warmth of Jace's arms around her waist. Startled, she jumped. He tugged her, pressing up against her back. Dropping his head, his breath at her neck, he kissed her below her ear.

She loved when he did that. He did it often enough, whenever she was too wound up, and it always had the desired effect. Sighing, she relaxed in his arms.

"Everything's good between me and Army, baby. He hit me. I hit him. We're even, and it's forgotten. We'll move you into my room at the compound, and then we'll tell the club, 'kay?"

Her man and her brother were good. She would move into the compound with Jace. They wouldn't have to hide, not anymore. It'd be like when Ty was away, but better.

She smiled. "Okay."

He feathered another kiss under her ear. "You making my favorite?"

She glanced at the chocolate chips on the counter and realized without thought, she had been. "Yeah, honey."

He tightened his arms around her. His hand gripped her chin, turning her head toward his, and he pressed a soft kiss to her lips.

She loved it when he did that, too. He kissed her lightly often, just because.

Jace drew away from her lips slowly. Smiling, he ran his thumb over her lips. "Thank you, baby."

She caught her brother's gaze dead on them. "What?"

Ty smiled, then mumbled, "Nothing."

****

Trig entered the meeting room and scanned the faces of his brothers. Some stood, some leaning against the walls or on the backs of the chairs.

He took a deep breath, steeling himself for what he'd hear. The meeting was about Allie, *his* Allie. He had Army's approval. He wouldn't lose his friend, his brothers, or the club, and Allie was his—the best possible outcome, but it didn't change the fact Allie was in trouble. Her ex-fiancé wasn't letting go.

He'd been terrified he'd lose her. He'd lived with that deep-seated fear for a month. Every morning he'd woken thinking that could be the day she realized he was trash and ended what they had. And the fear, despite the sleepless nights, was heaven compared to knowing her ex was fighting back.

Her ex was a man with money, with resources, and men like that usually got what they wanted. It meant his Allie's ex could possibly find a way to get her back, and the ex wouldn't go without punishing her. A man who beat a woman, who took out his frustrations on her would, and it meant for every punch Trig'd gotten in, Allie would get twice. He couldn't let that happen.

After she'd made them breakfast, they packed as much of her stuff as possible into their SUVs. Two of the prospects drove a truck to Allie's where they'd loaded the large pieces of furniture: her bed, couch, and dining room table. They unloaded it at the compound, placing her furniture in one of the empty rooms downstairs and her clothes, purses, and shoes into his room. It took about three hours. In reality, Allie didn't have much. Her apartment was small and didn't take much to fill it. What took the longest: packing her clothes and undergarments, and she insisted on doing it herself.

"Allie okay?" Cuss asked Army.

"Yeah, moved her in."

Cuss smiled. "Yeah, noticed. Noticed where her stuff was moved to, too."

Army didn't get the chance to respond. Prez cut him off.

"Need to discuss couple of things. First, Allie." He leaned both hands against the table. His stare dead on Army. "Her tires were slashed yesterday outside her work. She got a note on her car two weeks ago, and a rock was thrown at her window more than a month ago. We voted to protect her when her dick fiancé hit her in broad daylight. Some of you weren't here, but we had majority. She's Army's sister, but this—"

"She's mine. She's protected."

All gazes focused on him. He kept his on Prez, who straightened and quirked a brow. Prez's gaze then darted to Army.

"Lucky son of a bitch," Blaze muttered under his breath.

Bud ran his fingers through his hair. "Guess it makes sense."

His gaze snapped to Bud.

Bud grinned. "Been in too good a mood, figured something had to be goin' on."

"You patchin' her?" Wild asked.

If he had it his way, he would do more than patch her. He'd tattoo his name on her. He'd put a ring on her finger and marry her, but he wouldn't say it aloud. "I said she's mine, means I'm patchin' her."

Trick grinned. "Thought she was off limits. I'd have known, I'd've put on the charm."

Trig's muscles tensed. Eyes hard, he took a step in Trick's direction.

Army put his hand over his chest, stopping him. "Wouldn't have mattered, Trick."

Trick's eyes on him, he laughed. "Fuck, brother. Just messin' with you."

"Guess that answers whether you'd given approval," Rake told Army.

Shaking his head, Mellow, another one of his brothers, chuckled. "Never thought I'd see the fuckin' day. Trig with an old lady, and they say miracles don't happen."

"Wait, you patchin' her after knowing her three months? You fuckin' crazy, brother?" Hash, a typical comment from him. He liked women, lots of women, and enjoyed them together, two or three at a time. "I mean, fuck, three months?"

Dash's eyes glimmered. "I'd patch her in two. She's fuckin' hot."

They were doing this shit on purpose, trying to see how far they could push before Trig lost it, so he knew he should ignore them. They were wasting time, time better spent on planning what to do about Allie's ex. Because it was Allie though, he couldn't let it slide.

He launched himself at Dash, slammed him hard against the wall. "Didn't you hear me say she's fuckin' mine? Means you don't fuckin' say fucked shit, means you don't even think fucked shit unless you want me to gut you."

Dash, unfazed, lifted his arms in surrender, then smirked. "Got it, brother."

He shoved him hard against the wall, then released him.

"Gotta keep a closer eye on her." Army cut to the chase.

He turned, facing Army. "I'm hiring a PI." After Allie fell asleep last night, he'd stayed up and thought about their predicament. He came to the conclusion a man like Wyatt had to have skeletons in his closet, bad ones that, if uncovered, would tarnish his reputation and his family's. With luck, a PI could uncover it, and then they could use it as blackmail.

"The guy's got money and loads of it. What makes you think you'd find anything?" Strike asked.

"'Cause he's got money is why I think it's what's best. Everyone has skeletons. He's got money means he can hide those better than anyone. I know we hire the right guy, he'll find something. Besides, a man who hits a woman…" His jaw hardened. He shook his head. "He's probably done it before, and he'll do it again. Find them and it could be that easy."

"Doug," Army said.

Trig thought the same thing. Doug was a vet like them. After his fourth tour, he'd become a PI. Trig hadn't spoken to him for about a year, but Doug was good at his job. He'd hired him to find Della's father two years ago. Few days later, Doug called and told him where to find him. He'd paid him a visit.

"It's gonna be pricey," Cuss said.

He knew it would. Allie's ex had money and lived in New York in a fancy apartment with a doorman and security. Doug had to fly out to New York to do the job. Even knowing Doug, it would be expensive. He had some in his savings. Trig would take several guard jobs to make the money. Whatever it took. Most important thing was Allie's safety.

"Don't care how much it costs. I'm doing it."

Cuss patted his back. "We back you no matter what, brother."

He knew it. He didn't need to hear it, but hearing it helped. Truth be told, he was fucking terrified Wyatt would get his hands on Allie. He still didn't know how he'd managed to do what he had. He assumed her ex had hired someone or several to do his dirty work.

He glanced at Cuss, and then he scanned the room, meeting his brothers' gazes. He nodded.

"All right then, two brothers on Allie at all times."

Prez met his gaze. "Tell her. Make sure she doesn't try to ditch 'em."

"She wouldn't—" Army began.

Prez shrugged. "You wouldn't like having anyone watching your every fuckin' move."

He and Army exchanged a look.

"Now…" Prez's tone lowered. "Got a call from Chip…"

The tension in the room heightened so much so it was palpable, and the quiet deadening. Chip was the president of the rival motorcycle club, Chained Disciples, though Chained Disciples MC was more like a gang than a club. Biker nomads who went where the wind took them, they had to be that way because they were heavily involved in criminal activity.

Chained MC and Hell Ryders hadn't always been at odds. Before Prez took over the club and ended the club's involvement in criminal activity, they'd worked together. It presented a problem. Chained MC wanted to continue running guns and drugs through their town.

Despite Prez's request they run their business elsewhere, they hadn't, forcing the brothers to post up around town. It ended one night in an all-out brawl, and the clubs had severed ties for good. He'd been a prospect then, so he hadn't known the details until months later when he'd been patched. Last the club heard, Chained MC had taken off to Nevada.

Still, Chained wanting payback was not far-fetched. It had been five years, but there was no time limit on revenge. Chained was a threat and treated as such. They were one of the reasons they had "runs," posting up around town at night, making sure they kept their eyes and ears open.

"What the fuck does that dick want?" Ripper, face flaming, asked, his tone deadly.

Trig knew Ripper would be the first to speak. They all knew. For Ripper, this was more than club business. It was personal. Chip's cousin, Emelia, had been Ripper's old lady for two years. When shit hit the fan with the clubs, she took off. No one knew where she'd gone, not even Chip. A week after the brawl that ended their ties, Chip rode up to the garage alone, found Ripper sitting astride his bike out front, and beat the living daylights out of him. Ripper let him. It wasn't until several of the brothers dragged Chip away, Chip explained Emelia wasn't answering any of his calls. Ripper admitted she'd packed her stuff and left three days before. None of the brothers had known. It made perfect sense, too. None of the brothers had seen him for that long.

Ripper had never been the same. He'd always been a dick, but after Emelia, something in him died. They all knew it. Just no one ever spoke of it.

Trig never understood it, had never been able to wrap his mind around how a woman could change a man. Ripper loved Emelia. It was clear as day every time he saw them together, but he'd never known what it was to love like that. Now, he knew. Because of Allie. He loved her, and if he lost her, something inside him would die too.

"Wants to talk. Says it's important."

"Bull-fuckin'-shit!" Ripper raged. "I don't want anything to fuckin' do with them."

Fuck. He still loved her.

"It's for the club to decide," Prez said. "Know you got a history with—"

"It ain't about that shit."

"Just proved it was."

Clenching his jaw tight, Ripper took a step in Prez's direction. Pound, standing next to him, tensed. Before he could react, Ripper snarled, "Fuck you."

"It's a club matter, and we vote. Don't know what he has to say. I'm thinking that club's still dirty. We aren't. Means they won't be welcome in our town, but think we can agree we should hear what he has to say."

"I don't fuckin' agree."

"Think about it." Prez scanned the room. "We'll vote Friday."

Ripper closed the distance between himself and Prez, snaring his attention. "Don't matter if you give me five fuckin' decades. Ain't gonna change my mind."

Prez's eyes narrowed. "It isn't about you. It's about the club."

Chapter Thirty

Allie, standing by the refrigerator filling a glass with water, turned when Lynn called her.

Lynn smiled widely. "Wasn't expecting to see you here."

She took a sip of water, and then placed the glass on the counter. "Moved in."

"What?" Mia asked, peering into the kitchen.

She smiled wider. Mia closed the distance between them.

Pausing, she blurted, "Ty knows."

Mia's jaw dropped. Lynn gasped loudly. "Wait, wait…you told him?"

She shook her head, her face reddening with the memory. "We were going to today, but…He showed up at my apartment early this morning, and…Jace was there…in my room…in bed…with me…We weren't dressed."

"Oh my God!" Mia screeched.

"I can't believe it."

She shrugged. "Yeah."

"So, wait, that means you've moved in?"

She shook her head. "Well, no, the thing is my tires were slashed yesterday. Ty said I had to move back in, so he can keep an eye on me, but then he caught Jace and me. So now, I've moved into Jace's room."

Lynn's eyes widened, smiling, then rushed her,

305

wrapping her arms around her shoulders, hugging her. "I'm so happy for you guys!"

She released her, and then Mia hugged her. "Me, too."

"Don't get too excited." She was living with Jace, but it was temporary. Jace hadn't asked her to move in. The club was protecting her and moving into Jace's room just made more sense. After this was over, who knew?

Mia's brow quirked, "Why?"

"This is temporary because of the tires and—"

"Please tell me you don't believe that." Lynn smirked. "It's Trig. He's never—"

"Don't get her hopes up. We all know Jace."

Mia and Lynn turned, letting Allie get her first glimpse. A woman she'd never seen before, tall, at least 5'8, wearing a denim mini skirt, a cleavage-baring red shirt, and five-inch heels. Blonde hair cascaded down her shoulders past her breasts. Her steely, narrowed, gray eyes pinned Allie on the spot. Attractive, no doubt about it. She could be beautiful if she didn't have makeup caked on and if she'd left some of her best assets to the imagination. It hinted she was a tap, and yet, Allie knew she wasn't. Taps didn't talk to the old ladies. Taps didn't walk around the compound with free rein, not on a Saturday afternoon, not ever.

The woman strutted to her, her gray gaze never leaving hers. "Jace will say and do all the right things, but then he leaves. He always leaves, so don't get attached."

Her heart dropped to the pit of her stomach.

The blonde wasn't a tap. She'd once been with Jace, and he dumped her. She couldn't help but wonder if she'd once ridden on the back of his bike, if he'd told her he would make her his old lady like he'd told her. She hated doubting Jace. She loved him, but she couldn't help it when doubt stared her in the face.

"That's not true, Lilliam," Mia sniped, her tone harsh.

Lilliam narrowed her gaze on Mia. "Really? When has Jace ever been serious about a woman?"

Further proof, Lilliam called him Jace again. Every time, she wanted to cringe. It proved they'd once been something, and the knowledge of Jace with another woman made her stomach turn. It shouldn't. He was a man, who'd once been single and wasn't a saint.

"It's not the point—" Mia began.

"Oh, I think it is." A mean glint in her eyes, Lilliam flipped her hair behind her and set her steely gaze on Allie. "Jace doesn't stay. Jace doesn't make anyone *his* old lady. He makes them think he is, and then he throws them out on their ass."

"Allie isn't you," Mia shot back. "Trig—"

Lilliam wasn't paying attention to Mia. She was smiling widely, her eyes on her. "Jace fucked me every night for three months straight, then left. I know he likes blondes with bods. I don't want to be mean. I'm just trying to warn you. You aren't his type. I give it a month tops."

God, that hurt. A searing ache in her chest like she'd been burned from the inside out, and that pain spread through her limbs and up her throat.

Like that morning, she wanted to deny it, wanted to believe Jace would never do that to her, but the pain burning her throat wouldn't let her. A pain clear in her face because she couldn't fight it or hide it.

Lilliam got too much pleasure telling her this and watching her crumble. Allie could see behind the mean glint in Lilliam's eyes, she was laughing, loud. Lilliam was the worst kind of person, the kind who got off on hurting people. For that reason too, Allie wanted to tell her where to shove it, but the pain hadn't numbed, it compounded with anger, and only made it harder to keep her emotions in check. If she stayed any longer she'd cry, and no way in hell she'd let Lilliam see her cry.

Without word, she lifted her chin and sidestepped to pass her. Mia jumped to her defense raging at Lilliam. Lynn called out to her, but she kept walking. Her chin down, she strode out of the kitchen and into the hall, not paying attention like she should've. Next thing she knew, she walked into a mass of muscle. The familiar scent of him wafted into her senses.

"What... Allie?"

She didn't look at him. She couldn't. A fresh wave of tears hit her eyes. She had to hold them back.

"Allie?" Jace stilled. He lifted her chin with his finger until her gaze met his.

God, he was handsome. If he left her, she'd still think he was a mistake worth making. Her eyes on his, she watched in sheer fascination as those dark eyes turned cold, his jaw clenching so tight she wondered how it didn't crack.

He grabbed her wrist and hauled her, backtracking her steps. She realized too late where he was taking her. When she did, she resisted, pulling herself in the other direction. He stopped and turned. His rage-filled gaze hit her, and then he leaned into her. His face inches from hers. "Not fuckin' happy, Allie. You don't wanna fight me when I'm this pissed." He dragged her into the kitchen.

She caught glimpse of Lilliam's back and Mia, livid in a totally cute way only Mia could pull off. Mia's gaze shot to Jace then to hers and softened, and then she moved away from Lilliam.

"You're a fuckin' cunt."

Lilliam spun. Still, she didn't wipe the smirk off her face. Instead, she jutted her chest forward, stepped closer. "Hi, Jace."

He tightened his hold on Allie's wrist, yanked her to his side until her front was plastered against him. He then wrapped his arm around her shoulders, gripping her tightly. She loved it when he held her, always, but right then, he was so angry she couldn't help but be a little worried.

"No one calls me Jace. No one's ever called me Jace. No one but Allie 'cause she's my woman. You were never my woman."

A warmth settled in her gut.

"You were a tap, a conniving cunt, who thought she could manipulate me."

Lilliam took a step in his direction. "You can't deny we were more than—"

"Back the fuck away from me and my woman," he screamed so loud his whole body shook. His voice seeped in rage. "You were and still are a tap. That's all you've ever been, all you'll ever fuckin' be. I fucked you 'cause you were easy pussy, and I'll regret it every day of my life 'cause you're a manipulative bitch. Further prove my point, you never rode on the back of my bike. You never slept in my bed. You never met my niece, my sister. I never ate your pussy, never took you out, and I never showed you my house."

A relief to hear, but it came with guilt for so easily believing everything Lilliam said.

Lilliam flinched.

"It was three fuckin' years ago. Let it the fuck go. You fucked my brother the night I heard you were getting ideas and broke off whatever it is you thought we had. You got knocked up, and married my brother, and you still fuckin' dress and act like a fuckin' tap. You're still a fuckin' manipulative cunt."

Lilliam's eyes widened. "Trig." Her voice hollow.

"This is the last time you'll ever see me or my woman and the last time you fuck with me or my woman. You aren't welcome here. You haven't been welcome here for a long fuckin' time. Nobody's fault but your own. You dug your own fuckin' grave. Now, by fuckin' with my woman, you've nailed your coffin 'cause everybody loves Allie 'cause she fuckin' sweet, smart, and beautiful."

Did that mean he loved her, too? The warmth in her gut spread to her chest and limbs.

With those last words, he turned, taking her with him. Oh God, they had an audience. Ty stood at the threshold, his jaw clenched and arms crossed over his chest. Beside him was Cuss giving Lilliam the coldest look. Behind them, a mass of bikers; none looked happy.

Shoving his brothers to get to the front of the mass, Dodge appeared. He scanned the room. His face went feral. "Where the fuck is my kid?"

It hit her then. Dodge was the brother who'd married Lilliam, and Lilliam was Cullen's mother. Dodge had a two-year-old son, Cullen. She'd seen them together at the cookouts. Cullen also attended the daycare where she worked. Dodge dropped him off and picked him up. She had never met Cullen's mother and had assumed Dodge was a single father. That Cullen had a mother came as a shock.

"I don't know. *You* should be concerned with what Trig said to me," Lilliam snapped, proving she was not only a bitch but a bad mother and crazy.

Dodge turned away from her, a frantic look in his eyes. "Cullen!"

"I got him," Lynn shouted over the throes of bikers.

Dodge looked down, took a deep breath, and finally met Lilliam's gaze. "We're over. You got till tonight to get your shit out of my house."

"You can't—"

"We're fuckin' done. Tomorrow, I'll have my lawyer draw the papers. Cullen's mine. Don't even think about fightin' for him 'cause you're a shitty mother, and I can prove it."

That was all she heard before Jace grabbed her wrist and hauled her through the mass of bikers. He dragged her down the hall, up the stairs, and into his room. He then closed the door and faced her.

She swallowed, knowing the angry look. Taking deep breaths, he tried to fight it. Lilliam had really pissed him off, and it hadn't yet abated.

Jace took a step in her direction. He went to take another, then stilled like he thought better of it. "You ever listen to me?"

Oh God, he was angry with her? Why? And where was he getting at with this question?

"Allie." His voice hard. "Answer the fuckin'

question."

"Yes," she said, instantly.

He shook his head. "No, you don't. Maybe you hear me, but you don't fuckin' listen."

She swallowed.

"It's that or you hear whatever the fuck you wanna listen for."

"I don't understand…"

His stare hardened. "Don't you think there's a reason why I'm so pissed?"

She really wanted him to get to the point. She hated when he was angry, hated it more when it was directed at her. Worse, when she didn't even know the reason.

Still, she answered the question. Not answering it would make him angrier. "Yeah."

"Why am I angry, Allie?"

Really? She obviously didn't know. "I don't know."

He took another step in her direction and leaned into her. "You fuckin' believed everything she said 'cause you don't fuckin' listen to me."

A valid point. Guilt flooding her, she bit the side of her lip. Still, she defended herself. "I listened. I heard what she said."

The wrong thing to say. The corded veins on his neck clamped.

"Proving my point, Allie. Never said you didn't listen. Said you don't listen to *me*."

"I'm sorry…I—"

"You remember when I told you I wouldn't mind having you in my bed every night? It was the first night, Allie, the first fuckin' night. Remember when I told you, you're mine and that's why I handle shit for you?

Six days in. Remember when I told you I'd never be done with you? That was seven days in. You remember last night on your couch I was lying over you and I fuckin' told you I needed you, that if it were up to me I'd patch you in a fuckin' second?"

Shit. He'd said it all, and still, she'd so easily doubted him. Why? Her mind scrambled for the answer. She couldn't grasp it.

"It isn't just about words, Allie. Everything I do proves it. I called you four fuckin' times, then showed up at a bar knowing you were there, knowing you were ignoring me. I gave you my cut to wrap around your waist 'cause the thought of someone seeing a piece of you makes me wanna rip out their fuckin' eyes. You weren't mine then, but I wanted you to be, so I put you on the back of my bike. I fuckin' *claimed* you. Do you understand the significance of that?"

Shit. He'd done it all, and pointing it out made her feel worse. She did understand the significance of it. Mia told her, and still, she'd doubted him. She remembered everything he'd ever told her and everything he'd done to show her, but doubt *always* reared its head. She didn't understand why, but she understood every time she doubted him, she hurt him.

She did the only thing she could do. She nodded.

"You're the only woman I've ever fuckin' cuddled with, the only woman I've slept beside, and the only woman I call and text fifty times a fuckin' day 'cause I can't help it. I've never had a steady woman. You're the only one, the only woman I've ever made *mine*."

It hit her, the magnitude of what an absolute, insecure nitwit she was. She'd known it for a while, but she hadn't known how deep that insecurity went. He made it clear it went beyond her skin. It was deeply ingrained in her heart, body, and soul.

"I-I'm sorry, Jace." Her voice cracked. "I know...I..."

"I'm not him, Allie. I'm not any of them."

Her heart clenched. Her eyes watered. God, he was so right. It was about them, about Wyatt whom she'd never been enough for. He had to go elsewhere, several elsewheres. Primarily though, it was about her dad. She'd never been good enough either, in the worst possible way. She hadn't been good enough to make her own decisions. Her father didn't trust her. He didn't love her. How crappy a person are you when your own parent can't love you?

His eyes darkened. The next moment, he held her close, his arms around her back, his chin resting on the top of her head. "You're fuckin' beautiful, Allie, so beautiful, it's hard to stop lookin' at you."

With his body still pressed against hers, he cupped her cheeks and angled her face to his. "You're smart and sweet as fuckin' sugar, too, but you don't know it, and that, baby, terrifies me."

Her eyes widened.

"One day you'll realize it, and I don't know if you'll want me then."

"I..."

He pressed his lips to hers, softly, and then he met her stare. "I love you, Allie."

The air rushed out of her. She couldn't do anything but stare blankly at him, his declaration replaying in her mind.

She must've stood there for a while not saying or doing anything. His eyes changed, an ache glimmered in the darkness despite the beauty he'd just handed her.

With tears spilling down her cheeks, she finally smiled. "I love you too, Jace. It took me just a week to realize it."

Jace smiled. "One look, Allie, and you'd snared me." He hauled her against him for a kiss that turned into much more.

Chapter Thirty-One

Parting the door to his room at the compound, then shutting it behind him, Trig scanned the room. "Baby?"

"Yeah, honey."

He strode toward his bathroom, and found her with a towel wrapped around her, her hair in a messy knot at the top of her head.

Her gaze darted to him. She closed the distance between them and got on the tips of her toes to give him a kiss. He compiled, leaning down, wrapping his arms around her waist, and pressing his lips to hers.

Still close, she asked, "How was your day?"

His day was shit. He'd gotten a call from Doug, his Army buddy and PI, who'd informed him he'd gotten nowhere. Wyatt was not only filthy rich, but smart because somehow he managed to hide anything linking him to Allie's misfortunes. Wyatt was in New York. It meant he'd hired someone to slash Allie's tires, leave the note on her car, and throw rocks on her window. The problem: Doug searched Wyatt's bank accounts and found no large withdrawals of money to do the jobs. Covering all his bases, Doug had one of his men in New York watching Wyatt's every move. This frustrated Trig. He'd figured over a week in, Doug would've found something, anything. He was that good. The fact Doug hadn't made him feel helpless.

Still, right then and there, standing close to Allie,

he couldn't find the strength to tell her his day had been a disappointment. She was in his room at the compound, smiling at him, looking like a million bucks even with her hair a mess, and she was safe. He'd known all day his day would end with her. He knew she'd be waiting for him, greeting him with the same words, giving him a kiss, so his day was fucking amazing.

"Cuss brought you home today?"

"And Ty."

He nodded. Since the tire slashing incident, it's what they'd agreed on, two brothers on Allie at all times. She took the news easily. He'd tried to be one of the two, but sometimes, he couldn't. Days like today when he'd had to pick up Della at school since Tina had to work late, someone else, usually Cuss or Blaze, volunteered.

"How was your day?" he asked, belatedly.

She smiled. "Can't get in too much trouble at a daycare center…Want me to make you dinner? I was going to make—"

"Got a run tonight, Allie."

Her eyes rounded. Looking away from him, she nodded softly.

He expected it. She always did that when he told her he was going on a run. Though it had been ten days since they'd become public, he still hadn't told her exactly what they did. Knowing she wouldn't like it, a part of him didn't want to tell her. Another part of him hoped if he told her she wouldn't worry as much, so he'd never again have to see that look on her face. Truth was he didn't want secrets between them. He couldn't tell her everything about the club, but he could tell her more than she knew.

"Get dressed. We should talk."

He sat on the edge of his bed. She headed into the closet. A moment later, she reappeared wearing a pair of hip-hugging shorts and fitted T-shirt. He motioned for her to come closer, then wound his arm around her waist and settled her on his lap. Her hip pressed against his stomach.

"Gotta talk about the club. What I do."

She nodded.

"You know about our runs, but you don't know what they are. To tell you that, I first need to explain. The club wasn't always what it is now. Before Army and I were prospects, the club was heavily involved in running drugs and guns. After a while, it led to bad shit coming to Wadden. There was violence, a lot of it, and it was escalating."

He paused, waiting for a reaction. "Club voted. They decided they didn't need to do that shit anymore 'cause the garage was making good money."

"But Ty told me some of the stuff is not legal," she said, softly.

"Not completely."

She sighed heavily. "Either it is legal or it's not, Jace."

He ran his fingers over her lips. "Not everything's black or white."

She held his stare.

"Six years ago, club voted. It took a while, about a year, but club got free of it. It took work to get the gangs, dealers, and prostitutes out. It's what we do. Make sure they're off our streets, make sure no one with a vendetta comes back. It's easy most nights 'cause like I said, it's been a while."

Her eyes widened.

"'Sides that, we take side jobs. We call them 'guards.' Protecting people, we get good money. Sometimes it takes us outta town. It isn't entirely legal either 'cause sometimes we get paid to rough someone up or—"

"Who?"

"People who deserve it."

"How do you know—"

"Make sure of it."

Her mouth parted then closed. "Do you get paid to kill people, too?"

Fuck. This was a mistake. They didn't get paid for hits, but he had killed before, so it was a big mistake, one he couldn't take back. All he could do was explain and pray for the best. He hesitated, mulling words over in his head.

It was long enough she pulled away from him. Her eyes wide and pained, she whispered, "You do."

He gripped her hips, holding her still. "Allie, club doesn't get paid for hits. We do *not* kill people. We do rough them up, but you do realize I was in the Army and served three tours overseas, right? I've killed. I'm not proud of killing, but I'm proud I served my country."

Relaxing in his arms, she let out a small breath. "That's different."

His eyes hardened. "Killing is killing."

She shook her head. "It's survival."

"I was a sniper. It wasn't survival. It was killing." He didn't know why he said that. Had he been thinking clearly, he wouldn't have. It would serve only to push her away. Deep down though, he'd done it because he wanted her to know all of him. If she left, better now than later. It'd hurt still, but it'd hurt less than spending years with her and having to let her go.

"It's war. It was for your country."

Fuck. She wasn't stupid. She was smart, sweet, beautiful Allie, and yet, she so easily and quickly justified that he'd killed.

She did love him. She loved him for the good and the bad.

Maybe as much as he loved her.

He meant to tell her, then show her how much, but his heart clenched painfully. It felt like it was bursting, like he loved her too much and all that love didn't fit.

She looked away from him then met his gaze. "Are you supposed to be telling me this stuff?"

Worried about him. His Allie. He blinked, then swallowed past the lump in his throat. "Not telling you any club secrets. You're mine, you should know."

"Why didn't Ty tell me?"

"'Cause you're not his old lady. You're mine. I tell you. Don't know how much the others tell their old ladies, Allie, but I'm gonna tell you as much as I can, so you don't worry too much."

She smiled a soft smile then lifted a brow. "You think telling me this won't make me worry?"

"I'd hoped it put you at ease. Was I wrong?"

She smiled. "I'll still worry, but you're right. Knowing is better. You can't imagine what I've considered."

He grinned. "Care to share?"

She shrugged. "Drugs, prostitution, human trafficking…"

"Creative."

He stared at her for a long time. "Gotta present for you. Know what it is, baby?"

She shook her head.

Trig ordered it days ago, picked it up yesterday, and had it wrapped. He hid it, waiting for the perfect time to give it to her. He nodded toward his dresser. "Open the top drawer."

Smiling, she stood and opened the top drawer. She pulled out a wrapped box, then headed back to him, and settled on his lap. Her head down, eyes on her gift.

He wrapped his arm around her waist, tucked her against him, leaned into her, and whispered against her ear, "Baby, you gonna open it?"

She tore her gaze away from the box to look at him.

"What're you waiting for?

She smiled and began tearing the wrapping paper. His eyes on her face the entire time because he wanted to see the look on her face. Finally, she opened the box, and shifted through the tissue paper. Her face softened. She pulled the leather cut from the box, clutched it to her chest, and dropped her head. A tear slid out of her eye.

He cupped her cheeks, pulling her face to his. "Thought you be smiling, baby, not crying."

She kissed him softly. "Happy tears. Thank you." She hopped off his lap and put on the cut. With her back facing him, he could see the Hell Ryders insignia and read the inscription: "Hell Ryders, Property of Trig."

"Look beautiful, Allie. Always."

She turned, closed the distance between them, and

sat on his lap. Burying her face in his neck, she wrapped her arms around him. "I'm yours."

His hand at her hip trailed up her back. When he heard those words, his fingers gripped her.

All he could do was agree.

"Yeah, baby, you're mine."

****

Allie fell asleep without him. It happened two to three times a week, always when he was on a run or on club business.

She hated it because she loved cuddling up next to him, loved falling asleep with her head on his chest, listening to his heartbeat. The sound lulled her, making it easy for her to drift. She'd gone without last night. Every morning when she woke, he'd be in bed with her. He'd wake her kissing her lips, her chest, her neck, so every night she went to bed without him, she reminded herself the reward would be waking with him.

But he wasn't in bed. The alarm had been raging for a full ten minutes. She threw the covers off her, silenced the alarm, and scanned the room. Pulling on a robe, she tied it at her waist, grabbed her phone, and dialed his number. Her heart beating rapidly, her throat went dry, and then his voice message came on.

Fear choking her, she darted out of her room and knocked on Ty's door. He opened a moment later, his hair tousled, his eyes half-mast.

"Where's Jace?" Panic streaked her voice.

He shrugged, rubbing his eyes. "Don't know."

"He was with you last night?"

"Yeah, we got back around four."

"Baby?"

She spun and caught sight of Jace, perfectly

unharmed, wearing a pair of athletic shorts and wife beater, holding a cup of coffee in his hand. She released a loaded breath and dashed toward him, wrapping her arms around his waist.

He threaded his fingers through her hair. "What's wrong?"

She pulled away from the embrace to look him in the eyes. "I was worried. You weren't in bed."

His face softened. "Just getting you some coffee."

She nodded, then swallowed past the lump in her throat.

They'd been living together for nearly a month. Life with him had become habit. Every possible waking hour, they spent together. When he visited Della and Tina on Mondays and Wednesdays, she went along. Tuesdays and Thursdays, he had runs. Fridays, he took her out to dinner or a movie or they stayed in. Saturdays, they spent with Della. Each Sunday, they went for a ride. She wore her cut, and the helmet he'd bought her.

She was happy and content, the happiest she'd been her whole life, so despite her scare, she smiled. "Thank you, honey."

Chapter Thirty-Two

"Feels like it's been forever since we hung out." Lynn took a sip of her martini.

It had been. Since she and Jace became public and she'd moved into the compound, Jace hadn't let her out of his sight. She understood why and didn't mind. But it had been almost a month since her tires had been slashed and nothing had happened. It didn't mean she wasn't constantly surrounded by bikers, and it didn't mean this was the typical girls' night either. It meant Jace and Ty had let up enough that when she'd brought up girls' night, they didn't shut her down immediately. After nagging them for an entire day, she'd softened them, and they'd agreed. Since Jace and Ty were on a "run," it meant she, Lynn, Mia, and Tiffany sat in a booth at the far end of the bar, and Cuss, Blaze, Wild, and Stone sat in a high top table six feet from them.

"It has been."

"Well, can't say I didn't see it coming," Mia said. "I'm actually surprised you're even here tonight, and I don't mean because of your issues with the ex. I mean because Trig's crazy about you and doesn't like to share you even with us."

Jace was no longer ignoring Mia. It took no convincing on her part. After the encounter with Lilliam, she'd asked Jace to make up with Mia. He agreed instantly, surprising her. He explained, "Stuck up for you, Allie."

"I don't like to share him either, but I don't have a choice."

"How are you holding up?" Lynn asked.

"Good. Jace explained some things to me about what they do. I'm not as worried as I used to be, but still, I am, you know?"

"Yeah," Mia said. "It's the way of this world. You never stop worrying, but if you love him and he loves you, it's worth it. And we all know you love him, and he loves you."

She smiled.

Lynn laughed. "He gave you a cut in a month and a half. That has to be some kind of biker record."

She laughed softly, and then the smile died on her lips. "It's soon but it feels right. It feels perfect."

"There's no question he's crazy about you, Allie." Mia popped a chip in her mouth. "Like there's no question you're as crazy about him."

It had been only a short period of time, but Allie couldn't picture her life without him. She glanced at each of them and smiled.

"He looks at you the way every woman wants to be looked at," Tiff said softly, her eyes glued to her drink.

Allie swallowed. She'd never noticed the way Jace looked at her; knowing Tiff noticed it warmed her heart. If only Tiff realized someone looked at her like that too. She rested her hand over Tiff's. "Open your eyes, Tiff."

Tiffany's gaze met hers, and then almost as if she couldn't help it, they went to Cuss. It said it all. Still, Allie found it hard to believe. The two of them cared about each other, and for years, they hadn't done a thing about it. How could Cuss not realize it? Why hadn't he made a move? She would have a talk with him.

Finishing her martini, she stood. "Have to use the restroom. Be back." She spotted Blaze standing behind her.

"Where you goin'?"

She quirked a brow. "I can use the restroom, can't I?" she teased, if only to lighten the mood. She couldn't imagine how boring it must be for them watching her every move.

He smirked. "Yeah, but it means I gotta wait outside for you, Classy."

"Scared the toilet will swallow me?"

"Terrified," he mocked with a smile.

Allie shook her head, smiling. The restroom was small, three stalls, and empty. She parted the door into the first stall, did her business, and washed her hands. Sparing a glance in the mirror, she spotted him. The tall, thin, dark-haired man stepped out of a stall and headed for her. He wore a T-shirt and jeans, but you could tell he didn't feel comfortable in either.

"You're in the women's restroom."

"I know." His voice accented, a New Yorker.

The determined look in his eyes, the menacing sound of his voice, he wasn't there by accident. She should've run or screamed or done something, anything in that split second, but she froze solid, panic choking her.

He pulled a gun from his waistband. "You try to run or scream, and I shoot you. Then I'll shoot your biker friends."

Her eyes on the gun, her hands shook. Her pulse

jackhammered at the base of her neck. There was nothing she could do. She nodded.

He lifted his chin and pointed the gun to the back of the restroom where there was a window. Taking the cue, she walked toward it.

"Open it. Jump out."

She pushed the window up, looked out, and spotted another man waiting—another man she didn't recognize. He was shorter than the other with a slightly bigger build. Placing her hands on the window sill, she jumped out. The man grabbed her arm roughly and yanked her forward so quickly she tripped, landed on her hands and knees. He heaved a frustrated sigh, his hand still firmly gripping her.

"Fucking idiot."

She stood and turned.

He hadn't been talking to her. His gaze on the other man. "She's not delivered in perfect condition, we don't get paid. Remember?"

The man loosened his grip on her arm. "Sorry, boss."

Good to know. Not that it would help her now. Not that it mattered, they'd take her to Wyatt, and he wouldn't think twice about hurting her.

"Fucking worthless," he sniped. "Get the fucking car."

"Right." He released her and took off.

A black SUV pulled up a moment later. Blaze shouted her name. Anxiety streaked her. The man pushed the barrel of the gun against her lower back, and she jumped.

He threw the car door open. "Not a fucking sound. Get in."

She did and quickly.

Because she didn't want Blaze to find her.

Because she had no other choice.

****

Army patted him on the back. "She's gonna love it, Trig."

Trig pulled his gaze away from the diamond ring and met Army's gaze. "Yeah?"

Army nodded. "Yeah, fuckin' positive."

Last week, he'd been heading to the compound when he took a detour. He didn't realize where he was headed or what he meant to do. Somehow, he ended up at a jewelry store. He walked in and looked at several rings. When he set eyes on the two-carat, princess-cut diamond, he knew it was the one for Allie. He picked a simple band, had it sized, and maxed out his credit card to pay for it. It cost a fortune because it was two carats and because of the color, clarity, and some other bullshit the saleswoman explained he hadn't paid much attention to, but he wasn't leaving the store without buying it. It was Allie's. What it cost didn't matter. It was worth it. She was worth it. He'd take several guard jobs, and it'd be paid in full.

The saleswoman called him that morning and told him the ring could be picked up. He brought Army along because Army was his best friend and because as her brother, he wanted his approval.

It was soon, too soon to be thinking about proposing, but he wasn't changing his mind about her, not in a month, not in a year, not in a decade, not in a century. She was the one for him, the only one. He wasn't going to waste time. In the biker world and life, they were as good as married, but Allie was beautiful, sweet, and smart. She didn't grow up in the biker world and didn't fully understand it. Most importantly, she deserved to wear a white dress and walk down the aisle in a church. Women dreamed of doing that, and he wanted to make all her dreams come true.

"Telling you it's perfect. She's gonna fuckin' ball when she sees it."

He drew his gaze away from the diamond to look at Army. "Don't want her fuckin' crying."

Army chuckled, shaking his head. "It's what women do, brother. They're upset; they cry. They get emotional; they cry. They're really happy; they fuckin' cry. Get used to that shit now."

"It's true."

His gaze snapped to the saleswoman, Giselle, a short blond with pale blue eyes.

"I know because I'm a woman and all."

He looked back to the diamond ring. He grinned.

"Is she expecting it at all?"

"She's not," Army answered.

"Then she'll definitely cry, but it'll be a good cry."

"Haven't even thought how I'm gonna do it."

"That's easy."

He looked at her.

"Some men go all out, do something spectacular, but she loves you, she won't care whether you ask her in a fancy restaurant, at a concert, or in the middle of a bar." She smiled. "Trust me."

"Thanks."

His phone rang. He dug into his pocket, answered it, and brought it to his ear.

"Got some news," Doug said.

He handed the ring to Giselle, so she could

package it, and said to Doug, "Spill it."

"This info was hard to come by because the bastard's smart. Discovered he has an off-shore account, got millions in it under a fake company. That company makes deposits into other off-shore accounts. Looked into them and found out those companies are also dummy companies. Got sites with addresses, but the buildings are empty. It was a fuckin' pain in the ass, but discovered those off-shore accounts belong to judges in New York. Get what I'm saying?"

He got it. The ex was paying off judges. This information leaked, the ex would be facing jail time and lots of it. Trig wouldn't need to worry about the bastard messing with Allie's life because his life would be in shambles, and his Allie would be safe.

He smiled. "Don't need to tell you to leak it."

"You don't. Just sent a slew of emails to all the right people including the media, meaning agencies in charge of sorting this shit out are gonna wanna do it fast. All we gotta do now is wait for his ass to get arrested."

Fuck. Best day ever.

He'd move Allie into his house this weekend, and then he'd propose. They'd get married and have a couple of kids, and he'd never go a day without her.

"You haven't said a fuckin' word for like two minutes. If I didn't know any better, I'd say you were in shock." Doug chuckled. "Now, to some bad news, haven't been able to figure out who's been messing with her. Found nothing on that. That said, guy's a defense attorney, so he knows plenty of shady people willing to do anything for the right price, and he's got money, so, not that I have to warn you, but keep eyes and ears out for that, least until he's arrested and whoever he's paying to mess with her realizes he isn't getting paid."

Doug was right. He didn't have to be warned. It didn't matter, not anymore. By this weekend, he'd have her settled in his house. He had a state-of-the-art alarm system, and he'd be there. Nothing would touch his Allie. "You're right. You don't."

"Gotta let you go. Got another call."

He hung up, looked to Army, and grinned. Army handed him Allie's diamond. As they strode out to their bikes, he explained what Doug found.

Sitting astride his bike, his phone rang again. He read Blaze's name on the screen before he answered it.

"She's fuckin' gone, Trig."

The worst fucking greeting of his life, the worst words he'd ever heard in the same sentence turning the best day of his life into the worst.

Gone.

He didn't need to ask who. The moment he'd heard the words, he felt a deep pang in his chest.

"Trig! She's fuckin' gone, brother. Don't know what the fuck happened. She went into the bathroom and never came out. Don't fuckin' know how the fuck—"

His throat dry, fear clogged it. Still, he managed to say, "Compound." He barely recognized the sound of his own voice, streaked in anguish and fear, mirroring how he felt inside. He caught Army's gaze and was thankful, his brother could read him. He wouldn't have to force himself to say it a loud. Army read the agony he felt churning his whole body in his expression.

Allie was gone.

Chapter Thirty-Three

They drove for what seemed like hours. Then again, it probably seemed like hours because Allie was terrified and couldn't see where they were headed. In a sense, she didn't need to know. Wherever it was, Wyatt would be there. Nothing else would matter after that. He may have told her kidnappers not to hurt her, but he would.

Once in the SUV, the man holding the gun shoved it in her face and instructed her to get on the floor. Her mind racing, her heart palpitating, she did. Finally, the car stopped. The man beside her, grabbed her elbow, and hefted her up, pulling the gun in her face. "No fucking screaming. No fighting. No trying to get away. Your man's paying me good money for this fucking job, and I need it."

She swallowed the fear choking her and nodded.

He opened the door and dragged her out of the car. She glanced around, not recognizing any of it. An industrial area, a large building with several warehouses lined side by side, but it looked abandoned: no cars, no people, no life.

"Move." He pressed the butt of the gun to her lower back.

She followed the other man into one of the warehouses. Inside, it was dusty and as she'd assumed, abandoned.

"Move. Far corner, then sit."

She nodded, walked the distance to the corner, and sat on the floor, facing the men who took seats in two chairs in front of her. She wrapped her arms around herself attempting to stop shivering.

The leaner man pulled out a cell phone, dialed a number, and brought it to his ear. "Fuck." He hung up. "Bastard isn't picking up."

"Probably means he's on his way. Take a while though."

The leaner man turned. "Figured that, smartass, but don't think you fucking realize I don't want to be sitting here for hours till he gets here. I need to get this shit over and done with and get back to New York before my parole officer realizes I'm gone. He better be fucking good on his word, pay me my fucking money, and get me off those fucking charges. Prison isn't fun."

"Can say that shit again."

None of this information bode well for her. First, they were criminals. She didn't know what either of them had been to jail for, but Wyatt was paying them and promised to get one of them off charges. Chances were for the right price, they'd do just about anything, even getting rid of a body.

They might need to do that, too. There was no way in hell she was going anywhere with Wyatt.

****

Army went right for Blaze. "Why the fuck was she alone?"

At the garage, two uniformed officers stood a couple of feet away, talking to Blaze. Most of the brothers were there. The rest, Trig knew, were on their way. Mia, Lynn, and Tiffany were also near, huddled together.

"We fuckin' agreed. We fuckin' voted. Two fuckin' guys on her all the time."

Blaze, brows drawn, shook his head. "She had to use the bathroom. Did you expect me to go in there?"

Army advanced. Instead of backing away or fighting back, as if he thought he deserved it, Blaze steeled himself.

Trig grasped Army by the shoulder and dragged him away. "We aren't gonna stand here, fighting over what should've been done. It's fuckin' done, and Allie's fuckin' gone." His voice cracked. "More time we spend fighting, less time we spend lookin'."

Army relaxed, but his jaw clenched. "Why wasn't one of the women with her?"

"Fuckin' better this way," Cuss said. "We'd be lookin' for two instead of one."

"No telling what they'd do to someone they don't want who's extra weight."

His phone rang again. He fished it out of his pocket, turning away from them, and brought it to his ear.

"Been calling you. Wyatt got on a private jet about an hour ago. My guy's trying to find out where he's headed," Doug said.

Too little, too late. "She's gone," he managed to say. His voice hollow.

"Fuck. What do you know?"

"Nothing so far."

"Flight's eight hours. You got time."

Yeah, except that all that time Allie would be with God knew who, terrified out of her fucking mind. Nothing he could fix. Nothing he could do.

"Call you back, let you know if I can find out where he's landing. Whoever's flying the plane didn't file a flight plan. Don't know how the fuck they managed that. Suppose everyone and everything has a price. It'll take time to figure this out. I'm gonna check to see if he owns any property in the area. Might be your best bet."

"Yeah." He hung up, turned to his brothers and the cops, and explained what Doug said.

"You sure it's this Wyatt guy?" one of the cops, George Conaway, asked. The club knew most of the cops. Before the club had been clean, they knew them because they avoided them. Now, they knew them for different reasons. Cops knew, like the whole town knew, the club was the reason their streets were clean. They didn't work with them, and they didn't condone what they did, but the cops on some level, were glad for it.

"It's him," Trig said, instantly. "I know it's fuckin' him. We know it's fuckin' him. Don't waste your time, our time, and her time lookin' at anyone else."

"No reason why she would've left?" The other cop asked. Young and new to the force, Trig didn't know his name.

The question directed at him, but hung in the air. He wanted to respond quickly, but the pang in his chest deepened.

"She wouldn't have left," Army answered. "No way in fuckin' hell she would've left."

"She's over eighteen, hasn't been missing for more than an hour. Our hands are tied."

Rage building inside him, he took a step in the cop's direction. "She was fuckin' kidnapped. We're telling you, means your hands aren't fuckin' tied."

"There's no proof."

"How would she have left?" Blaze asked. "I drove her there. She doesn't have a car, and she left her purse in the booth where she'd been sittin'."

George opened his mouth to speak, then stopped when he lifted his phone out of his pocket and answered, "Conaway."

They stood in silence waiting for him to finish.

He hung up. "Someone reported a black SUV driving in the back of the bar near the bathroom window they found open. Anyone of you owns one?"

He fisted his palms tightly. "Most of us got black SUVs or trucks. None of us took her, so make the fuckin' calls you need to make, and find my fuckin' woman."

The cop's eyes hardened. "I'm the fuckin' law. I gotta ask these questions."

He took a step in his direction. "Get that 'cause I'm not blind, but it isn't your fuckin' woman who's been kidnapped. It's mine, so I don't fuckin' think you understand she's fuckin' terrified and alone. When her ex gets his hands on her, he's gonna be pissed she left New York. He's gonna be pissed we roughed him up for slapping her in broad daylight, and he's gonna be livid she's with me. It means he'll be outta fuckin' control, so out of it, he'll fuckin' beat her until she's isn't breathing, and if my woman ain't breathing, neither will he."

"It's plain stupid to say that to a cop."

"I'm not fuckin' stupid. I'm fuckin' pissed I'm having to convince a fuckin' cop to find my woman. I'd known, we wouldn't have called the fuckin' cops, and it don't matter what the fuck I tell you 'cause she's not breathing means I'm not living just fuckin' existing. I can exist fine behind bars."

It was something he said, the way he said it or maybe it was the anguish that clung to him clear in his face, but it worked. George held his gaze for a long moment, and then, he pulled his radio from his waist and reported the kidnapping and the possible suspect's car description.

"We'll keep in touch," the cop said, and they left.

****

Allie didn't know where she was or how long she'd been there, and she was still shivering. She'd cradled her knees and rested her head on them. It served a dual purpose. She wouldn't have to look at the gun or the men who'd taken her.

She closed her eyes, and willingly, Jace's face came to mind. Since she'd been taken, she tried her hardest not to think about him. She knew thinking of him would serve only to remind her what she'd miss the most, and then it'd be much harder to keep the tears at bay. At that moment, she didn't care if she cried.

She wanted to remember everything, everything he'd said, everything he'd done. She wanted to remember the look in his eyes every time he told her he loved her, the way he held her every night and every morning, the way he said her name.

So she did.

And she cried.

****

No news.

Still.

It had been seven hours. Seven hours since she'd

been taken, seven hours she'd been terrified, probably trembling and fucking alone. In a little over an hour, her ex's private plane would land, and he'd find her wherever they'd hid her, and then, he'd fucking hurt her.

The ache in his chest strengthened. He braced, shaking his head, trying to force himself to focus.

They'd had no leads to her whereabouts. Not the club, not the cops, not Doug. Because of it, the brothers separated into groups, each going to a different airport and private landing strip to wait.

Waiting was the worst. Every second, the panic grew; the dread compounded. His heart beat so hard and fast, any moment he swore it would explode inside his chest.

He'd lived through a war and seen death. He'd stood at the end of a barrel too many times to count. He'd been shot at, stabbed, and too close to exploding IEDs, but he'd never been more terrified in his life than he was then.

If he didn't get to her in time, he'd be like Ripper, angry and bitter, existing without living, fucking dead inside.

"Gonna find her."

He spared a glance at Mellow and prayed for the millionth time for his Allie.

Chapter Thirty-Four

The door into the warehouse crept open. Allie lifted her head, and her gaze locked with Wyatt's. Her eyes watered.

He rushed toward her and kneeled in front of her. "Alyssa? Did they hurt you?"

She shook her head then managed to whisper, "No."

"Why are you upset?"

She swallowed. "How long have I been here?"

He turned to the two men who responded, "Nine hours."

Wyatt faced her. "You hungry?"

Hungry? No! She was scared, shaking, and she wanted to go home to Jace. Saying it would be suicide, so instead, she took a deep breath. "I'm not hungry. I'm tired, and I'm scared. Ty is worried about me—"

"Don't fucking mention him," he snapped. "Or your lover. They took you away from me, and they beat me. I was in the hospital for a week, Alyssa. I had a cast on for a month and a half. They're animals."

"They didn't take you away from me, Wyatt. I left. I left because you hit me."

He slapped her hard across the face, the impact sending her head into the wall. Pain exploded at her temple making her eyes water.

"Fuck. Tell me you're fucking kidding me?" One

of the men asked. "Tell me you didn't have me kidnap this woman, so you could beat her. I'm a fucking drug dealer, but I'm not a fucking—"

"You'll do what I say and you won't say a word because I'll report you to your parole officer. You'll end up in jail, and you won't get that money you want so bad." Wyatt spun.

She took one look at his face, at the menacing gleam in his eyes, and she knew what would come and knew it would hurt. Closing her eyes, she pictured Jace and braced.

Then the beating began.

****

Trig brought his palms to his temple and squeezed with all his strength. He then slammed his fist through the driver's side window. It shattered, cutting his hand. Blood poured out and onto the ground.

It didn't hurt.

It didn't alleviate the throbbing pain in his chest either.

He was losing his fucking mind. No, he'd fucking lost it already.

It had been nine hours, nine long, agonizing hours suffering the unbearable ache in his chest, hours without Allie, with Allie terrified and alone.

They'd missed him.

Doug called to tell him the private jet the bastard took off in New York was in Washington. A flight plan had just been listed, and the jet was now headed to New York. More than likely, since flight plans were required for out of state flights, the plane Wyatt took off in landed in another airport in New York. He'd switched planes, evading the PI. Wyatt could've then flown directly to California, making it impossible to track him since they hadn't known which plane he'd taken off in. It meant he'd probably already landed in California, probably one of the larger airports, so he wouldn't be spotted. Because they didn't know he'd switched planes, there was no way to find out where the plane landed. Not that it mattered, the plan had been to follow him to wherever he went, which would've led them to Allie.

His phone rang, and he brought it to his ear.

"Gotta report about a black SUV in an abandoned warehouse in Santa Rosa. It's out of our jurisdiction—" George said.

Fuck. Hope. His heart pounding louder, he cut him off, "Address."

"Can't—"

"Gimme the fuckin' address or I swear to fuckin'—"

"Not smart to threaten a cop."

He sighed, tears forming in his eyes. Clutching his phone to his ear, he did something he'd never done before. He begged. "It's been nine fuckin' hours. She's been alone. He's there already. I fuckin' know it. I need to find her before…Please, give it to me."

George must've heard the desperation in his voice. "Giving you some advice, don't fuckin' kill him. You'll end up in jail, and if she loves you half as much as you love her, you'll be punishing her." He gave him the address.

Trig wasted no time. Jumping in his SUV, Mellow hopped in beside him. While he drove, Mellow made calls to his brothers.

It took ten minutes to get there. He parked and

reached for the gun in the glove compartment.

Mellow gripped his hand, stopping him. "We go in together."

"Don't know how many—"

He shook his head. "Not lettin' you go in there alone, brother. The faster you agree, the faster we're in."

He nodded, hopped out of the SUV, and sprinted to the door. He slung it open and spotted three men. Two were toward the middle of the warehouse facing him. The other was the ex, the fucking bastard's back facing the door, hovering over her, his beautiful-beyond-anything-in-the-world Allie. She lay motionless on the floor.

He swallowed the anguish, fighting the tears pooling in his eyes and roared, "Get the fuck away from her! Now or I'll fuckin' shoot all of you!"

The two men lifted their hands immediately. Wyatt's back shot ramrod straight, but he didn't turn.

"Don't know if you fuckin' know but I was a sniper. It means I can shoot you between the eyes from behind, so put your fuckin' hands up and face me."

Wyatt turned. His eyes, dark and menacing, met his.

"Don't fuckin' think about reaching for that gun," Mellow said from beside him. He walked toward one of the men and removed the gun from his waistband. "Check Allie."

He didn't need to be told, already half-way there. Reaching Allie, he knelt. On her side, her dark hair sprawled across the floor, her arms covering her head, like she'd been trying to protect herself from the asshole's blows.

Slowly, he drew her arms away from her face. Unconscious, the right side of her face swollen, her lip bleeding. His heart clenched. He checked her pulse, slow and steady. Alive and breathing, he sighed in relief.

She was safe. He heard the faint sound of sirens but paid no mind to it. Putting his gun on his waistband, he wrapped one arm around her back, the other under her knees and lifted her. Her body slumped against him. His arms tightened around her. His eyes glued to her face, he caught sight of her eyelids fluttering open.

"Jace…" she whispered.

She knew he was there.

She knew she was safe.

"Yeah, baby, I'm here."

She smiled, softly.

He looked up. Army, Cuss, Blaze, Trick, Wild, Stone were there now too. Three had guns drawn, aimed at Wyatt and the two others.

Army strode to him, took one look at Allie's face and tensed. "She's gonna be fine. She's gonna survive this. She's gonna move on." He said it trying to reassure himself.

Trig spared a glance at Wyatt. "I'd kill you, but rather let you rot in hell."

"She'll never testify." Wyatt laughed. "Besides, I have money and *friends*. I'll get off."

He shook his head, his eyes hardening to slits. "Not when they find out you been paying off judges."

Wyatt's face blanched.

He glared at the two others and strode away.

Chapter Thirty-Five

Allie didn't want to open her eyes. She didn't want to wake up. Her head hurt. The only way not to feel it was to go back to sleep, but it was too late. She was conscious enough to know Jace wasn't in bed with her.

Her eyes fluttered open and met white walls in an unfamiliar room. The antiseptic smell made the memories flood her: the man in the bar's bathroom, the warehouse, Wyatt, the beating. She touched the side of her head and felt the bump.

"Baby?"

Jace.

She shifted her head toward the sound of his voice. He sat in a chair at her right side. His eyes were red like he hadn't slept, wearing an expression she'd never seen before—pained, concerned, and defeated at the same time.

He leaned forward, took her hand in his left, and brought it to his lips, but he made no move toward her. "How do you feel?"

"I want to go home." Her voice soft and shaky.

"Yeah, baby, you're gonna go home soon, but the doctor needs to check on you again."

She nodded, wondering why he wouldn't close the distance between them, wondering why if he'd been there, he hadn't lain beside her.

"How do you feel?"

"My head hurts."

"You have a concussion."

"Makes sense. Anything else?"

He swallowed. "Your cheek's swollen, your lip's busted, and you got bruises, a lot of them."

She nodded. "Did anyone get hurt?"

His eyes darkened, anguish shining through. "Yeah, Allie, you. You got fuckin' hurt." His voice so rough it pained her.

"Besides me."

Looking away from her, his jaw went hard. "No."

She nodded.

"And Ty's—"

"He's fine."

She couldn't stand the nagging feeling something was off about him. "Is there something you're not telling me?"

He met her eyes. "Tell you just about everything, Allie."

It wasn't what she meant, so she tried to rephrase. "Why…why are you…"

"Why am I what?"

"Why are you acting different?"

"Scared outta my goddamned mind, Allie. Fuckin' lost it."

Shit. He'd lost it. A memory flooded her, a memory of Jace, carrying her, saying in a deep ragged voice, "Yeah, baby, I'm here."

He found her.

He saved her.

What else had he done?

"Did you kill him?"

He released a breath. "No, didn't kill any of them.

345

Let the police handle them."

Eyes falling away from his, she exhaled in relief.

"He's facing kidnapping, conspiracy to commit kidnapping, assault and battery charges, and a bunch of other unrelated shit. He's not getting off."

"What other stuff?"

"After your tires were slashed, I hired a friend that's a PI to look into him. He found out the bastard's been paying off judges."

It came as a shock. Not the fact Jace hired someone, but the fact Wyatt had paid off judges. It seemed so out of character. Then again, Wyatt was good at disguises, concerned for her one minute, shamelessly beating her the next.

Lost in her thoughts, she barely caught it. A brief moment before Jace could blanket it from his expression, she saw it—the pain, the reason he kept his distance. He loved her. He told her, but most importantly, he showed her, every single day. After all she'd been through, that hurt the most. That it hurt the man she loved the most.

"Hold me."

"Want nothing more, but don't want to hurt you. Wanted you to get some rest, too. You need it."

She smiled. "Don't you know after all this time that what I need most is you?"

He fought a grin and lost.

"You can't hurt me, and I sleep better with you."

He pressed his lips to her palm, closed the distance between them, and settled beside her. Wrapping an arm around her shoulders, he pressed her head against his chest.

She caught glimpse of the bandage on his hand.

"What happened to your hand?"

"Lost you. Lost my fuckin' mind," he whispered into her hair.

He didn't elaborate. She didn't push. If he didn't want to say, she didn't want to make him relive it.

"Love you, Allie."

Tilting her head up, she looked into his eyes. "I love you, honey." She then settled against his chest, and in seconds, she fell asleep.

****

Allie.

Even with the nasty bruise on her cheek and her busted lip, she was beautiful. His beautiful, smart, sweet Allie.

He held her against his chest. She'd fallen asleep in seconds. She needed it. Apparently though, she slept better with him. Softly threading his fingers through her hair, he smiled.

The door to the hospital room opened. Army walked in. "She wake yet?"

He nodded. "Up for five minutes. Long enough to make sure we didn't kill anyone, ask if everyone was safe, ask about you, and tell me she loves me."

Army smirked. "Never thought the man who saved my ass in Afghan was the man for my baby sister."

"Never thought the baby sister of the man who'd saved my ass in Afghan would be the one for me."

"When you making it official?"

"Want to move her in and give her some time." He wanted to make sure there was no backlash either. She'd seemed fine when he spoke to her, but she'd been kidnapped, held against her will for more than nine hours, and beat by her ex. He'd be stupid to think the experience wouldn't affect her.

Army nodded. "You got something good, both of you, together. Everyone knows it." He chuckled. "When I found out, remember you told me you were different with her?"

He nodded.

"I didn't believe it, but then I saw it. You're different, not just with her, with everyone 'cause you have her, but you know shit gets fucked sometimes. Sometimes it's our own doing. Sometimes, it's shit we let get to us. Don't let this eat at you, brother. You could ruin what you've got with her, and then you'd have no one to blame but yourself."

He'd already let it get to him, and Allie sensed it. There was nothing he could do but thank Army. That's what he did.

****

"Where are we going?"

Jace pulled his gaze away from the road to glance in her direction. "Home."

Allie had just been discharged from the hospital and could not hide her relief. She'd been there only a day, but she'd suffered through eating horrible hospital food and didn't think she could take any more of it. Her head still hurt, but she felt better than the last time she woke.

"But we just passed the garage."

He grasped her hand, squeezing it lightly, and placed it on his lap. "Our home, Allie."

They had a home? "Um…okay."

A moment later, he pulled into the drive of his house. Finally understanding he meant his home.

"Honey, I don't have clothes here."

He parked, then angled his body until he faced her. Smiling his amazing smile and without saying a word, he opened the driver's side door and hopped out. Walking around the car to open her door, he helped her out and wrapped his arm around her shoulders. Together, they strode up to the door. He unlocked it, opened it, and allowed her in first. From behind her, he wrapped his arms around her waist, buried his face in her neck, and kissed under her ear. "Welcome home, baby."

She turned, her chest to his, tilting her head up to meet his eyes. "Jace, umm…are you saying you want me to live here with you?"

His eyes twinkled with humor. "Yeah, Allie, that's what I'm saying."

He wanted her to live with him? In his beautiful house? He didn't ask her. He brought her and let her figure it out. She should've guessed. He was a biker, and bikers told you to do stuff instead of ask.

She smiled. "I don't have any of my stuff."

"Mia, Lynn, and the guys took care of that."

"But it's been like…two months…I mean…isn't it too fast?"

His brows drew together. "Allie, when we began dating, we were living together. I had to go without for weeks, and I nearly fuckin' went crazy. I got that back when you were living with me at the compound. For a month straight, slept with you beside me, woke with you beside me, got home and you'd give me a kiss and ask how my day was, and then you'd fuckin' make me an amazing meal. You think I'm gonna let you move into your own place, you're fuckin' wrong."

"It's because I cook for you, huh?" she teased.

He fought a smile. "Agreed?"
"Do I have a choice?"
He smirked.
She smiled. "Yeah, honey."

****

Allie woke in the middle of the night. Her head lay across Jace's chest, her hand on his stomach, the smell of him filling her.

It'd been a week since she'd been kidnapped, and a week since she'd moved into Jace's house. As it was with them, everything was perfect. Well, except she caught him staring at her several times. It wouldn't bother her because she loved it when he looked at her and because she loved looking at him too, but it did bother her.

As of late, when he looked at her there was a sadness in his eyes. She knew in those moments he was reliving it, thinking of what could've happened. He'd been overprotective, too, hovering over her every move, getting things for her she could get herself. She couldn't blame him and accepted it with ease, hoping with time it would pass.

She couldn't accept his sex ban though. He held her all night, told her he loved her, but he never made a move. She had several times, and he'd made some silly excuse. When she finally pushed for the real reason, he admitted she was bruised, and he didn't want to hurt her. She could not accept this, so daily she attempted to seduce him. So far, she'd been unsuccessful. She tried it all. Almost.

Allie lifted her head and tilted it up to meet his face. The hard angles relaxed in sleep. She moved, angling her body over his, straddling him. His arm around her back tightened.

She pressed her lips against his softly, then trailed her mouth down the length of his body. Reaching the top of his boxers, she tugged them down, took the length of him in her hand, and watched as he hardened before her eyes. She took him in her mouth.

His eyes snapped open and widened, groaning. His fingers pressed into her shoulders.

She continued to take him in her mouth, pressing her tongue against the length of him. His hands grasped her arms and hauled her over him until her lips were pressed against his. He rolled until he'd nestled her under him, his shaft pressing at her core. Her legs instinctively pushed him toward her, a silent demand. With his tongue in her mouth, the warmth of his body over hers, he pulled up her nighty, yanked her thong off, and filled her slowly.

Yes, exactly what she wanted, what she needed. Ecstasy rippled through her. Her eyes widening, she moaned into his mouth. Her fingers gripped the skin on his back.

"Missed having this, baby. Missed having you so fuckin' much," he whispered against her lips.

He pulled out of her, then pushed into her again, slowly. In that slow pace he set, he stayed, making love to her. She didn't ask him to go faster or harder. She couldn't. His eyes held hers captive, making her heart squeeze in her chest.

Then and there, she fell in love with him all over again.

****

Allie liked it hard. She liked it fast, but he also knew she'd take it however he gave it to her.

Trig had been without for more than a week. She'd been banged up and bruised, and he hadn't wanted to hurt her, so tonight, he'd take his time. He wanted it to last so the memory was seared in his mind.

He slid into her, then out of her, keeping his slow pace. The entire time, her eyes on his like she, too, wanted to burn the memory in her mind.

"Heaven, baby."

Her lips parted. She moaned, and her nails bit into his skin, her legs tightened around his waist. She lifted her hips to take more of him in, keeping his pace. He was already close. She had that glassy look in her eyes, so he knew she was too.

"Come with me."

Her arms tightened around him, and then, she moaned his name. He let loose, his cock jerking inside her. She clenched him.

"Jace…"

His fingers gripped the back of her neck, his whole body shook from the force of his release, hers shivering under him. It seemed to last forever. He savored every bit until it slowly dissipated. Panting and catching his breath, he held her eyes.

She smiled, ran her finger along the scar on the side of his lip, and whispered, "Love you, honey."

Love. What he felt was so much more, and every day it grew.

Without responding, he drew away. Her eyes saddening, she reluctantly unwrapped her arms and legs from him. He hated to let her go, to see the look on her face, but his body moved. Reaching into his nightstand, he pulled open the drawer, and removed a black jewelry box. He settled in between her legs with his head near her stomach, and then he placed the box between her breasts.

Her eyes widened. Her gaze shot from the black box to him, then back again. She didn't make a move, but the question hung in her eyes.

He hadn't prepared what he'd say because he hadn't intended on proposing so soon. He wanted to give her time to adjust to living in their home and get over what happened, but like when he bought the ring, he acted without thought, without giving his brain time to think, process, and plan.

Her gaze went to him again.

"Marry me."

She let out a small gasp. Her eyes watered. When she whispered, "Yes," tears drifted out of her eyes.

He smiled.

She leaned down, cupped his cheeks, and pressed her lips to his. "Yes. Yes. Yes."

He chuckled. "Baby, you wanna see the ring?"

Drawing away from his lips, she nodded. He grabbed the box, pulled it open toward her.

Her eyes widened. Without blinking, more tears drifted down her cheeks. "It's beautiful, Jace."

He removed it from the box and placed the diamond ring on her finger.

Her gaze on her hand then met his. "We're getting married, honey."

He grinned. "Yeah, baby, we are."

Her eyes glimmered. "I'm going to be Mrs. Jace 'Trigger' Warren. I'm going to be Alyssa Marie Warren."

Heart tightening in his chest, he took a deep breath, loving the sound of that, loving it more she wanted to take his name.

"Yeah, baby, you are."

He was the luckiest trailer trash on earth.

Epilogue

Four months later…

Allie descended down the stairs. Her mind on her dress, the beautiful, white, mermaid, lace gown. She couldn't think of Jace. If she thought of Jace, she'd remember in minutes she would be married to him, and it got her emotional in a very happy way that would make her start crying and ruin her makeup. She knew this, but Mia, Lynn, and Tiff had to remind her every time she let herself think of Jace.

"Allie?"

She turned and met Ty's gaze. Her hand resting on his elbow, he stood beside her, helping her down the stairs.

"Can't believe you're getting married."

"Me neither, Ty."

He smiled. They reached the bottom of the staircase. "You make a beautiful bride."

He told her this multiple times. She'd thanked him multiple times. Right then, she just smiled.

Together, they walked toward the French doors leading to the backyard of her and Jace's home. He pulled the door open and held it out.

She paused and looked at her brother. "Thank you, Ty."

His brows drew together.

"If it hadn't been for you…" Tears hit her eyes.

Her voice trailed off.

He shook his head. "Anytime, anyplace, Allie."

"I love you," she whispered.

"Love you, too." He quirked a brow. "Dry them tears."

She laughed, shakily.

In the backyard under one of the willow trees, stood the white gazebo decorated with roses and calla lilies. An aisle, with rose petals scattered on it, led to it. White chairs lined each side, flowers at the end of each row.

Simple.

Perfect.

She reached the end of the aisle with Ty by her side, forced her gaze toward the front, and caught her first glimpse of Jace, wearing a tie and a tailored, black suit he filled out perfectly. Clean-shaven, his dark hair lightly gelled. Always handsome, she knew this, but Jace in a suit was beyond it. Then she let her gaze meet his.

Again, she couldn't help it.

Her eyes watered because she saw it.

The way he was looking at her.

It was the way every woman wanted to be looked at.

Like the sun rose and set on her.

****

She was fucking beautiful, so beautiful Trig couldn't peel his eyes away even if his life depended on it.

She'd always been beautiful, he knew, but fuck him, she looked like a fucking angel in the white fitted dress with her hair loose in soft curls around her.

The moment he saw her at the end of the aisle, his heart squeezed so hard he'd thought it'd take him to his knees. He had to fight his body. More than anything, he wanted to meet her in the middle, take her in his arms, and kiss her.

He couldn't do that. He had to wait, so while she walked down the aisle with tears in her eyes and a smile on her face, he waited impatiently.

"Who gives this woman to this man?"

"I do." Army kissed Allie's cheek and placed her hand in his. Then he took his spot next to him as best man.

Trig said his vows, watching her beautiful face as tears drifted down her cheeks. Wiping them away, he cupped her cheeks. When he finished his vows, he pressed his lips against her forehead.

She waited until he met her stare to say her vows. His whole body filled with warmth until he thought his chest would explode. She cried then, too. He wiped her tears away, smiling. They exchanged rings, and then, finally, they were pronounced husband and wife. He kissed her soft and slow, then hard and rough, ignoring the hooting and hollering.

When he pulled away from her lips, he rested his forehead against hers, locking eyes, and whispered, "I love you, Allie. Always will."

She smiled. "I love you, Jace."

He knew she meant it.

It's how he knew he really was the luckiest trailer trash on earth.

About the Author

J.L. Sheppard was born and raised in Miami, Florida, where she still lives with her husband and son.

As a child, her greatest aspiration was to become a writer. She read often, kept a journal, and wrote countless poems. She graduated from Florida International University in 2008 with a Bachelors in Communications. During her senior year, she interned at NBC Miami, WTVJ. Following the internship, she was hired and worked in the News Department for three years.

It wasn't until 2011 that she set her heart and mind to writing her first completed novel, which was published in January of 2013.

Besides reading and writing, she enjoys traveling and spending quality time with family and friends.

Note from the Author

Thank you for reading Running Wild. I hope you enjoyed Jace and Allie's story as much as I enjoyed writing it. Up next in Hell Ryders Series is Cuss's story.

If you haven't read any of my previous releases, check them out: Burdened by Desire, Heavenly Desire, and Awaiting Fate.

Honest reviews are always welcome and very much appreciated.

~*~

Visit J.L. at

http://www.jlsheppard.com

~*~

To chat with J.L. Sheppard and other Wild Rose Press authors of erotic romance, join us at
www.groups.yahoo.com/group/thewilderroses.

Also Available

Awaiting Fate

by

J.L. Sheppard

http://amzn.com/B00TZ9ZI36

Cain Thaler's lived more than four hundred years fighting rogue immortals, avenging the family he'd lost. It's all he's needed, all he's wanted. That changes the fateful day he lays eyes on his fated mate.

Olivia Waden, a werewolf princess, is nothing like him. Unwilling to give her up, he sets a plan into motion: ignoring his need to claim her, he befriends her.

Despite Cain's best efforts at friendship, Olivia has fallen hard for him. It is him she dreams of, him she wants as her fated mate. But she is sure he doesn't feel the same way. In way over her head, she has no option but to run away from the only man she's ever loved. Will Cain find Olivia before it's too late or will their differences tear them apart?

Also Read

Deep Down

by

Mia Hopkins

http://amzn.com/B016ZGXS4M

Resilient and disciplined, tsunami survivor Eve Ono moves to California from Japan looking for a position as a sushi chef. When she's suddenly fired from her restaurant job, desperation drives her to find work on a fishing boat despite her fears of the ocean. To make matters worse, she's stuck in close quarters with her new captain—a man whose raw physicality drives her out of her mind with lust.

Free-spirited and roguish, Sam Lamont is a commercial fisherman aboard his own dive boat, the Bravado. When he makes a bad deal with a deadly loan shark who threatens to take his boat, Sam is in danger of losing both his business and his way of life. On top of that, he's got to train his new deckhand—a beautiful hard-ass who just so happens to be sexy as hell.

A female sushi chef with mad knife skills. A deep-sea diver who's pissed off a Mexican drug cartel. Together, they're in trouble, and the only way out is down.

Thank you for purchasing this
publication of The Wild Rose Press, Inc.
If you enjoyed the story, we would appreciate
your letting others know by leaving a review.
For other wonderful stories, please visit our
on-line bookstore at www.wilderroses.com.

For questions or more
information contact us at
info@thewildrosepress.com.

The Wild Rose Press, Inc.
www.thewilderroses.com

Stay current with The Wild Rose Press, Inc.
Like us on Facebook
https://www.facebook.com/TheWildRosePress
And Follow us on Twitter
https://twitter.com/WildRosePress